GRAND CENTRAL
PUBLISHING

LARGE
PRINT

CROOKED RIVER

A Pendergast Novel

DOUGLAS PRESTON & LINCOLN CHILD

GRAND CENTRAL
PUBLISHING

LARGE PRINT

By Douglas Preston

The Lost City of the Monkey God • The Kraken Project • Impact • The Monster of Florence (with Mario Spezi) • *Blasphemy • Tyrannosaur Canyon • The Codex • Ribbons of Time • The Royal Road • Talking to the Ground • Jennie • Cities of Gold • Dinosaurs in the Attic*

By Lincoln Child

Full Wolf Moon • The Forgotten Room • The Third Gate • Terminal Freeze • Deep Storm • Death Match • Lethal Velocity (formerly *Utopia*) • *Tales of the Dark 1–3 • Dark Banquet • Dark Company*

CROOKED RIVER

Copyright © 2020 by Splendide Mendax, Inc. and Lincoln Child

Cover design by Flag. Cover art credits: digital imaging by Scott Nobles; photograph of birds by Jes Aznar/Stringer/Getty Images, buildings from Shutterstock, clouds from iStock/Getty Images Plus. Cover copyright © 2020 by Hachette Book Group, Inc.

Grand Central Publishing
Hachette Book Group
1290 Avenue of the Americas, New York, NY 10104
grandcentralpublishing.com
twitter.com/grandcentralpub

First Edition: February 2020

Grand Central Publishing is a division of Hachette Book Group, Inc. The Grand Central Publishing name and logo is a trademark of Hachette Book Group, Inc.

The publisher is not responsible for websites (or their content) that are not owned by the publisher.

The Hachette Speakers Bureau provides a wide range of authors for speaking events. To find out more, go to www.hachettespeakersbureau.com or call (866) 376-6591.

Library of Congress Control Number: 2019953904

ISBNs: 978-1-5387-4725-4 (hardcover), 978-1-5387-4726-1 (ebook), 978-1-5387-5137-4 (int'l), 978-1-5387-0295-6 (large print), 978-1-5387-0297-0 (B&N signed edition), 978-1-5387-0298-7 (signed edition)

Printed in the United States of America

LSC-C

10 9 8 7 6 5 4 3 2 1

*Lincoln Child dedicates this book to
his parents, Bill and Nancy*

*Douglas Preston dedicates this book to
Steve Elkins*

CROOKED RIVER

I

Wᴀʀᴅ Pᴇʀsᴀʟʟ ᴡᴀʟᴋᴇᴅ along the narrow beach in a deliciously cool strip where the waves slid up and down on the glistening sand. He was just seventeen, short and skinny for his age and acutely aware of both. It was a cloudless day, the surf creaming in from the Gulf of Mexico. His flip-flops sank into the wet surface, the pressure oddly pleasing, and with each step forward he flung a small gobbet of sand from his toe.

"Hey, Ward." It was his dad speaking, and Ward turned to see him, sitting alone in a beach chair a dozen feet back from the water, Nationals baseball cap on his head and beach towel draped over his legs. The fat green Boorum & Pease notebook that never seemed to leave him lay open on his lap. "Keep an eye on your sister, okay?"

"Sure." As if he hadn't already been doing that for almost a week now. Besides, Amanda wasn't going anywhere. Certainly not into the ocean. She was a little farther down the beach, shell hunting, crouched over in what he'd learned was called the "Sanibel stoop."

Ward let his eyes linger on his father as the man turned back to his notebook, writing equations or notes or other things he never let Ward see. His father worked for a private defense contractor in Newport News, and he made a big deal of not being able to tell his family over dinner about how each workday had gone and what he had done— all very top secret—which only helped widen the gulf between them. Funny how Ward was beginning to observe things like this—things that had always been there, but that he'd never been able to articulate exactly, like the reason his father always wore baseball caps (to cover his baldness), or the way he covered his pasty legs with the beach towel (to avoid the skin cancer that ran in the family). He supposed his mother had seen these things and a lot more, too, and no doubt that had contributed to the divorce three years ago.

Now his sister ran back to him, pail in one hand and plastic shovel in the other. "Look, Ward!" she said excitedly, dropping the little shovel, digging her hand into the pail, and bringing something out. "A horse conch!"

He took it from her and peered closely. To his left,

the repetitive sound of the surf continued, unceasing. "Nice."

She took it back and replaced it in the pail. "At first I thought it was a cantharus with all its bumps smoothed off. But the shape is kind of wrong." And without waiting for his reply she returned to her shelling.

Ward watched her for a few moments. It felt better than watching his father. Then he glanced around quickly to make sure no new treasures had washed ashore while he was speaking to her. But this section of Captiva Island beach was quiet, and competition was minimal: no more than a dozen people were in sight, walking along the verge of the surf in that same curious position he and his sister had adopted.

When they'd first hit Sanibel Island five days ago, Ward had been hugely disappointed. The ocean vacations he'd taken before had been to Virginia Beach and Kitty Hawk. Sanibel seemed like the end of the earth, with no boardwalk, few shops or amenities, and worst of all, lousy internet connectivity. But as the days had worn on he'd grown used to the quiet. He'd downloaded enough movies and books to last the week, and he didn't need online access to compile new builds of the side-scroller he was developing for his class in Applied Python. Since the divorce, his dad didn't get many chances to take them on vacations—with the alimony and everything, there wasn't a lot of extra money—and when some work friend had offered him a week at his small Sanibel beach house, just off Gulf Drive, he'd said yes. Ward knew even that was a financial stretch, with the plane tickets and restaurants and everything, and he'd been careful not to complain.

The shells had helped.

Sanibel and Captiva Islands, off the southwestern coast of Florida, were known for some of the best shelling in the world. They reached out into the Gulf of Mexico like a net, catching all sorts of mollusks, dead and alive, and strewing them along the sand. A brief storm had passed through the night before they'd arrived, which turned out to be a piece of luck: apparently, that always brought in more shells. Their first day on the beach had revealed an almost unbelievable treasure trove of unusual and beautiful specimens—not the crab pincers, broken scallop shells, and other crap you found on the Outer Banks—and shelling fever had claimed both him and his sister, Amanda in particular. Already she'd become something of an expert, able to differentiate cowries from whelks from periwinkles. Ward's own fascination had cooled after a few days, and his eye had grown much more discerning. Now he only picked up a few really good specimens here and there. His father had limited them to one bag of shells each for the flight back, and Ward knew that tomorrow night's culling—and Amanda's protests—were going to be hell.

The tide was coming in, the wind had picked up, and the surf was beating against the shore with a little more energy. A wave broke across Ward's feet, sending a spiral-shaped pink shell rolling and bouncing over his toes. As he picked it up, another sheller hustled up behind him—bright colors in the shallow water drew them like flies—and peered over Ward's shoulder, breathing heavily.

"Rose petal?" the man asked excitedly. Ward turned to look at him—maybe fifty, overweight, with a Ron Jon sun visor, cheap sunglasses, and arms sunburned from the elbows down. A tourist, of course, like everyone else around. The locals knew the best times for beachcombing, and Ward rarely saw them.

"No," said Ward. "Just a cone. Alphabet cone." His sister, instinctively alerted to a possible Find, came skipping over, and he tossed it to her. She gave it a quick glance, made as if to fling it into the water, then on second thought dropped it into her pail.

The man in the sun visor fell back and Ward walked on, trailing Amanda, the bones of ancient sea creatures crunching beneath his flip-flops. Thoughts of packing up reminded him they'd be home the day after next, which meant resuming his life—finishing his junior year, then starting the grind of tests, essays, and college applications that would inevitably follow. Recently, he'd begun worrying about ending up like his father—working like a dog but somehow never getting ahead, overtaken by younger people with shinier degrees and more marketable skill sets. He didn't think he could stand that.

Another wave broke over his feet, and he automatically corrected course, veering inland. Fresh shells went tumbling back with the undertow: an auger, a conch, another auger, yet another. He'd already collected enough damn augers to last a lifetime.

Another wave, heavier still, and he looked out to sea. The water was definitely getting rougher. That was probably a good thing: tomorrow was their last full day, and maybe they'd get another storm that would bring in a bonanza like when they'd first arrived—

Just then, his eye caught a flash of green directly ahead. It was a lighter shade than the turquoise water, and it was rolling end over end, receding with the surf. And it was big. A fighting conch? No, the color was wrong. It wasn't a whelk, either.

In a moment, his jaded attitude evaporated, replaced by a collector's lust for rarity. He glanced furtively up and down the beach. Neither his sister nor the man in the visor had noticed it. He casually increased his pace. It would be back again on the next wave, or maybe the next.

Then he saw it again, half-submerged, about six

feet out from the shore. And this time he realized it was not a shell at all, but a sneaker. A brand-new, light-green sneaker. Not quite like any he'd seen before.

Even if he couldn't afford them, he knew from high school that certain sneakers were super collectible. Balenciaga Triple S or Yeezys often sold for three or four hundred dollars, when you could find them in stock. And if you were really lucky, and scored a rare pair like the Air Jordan 11 Blackouts, you could sell them used on eBay for four figures, easy.

For all Amanda's shelling, the best specimen she found all week might get ten bucks, tops.

One sneaker, just one, and a uniform green. What the hell brand was this? It was rolling in to shore again and he'd know in a moment.

The surf swarmed around his ankles with a muted hiss. Deftly, he snagged the shoe from the water. Shit, it was heavy—no doubt waterlogged. Still, it was in great shape. Automatically he turned it over to check the sole, but there was no logo or brand on the rubberized surface.

He sensed more than saw Amanda and the fat guy in the visor approaching him again. He ignored them as he stared at the sole. Maybe it was a proto-type. They probably tested them out down here on the beach. People would pay even more for a proto-type. Instinctively, his eye traveled back to the line of surf. If the mate was floating nearby, this single discovery just might turn a so-so vacation into something special, even...

Suddenly, his sister screamed. Ward looked at her, frowning. She screamed again, even louder. For some reason, she was staring at the shoe in his hand. Curiously, he glanced down, twisting his wrist to get a better look.

He could now see inside the sneaker. It was filled with something, a pulpy red-pink with a shard of pure white projecting up from the middle. Ward froze, his mind not quite able to process what he was staring at.

His father was on his feet and running toward them. From what seemed very far away, Ward could hear the man in the visor cursing, and his sister squealing and backing up, then vomiting into the sand. Abruptly released from his paralysis, Ward dropped the shoe with a convulsive jerk and staggered backward, losing his balance and falling to his knees. But even as he did so, his gaze turned instinctively out to sea, where he could now make out—rolling among the creamy swells—more sneakers, dozens and dozens of them, bobbing lazily, inexorably, toward shore.

2

P. B. PERELMAN PULLED his Ford Explorer into the public parking area of Turner Beach. It had taken him only five minutes from the first PSAP squawk to get there—his house on Coconut Drive was less than a mile away—but he was relieved to see two of his beach patrol officers, Robinson and Laroux, already on the scene. Robinson appeared to be clearing the beach, getting people back into their cars prior to roping off the lot with crime scene tape. Laroux was perhaps a quarter mile down the sand, talking to a small knot of people. As Perelman watched, the officer looked back toward the water, then turned and ran down into the surf, plucked something out, and set it carefully on the sand, out of reach of the waves.

What—as Dorothy Parker used to say—fresh hell was this? All dispatch had told him was "beach disturbance." But he knew from personal experience that, even in a place as sleepy as Sanibel and Captiva, those two words could include anything from drunken weekenders beaching their speedboats in the dark to equinoctial ceremonies held by the blue-rinse North Naples Nudist Colony.

Perelman walked from the Explorer across the thin line of dune grass and sea oats and onto the beach. As he did so, he passed Robinson, briskly escorting two stricken-looking families—blankets, beach chairs, coolers, boogie boards, and all—toward the parking area.

"Better call in the cavalry, Chief," Robinson murmured as they passed each other.

"Everyone?"

In response, Robinson just nodded toward Officer Laroux.

Perelman proceeded down the beach, walking faster now. Laroux, who had returned to the small group of people, broke off again and ran back down to pluck something else out of the surf. As Perelman drew closer, he could see that it was a shoe or slipper of some kind, made of light-green material.

Laroux, catching sight of him, stopped. When Perelman approached, he saw that the shoe had a foot in it. A severed foot, by all appearances.

Laroux showed it to him in silence and then gently placed the shoe in the sand. "Hello, Chief."

Perelman didn't answer for a moment, staring

downward. Then he turned to his deputy. "Henry," he said. "Mind getting me up to speed on the situation?"

The officer looked back at him, a strangely blank look on his face. "Reece and I were in the DPV, headed for Silver Key. Just before we reached Blind Pass I saw some kind of commotion here on the public beach. I called it in and we pulled over to—"

"I mean *that* situation." And Perelman pointed to the shoe.

Laroux followed his gaze. Then, with a kind of helpless shrug, he gestured over his shoulder.

The chief followed the gesture. And he now saw many shoes, lined up above the high tide mark. They all appeared to have feet in them. And as he turned his gaze seaward, he spied several others, rolling and tumbling around loose in the surf. Seagulls were beginning to circle above them, crying loudly.

Perelman grasped why his officers had been too busy, too overwhelmed with surprise, to do more than make a flat call when they pulled over in their DPV five minutes ago. He felt it, too: an unexpected nightmare so bizarre and outlandish it was hard not to struggle with disbelief. He closed his eyes and took in a deep breath, then another. Then he pointed at the small group up by the dunes. "Is that the party that found the, ah, first foot?"

Laroux nodded.

The chief looked around again. Laroux's instincts were good—until they had more resources, the best he could do was pluck the feet from the gulf and place them on higher ground, roughly in line with where they had come ashore.

"Get much out of them?"

"They didn't have much to say, beyond what we're seeing ourselves."

Perelman nodded. "Okay. Good job." He glanced toward the surf. "Keep at it, save every single one, and remember: we're dealing with human remains."

As Laroux headed back toward the water, the chief pulled out his radio. "Dispatch, this is Perelman."

"Dispatch. Go ahead, P.B."

So it *was* Priscilla doing desk duty that morning. He thought he'd recognized her squawk. Nobody else would have the temerity to call him "P.B." Not only did she call him by his initials, but since he never told anybody what they stood for, she enjoyed guessing whenever he was in earshot. Perhaps she believed his being the unlikeliest of police chiefs gave her license to be a smartass. Anyway, she'd run a few dozen by him—including Parole Breaker, Peanut Butter, and Penis Breath—without getting close to the truth.

He cleared his throat. "Priscilla, I'm calling a condition red. I want you to bring in everyone with a gun or a badge."

"Sir." Priscilla's voice tightened considerably.

"I want both lieutenants on duty, and all sergeants on full alert status, in case we have to impose a curfew on short notice. They know the drill. Tell them to handle it quietly; we don't want to panic the tourists. We're closing down the entire Captiva beach and western shoreline now. Have them make preparations for the possible evacuation of Captiva Island. And alert the mayor, if she doesn't know already."

"Sir."

Perelman was speaking fast now. It seemed his words were accelerating with each passing second. Meanwhile, Laroux had fished out another four or five shoes. At a rough estimate, that made about twenty-five, with more washing in. Now the officer was chasing away seagulls that were trying to make off with some of them. Robinson had escorted the last shellers and sunbathers from the beach and was taping off the access points.

"I want a checkpoint at the mainland end of the Sanibel Causeway, and a second at the Blind Pass Bridge. The second is to allow access to Captiva residents and renters only. Notify the Office of the District Twenty-One chief M.E., and get them out here, ready to handle significant human remains at Turner Beach."

"Sir," Priscilla said a third time.

"Get on the horn to the Coast Guard command in Fort Myers. Tell them to send a cutter ASAP; I think the USCGC *Pompano* is temporarily berthed in Station Cortez. Have the command staff liaise with me directly. And TFR the airspace above Captiva for emergency operations only, no media helicopters. Got all that?"

A brief silence in which Perelman heard the scratching of a pen. "Roger."

"Good. Now, once the islands are secure and checkpoints up, have every free officer report to me here at Blind Pass. Perelman out."

He replaced the radio and glanced again in Laroux's direction. The officer was moving as fast as he could now, plucking shoes from the sea, but the seagulls were swarming in force, screaming and wheeling, and Laroux was outmanned. Distantly, Perelman was aware of how impossibly strange the situation was, but despite that, his attention was fixed on getting things under control. Twenty-five shoes, twenty-five *feet*, washed up on his beach, and from the looks of it plenty more coming in with the tide. It would be easier just to pile them together, but Perelman knew every clue here would be important and that the shoes should stay as close as possible to the point where they came ashore.

He pulled his departmental camera from his pocket and, ranging down the beach, took pictures and short video clips of the scene. Then he glanced back at the eyewitnesses, now behind tape, a small, spectral-looking group. He badly wanted to interview them—although he doubted there was much he'd learn—but for now his task was to stabilize and protect the scene until reinforcements arrived.

More seagulls were converging, the air thick with their cries. Perelman saw one land beside a shoe.

"Henry! Fire at the gulls!"

"What?"

"Shoot at the gulls!"

"There's too many, I can't bag—"

"Just fire in their direction! Scare them off!"

He watched as Laroux broke leather, pulled out his Glock, and fired up and out toward sea. A huge cloud of screaming gulls rose wheeling into the sky, including the one that had almost snagged a shoe. Looking farther down the shore, he saw with a sinking feeling that even at a distance there were shoes rolling in. The entire western shore might need to be taped and locked down as a crime scene.

And now Perelman began to see figures appearing at intervals along the top of the dune. They did not try to approach; they simply stared without moving, like sentinels. More rubberneckers. His heart sank. These weren't tourists; these were locals. People whose homes were on Captiva Drive, whose beach was being violated by this strange and awful tide.

Glancing at them one after another, he realized he knew at least half of them by name.

Death's a fierce meadowlark . . . The mountains are dead stone . . .

There was a sudden commotion; a yell and a curse, followed by furious barking. Looking around, temporarily disoriented by the unmanageable scene, Perelman saw a blur of copper: a dog had just darted past him, a shoe gripped in his mouth, headed northeast toward the preserve—an Irish setter named Sligo.

Son of a bitch.

"Sligo!" he shouted. "Sligo, come back!"

But the dog was running flat out away from them. Running with a mouthful of evidence: human remains. If Sligo reached the preserve, they might never see that evidence again.

"Sligo!"

It was no good: the dog, excited by all the activity, hunting instincts fully aroused, was beyond obeying.

"Sligo!"

Maintain the chain of evidence, his training practically shouted in his ear. *At all costs, be respectful of human remains.* The ultimate responsibility stopped with him as chief.

Perelman drew his service piece.

"What are you doing?" shouted a voice from the line of observers.

"No! No way!" someone screamed.

Perelman aimed; took in a long, quavering breath; held it; then—as the dog was about to plunge into the brush—he squeezed off a shot.

The dog flipped over without making a sound, landing on his back, the shoe tumbling out of his mouth. A terrible moment passed and something like a groan rippled through the people standing atop the dune.

"Oh my God," someone said breathlessly, "he shot that dog!"

Perelman slipped his weapon back into its holster. *Son of a bitch*.

More shots echoed behind him: Laroux was chasing away the seagulls as he worked desperately to grab more shoes. Robinson was now jogging over to help him. In the distance, Perelman could hear the whir of a helicopter and the thrum of a marine engine cutting through water.

"Hey you, *mister*!" came a loud, accusatory voice. Perelman looked over toward the row of onlookers.

"You shot that dog!" It was a woman, about fifty years old, her finger pointed at him, shaking accusatorily. He didn't recognize her; perhaps she was there for the season.

He said nothing.

The woman took a step forward, to the edge of the tape. "How could you? How *could* you *do* it?"

"I couldn't let him get away with the evidence."

"Evidence? *Evidence?*" The woman flapped her arm at the beach. "Isn't there enough for you already?"

Abruptly, something—maybe the way the woman pointed so contemptuously at the motionless lumps of flesh placed here and there across the sand, maybe the very absurdity of the comment—made Perelman issue a bitter laugh.

"And now you think it's funny!" the woman cried. "What's the owner going to say?"

"No, it's not funny," Perelman replied. "Yesterday was his birthday."

"So you *knew* the dog!" The woman stamped furiously. "You knew him...and you shot him anyway!"

"Of course I knew him," the chief replied. "He was mine."

3

AFTER LEAVING MIAMI, the FBI helicopter dropped low over the blue-green water of Biscayne Bay, heading south, then trending west as it reached the long green finger of national park marking the upper terminus of the Florida Keys. Assistant Director in Charge Walter Pickett, strapped into the copilot seat of the Bell 429, traced the route on a map he'd set atop a thin briefcase, which in turn rested on his knees. It was not quite two in the afternoon, and the brilliant sun, reflecting off the placid water below, was overpowering, despite his sunglasses and the tinted glass of the chopper. Sea plants and coral reefs gave way to a skinny chain of tropical islands linked, like beads on a string, by a single four-lane road. Groomed driveways appeared, then quite suddenly, mansions and yachts. These in turn gave way to what appeared to be a picturesque fishing village, then rows of identical condominiums, and then ocean again. And then another island; another thin ribbon of highway, surrounded only by water; yet another island. *Plantation Key*, ADC Pickett guessed: the speed of the chopper, and its low altitude, made it difficult to follow along on the map.

Now the chopper veered sharply east, heading away from the string of keys and out over open water. They flew for so long—ten minutes, maybe more—Pickett began to wonder if the pilot was lost. Ahead lay only blue, stretching out to the sea horizon.

But no—that was not quite true. Squinting through his dark glasses, Pickett could just make out a tiny speck of green, appearing now and then almost coquettishly over the most distant waves. He looked a moment longer, then reached back into the passenger compartment and grabbed the heavy marine binoculars. Through the glass, the speck turned into a self-contained oasis of greenery, a tiny ecosystem amid the ocean.

He lowered the binoculars. "Is that it?"

The man nodded.

Pickett glanced down at the map. "There's nothing on the chart."

The man nodded again, this time with a grin. "I'm still wondering how much that little bitty piece of land cost."

Pickett took another look at the island as the chopper skimmed over a coral reef. It was approaching quickly now, the placid water turning pale emerald as the bottom shallowed. What had seemed a riot of jungle sorted itself into palm trees, as trim and serried as lines of grenadiers. He could make out shapes between the trees, bone-white against the green: strategically placed guard towers, discreet but equipped with machine guns. And now a long, low boathouse appeared, artfully hidden in the verdant growth, two vessels barely visible within, next to a long pier that stretched out into the turquoise.

The chopper slowed, banking around the boathouse. On the far side of the pier, a pair of helipads had been built out over the water. They sparkled as if barely used.

The pilot circled as he descended, then landed neatly on one of the pads. Pickett grabbed his briefcase, opened the door, and stepped out into the blinding sun. As he did so, two men appeared from the shade of the trees and walked down the dock to meet him. Their skin was the color of cinnamon, and they were dressed in black berets with bloused olive shirts and matching shorts, neatly pressed—straight out of the British Raj, with a touch of Caribbean.

They smiled and shook hands, then led Pickett back up the dock and along gracefully curving paths of crushed shell, punctuated by marble benches set into the foliage, heavy with tropical flowers. They climbed a set of marble stairs, went down another pathway, climbed again. Despite the sun, it was cool under the palms, and a gentle but constant breeze stirred the flower-fragrant air. Now and then, Pickett spied buildings between the trees: alabaster marble, like every other structure. Here and there a peacock strutted across the walk, and huge parrots stared down at them from bottlebrush trees. The island appeared sparsely occupied, just a few men and women whom Pickett infrequently glimpsed at a distance through openings in the trees, or across long, verdant areas of grass, dressed in the same garb as his guides.

At last, after mounting yet another staircase, grander and longer, and skirting a sculpture of Poseidon, the two guides stopped before a shadowy passage. They indicated he was to go on alone. He thanked them, paused a moment, then walked forward through the archway.

He found himself in a roofed colonnade, supported by Corinthian columns of the same snowy marble. As he began to walk down its length, stripes of sun painted the walkway, and a distant murmur of conversation from ahead was almost drowned out by birdsong. At the far end, the colonnade opened into a peristyle surrounding a courtyard lined with potted plants. At the center, two artfully poised cherubim fountains sent streams of water puckishly at each other.

At the rear of the courtyard, several chairs had been placed beneath a vined trellis, and it was here Pickett at last spied Special Agent Aloysius Pendergast. He was wearing a white linen suit similar to the one Pickett recalled from their meeting a fortnight or so earlier at a rooftop bar in Miami Beach. One leg was flung over the other, and beautifully made loafers of buttery leather were on his feet.

Two men in the same omnipresent uniform stood on either side of the trellis. But there was another person present as well. To Pickett's surprise, a woman occupied the chair nearest Pendergast. She was young, in her early twenties, and as Pickett approached he saw she was strikingly beautiful, with violet eyes and dark hair cut in a short, stylish bob. She was dressed in pale organdy and was holding a book in one hand—a French book, apparently, titled À rebours. She looked him over with a cool impassivity that for some reason made Pickett uncomfortable. This must be Constance Greene, Pendergast's ward. He had heard a little about her, and had tried to learn more, but there seemed to be scant information, even in the FBI databases. There was something almost otherworldly about her that he couldn't put his finger on. Maybe it was the eyes. It was as if, Pickett thought, those eyes, so cool and steady, had seen everything, and were thus fazed by nothing.

The girl cleared her throat to speak and, realizing he was staring, Pickett glanced away.

"Look, my lord," she said in a surprisingly deep, velvety contralto. "It comes."

"Angels and ministers of grace defend us," Pendergast murmured.

"I'm sorry?" Pickett asked after a moment, taking a step forward.

"You must forgive Constance her little jokes." Pendergast turned to her. "My dear, I'm afraid ADC Pickett does not share your fondness for literary allusions."

She nodded. "Perhaps it's for the better."

Pendergast motioned Pickett toward an empty chair. "Please, have a seat. And may I introduce the two of you: Assistant Director in Charge Walter Pickett of the FBI—my ward, Constance Greene."

Pickett took her hand and sat, placing his briefcase down. In the silence that ensued, he glanced past the courtyard and down the colonnade, flanked with its stately palms. He could see the light jade of the ocean in the distance, beyond the line of greenery. It was a beautiful spot: impossibly private, impossibly tranquil—and no doubt impossibly expensive.

Pickett disliked unnecessary opulence. But this place nevertheless appealed to him on a visceral level. It seemed as elegant, and as rarefied, as a rainbow arcing over a waterfall. Yes, he could indeed get used to it.

"Would you care for a drink?" Pendergast raised his glass, containing a cloudy crimson beverage.

"What is it?" he asked.

"I haven't the faintest idea. Our hosts tell me it's a native concoction, good for the digestion."

"Don't try it," Constance warned. "I've had a sip of the 'native concoction,' and it tasted like brined formaldehyde." She gestured at Pendergast. "He's been drinking them practically since we arrived. Don't you notice his head beginning to shrink already?"

In response, Pendergast took a deep sip. "Constance, don't make me send you to your room without supper."

"May I ask what you're drinking?" Pickett asked her.

"Lillet Blanc with a wedge of key lime."

Pickett wasn't inclined to take a chance on that, either.

Pendergast called over one of the uniformed men, who asked for Pickett's order. "Daiquiri," he said. The man retreated with a faint nod, almost immediately returning with the drink.

"Leave it to you to find this place," Pickett said. "Something about it makes me think of Atlantis."

"And like Atlantis," Pendergast replied in his honeyed drawl, "nature will no doubt ensure it shall soon be submerged. Now seemed the ideal time to enjoy it."

"I hadn't expected to be back in Florida so soon," Pickett said. "But I was summoned to appear before a grand jury yesterday afternoon. In the Broken-hearts case."

Pendergast nodded. "My presence was requested as well. I gave my testimony earlier in the week."

Pickett had already known Pendergast had ap-peared before the grand jury and that he was still in Florida—what he hadn't known was where. Finding that out had taken him more time and effort than he cared to think about.

"Most kind of you to drop in for a visit like this on our vacation," Pendergast said. "I assume now you'll be heading back to New York?"

Goddamn it, would the guy never tire of busting his balls? Pendergast knew damn well Pickett wasn't paying a social call. This thing had happened at the worst possible time: right when he was hoping to transition to a leadership position in Washington. "Actually, I'm not heading back north quite yet. I'm heading for Captiva Island."

Pendergast sipped his drink. "Ah."

Pickett gave a brusque little nod. "There's a case unfolding as we speak: a very unique case. This morn-ing, a large number of feet—human feet—washed up on shore, each encased in a green shoe."

Pendergast raised his eyebrows. "How many?"

"They're still coming in with the tide. Somewhere in the upper forties, at last count."

Both Pendergast and Constance Greene remained silent. Pickett reached over and unlatched his brief-case. He felt a little uncomfortable sharing confidential information with Pendergast in front of Ms. Greene. But he'd heard she was as much Pendergast's amanu-ensis and researcher as she was his ward. Besides, he sensed asking her to leave would not be helpful to his mission—to put it mildly.

"Nobody knows where the feet came from, why there are so many, who they belonged to, or any-thing else," he went on, taking a manila folder of photographs out of the briefcase and handing it to Pendergast. "That's why the FBI is getting involved with the case, along with the Coast Guard and local authorities. We'll be forming a task force."

"Have any commonalities been identified?" Pen-dergast asked as he flipped through the photographs. "Age, sex, race?"

"Too early to say. Law enforcement resources are still arriving and the remains are being transferred to the M.E.'s office in Fort Myers. It's not an easy crime scene to secure. We'll know more in twelve to twenty-four hours."

Constance Greene sat forward in her chair. "You called it a crime scene. How can you be sure of that?"

Pickett started to reply but then stopped himself. The question seemed either very shrewd or very stupid. What could this be, if not some horrific mass murder? "The feet show indications of extreme trauma: torn flesh, broken and chopped bones. I can't imagine any accident or other circumstance that would cause such injuries."

"Only feet have been washed ashore, you say? No other body parts?"

"None. The rest of the remains have yet to be discovered."

"You speak of 'remains.' How do you know the people who once possessed these feet are, in fact, dead?"

"I—" Pickett fell silent a moment. "We don't know. As I said, this case appears to be unique." As annoyed as he was by these probing questions, he was careful to add special emphasis to the word *unique*.

"I would imagine it is. Thank you, Mr. Pickett." And Constance sat back in her chair, like a lawyer completing a cross-examination. Pendergast handed her the folder of photographs. Pickett winced inwardly but said nothing.

"Fascinating," Pendergast said. "But I assume you didn't go so far out of your way just to exchange pleasantries about an odd case."

"No." Already Pickett was growing accustomed to the novelty of the surroundings, and he felt a good ground of command once again beneath his feet. "Actually, it's not that far out of my way. As I said, I'm headed to Captiva now. And I'd like you to go with me."

"I see," Pendergast replied after a silence. "And why is that, may I ask?"

"This has all the makings of an exceedingly unusual and difficult case. I think your experience would be...useful."

"I'm gratified by your faith in my experience. But, as you can see, we're on vacation."

Constance, Pickett noticed, was looking through the photographs with undisguised interest. "I would think you, of all agents under my command, would find it intriguing," he said.

"Under normal circumstances, perhaps. But Constance and I have not completed our holiday."

Pickett took a deep breath. "Nevertheless, I would like you to have a look at the scene." He knew he could order Pendergast to take the case, but it was a tactic that would surely backfire.

Pendergast finished his drink. "Sir," he said, "I assume you don't mind my speaking freely?"

Pickett waved a hand.

"You already ordered me to uproot myself from New York and come down to Florida to work on one case. And now you are asking me to 'have a look' at a second. To be frank, I don't much like the idea of taking up cases in distant locations at a whim. I would prefer to return to my field office of record—that is, New York City. Besides, based on what you've described, this problem seems outside my area of competence. It doesn't sound like the work of a serial killer. The circumstances may be interesting, but I don't see any deviant psychological angle. It would hardly be gentlemanly of me to leave Constance here unchaperoned."

"You needn't worry, Aloysius," Constance said, handing back the photographs. "You can hardly call this place 'unchaperoned.' Besides, I have Huysmans to keep me company." With a brief nod, she indicated the book by her side.

Pickett was thinking. He could assign Gibbons, or Fowler, or Singh. But he had a gut feeling that this case was so bizarre—so sui generis—that Pendergast would be by far the best tool in his belt. The Brokenhearts case had already demonstrated that. He reconsidered ordering Pendergast to come with him. Fact was, this bantering refusal of Pendergast's bordered on insubordination. Pickett's habitual impatience began to reassert itself. He'd come all the way down here. He'd humored Pendergast, dangling tasty tidbits in front of him. *He* wanted to get back to New York, too, and time was passing. He stood up.

"Listen, Pendergast," he said. "Come with me. I've

got a chopper waiting. We'll look at the scene. Just *look* at it, for Chrissakes. We can argue about the details afterward. Over stone crabs."

Pendergast, who had been idly regarding his empty glass, looked up slowly. "Stone crabs?"

4

THE CHOPPER LANDED on the fourteenth green of a golf course at the far northern end of Sanibel Island. Pendergast unbuckled his harness and stepped onto the greensward, looking around. It appeared that someone, either Pickett or a lackey, had done the advance work well: a motor launch was waiting at a dock just past the fairway rough, and once they had climbed aboard, it backed immediately into Wulfert Channel, then turned and made its way west under the low bridge through Blind Pass, the narrow passage between Sanibel and Captiva. On the ride over the Florida Everglades, Pickett had told Pendergast what he knew of the two islands: they were tourist meccas, known— unlike Palm Beach or Miami—for their relaxed atmosphere, extensive nature preserves, resistance to commercial development, and some of the best shelling in the world.

None of these attributes was evident as they came around Blind Pass and within sight of Turner Beach. Three Coast Guard vessels—a cutter and two patrol boats—were visible offshore. The cutter was keeping curious pleasure boats away, while the two patrol boats roamed back and forth a few hundred yards off the beach, like beagles sniffing for a scent. As Pendergast watched, there was a yell from one of the patrol boats; it stopped, and a man with a long pole and net reached out and snagged something.

Other police and emergency vessels clogged the channel beyond Blind Pass, and their launch was forced to come ashore at the closest end of the beach, where the sand abutted a breakwater. The beach itself was a scene of frantic activity: half a dozen knots of people, speaking animatedly; EMS and crime scene personnel moving back and forth, taking notes, gathering evidence, kneeling in the sand; Coast Guard officers speaking into radios. Traffic was backed up behind a police checkpoint, cops checking documents and directing a single lane of backed-up vehicles over Blind Pass Bridge. And at least a mile of the beach itself was roped off with yellow tape, dozens of evidence flags fluttering above the high tide mark.

"Looks like a goddamn anthill somebody just kicked open," Pickett said as he and Pendergast stepped out of the launch and onto the sand. He looked around a minute. "Let's start with them," he said, indicating the largest huddle on the beach.

Beyond the police cordon, throngs of people were clustered along the main road of the island, standing on tiptoe, phones held high to get a view of what they couldn't see themselves. Others were staring out of second- and third-story windows of houses and condos. Some even had telescopes. There was a mass of press kept behind the bridge checkpoint. Police were now beginning to unspool and prop up a heavy curtain of white plastic sheeting along the line of crime scene tape in an attempt to shield a portion of the lower beach from view.

Pickett reached the group and introduced himself, passing out a few cards. He turned to introduce Pendergast, but Pendergast had continued walking on past, threading his way through the confusion to a higher spot on the dunes where he could get a view of the entire scene. He noticed that someone had reached the place before him: a tall, tanned man in shorts and a polo shirt. He was perhaps fifty, with sun-bleached hair and eyes and two vertical creases down his weathered cheeks. The only signs of authority were the thumb-break holster and police radio attached to his belt. He stood in a shaded spot beneath a stand of palms, arms crossed, watching the activity with an almost melancholy expression.

He nodded as Pendergast approached, giving the

agent a faint smile and, with a glance up and down, taking note of his suit.

"Good afternoon," Pendergast said, bowing and touching his Panama hat with one finger.

"Do you really think so?" the man replied.

"No," Pendergast said. "But one must maintain the pleasantry of manners, even in the face of the grotesque."

"I can't argue with that." The man extended his hand. "Chief Perelman, Sanibel PD."

"Special Agent Pendergast, FBI."

"I knew it." Perelman nodded toward the knot of people Pickett was commandeering. "I saw you arrive with that fellow."

"Ah." Pendergast nodded. "You knew he was coming?"

"He made sure everyone knew he was coming. You might want to pull your badge out and put it on a lanyard, you know, just to keep from getting challenged."

"I find it much more interesting—and revealing— to go incognito. But I notice you, too, are in mufti."

Perelman looked down at his polo shirt. "Actually, this is my usual uniform. And everybody already knows who I am. Sanibel isn't your typical Florida resort, Agent Pendergast. In fact, it isn't your typical town anywhere. We count eight best-selling authors as residents, along with three world-famous painters, a Nobel laureate, a Pulitzer poet, and two ex-directors of intelligence services. There's plenty of money here, but it's not usually on display. If you want to see conspicuous consumption on a world-class scale, Naples is just over the causeway and south a few miles. We like our streets quiet, our beaches clean, and our tourists civilized."

This last, apparently a town motto, was delivered with the slightest touch of irony.

There was a cry from the line of surf, then another; several uniformed cops and Coast Guard officers darted toward the sounds. Both men looked in the direction of the commotion. More feet, it seemed, were rolling in.

"Looks like two more," the man said. "That would make fifty-seven."

"Has there been any regularity or pattern to their arrival?" Pendergast asked.

The chief shook his head. "As best as we can tell, there were two initial waves. The bulk of them came in then. But, as you can see, it's a gift that keeps on giving. Until now, the last one was almost an hour ago. Maybe a third wave is about to land."

"And they've remained confined to this stretch of barrier island?"

Perelman nodded. "So far."

"Isn't that rather unusual?"

"Actually, it isn't. When the tides are right—as

they are now, just on the ebb—any floating debris tends to stick together and not disperse before reaching land. These islands are uniquely located in terms of ocean currents, which focus flotsam into a narrow lane and cause immense quantities of shells to wash up."

The man's radio squawked. Perelman plucked it from his belt, listened for a moment, then muttered a brief string of orders and returned it to its clasp. Down at the surf line, the officers had retrieved the newly discovered feet and were placing them carefully on the sand, marking them with flags.

Pendergast looked around for a moment. "If I may ask an even more intrusive question: why are you back here observing, rather than over there involving yourself in the thick of command and control?"

"Do you see that knot of people around ADC Pickett? In particular, that man with all the gold braid on his uniform? He's the deputy sector commander of the Coast Guard. The slender woman next to him is the mayor of Sanibel and Captiva. And that other fellow, the mustachioed bald man with the crutches, is chief of the Fort Myers police. With an incident of this magnitude in Lee County, Fort Myers automatically takes command—along with their detectives, homicide investigators, and forensic teams. So my duty is to direct my officers, keep the residents and visitors calm, and make sure we get through this as best we can. *Non omnia possumus omnes.*"

Pendergast glanced at him with faint amusement. "Are you a Latin scholar as well as a police chief?"

Perelman shrugged. "Some things were best said by Virgil."

"Quite so. And now, would you excuse me?" And, bowing again, he made his way slowly down the beach in the direction of the water, pausing here and there to glance around. His pale eyes took in everything, large and small: the knots of people working the scene; the boats maintaining their vigil off the coast; the flight of the gulls; the little flags fluttering along the shore. He stepped up to one of the flags. Beside it was a shoe of a uniform light-green color, an amputated foot nestled coyly inside.

He knelt. It wasn't a sneaker exactly, nor was it a slipper. There were no laces, it being of an elastic, slip-on style. The sole was stamped in a nonskid waffle pattern. It was the kind of inexpensive, even disposable footwear someone who worked in a manufacturing clean room or a hospital ward might wear.

Reaching into a pocket, he pulled out nitrile gloves and a mask and put them on. Then he plucked the shoe from the sand, looked at it closely, turned it over in his hands. It wasn't only the design but the material that seemed unusual.

While he was poking a finger inside to palpate the flesh, he heard someone call loudly. "Hey! Hey, you!"

Pendergast turned to see the man in the gold-braided uniform—the one the police chief had said was a Coast Guard commander—gesturing at him, a hard look on his face.

Pickett said something and then called out to Pendergast. "Agent Pendergast, would you mind?"

Pendergast carefully replaced the shoe, walked across the beach, and approached the group, pulling off the mask and gloves as he did so.

The Coast Guard commander was glowering at him. "You shouldn't be touching crime scene evidence without—"

"Agent Pendergast," Pickett interrupted, his voice edged with impatience, "this is Deputy Sector Commander Baugh of the U.S. Coast Guard." He then introduced Pendergast to the mayor of Sanibel and the police chief of Fort Myers, both of whom seemed a little cowed by the red-faced bluster of the commander. "Commander Baugh will be taking overall charge of the investigation."

"That's correct," said Baugh. "And any evidence handling will be done by teams designated for the task. This is a fluid situation, and we need to set up a clear chain of command, division of responsibilities, procedures, and timetables. Only then can we proceed with the investigation."

"Speaking of timetables," Pendergast said, "it appears these feet have been in the water about three weeks. I'm curious to know how that fact will drive your investigative plans."

There was a sudden silence. The commander looked at him, his frown mingling with uncertainty. "Three weeks? How would you know that?"

"Or perhaps four, on the outside—the laboratory examination will provide more specifics. You see, Commander, the life cycle of the lowly barnacle is most useful in matters of forensic marine biology. They develop on a set schedule, and a juvenile barnacle in the early sessile phase was visible on the sole of the shoe I was examining. Barnacles— something you should look into at your earliest opportunity."

When Baugh turned to the bald police chief from Fort Myers and asked why this barnacle observation had not yet been reported, Pickett took Pendergast a few yards away from the group. "You can see how it is," he said, an irritated crease in his brow. "Already the jackasses are out in force. The case is so bizarre it's thrown all the local agencies into confusion. Commander Baugh is claiming jurisdiction, given that these damned feet are coming in from the sea. Naturally, it's important for the FBI to be represented."

"Naturally."

"No doubt a task force will be set up, and I'll bet dollars to doughnuts that Commander Baugh will be put in charge. You'll have to appear subordinate to the commander. I'll expect regular reports."

Pendergast took a deep breath. "Sir, are you forgetting what I said earlier?"

"I remember what you said. But tell me: have you ever seen anything like this before?"

"No."

"Never in your experience? Nothing remotely like it?"

A pause. "No."

"Do you have even the slightest idea of a reason why sixty, seventy human feet would wash up on a beach in the middle of a Florida resort island?"

"Not the slightest."

"And yet, you're not curious about it?"

Pendergast did not answer the question.

"There you go." Pickett looked pleased, as if he'd just checked a chess opponent. "*That's* why you must take this case. Because it is absolutely outside of all our experience. You *have* to know."

"I do not particularly like boats or the sea."

"Dramamine," said Pickett. "And I was thinking you could use some help on this case. Like last time, I mean. A partner."

Pendergast went quite still.

"It's worth mentioning that Agent Coldmoon's

still around. He's applied for a posting to Colorado, and if it's approved—which it will be—it will take a few weeks to process." Pickett paused to brush some sand from his cuffs. "And after all, you worked so brilliantly together."

Pendergast remained still. "I made every effort to be accommodating to Agent Coldmoon. Are you implying I could not have solved the Brokenhearts case on my own?"

The long silence answered the question. "We're dealing with something quite different here," Pickett went on, "but equally baffling. Coldmoon is an agent whose qualities complement yours."

"As I recall," Pendergast said coldly, "through haste and impetuousness, Agent Coldmoon fell into a pit and I had to rescue him."

Pickett held up his hands. "All right, all right, let's forget about Coldmoon. You know I always believe partnering is the better strategy, but never mind. If I give you free rein to explore this on your own, using your own methods—observing the task force chain of command, of course, but with total freedom from our end—will you agree to investigate?"

As Pickett asked the question, a look came over Pendergast's face. This expression, too, resembled one commonly seen in a chess match, when checkmate was at hand. "If those are your orders, then I would have no objection to remaining a few days, merely to satisfy my curiosity. Sir."

"Then let's inform Commander Baugh at once." And putting one arm lightly over Pendergast's shoulder, Pickett began leading the way back to the group clustered nearby on the sand.

5

Roger Smithback, reporter for the *Miami Herald*, hadn't waited to get his editor's green light on the story. When his police band scanner picked up news of feet washing up on a beach on Captiva Island, he had jumped into his Subaru and driven like hell across the Florida peninsula, his radar detector and laser jammer both working overtime to avoid the cops. Smithback was familiar with Sanibel from having taken an expensive vacation there with a girlfriend (now ex—and a pox on her), and he realized it posed a serious access problem. As he drove, he pondered the logistics of reaching the crime scene and getting the scoop. First, he was going to be hours late. There were plenty of newspapers and other media outlets closer by who would be sending out reporters. The Fort Myers *News-Press* was going to get at least a two-hour jump on him, not to mention the *Tampa Bay Times*, the *Sarasota Herald-Tribune*, and the *Charlotte Sun*. The other problem was physically getting onto Captiva Island. The cops would certainly have set up checkpoints. One would no doubt be at the Sanibel Causeway, which he could probably lie his way through. The bigger problem was getting from Sanibel to Captiva. There was only one connection between the two islands, the Blind Pass Bridge. If memory served, that bridge ended right at the beach where the feet were washing up. It was sure to be locked down tight.

But no way was Roger Smithback, senior reporter of the *Herald*, going to join a crowd of miserable journalists sweating behind some barrier, pleading for a crumb of a story. He was going to get onto Captiva Island if it was the last thing he did—and the logical way to do it was by boat. As he drove, he poked away at his smartphone, made a few calls, and soon had a plan worked out. Instead of driving onto Sanibel, he would take the nearby causeway to Pine Island, drive south to St. James City, and from there hire a boat to take him across Pine Island Sound to the Captiva Island Yacht Club. The yacht club had a courtesy car available for yachtsmen, which would drive him wherever he wished on the island. All he had to do was act like some rich yachting bastard, passing out lots of twenties as tips.

Smithback then texted Kraski, his editor, and told him he was covering the story—just so it wouldn't get assigned to anyone else. Screw proper channels: this one was his. Feet washing up on a beach—he fairly tingled at the ghastly appeal of it.

Three and a half hours after leaving Miami, his plan executed perfectly, Smithback found himself waving goodbye to the nice gentleman from the yacht club who had dropped him off near the southern end of Captiva Drive. Captiva was a narrow island, exclusive, with a single road down the middle, driveways on either side leading to million-dollar waterfront houses. In scoping out the scene from afar, Smithback had decided the best way to get close to the action would be to sneak through someone's yard to reach the gulf-side beach. Access from the public parking lot would surely be closed off and swarming with cops.

He picked a house that looked unoccupied and slipped down the driveway, skirted around the side, then across a backyard to a path that ran through sea grape and hopbush to the broad expanse of beach beyond. He paused in the shrubbery to take off his shoes and socks, shove them in his reporter's bag, and roll up his pants—to create the appearance of a local beachcomber.

Where the path joined the beach, it was blocked with fluttering strings of yellow crime scene tape. As he looked up and down the shore, he could see that

the entire beach had been taped off—and the law enforcement response was massive. There were several
Coast Guard vessels cruising back and forth near the
shore, with Coast Guard servicemembers dipping
nets into the sea, fishing out feet. The beach itself
was patrolled by police dune buggies and officers on
foot. It looked like multiple departments had turned
out—Fort Myers and Sanibel at the least—and there
were also a number of Coast Guard Auxiliary regu-
lars in blue jumpsuits. Two Coast Guard helicopters
circled above, but there were no media choppers
anywhere. Good.

Behind the tape strung along the back of the beach,
he could see a number of people watching the action,
talking excitedly, taking pictures and selfies. But as
he scanned the crowd with his binocs, he couldn't
make out any obvious journalists. All those jokers
were no doubt penned up like sheep at the Blind
Pass Bridge. He alone had made it to the island...or
so he hoped.

At the far end of the beach, near the inlet, he could
see what looked like a temporary command post. A
white plastic screen fenced it from view. That was
where the heart of the action was—and where he
needed to be.

Walking fast, he worked his way south through
the onlookers. He would need to get some choice interviews from these witnesses—the more hysterical

the better. But that could come later. Within ten minutes, he'd reached the point closest to the command center, where the white screen fence began. Scanning with his binocs, he could now get a general idea of what was happening. Dozens of light-green shoes were being brought in, logged, tagged, and placed in refrigerated evidence containers, which in turn were being loaded into the back of an ambulance. They all seemed to have feet still inside them. His heart quickened at the same time that his gorge rose.

He couldn't hear what was being said over in the tight knot of brass. He needed to get closer. Scouting around, he realized one section of the barrier was visually screened by a row of parked cruisers on the beach. If he could get inside at that point, he might not be noticed, and then he'd be able to mingle with the technicians, detectives, and others who were not in uniform. Almost all had IDs on lanyards around their necks. He had a lanyard, too—which held his press credentials. He pulled it out of his bag, removed the press card, and shoved in his PADI diving certification card. It looked official from a distance, and even if someone checked they might just think he was some kind of authorized diver.

He rolled his pants back down, put on his shoes and socks, slapped the sand off, smoothed his hair, and hung the lanyard around his neck. His reporter's case would add to the look of someone engaged in legitimate business.

The sun was hanging lower over the gulf, and the parked cars cast long shadows. He sauntered along the barrier to where the view was obscured by the cruisers; then in one quick movement, he pulled out his pocketknife, cut a flap in the barrier, then ducked through and walked quickly to where the cars were, keeping out of sight behind them. So far, so good. Then, mustering a look of purpose, he strode out from behind the cars and angled toward the command tent, walking decisively.

Nobody challenged him. And here he lucked out: at a table where various evidence-gathering items were spread out, there was a box of gloves. He quickly pulled out two and drew them on, then grabbed a face mask and hairnet and donned those as well.

His heart quickened as he realized he was actually going to succeed. Slipping out his cell phone, he pretended to be checking it, while taking dozens of photos of the action—the boxes of shoes, the comings and goings of the cops and technicians, the hastily assembled command center—he got it all.

He edged over to where the feet were being placed in refrigerated coolers. Again pretending to be checking his phone, he took another slew of photographs. He even got in a short video. God almighty, Kraski was going to love this—he was always moaning about not having enough video for the website.

He heard a yell and spun around. Strong arms seized him and his phone was manhandled away by a Coast Guard officer, blazingly angry, quickly joined by another. They looked like identical twins except one was red-haired, the other black-haired.

"What the hell do you think you're doing?" Red Hair yelled.

"He's a journalist. Taking pictures," said Black Hair, pulling off the mask and hairnet.

"Give me back my phone!" Smithback tried to sound authoritative, but his voice cracked. What had given him away?

Red Hair seized his lanyard. "What's this bullshit? A diving ID?" He snorted. "I'm gonna delete these photos."

"Please don't! The public has a right to know!"

"Look, pal, you better be glad we're not going to arrest your ass. We've got enough shit to deal with."

Smithback felt himself being propelled forward by the two officers, one on each side. "Let's go, asshole. You're out of here."

Suddenly the two men halted and Smithback heard a honeyed voice: "Bless me, if it isn't my old acquaintance Roger Smithback."

Smithback twisted around to find himself face-to-face with none other than Agent Pendergast. He was temporarily speechless.

The Coast Guard men seemed uncertain, loosening their grip.

"Hold him fast, gentlemen," said Pendergast, flashing his badge. "He's a slippery one. I've had dealings with him before."

"We caught him photographing everything—even the feet."

"Shameful," said Pendergast, holding out his hand for the phone. "I'll erase those photos, if you please."

"Sure thing."

Pendergast took the phone and began flicking through the photographs with an amused look. "Mr. Smithback, I see you're truly a man of many talents. Such masterly use of depth of field. Pity you can't keep these."

Smithback pleaded. "Agent Pendergast, don't do it. For old time's sake."

"I don't know which 'old time' in particular you're referring to. In any case, I'm afraid you are trespassing on a crime scene and will have to be escorted out. And these photographs destroyed."

"I'm just doing my job."

"And we are doing ours."

Even as he pleaded, he could see Pendergast deleting the pictures. The two Coast Guard officers watched with approval.

"I thought we were friends!" Smithback said, almost at a wail. "Don't!"

"It is done," said Pendergast, wagging his phone. "You shall have your phone returned when you're safely behind the barriers."

Son of a bitch, thought Smithback. But maybe he could get a statement, if nothing else. "Agent Pendergast, can you at least tell me what's going on? Do the police have any theories?"

Pendergast turned and gestured to the Coast Guard men. "Please escort him to the perimeter."

"Wait! Just one question!"

The two men took his arms and led him away, Pendergast following.

Smithback tried again. "Any ideas? Even a guess? One little statement is all I need!"

Pendergast didn't reply.

"How many feet? For the love of God, Pendergast, just give me a number!"

No answer.

They reached the crime scene tape and Pendergast held it up while Smithback was shoved under it. He turned and Pendergast handed him back his phone.

"If you trespass again," Red Hair said, jabbing his finger hard into Smithback's chest, "we'll arrest you. You got that?"

All three turned and walked away. Smithback watched them go, sweating and cursing under his breath. Then he examined his phone, morosely flipping through his photo gallery. The pictures were indeed gone. But wait: a freshly typed message was sitting on his notepad. It said simply: *Check trash. This once.*

And there, waiting in the trash, was a small but extremely well-chosen selection of his photographs.

6

I'T'S LIKE A damn fish market in here," Moira Crossley heard one of the autopsy technicians mutter as he
unpacked a refrigerated crate full of feet, which had
just arrived via ambulance. He arranged them on a
gurney, where other technicians were logging and
photographing them, assembly-line fashion. Crossley was the chief medical examiner for the District
21 office, and she thought she had seen everything
in her many years on the job. All kinds of full or
partial remains had washed up on beaches in her
time, some with pretty bizarre characteristics. But
this...this was beyond the beyond. More than sixty
feet—on a preliminary inspection, at least. Did this
represent sixty-plus homicides? If that were the case,
they might be dealing with one of the worst mass
killings in Florida history. If the individuals were
still alive, however...then where were they? And
what had happened? It defied all explanation.

Crossley's normally quiet and orderly laboratory was a beehive of activity, and it did indeed smell like a fish market—its wares gone bad in the sun. Rivulets of seawater ran down the floor to the central drains, mingled with wriggling shrimp and other sea creatures that had been feeding on the feet, now dislodged by handling.

Another ambulance had just pulled in with two more crates, bringing the total to—sweet Lord in heaven—more than ninety feet, all encased in the same green coverings. She had called in her entire staff, four technicians and two assistant forensic pathologists, to handle the influx. Chief Perelman of the Sanibel Island PD was also there, having arrived with the last batch, along with two of his detectives. Fort Myers homicide was also involved, not to mention several Coast Guard staff in operational dress who appeared to have no clue about what they were supposed to be doing, standing around with furrowed brows, trying to look occupied.

But among the group milling around, one figure stood out like a sore thumb: a tall, pale man in a white linen suit, crisp white shirt, and black tie. He had a chiseled face and a pair of eyes that glittered like polished dimes. While the man himself was as immobile as a Greek statue, those eyes roamed restlessly about, taking in everything.

Crossley turned to her assistant, Paul Rameau. "No time like the present," she said.

"For what?" he asked. Paul was a great big teddy bear of a technician, practically bursting from his scrubs, with a beard like a Viking's. He was a hard worker, eager to please, but not, she had to admit, the brightest bulb in the room.

"Grab one of those and bring it to Bay One. We're going to do a dissection."

"Now?"

"I was actually thinking the Thursday after next."

"Right, okay, sorry." Using forceps, Paul gingerly picked up a foot, put it in a container, and carried it into one of the small exam stations set along one wall. As she removed it and placed it on a dissection table, Rameau set up the video recorder and tested it.

"Implements."

Rameau filled a rolling trolley with dissecting tools and wheeled it over. Crossley slipped her mask up and selected a small pair of tweezers.

"I beg your pardon," came a voice from behind her, smooth as satin.

She turned to see the pale man. "Yes?"

"I should like to observe, if that is possible."

She had no idea what he was doing there. He looked like nobody she had ever seen before in law enforcement—or medicine. "And who might you be?" she asked.

A hand slipped into the suit and out came a leather wallet, which dropped open, exposing a gold-and-blue shield below and an ID above.

"Ah, FBI," Crossley said. Whatever else he was, he was probably—almost surely—a rung above the others on the ladder. He certainly radiated authority.

"Special Agent Pendergast," said the man, with a slight nod. The accent was unmistakable and unlike any other Southern intonation, and she quickly recognized it from her childhood as that rarefied upper-class New Orleans accent possessed by only the oldest of families. Pendergast . . . the name was vaguely familiar, too, and not in a pleasant way.

"Chief Medical Examiner Moira Crossley," she said briskly. "You're welcome to watch. But gown up and stay well out of the way."

"Certainly."

She turned her attention to the foot on the table and, with the video now rolling, began the gross examination, starting with a description. She examined the end of the bone, noting that the amputation was crude in the extreme, effected by a dull, heavy-bladed instrument that left cut marks and splintering. It appeared that a series of such blows—at least six, judging from the marks on the tibia and fibula—had separated the foot from the body about two inches above the ankle joint. Sea life had stripped the area above the joint of flesh, leaving only bone. But below that the flesh, protected by the covering, was still present. It had swollen badly and was squeezing out of the opening. Clusters of tiny sea animals were still clinging to the raw flesh—worms, amphipods, cyprids, and sea lice. The flesh was all chewed up and she could see oozing holes where larger creatures had burrowed.

"Paul, bring me an ethanol specimen jar."

Paul lumbered over with it and, using the tweezers, she carefully removed as many different specimens as she could find and dropped them in for later examination.

"May I ask a question?" came the cool voice from behind.

Crossley felt a twinge of annoyance. "Yes?"

"From what direction did the blows originate?"

Good question. She examined the foot again. "The blows were directed from above, to the right anterior side of the leg in a haphazard fashion, at an angle of approximately forty to seventy degrees from the horizontal."

"Thank you."

Chief Perelman had also gowned up and was watching as well. She was glad of it. She liked working with the chief and hoped he might be of use in keeping back the plague of other investigators, not to mention press.

She continued her gross examination, going down

the list of requisite observations. When that was completed, it was time to remove the shoe, dissect the foot, and take samples for the toxicology and histology labs.

"Another question?" came the honeyed voice.

"What?"

"Is there a way to tell if the flesh has previously been frozen?"

Crossley was startled by the question. That test would never have occurred to her, but on reflection, she thought it could and probably should be done.

"Yes, it's possible to test for that, and I'll add it to the histology lab request." She turned to Paul. "Shears."

Paul handed her a pair of shears, and she began cutting off the shoe.

"I beg your pardon," the voice intruded again, "but may I have the footwear as evidence when you are finished?"

"No." She continued cutting. The flesh strained from below the ankle like an overinflated balloon.

Snip, snip. Gray and pink flesh bulged alarmingly. The skin seemed to be moving, as if alive.

Snip, snip—

And then, like the bursting of something rotten, a creature came whipping out. It was a hagfish, the most hellish of nightmares. Because of the sudden release in pressure, a spray of hagfish slime splattered across her chest and struck Paul full in the face and beard. With a piercing yell the technician jumped backward, pawing at his face, while the hagfish landed on the floor, wriggling and spewing more mucus from its slime glands as it slithered into the center of the room.

"Oh God, *no*—!" she cried as Paul, blinded, slammed into the long gurney on which the feet had been arranged, knocking it to the floor with a massive crash of stainless steel. The feet tumbled through the air and hit the ground, bouncing every which way, dislodging more hagfish, crabs, and eels, which scuttled and writhed, snapped and slithered across the tiled floor along with a rush of seawater, chewed-up flesh, and a stench revolting beyond belief. There was a huge uproar as people surged back, trying to get away from that slimy tide, slipping and falling everywhere.

Crossley looked on in dismay as the brisk and professional operation she had organized collapsed into the slapstick chaos of a Three Stooges two-reeler.

She turned to see Agent Pendergast standing well back from the imbroglio, surveying the scene with an amused expression. He turned and observed her scrubs, dripping with hagfish slime. "In all things of nature," he drawled, "there is something of the marvelous."

"You call this marvelous?" Crossley asked.

Chief Perelman suppressed a laugh. "Aristotle would be amused."

"Well," said Crossley, mightily annoyed, "I've got a god-awful mess to clean up in here. Since the dissection is effectively over, would you two please clear out of my lab?"

As they turned to go, she said: "And, Agent Pendergast? You may have the damned shoe."

7

To Chief Perelman's infinite relief, the task force was set up inside the capacious Fort Myers Police Department on Widman Way instead of his own cramped offices behind the Sanibel public library. He pulled his Explorer into a space. He and his two lieutenants, Towne and Morris, got out. Perelman liked to drive himself as much as possible, abhorring a dedicated driver, even insisting on chauffeuring his subordinates around when he could.

The first meeting of the task force had been scheduled for eleven, but he arrived thirty minutes early, partly in case of traffic, but mostly because he wanted to get a feeling for the task force commander, Baugh, and how this whole thing would work. He'd never been part of a task force before, and his impression of Baugh hadn't been favorable, but Perelman believed in giving everyone a second chance. After that, they were irredeemable in his book.

"Honor, Ethics, Accountability, Respect, Teamwork," said Towne, staring up at the façade of the building, where those words had been inscribed in giant letters. "I hope to God that's more than just hot air."

"We're going in assuming the best," said Perelman.

He entered with his lieutenants and was directed by a dour secretary to the task force staging area, a large conference room in the back of the building, with an adjacent office of open-plan cubicles, swarming with technicians and workers setting up desks, computers, big screens, and whiteboards. It looked, at first glance, like a reasonably efficient and organized operation. Hope sprang up in Perelman's breast: more evidence this was a good start. In the hall outside, a coffee, tea, and ice water station had been set up.

Perelman made a beeline for it. He poured himself a cup, then dumped in three half-and-halfs and the same number of sugar packets. He sipped the coffee. Decent. Quite decent. Towne and Morris helped themselves as well, and they carried their steaming cups into the conference room, claiming seats in the front. Pretty soon others began to arrive— a captain and two lieutenants from Fort Myers PD, who greeted Perelman, along with a small cluster of uniformed cops. Caspar, the Fort Myers chief, wasn't with them. That was typical of Caspar; even though he had nominal charge of the police aspect of the investigation, he was counting the months to retirement, currently laid up with a bad case of gout, and would be happy to let his most senior staff— and the Sanibel police force—get their hands dirty. If the investigation was ultimately successful, he'd inevitably get involved in its final stages, limping in to claim more than his share of credit.

Next in the informal parade was Kyra Markson, mayor of Sanibel, wearing her trademark tennis whites despite—or more likely because of—the tragic events. Her grim expression eased a little when she caught sight of him. Perelman nodded back. In earlier years, Markson had been a top executive in a public relations firm, and this—along with her family's history at Sanibel, dating back to the days of the ferry—had been an unexpected but ideal qualification for mayor. She had evidently seen unusual qualifications in him as well, because she'd been instrumental in his becoming chief. They functioned well together by respecting each other's territory: she kept the people happy, while he kept them safe. He knew Markson, at least, could be relied on to stay out of his way on this unless he needed her administrative firepower.

A moment later, Chief M.E. Crossley arrived with two assistants. Her face was rather drawn, and Perelman wondered what else might have happened besides the hagfish incident after he left her lab the evening before.

He looked around, curious where that fellow Pendergast was but not seeing him.

And then, arriving in tight formation, came the Coast Guard contingent, led by Commander Baugh in service dress blue, followed by other personnel in dress blues or operational uniforms. It was an impressive-looking crowd. Baugh went up to the front while the rest seated themselves. A tech wired him with a lavalier. The room fell silent as Baugh walked to the podium and withdrew some notes from his jacket. Exactly at the stroke of eleven, Agent Pendergast slipped in and, instead of taking a seat, stood leaning against the back wall of the room, arms crossed. He was wearing another white suit, this one apparently silk rather than linen. It seemed to have the faintest shade of coral to it, but in the lighting Perelman couldn't be sure. What he was sure of was that he'd never known an FBI agent to dress in such a way.

"Welcome," said Baugh, looking around. "I am Deputy Sector Commander Stephen Baugh, Sector Seven of the United States Coast Guard, and I will be heading Task Force Captiva. The task force consists of the Coast Guard, the Fort Myers Police Department, the Sanibel Police Department, the Federal Bureau of Investigation, the District Twenty-One Medical Examiner's Office..."

Perelman tuned out the detailed description of

command structure and responsibilities. When it was over, Baugh paused dramatically, looked fiercely around the room, and, gripping the podium, began to talk about the crime itself.

"So far," he said, "ninety-nine green shoes have washed up on a one-mile stretch of Captiva Island, each one with a human foot inside, crudely severed above the ankle. You're familiar with the details— which, pending further analysis and tests, are few— so I won't go over them again here. The key fact is that the feet have been in the water about twenty-five days, give or take. We know this from the development of associated marine organisms. What I'd like to do now is go around the room and ask each chief a simple question: do any theories suggest themselves to you? I'll give you all a moment to confer with your people."

Perelman glanced at his lieutenants. "Any ideas?"

"Well," said Towne, "I was thinking maybe this is some crazy cult. You know, like the Kool-Aid guy, Jim Jones, or those Heaven's Gate people who thought they were going to join an alien spacecraft."

"Hmm. Interesting. And you, Morris?"

"Totally baffled, but the idea of a cult seems as good as any."

Perelman nodded.

"What about you, Chief?"

"I've no idea, so let's go with the cult."

Now the commander raised his head. "Are we ready? Assistant Chief Dunleavy, Fort Myers PD?"

Chief Caspar's stand-in rose, a black woman in her fifties. "We were wondering if these feet may have come from some medical experimentation, maybe drifted up from Central America. I say that because those shoes look similar to the kind nurses wear in hospitals. But that's sheer speculation."

"Thank you. Chief Perelman?"

"With the same caveat—that this is speculation— we wondered if it might be from a doomsday cult. One whose initiation required the removal of a limb, by a priest or whatever."

"Thank you. Special Agent Pendergast?"

A long silence. All eyes were turned to the figure standing at the rear of the room. He slowly uncrossed his arms and said, simply, "I would rather not speculate."

"No one's going to hold it against you. That's what I want—speculation."

"And that, Commander, is what I do *not* want."

This fell into a leaden silence and the commander rolled his eyes. "You're entitled to your opinion. And now, I'll direct the question to myself."

Perelman saw this was where the commander had been going all along.

"I want to draw your attention to the crudity of the amputations," Baugh began. "To the institutional sameness of the shoes. To the fact that all washed up essentially at once, which means they were released into the ocean at the same time." He paused. "Think about it: What nearby country would be capable of such a barbarous act? What country has one of the highest incarceration rates in the world? What *country* is ninety miles off our shores?"

This was followed by a long silence.

"Cuba."

He let that sink in and went on. "They have more than one coastal prison, and some, like the Combinado del Este, are among the most brutal in the world, where political prisoners are jailed, tortured—and executed." He leaned forward. "While we don't have any direct evidence yet, I would propose the most likely conclusion is that, one way or another, this load of feet came from Cuba as the product of torture."

Perelman had to admit this was not a bad hypothesis. But Baugh's certainty made him uneasy. He'd been a cop too long to put any stock in a theory without supporting evidence.

Baugh left the podium and walked over to a nearby table covered with charts and maritime volumes, manned by a rather unprepossessing-looking Coast Guard lieutenant. A murmur of conversation rose in the room and Baugh held up his hands. "So let's talk broad assignments. The Coast Guard will be in

charge of all seagoing investigations and operations."
He grasped the top chart and held it up. "Our
first priority will be to do a drift analysis, retracing
currents, waves, and wind forces to see if we can't
pinpoint *where* those feet originated in Cuba. We'll
liaise with Homeland Security to get classified satellite imagery of all sites of interest." He cleared his
throat. "Sanibel PD will be in charge of maintaining
the security and integrity of the immediate crime
scene, patrolling the beach, and picking up any stray
shoes. The District Twenty-One Medical Examiner's
Office will continue to process and run laboratory
tests on the remains and associated evidence. Fort
Myers PD will gather witness statements, manage
the press, and run overall law enforcement efforts
from the task force's back office. And the Federal
Bureau of Investigation—" he paused to peer at
Pendergast— "will be asked to scour the NCAVC
databases for any similar crimes, as well as to analyze
the shoes and track them back to their source of
manufacture."

At this, Perelman noted that Pendergast raised his
index finger in a querying fashion.

"Yes?"

"Commander Baugh, may I ask the dates of those
charts?"

"Dates? You mean, when they were created?"

"Precisely."

"I fail to see why that's relevant. These are the most accurate charts available. All the merchant mariners and Coast Guard captains use them. The tides and currents simply don't change much over the years."

"Yes, but the dates, please?"

"As a sector commander in the Coast Guard, I have over ten thousand command hours on these waters as the captain or master of a vessel. I use these charts every day with complete confidence." Baugh smiled. "Agent Pendergast, have you had any seafaring experience?"

"I believe I am what you might term a landlubber. Nevertheless, I would very much like to know the *dates* of those *charts*."

With an irritated gesture, Baugh turned to the lieutenant at the table. "Darby?"

The man examined the lower corner of the top map. "Nineteen sixty-one," he said in a reedy voice. He shuffled to the next. "Nineteen sixty-five." Another shuffle. "Nineteen fifty-nine."

"Thank you, Lieutenant." Baugh looked back at Pendergast. "Satisfied?"

The expression on Pendergast's face betrayed anything but satisfaction.

"Agent Pendergast, you've already confessed your lack of knowledge of the sea. So may I suggest you focus on the NCAVC databases and the manufacturer of those shoes—and leave the oceanographic science to us? Or perhaps there is something unclear about your assignment?"

"Nothing."

"Thank you. Okay, people, let's get this done."

As the meeting broke up, Perelman looked around for Pendergast, but the man seemed to have vanished. Baugh had come down on him a little hard, and Perelman sensed Pendergast was a man who could be pushed only so far before something happened— something perhaps quite ugly.

8

IRONICALLY, AFTER SEARCHING around for Pendergast without success as the meeting broke up,
Perelman found the FBI agent in the parking lot—
leaning up against the chief's unmarked Explorer.

"Looking for me?" Perelman asked as he approached.

"Indeed I am," Pendergast said. "I wondered if we
might have a chat."

"Sure. Care to grab some lunch?"

"Not especially. I was thinking that perhaps we
could take a stroll along Turner Beach."

At first, Perelman thought this was a joke. But
Pendergast's smile was at present too faint to support
even the driest pretense at humor. Upon leaving the
station, the man had donned an expensive pair of
Persol sunglasses and a wide-brimmed Panama hat.
Now he looked even less like a law enforcement
agent and more like...well, a member of the polo
club, maybe, or perhaps even a stylish drug lord.

In his job, Perelman had grown used to eccentricities of all kinds. Besides, he felt rather curious—he wasn't sure why—to see what Pendergast would do next. His beach patrol officers were already "maintaining the security and integrity of the immediate crime scene," as Baugh had directed, leaving him temporarily free to examine the case from a broader perspective. Towne and Morris could bum one of half a dozen other rides back onto the islands. So he merely shrugged. "Sure. Would you like to ride with me?"

"If you don't mind."

So Pendergast presently had no transportation, either. Perelman shrugged this off as well and they got into the police SUV. He started the engine, made his way to McGregor Boulevard, then turned south toward the Sanibel causeway.

"Do you mind the open windows?" Perelman asked. The temperature was hovering around ninety, with 100 percent humidity, but Perelman disliked air conditioning.

"I prefer it, thank you."

They drove in silence for five or ten minutes. Pendergast, who was gazing out at the palm-lined street, seemed in no hurry to talk. Finally, Perelman asked: "How did you know this was my car?"

"I suppose I could give you a long list of potential giveaways: the unobtrusive spot lamps, the hidden door lock plungers in the backseat, the empty shotgun mount, other unmistakable accoutrements of the Ford Police Interceptor Utility—but it was the gold-edged 'SPD' parking sticker on your windshield that rendered further examination unnecessary."

Perelman chuckled, shook his head. He was driving fast, and they were already past Cape Coral and nearing the causeway. They navigated their way past a series of traffic cones and temporary road signs bordering the first roadblock. Minutes later they were on the island, driving along Sanibel Captiva Road toward Blind Pass. The shock of yesterday's events—and the official reaction, flashing lights and ambulances and an almost endless chorus of sirens—had abated somewhat, and to an unpracticed eye the little downtown would have looked almost normal. As they drove along, Perelman was flagged down three times by residents. All of them asked the same questions, and Perelman gave them all the same amiable non-answers.

"Delightful village," Pendergast said.

"Thank you."

"How did you become its police chief?"

"As in, *you* of all people?" the chief asked.

"You are the first police chief I've met to quote Virgil."

Perelman had to think back to their first meeting before he understood. He shrugged. "I've always been a fan of Virgil."

"But then there's the fact you're the first police chief I've met who also dropped out of Hebrew Union College in New York—and just months before completing a master's in rabbinical studies."

Perelman didn't know if he should be surprised or flattered this agent had taken the time to dig into his background. "There's this thing called an 'existential crisis.' I went through one late in grad school. I didn't know whether I wanted to be a cantor, or a Talmudic scholar, or a wandering minstrel or what. The idea of being a Visigoth was also appealing— I would have been good at sacking Rome—but the timing was off. But, yes: I left the East Coast, wandered west until I reached Northern California. And there in Humboldt County, in a redwood forest, I came across a riot about to break out, between loggers and a bunch of environmentalists camped way up in the trees. Don't ask me why, but it felt like my destination. There were two opposing forces— the law and the advocates of nature—and I wasn't sure which side I felt like joining."

"Which did you ultimately choose?"

"Neither. I turned into the go-between, sitting in no-man's-land talking to both sides. I felt everyone had a point: it wasn't right to break the law, but there was no reason humans had to go about destroying nature for profit, either. I joined the Forest Service. It seemed the best way to mediate things.

And from there, I somehow drifted into straight-up law enforcement."

"I imagine that required mediation, as well."

Perelman grinned. "Some laws are stupid. Some people are stupid. My job was to show people why peaceful coexistence was better than getting jammed up or thrown in jail."

"A Zen master with a badge."

"Sometimes I have to raise my voice, though."

"And Sanibel ended up a good fit?"

"I hadn't planned on coming down here. But one thing led to another. And to be honest—I was born to live in a place like this."

They passed through the checkpoint and over the bridge, then pulled in at the command center set up in the Turner Beach parking lot. The beach was still off-limits, of course, but most of the heavy work had been done. Some leftover crime scene investigators were fussing here and there in the sand. Coast Guard boats were still patrolling out past the breakwater, keeping a small flotilla of pleasure craft away.

They got out of the car and Pendergast paused a moment, taking in the scene with his peculiar silver-blue eyes.

In the command tent were several Department of Sanitation workers and a few of Perelman's officers, including a sergeant by the name of Cranfield. They were sitting around a folding table, drinking coffee.

As Pendergast and Perelman entered, the group began to rise.

Perelman motioned for them to remain seated. "This is Agent Pendergast of the FBI. Some of you may have met him yesterday." He turned to Cranfield. "Anything else horrible wash up?"

"Just one foot in the last eight hours."

"How's it going otherwise?"

"The usual hassles with traffic, rubberneckers, and the odd journalist."

Perelman nodded. "Let's keep our status at condition yellow, then. We'll review it again in another twelve hours." He turned to Pendergast. "Want to take that walk?"

They stepped out into the merciless sunshine, crossed the asphalt, then ducked under the yellow tape and onto the sand. Pendergast paused again. "A shame to see so much trash on such a lovely beach," he said.

"You can't clean an active crime scene. We haven't been able to run the raking machines since all this started."

"Well, it would seem all the important evidence has been taken away. Surely it wouldn't hurt to have your men help us pick up some of this refuse?"

Pick up trash? Perelman, trying to keep a neutral look on his face, unhooked his radio. "Cranfield?"

"Yes, Chief?"

"Please send Dixon and Ramirez out. With trash bags."

A brief pause. "Ten-four."

A minute later, two of the sanitation workers emerged from the tent, carrying large black bags. The four started slowly down the beach, Pendergast still in his expensive shoes. Ramirez bent down to pick up a plastic plate.

"That one won't be necessary," Pendergast said. "I will do the trash picking, if you please."

And so they proceeded in fits and starts, pausing every now and then for Pendergast to pick something up—a potato chip bag, plant debris, pieces of driftwood, a plastic drink cover—and drop it into one of the bags the two sanitation men were holding. There seemed to be no rhyme or reason to his choices. This had to be the strangest "stroll" Perelman had ever taken.

"Do you have that map I requested?" Pendergast asked while examining a rubber gasket, which he tossed back onto the sand.

Perelman brought out a piece of paper and gave it to Pendergast. It was a map of the beach, hand-drawn, with red dots documenting where each foot had washed up before being placed above the high tide line, along with the estimated time of arrival. The agent had asked for it yesterday evening, just before leaving for the morgue.

Pendergast paused to examine it. "This is most excellent, thank you."

"My patrol officer, Laroux, made it. He fancies himself quite the artist."

Pendergast kept it in hand while continuing down the beach, but it did not seem to alter the randomness of his progress. They walked on, the agent stopping every now and then to look over an evidence flag or pick up a piece of trash, examine it, and put it in the bag or toss it back onto the sand. While he proceeded, he peppered Perelman with questions: Had anything like this ever happened before—not with human feet, of course, but a strange and concentrated gift from the sea? Would it be worth interviewing the local fishermen? Did a lot of trash and seaweed usually wash up, in addition to all the shells? How often did they have to rake the beach? Perelman did his best to answer.

They were now nearing the far end of the beach, and Pendergast stopped to point out a large, old house on the dunes beyond the crime scene tape. "What a charming example of shingle-style Victorian architecture."

"The Mortlach House," Perelman said.

"An almost ideal location—although, situated beyond the dunes as it is, the house does seem rather exposed." He paused. "It's a trifle out of place—at least, compared to the other buildings around. Who lives there?"

"Nobody. In fact, it's scheduled to be torn down."

"What a shame." He picked up a plastic tag and dropped it into one of the now-bulging trash bags. Then he straightened up. "Shall we return? I think I have enough trash."

"Fine with me."

They turned around and headed back, Ramirez and Dixon lugging the two full bags.

"Chief Perelman, I must admit that I'm curious. What are your thoughts on the commander's theory?"

"He's an experienced seaman—logged ten thousand hours on the water as a captain, just like he said— and his abilities are without question." That wasn't quite an answer, and Perelman knew it. He hesitated a second, then decided Pendergast deserved his trust. Exactly why, he wasn't sure. "He's old-school, used to absolute command—obviously, that makes him a little proud and not always willing to listen. But I've worked with him before. I respect his experience: a lifetime on the sea. His idea that the feet originated in Cuba does, at least to me, seem quite possible. Cuba's changing but, sad to say, there are still many dissidents in prison."

Pendergast, walking beside the chief, nodded.

"On the other hand . . . well, we're not dealing with

the set, drift, and windage of a four-hundred-ton Coast Guard cutter here. We're dealing with shoes floating in the water. I'm not sure that falls within anyone's experience—even the commander's."

As he was speaking, Perelman noticed movement in his peripheral vision. A black town car had turned off Captiva Drive and then continued along the road that dead-ended in the beach parking lot, where it pulled over before the tape. He frowned. What fresh hell was this—yet another bureaucrat out for a photo op? He thought he'd already met with or spoken to every city manager, councilperson, and reservist brass in Lee County who could claim even a modicum of authority.

But then the rear door opened and he realized he was wrong. A woman stepped out into the shade of the palms. She wore a large, stylish sun hat and a pale dress of what looked like organdy, tailored to accentuate her slender figure. As she approached, moving out of the shade and into the sunshine, Perelman realized that she was not only very young—hardly twenty-three or twenty-four—but remarkably attractive. Perelman was a cinephile, and this woman's thin, curved eyebrows and bobbed mahogany hair reminded him of Claudette Colbert. No—even stronger in the chief's imagination was a resemblance to the legendarily beautiful Olive Thomas, the silent film starlet who died in 1920.

But then this vision from the past slipped gracefully beneath the crime scene tape, and Perelman's spell was broken.

"Just a minute, there!" he cried. In the distance, he could see a couple of his officers trotting in the direction of the black car.

A faint pressure on his arm. "It's all right," Pendergast said. "She's with me."

But the young woman had stopped of her own accord, unwilling to bury her heels in the sand, and was apparently waiting for them. Perelman called off his men and then the small procession—FBI agent, police chief, and two workers lugging heavy bags of trash—made its way through the sand toward her.

"Constance," Pendergast said as they drew near, "this is Chief Perelman of the Sanibel Police Department. Chief, allow me to introduce my ward and assistant, Constance Greene."

The young woman removed her sunglasses and regarded him with violet eyes. "Pleased to make your acquaintance." The deep contralto, with its mid-Atlantic accent, once again caused Perelman to feel a strange tug from the distant past.

"I'm surprised to see you here, though pleased," Pendergast told her. "What prompted you to leave Eden?"

"I believe it was encountering the tree of knowledge."

"Even the charms of paradise can pale with time."

"I finished *À rebours*. And it occurred to me—after the security chief finished explaining the finer points of handling his M60—that it was selfish of me to stay behind, wallowing in luxury, while you were presumably toiling away on this investigation. Whether or not I can lend assistance with that, at least I can lend you my company."

"Most kind."

"They told me you were staying at the Flamingo View Motel—" she pronounced the name as if it were some species of slug— "but when I arrived there, I assumed it was a misunderstanding and didn't venture inside to inquire."

"Not a misunderstanding, alas. I'm sure ADC Pickett had intended to book me into a more suitable place. I'll sort things out shortly."

"Don't make any changes on my account. I understand that sleeping in hovels builds character."

Pendergast turned back to Perelman, who had been following this exchange with curiosity. "Thank you for humoring me and my interest in trash. I enjoyed having a chance to talk. No doubt we'll see you again soon."

"Stop by in the evening, if you're free. If I'm not tinkering with my boat, you'll usually find me on my veranda, playing guitar, drinking tequila, and pretending to read poetry. Ms. Greene, it was a pleasure to meet you." And with a nod to his workers, Perelman turned back toward the command tent.

"One moment, please!" he heard Pendergast call. The agent gestured at the two bags of garbage. "Allow me to take those off your hands."

Perelman frowned. "What?"

"You were kind enough to drive me to the beach. These men were kind enough to carry the bags while I filled them with trash. The least I can do is spare you the trouble of disposing of them."

"But why—?" Perelman stopped, realizing he wasn't going to get a straight answer. He nodded to the two sanitation workers, who followed Pendergast and his ward back to the town car, where Pendergast directed the men to put the bags in the trunk. Then the workers returned to the chief and watched as the gleaming black car made a three-point turn and then took off south, over the bridge and toward the Flamingo View Motel.

9

ROGER SMITHBACK ASCENDED the outside steps leading to the dingy attic apartment, trying to be as quiet as possible and not wake the occupant of the first floor. The climb was more difficult than before: that fifth Johnnie Walker Black on the rocks had really done a number on his cerebellum.

He gained the landing and steadied himself a moment, breathing deeply and taking in the nocturnal landscape. Similar little Cape Cod–style houses spread out around him, lining the banks of a man-made canal. He could hear cars, singing, the faint crash of surf, and the endless drone of insects.

Opening the door, he turned on the light, then tacked across the room to an easy chair, which he flounced down into. He pulled his cell phone from his pocket and quickly hunted for the photos he'd surreptitiously taken that evening. Thank God, there they were—and decently exposed. Smithback knew how to deploy the more unsavory arts of reportage, but the darkness of the bar had made him worry.

He let his phone hand sink to the floor, then closed his eyes. Immediately, the room began to spin. He opened his eyes again and glanced at his watch. Just after nine. Kraski would still be in his office; he never left the place if he could help it.

After being unceremoniously escorted from the crime scene, Smithback had returned to the mainland, where he'd picked up his Subaru, then driven back to Sanibel—an ordeal in itself—intending to book a motel room. But with the influx of press, they'd become scarce as hen's teeth. Even the crappiest motels were showing NO VACANCY signs. In the end, he'd been forced to rent a "second-floor suite" from a private homeowner—a post office retiree—at an outrageous rate. The "suite" consisted of one room and a bath, as well as a landlord who would talk his ear off every time they ran into each other. Worse, it was in a frumpy section of Sanibel known as Gumbo Limbo—near the causeway and far from Turner Beach. The silver lining was that the "suite" came with a coveted A-class beach permit, marking him as a resident and, as such, free to wander...as long as he steered clear of that red-haired dickwad from the Coast Guard.

Of course, residents couldn't approach any closer to the crime scene than nonresidents, but at least his movements weren't restricted and he could get through the checkpoints.

That still left the problem of obtaining more information. Kraski had practically soiled his linen over the photographs and story, praising Smithback effusively for getting the exclusive. Praise from the editor of the *Herald* was rare, and Smithback had eaten it up. But that was yesterday's news. As good as it was, Kraski wanted more, and he had quickly reverted to his usual grumpy and demanding persona.

Unlike his deceased brother Bill, also a reporter, Roger Smithback preferred to keep a low profile when he worked. One of the skills he'd picked up while pounding the beat in Miami had been to quickly ID restaurants and bars—which ones were for tourists, which ones were for locals, which for cops, which for wiseguys, and so on. So he'd spent the evening hopping from one promising-looking bar on Periwinkle Way to another, drinking seltzer and keeping his ears open. And eventually, this strategy had led him to the Reef Bar and a certain Paul Rameau. Rameau was a friendly giant of a medical technician who'd seen enough over the past thirty-six hours to need to drown those sights in the flowing bowl: specifically, high-ABV dry-hopped craft beer. Smithback had managed to get a barstool next to him and they'd soon become, if not fast friends, at least drinking buddies.

Rameau, it seemed, had a capacity for beer that matched his enormous size. And so Smithback found it necessary, for reasons of comradeship and credibility, to switch from seltzer to scotch.

He shook his head, forced himself to sit up in the chair. Christ, he'd better call this in before he fell asleep. He took another quick look at the photos, then pulled up his contact list and pressed a button.

His phone was answered on the first ring. "Kraski."

"Hey, boss."

"Smithback. I've been waiting to hear from you. What you got for me?"

Just like a baby bird, beak wide, frantic with hunger. Already his coup of the previous day was ancient history. Smithback, who was interested in game theory, decided his best strategy was to play to Kraski's impatience and string him along a bit.

"It's rough out there," he replied. "Really rough."

"Yeah?"

"Something this unprecedented—well, there's nothing in the playbook. The authorities are working on instinct. Starting with a complete shutdown on information."

"Have you been drinking? You're slurring your words."

"In service of a lead, I assure you."

"All right. Go on."

Smithback didn't respond. He was mentally adding up how many beers he'd bought Rameau and wondering whether he could expense them all or not.

"Roger?" Kraski asked. "You there?"

"Yes, boss."

"So what you got?"

"The locals don't know anything; I've asked around. But I've rented a room and I'm well positioned if anything should come up."

"Now that you're on the crime beat, you know you've got to *dig*."

"They've got this one squeezed up tighter than a duck's ass."

Silence over the line. Then a sigh of exasperation. "Smithback, I admire how you jumped into this case. But being my best investigative reporter means you have to bring me *product*—and, on a hot case like this, daily, not next week. You showed real initiative yesterday—so where'd that go today?"

Best investigative reporter. That was more like it. Smithback knew he'd gamed Kraski about as far as he could with this no-info sob story. "I was just getting to that. I've got product."

"Yeah?" Instantly, annoyance was replaced with eagerness. "Like what?"

"Like the number of feet that washed up. The count's

broken one hundred—how's that? And they've been in the water a long time, close to a month."

"Holy shit. Where are they from?"

"Nobody knows. They're doing DNA and all kinds of other tests."

Smithback could hear the creak of the chair as Kraski rolled it up to his desk. "What else?"

"That's more than anybody else has." *And I had to spend an entire evening getting a shell-shocked technician drunk just to get that.* But he'd decided to hold back the really big scoop—or at least, what he hoped was going to turn into the big one.

"Okay." Kraski knew better than to ask for Smithback's source. "You'll write it up and send it to me, pronto?"

"On it now."

"That's some good work, Roger. Keep it up." And Kraski hung up.

Smithback sat back. It *was* good work.

But he'd done more. Much more. When Paul Rameau was at his drunkest and friendliest, Smithback had heartily suggested they exchange phone numbers. Rameau gave Smithback his number. Then Smithback suggested getting his contact info into Rameau's phone by calling it from his own.

Which accomplished exactly what he hoped: Rameau took out his phone to check it and kept it out when Smithback gushed about how much he liked the OtterBox case. That led to Rameau talking about how, in his line of work, he dealt with a lot of disgusting and corrosive fluids, which made the rugged OtterBox ideal, especially since he had to use it for work almost every day.

And then he laid the phone on the bar.

It was surely crammed with information. But how to get his hands on it? That was where Smithback got really clever: he made a series of urologic references, including how drinking beer made him piss like a racehorse, which was why he drank only scotch— which in short order had the desired effect of sending Rameau lurching off to the men's room.

As soon as he was out of sight, Smithback tapped the screen on the technician's phone to make sure it wasn't about to lock up, then pulled it over. He had sixty seconds to mine this baby. Email would be too time-consuming. He quickly dismissed voice mail or text for the same reason. But photos—did Rameau take photos of his work? Smithback tapped the photos app, and there they were: dozens of them. Smithback whipped through them—a whole slew of crisp, gruesome pictures of feet in every stage of dissection, from first incision to flayed and skeletonized. Rameau was a damn good photographer, too, every picture crisp and well framed.

They were all repulsive, but none revealed anything noteworthy. And then, with seconds to go, he struck gold. Three amazing photos, all in a row, of the same thing.

With his own phone, he quickly took photos of Rameau's pictures: one, two, three. And now as he mentally reviewed his coup, he was so pleased that, in the darkness of his "suite," he once again woke up his phone and scrolled through the shots he'd taken of Rameau's screen. The three pictures were close-ups of the top outer part of a foot, from the ankle up to where the leg had been severed. The skin around the amputation was shriveled and ragged, and the bone protruding from the sea-bleached flesh was revolting. But there, clearly visible on the skin, was a tattoo— almost all of one, anyway. It was a cross, surrounded by lightning bolts and some lettering. The lettering was a little blurry, but he could do something about that.

He wasn't going to go off half-cocked and tell Kraski about this. He needed to develop the lead. He'd download the photos to his laptop, then manipulate and sharpen them so he could read those letters. And then he'd ask around on the down low, hoping to identify the tattoo and maybe even where it had been inked. Because something about it looked familiar. And if he was right, this could lead to the biggest scoop of his career. It had to be said, Kraski was nearing retirement...and

"Roger Smithback, editor in chief" had a nice ring to it.

Pushing himself out of the chair, he shut off his phone, then made his way toward the room's lone table, where his laptop—and the story he'd promised Kraski for the *Herald*—was waiting.

10

PAMELA GLADSTONE GUIDED the R/V *Leucothea* from the Caloosahatchee River into the entrance of the Legacy Harbour Marina, heading toward the dock. It was a tricky landing, made worse by a twenty-knot offshore breeze. As she approached the pier, the High Point Place towers rose on her starboard side, casting late-afternoon shadows across the water. Approaching at the barest headway, she eased the bow of the vessel toward the dock and gently pinned it against the bumpers to keep it from blowing off, while throttling down and turning to starboard.

"Put over the aft tending spring line," she called to her postdoc and unwilling first mate, Wallace Lam, ready at the gunwale.

The line went over, a perfect throw for a change, and a pier crewman cleated it neatly.

"Hold the spring, I'm coming ahead on her," Gladstone said, keeping the starboard ahead and the port backing slow, bringing the forty-six-foot research vessel up snug against the pier face. She pulled the throttles into neutral. As the rest of the lines were cleated, she breathed a sigh of relief that the maneuver had gone well and she hadn't made a fool of herself, like last time, when she had smacked a piling with her stern. Total jackass carelessness, and naturally everyone had seen it and she had to fill out an accident report, even though neither pier nor ship had sustained any damage beyond an unsightly streak of black rubber on the boat's white gelcoat.

It had been a good trip. They had successfully retrieved both acoustic Doppler current profilers. To lose one of those twenty-thousand-dollar babies would be a disaster. Now she was eager to download the data and see if it finally confirmed her mathematical models.

She set the rudder to zero, and as she was putting all the controls on the helm to bed, she noticed through the bridge windows a man standing on the dock, tall and pale, the wind whipping his white suit. With a Panama hat on his head, he looked like an albino drug lord waiting for his shipment to come in. He was peering up at her boat and seemed to be looking directly at her through the bridge windows. She wondered how a weirdo like this had gotten onto the private pier, because he obviously was no mariner.

Once everything was in order and she'd filled out

the electronic log and shut down the breakers, she stepped out of the wheelhouse. Lam was finishing up as well, transferring the ADCP devices to a two-wheeled cargo carrier on the pier. The man in white was now approaching her directly. She turned her back, busying herself with straightening up a muddy bight, hoping he would go away.

"Dr. Gladstone?" came a smooth voice.

She turned. "Yes?"

"I am Special Agent Pendergast."

His hand was extended, but instead of shaking it, she held up both of hers, wet and smeared with tidal mud from the dirty line. "Sorry."

The man withdrew his hand and fixed a pair of glittering eyes on her. "I should like to have a conversation with you."

"Go ahead." She stood there. *Special Agent.* Did that mean he was FBI? "Wait—you got a badge or something?"

A hand slid out a billfold, displayed a shield, then returned it to his suit. "If we could perhaps withdraw to your laboratory, where we could speak in confidence?"

"What's this about?"

"Captiva."

"No way. Sorry." She turned, slung her duffel over her shoulder, and began walking briskly down the pier. Lam tried to catch up, pushing the carrier, and she again quickened her step, trying to escape the man in white. But he paced her, effortlessly.

"I understand you've been studying the pattern of gulf currents over the past five years," he remarked.

"I said no. I'm in the middle of a research project, my grant is about used up, the lease on my research vessel expires next week, my rent's increasing, my boyfriend dumped me—and I don't want anything to do with those feet washing up."

"Why not, if I may ask?"

"Because it's going to be a mess. A big, hot, political mess, in which the science—the *actual* science—will be lost. I've been through it before...trust me."

She walked still faster, but the man kept up without even appearing to quicken his gait. Gladstone was usually able to outwalk anyone, and this only served to increase her irritation.

"Dr. Gladstone, I'm glad you mentioned your research vessel. Aside from that ugly streak on the stern, it's a handsome boat."

They had reached the end of the pier. Lam was practically jogging in an attempt to keep up. Gladstone's Kia Soul was parked close in, thank God. She spied it, raised the key fob, unlocked it with a chirp, and made a beeline. She reached the door, pulled it open, and got inside. She began to shut the door, but the man's hand came to rest on it, holding it in place as he leaned in.

"Please take your hand off my car." She gave the door a pull, but he was holding it fast with remarkable strength. He gave her a little smile.

"Dr. Gladstone, I am sorry to hear about your other troubles, but at least you needn't worry about the lease on your vessel."

She paused. "What do you mean?"

"I paid a call on Caloosahatchee Marine Leasing. Your lease has been extended. And they kindly pointed me in your direction."

"Wait . . . why?"

"Because you see, Dr. Gladstone, the FBI is going to need that boat of yours. And, of course, *you*."

II

CHIEF P. B. PERELMAN sat in the back of the meeting room, flanked by Towne and Morris, listening with growing impatience as the Coast Guard oceanographer, a fellow named McBean or McBoon or something, droned on while plowing through an endless PowerPoint presentation, his green laser pointer flashing about like a cat chasing a mouse. In image after image, chart after chart, Perelman was getting a grand tour of the southern gulf and the Caribbean, focusing on Cuba.

Commander Baugh stood next to the oceanographer, in work blues, arms crossed, listening with his head tilted and a serious furrow in his brow.

The images flashed along, finally ending in an animated video that showed the complex swirlings and windings of the Loop Current, the famous oceanographic phenomenon that came up from the south and carried water into the Atlantic, where it joined the Gulf Stream.

What Perelman gathered from the presentation was that it was essentially impossible for the feet to have been carried by any combination of currents, winds, and tides from the Cuban mainland to Captiva Island—except for one area. As the main Loop Current drove northward along the Yucatán coast and into the gulf, a stable eddy, called the Mariel Stream, separated from the current and brushed the northeastern shore of Cuba, from Mariel Bay to Playa Carenero. In this twenty-mile stretch of shoreline, a floating object placed in the water at a tidal low had the possibility of being carried north toward the Gulf Coast of Florida, where it would encounter the natural prominence of the Sanibel/Captiva island chain. And, he concluded, a backtracking simulation of the Mariel Stream and Loop Current indicated that under certain conditions, such an object would require a travel time of about three weeks, plus or minus, to reach Captiva—which he wished to point out fit with the twenty-five-day estimated time the feet were in the water.

At the end of the presentation, the man retreated from the podium and the commander came up, face dark and serious. Two knotted hands gripped the podium and he glowered at the group, turning his head from one side to the other, displaying a fresh whitewall haircut.

"Thank you, Lieutenant McBath," he said in a gravelly voice.

He allowed a silence to gather in the hall.

"We all remember," he began slowly, "the Mariel Boatlift, where over a hundred thousand Cubans, released from prisons and mental hospitals, crowded on boats and headed northward, flooding the United States. It was so called because they hailed from Mariel Harbor."

He looked around.

"There's a reason why they came from that place. At the mouth of Mariel Harbor, on the gulf side of the bay, is the infamous prison known as El Duende. El Duende is a grim institution, long infamous for the incarceration and torture of political prisoners. Many of the inmates from El Duende joined the boatlift, which almost emptied the prison."

A satellite image, stamped SECRET, appeared on the screen, showing a vast prison complex surrounded by walls and fences, sprawling along the strand beyond the mouth of the harbor.

"But El Duende was soon refilled by the Communist regime in Cuba."

The commander started a new PowerPoint presentation with an aerial image of a sprawling facility along a shoreline.

"Here is a recent Homeland Security image of El Duende. It is thriving, if that's the word, home to an estimated twelve thousand prisoners."

He went through a series of satellite images showing buses arriving and leaving, prisoners getting on and off, yards filling with prisoners during exercise time, and so forth. Perelman listened with interest as the commander outlined the rumored horrors of El Duende. "Our number one hypothesis," he concluded, "is that these feet are the fruits of torture and large-scale executions at El Duende. Whether the feet were the product of an intentional or accidental mass dumping is an interesting but, for now, irrelevant question. One way or another, they ended up here—and it's our job to find the answers." He straightened up. "Any questions?"

There was a murmur of conversation and the questions came thick and fast. Towne leaned over to Perelman. "Not a bad theory, if you ask me."

"Seems as likely as any." Perelman had to admit it made sense, but he felt uneasy at how quickly the Coast Guard had settled on it to the exclusion of all other theories. He glanced around for Pendergast, curious whether he was going to make more provocative inquiries, but did not see him in the room.

As the questions trickled off, the commander resumed.

"So what is the next step in the investigation?

We've asked Homeland Security to provide a detailed analysis of El Duende, covering the time frame when the feet would have entered the ocean, to see if there was any unusual activity. DHS will also comb through SIGINT intercepts from that time frame, and tap ONI and HUMINT sources as well."

He looked around. "What I'm about to tell you is classified."

At this the room went completely silent.

"Over the next few days, the Coast Guard is going to send a national security cutter, under my command, to the Mariel coast to perform surveillance operations. We have a Sentinel-class fast-response cutter of the right specifications hailing from the Port Charlotte Station. It has a sophisticated S/SCIF, SEI sensors, increased data-exchange bandwidth, AIS data sharing, and other enhanced capabilities. The flight deck accommodates a DoD HH-60 helicopter, and it is fully integrated with the National Distress and Response System Modernization Program..."

Perelman tuned this out. God, what was it with these military guys and their acronyms? He knew that the Cuban coastline was routinely surveilled by the U.S. fleet, so this wasn't anything unusual. What did seem a bit unusual was that Baugh himself would command. But then again, he seemed just the kind of guy who would go for the glory. More power to him, if it advanced the case.

The briefing ended and the assemblage began to break up. Perelman rose along with Towne and Morris. "I wonder where Pendergast has gotten to?" he asked.

Towne chuckled. "He's an odd duck. What the hell is he doing with that garbage he lugged away? God, I'd love to have seen the Flamingo View Motel manager's face when he carried in those stinking bags."

"He's staying at the Flamingo View?" Morris asked. "You'd think the feds would have a bigger budget."

"Maybe he's combing through the garbage hoping to find Captain Kidd's treasure map," said Towne.

Perelman didn't respond. He'd thought about it for quite a while after Pendergast and his ward drove away, and ultimately he'd arrived at what felt like a pretty fair guess as to what Pendergast was doing with that garbage. He wondered why Baugh hadn't thought of doing the same—or why he himself hadn't, for that matter. An odd duck, for sure—but a damned clever one.

12

Pamela Gladstone unlocked the door of her lab and held it open for the FBI agent. It was a tiny space, almost entirely filled with electronic equipment—computers, screens, and an NOAA Automated Surface Observing System terminal.

"You can shift those manuals off that chair," she said, indicating a stool. "On the floor is fine."

Pendergast slipped them off but did not sit down. Instead, he looked around with his glittering eyes. Lam, wearing his signature red Keds high-top sneakers, came in and wedged himself into the cramped nook that served as his workstation. Gladstone sat down in her own capacious chair, leaning back with her hands clasped in front. She turned to Pendergast. "All right. You wanted to talk? Go ahead."

"I've consulted with a variety of sources, and it's my understanding you have some unconventional theories about currents and the sea."

Gladstone had to laugh. "Unconventional? Sounds like you're describing my political opinions."

"I loathe politics, presently more than ever. I'm solely interested in your oceanographic views."

She brushed her long blond hair out of her face. The salt air always made it unruly. "My theories. Okay. Well, they involve chaos. I mean, in the mathematical sense. You're familiar with the so-called butterfly effect? That the flapping of a butterfly's wings in Africa results in a hurricane in Florida?"

"I'm familiar with that fanciful idea, yes."

"Fanciful," Lam scoffed under his breath. She glared at him.

"It's overstated, true, but what it really means is that the tiniest change in the initial conditions of a system can snowball into gigantic effects later on. Wallace and I are just applying that mathematical concept to ocean currents. Unfortunately, most of my colleagues think we're wrong."

"Are you wrong?"

She hadn't expected this question. "That depends on how you define *wrong*. I know we're on the right track, but we're getting wrong results. It's a nontrivial problem. I need time. And more data. Those who think we're on the wrong track, that's a different thing. They lack imagination. They're...well...a little thick."

Pendergast's thin lips formed a dry little smile.

"Most people, in my experience, are a little thick. If not abundantly so."

Gladstone had to laugh, along with Wallace. This man, despite his severe look, had a droll sense of humor. She went on. "Ocean currents appear to flow in big, logical movements. The tide comes in and goes out. The Loop Current goes this way and that in a predictable fashion. It's all there in the charts. The problem is that, when you actually drop small GPS floaters into the ocean, you find you can't really predict where each individual floater will go. You can start them all together and they spread out enormously. Or you drop them far apart and they all end up on the same beach. So Wallace and I have been trying to develop a fractal mathematical model to explain that."

"*I* developed it, actually," Lam said. "On my own."

The man nodded slowly. She wondered how much he actually understood. It was hard to read his marble-like face.

"How does the model work?" he asked.

"Wallace? You're on—smartass."

Lam cleared his throat extravagantly. "Ahem. We start by turning the surface of the sea into millions of vectors and perform a fractal matrix analysis showing how each vector evolves over time—given various initial conditions of air and water temperature, wind, tides, waves, currents, solar gain, and other factors. It essentially draws a multidimensional Poincaré map of the ocean's surface. We do our calculations using the Q machine supercomputer at Florida Atlantic University." Lam tilted his head. "Am I making sense?"

Agent Pendergast tilted his own head back. "A Poincaré map? Is that all? Why on earth did you not consider a Ramanujan eleven-dimensional Matrix Attractor?"

Lam sat there, dumbfounded. "Um...what?"

"I think our guest is making a joke," said Gladstone.

"Oh," Lam said slowly. He was used, she realized, to having a monopoly on irony in the lab.

"No, I don't have any questions," said Pendergast, "for the simple reason that I have no idea what you were talking about."

"But I *tried* to make it simple," Lam said with a smirk, regaining his equilibrium.

"No matter." The agent turned to Gladstone. "How well do your models actually work?"

Gladstone smiled. "So far, I'm sorry to say— total shit."

The man winced and she saw, to her amusement, that the vulgarity had offended him. "But they *will* work, I'm sure of it. Let me show you the size of the problem. Wallace, could you please run the floater video?"

"Why not?" Lam came over to a terminal and

began tapping. Soon an image of the eastern Gulf of Mexico and the coast of Florida came up.

"What Wallace is going to show you is an animated video of the track of every floater for which we have data, going back twenty years. There have been thousands."

Black lines appeared on the chart, crawling every which way until a vast spiderweb covered the screen.

"You can see how crazy it looks." She pointed to a great hairy bundle of lines coming up from the Caribbean, running along the coast of the Yucatán Peninsula, curling up into the gulf, looping back down the west coast of Florida, brushing the Keys, and streaming out into the Atlantic Ocean, leaving many eddies and swirls in the gulf itself.

"That's the famous Loop Current," she said. "But as you can see, even though many lines follow it, there are hundreds that don't. It's the ones that don't— the exceptions—that I'm trying to fit into our mathematical model. Wallace is a genius and, as you've discovered, nobody understands his equations."

"We're making progress," Lam said. "And I wouldn't exactly term our recent results 'shit.' We've progressed to the 'half-assed' phase, at least."

Gladstone laughed. "Another thing is that the results of our models go against a lot of traditional old-salt wisdom about the gulf, accumulated by generations of grizzled seafarers. A young woman like

me and a Chinese American brainiac like Wallace—
well, what could we possibly know? We're not
popular, to say the least. So...how can we help you,
Agent Pendergast?"

"I wish to reverse engineer the journey these feet
took to Captiva Island. Trace them to their origin.
Can you do that?"

She had suspected this was where he was headed.
"I can try."

"And can you keep any data or information I share
with you two completely confidential?"

"For extending the lease on my boat, I'll sign an
NDA in my own blood."

"That won't be necessary. Tell me what you need
in order to do the analysis."

"For starters, I'll need all the data you have on
where each foot washed up, and when—as precisely
as possible. If there are any videos or photographs
of the event, that would be great. Did anything else
come ashore with them?"

"The usual flotsam and jetsam—seaweed, driftwood, and miscellaneous garbage."

"Anyone collect it?"

"Yes."

"Bring it to me."

"There are two garbage bags full."

"Wonderful. We love garbage that comes in from
the sea. Every piece tells the tale of its travels."

"Very good."

She frowned. "Isn't the Coast Guard also doing this sort of analysis? I sure as hell don't want to get crosswise with them. They don't like us as it is."

Pendergast paused before answering. "I think it's safe to assume that *everyone* involved should be doing this sort of analysis. It's the most obvious investigative path. However, the Coast Guard—at least those assigned to this mission—are, as the expression goes, 'old-school.' They have the latest technology, but they prefer to rely on their own experience with the sea—including making use of fifty-year-old paper charts. It is my belief they are underestimating the complexity of the problem—perhaps by a vast margin. I know enough about meteorology to realize that Earth's natural systems don't always run in predictable patterns. As a result, I would prefer to work with somebody comfortable with cutting-edge tools and theories—and unlikely to discard possible results simply because they don't follow received wisdom. In any case, your role will remain confidential."

"Fair enough. So...what *does* the Coast Guard think?"

"That the feet came from a Cuban prison."

"Sounds like a reasonable assumption to me."

"The problem is that it *is* an assumption. Having made the assumption, they're now trying to massage the data to prove it."

"And you think that's putting the cart before the horse?"

"It's the cardinal error of any criminal investigation."

She nodded. She was pretty sure this was going to end up a god-awful mess. She wasn't at all sure she could pull off the analysis—Pendergast was right when he said it was a complex problem. But she couldn't very well say no to the FBI, could she? And besides, there was something strangely magnetic—from an intellectual standpoint—about the pale man in the pale suit.

13

Loren Mayfield, Esq., was poring over the final pages of a particularly complex irrevocable trust when a knock sounded on the door of his inner office. He put the document down with relief and called, "Come in."

The door opened and Evelyn, his secretary, stuck her head in. "That woman who called you this morning for an appointment is here, Mr. Mayfield."

"Good. Please send her in." Mayfield pushed the trust document aside and straightened his tie. The woman had refused to say what she wanted to see him about. As a lawyer, Mayfield liked a mystery. The more mysterious, the greater the potential for a sizable retainer.

When the woman was shown in, however, Mayfield temporarily forgot about money. She was young, extraordinarily beautiful, and wore a dress that, although prim and conservative, could not hide the contours of her body.

He stood up, his instincts as a lawyer immediately reasserting themselves. *Down, boy.* "It's a pleasure to meet you. I'm Loren Mayfield. Please have a seat." He pointedly did not mention the fine weather they were having, or how well his visitor looked today, or any other ice-breaking small talk of that ilk.

"I'm Constance Greene. Thank you for seeing me on such short notice."

"My pleasure." Now that the initial surprise was wearing off, Mayfield realized that the woman's clothing was not just prim but downright old-fashioned. Nobody wore ankle-length dresses on Sanibel; just slipping into a pair of flip-flops was considered formal. He wondered if perhaps she was Amish, or a member of some other antique Christian sect. He glanced out the window but saw no three-wheeled bicycle parked outside. No matter; he'd find out soon enough. He rested his elbows on his desk and interlaced his fingers, giving her his full attention. "How may I help you, Ms. Greene?"

"I'm here about the Mortlach House."

"Ah." Perhaps that explained the dress. Did she want to use the house for some kind of photo shoot, maybe? If so, she'd have to hurry up.

"I was told to direct any inquiries to you."

Mayfield nodded. "I represent the current owner of the house, yes."

"Excellent. We wish to rent it."

"We?"

"My guardian and I."

"For what purpose?" A fancy-dress ball? Mayfield wondered. Something kinky?

"To reside in, naturally. It seems ideally situated."

At this, the lawyer had to chuckle. "I'm sorry, Ms. Greene, but I'm afraid that's impossible."

"Why? Is there a problem with the house?"

"No. It's been meticulously maintained."

"Are others living there? Or perhaps it's unfurnished, or requires cleaning?"

"In all cases, the answer is no. The Mortlach House cannot be rented because it is scheduled to be demolished in a matter of days."

This information did not surprise the young woman. She smoothed down her dress with remarkable composure. "So I understand. But certainly some accommodation could be reached."

Mayfield shook his head. "Ms. Greene, I wish you had walked in here five years ago."

"Five years ago I would not have been in a position to rent that house."

"No. What I mean is, five years ago an offer like yours would have seemed a gift from God. Now, however, I'm afraid it's simply too late."

Ms. Greene raised her eyebrows in mute inquiry. Lawyer though he was, Mayfield was tempted to forgo his natural reticence and mention a detail or two. Doing so would, at least, keep this attractive woman in his office a little longer and delay a return to the irrevocable trust.

"My client bought the Mortlach House not quite a decade ago, when it was somewhat the worse for wear," he told her. "He lives up north—in the greater New York area—and thought it would make a good investment property, winter rentals and so forth. He replaced the roof and some rotted timbers, had it furnished and redecorated and re-painted. But rentals turned out to be few and hard to come by." He leaned forward. "You know small towns and their gossip."

"I assume you're referring to the murder."

Mayfield sat back at once. "Yes. It took place in 2009. I don't know all the details, beyond the fact that the owner was murdered—with an ax, apparently, judging by the, ah, evidence left behind—and the murderer never caught. Naturally, the disappearance of the body made the gossip, if anything, even more active than it normally would have been." Mayfield pursed his lips. "The owner's estate really should have included this information in the seller's disclosure. Instead, they waited until things quieted down and then sold the property to somebody far away who didn't know the history."

"The buyer could have sued."

"I'm sorry, but I can't get into details of that sort,

especially since I did not represent him until after the sale was complete. Suffice it to say, my client believed a total restoration would take care of things. Unfortunately, that was not the case—again, thanks to these island folk and their gossip."

"Your secretary mentioned to me that no matter how many times they repainted the walls, blood kept oozing out. And that the few people who stayed overnight reported tapping noises and once or twice the clanking of chains, echoing faintly in the small hours."

He would have to talk to Evelyn about this. "Ridiculous, don't you think? In any case, my client has patiently kept the house in perfect shape, but with this nonsense refusing to go away, and seasonal visitors always getting wind of the stories somehow, it's become a money sink rather than an investment. Condominium developers have been interested in the parcel all along, and my client has determined the time has come to demolish the house and sell the land." *At a nice profit*, he thought privately. "It is, quite simply, an albatross of a property."

"But I've told you already. We would like to rent it."

Mayfield shook his head sadly. "I'm afraid things have gone too far for that now."

The office fell silent for a moment. Then Ms. Greene said: "It's a shame to raze such a beautiful structure. I'm surprised the local historical society isn't doing something about it."

"Oh, they've done all they can. Held candlelight vigils, put together one fund-raiser after another. But my client was determined and had the zoning laws on his side, and they weren't able to meet his price. Maybe if the murder had been solved, things would be different, but it's still on the books, and so..." Mayfield spread his hands in a gesture of futility.

While he'd spoken, his visitor had been writing something. "To my mind, an unsolved murder is merely icing on the cake. If you can have the house aired and cleaned, we'll move in tomorrow."

"But, Ms. Greene, I've explained to you that—"

There was a low sound as the woman tore away a strip of paper, then handed it across the desk. Mayfield saw it was a check, from a private New York bank, made out to his firm in the amount of ten thousand dollars. The handwriting was old-fashioned and self-assured. On the memo line was written *Week no. 1.*

Week number one.

"May I assume, Mr. Mayfield, that amount will stave off the bulldozers and wrecking balls—at least temporarily?"

Mayfield looked from the check to her and back again. "I..." he began.

Ms. Greene seemed to take this as assent, because

she rose from her chair. "Thank you so much for your consideration. We'll stop by tomorrow afternoon for the key. May I suggest four o'clock?"

And when the lawyer made no reply, she smiled, inclined her head ever so faintly, then turned and exited the office.

14

AGENT PENDERGAST STEPPED into the room—part
office, part laboratory—that Dr. Crossley had lent
him in the low, sand-colored building that housed
the district medical examiner for Lee County. Another man was there already—short and thin, in his
late forties, with dark hair parted carefully down the
middle as slick and shiny as an Eton schoolboy's. He
quickly stood up as the agent entered. There was a
wheeled tray beside him, on which sat four evidence
bags, their surfaces scuffed and cloudy.

"Ah, Mr.... Quarles, is it not?" Pendergast said.
"Thank you so much for agreeing to work with us
on this matter."

"My pleasure, Agent Pendergast," the man said,
shaking the proffered hand. "Peter Quarles, forensic
examiner, FTG."

"Yes, yes. FTG—?"

"Footwear and Tire Group."

"Yes, of course."

"As soon as your courier package arrived at Huntsville yesterday morning, I dropped everything and began an analysis of the specimens. The Bureau placed the highest priority on this case."

"Excellent. I look forward to hearing the results." Pendergast sat down and offered him a place across the room's small conference table. "Tell me about this, ah, Footwear and Tire Group. I haven't worked with that forensic subspecialty before at the Bureau."

"The most problematic tire work is done in Quantico, the rest in Huntsville. 'Footwear and tire' is a little deceiving, of course—because there are so many items that require specialized knowledge, each of us in the group had to develop broader areas of expertise. In addition to shoes, mine includes hats, neckties, and men's underwear."

"I see."

"Boxers only, however. Briefs are handled in Quantico."

"I would never have suspected."

Mr. Quarles nodded, pleased. "And may I compliment you on your own pair?"

"I beg your pardon?"

"Your pair. Of shoes. John Lobb, if I'm not mistaken. A beautiful example of bespoke handcraft."

"You are most kind." Pendergast crossed one leg

over the other and glanced pointedly at the evidence bags.

"But here I am, wasting your time with pleasantries!" Quarles rose, wheeled the metal tray over, and adjusted its height so that it hovered barely an inch above the table. The evidence bags on the tray, Pendergast knew, each contained one of the shoes that had floated ashore—two right and two left, in different sizes, including the one the M.E. had originally sliced up.

"I examined all four examples carefully. Since they're without question from the same source and identical, I'll simplify things by focusing on one," Quarles said as he pulled on a pair of gloves. Then he selected an evidence bag, slid open the seal, and removed a shoe. Although it was still in one piece— barely—it had been sliced, cross-sectioned, punched, and cut for samples so many times that it looked more like a flayed bird than a shoe. Quarles set the item before Pendergast. A faint smell of seawater and rotten fish reached Pendergast's nostrils.

"As one who appreciates fine footwear, you probably don't need me to describe the traditional shoemaking process to you: creating the last; stretching the shell; steaming the upper; adding the lining, tongue, and hardware on the stitching line; and so forth. This," Quarles said, shaking the shoe for emphasis so that it flapped, "is not that kind of shoe. It is a cheap, mass-produced item almost certainly made in China. It was created for a specialized environment rather than for everyday streetwear. It's clearly not a fashion product: it's strictly utilitarian. I don't find any match to this shoe in our databases."

"What kind of specialized environment?"

"There are many settings in which specific footwear is required. There are disposable, nonwoven foam 'scuffs' for spas, hotels, and the like, usually color-coded for size. On the other end of the spectrum are the kind of heavy-duty, polyethylene-coated shoe coverings used in biohazard environments or clean rooms. This is neither of those."

Pendergast nodded for the technician to continue.

"When a shoe resists easy analysis, we must turn to its component parts to look for an answer." Quarles picked up a small metal instrument from the tray, almost like a dental pick, which he used for demonstration. "The shoe—I use 'shoe' here in the most generic sense—is cheaply made, of inferior materials, and lacks many standard components, such as an inner lining. The top was formed through a process known in the trade as 'SMS'—meltblown polypropylene, sandwiched between layers of spun-bond polypropylene. Usually, such footwear would have three or four plies of material, but these have only two—more evidence of how cheaply they were made. The exterior layers are not woven into a breathable material. That gives them fluid resistance at the expense of comfort."

"Fluid resistance?"

"Yes. This shoe, or perhaps more accurately specialized slipper, would be used in an environment where there might be fluids on the floor, such as a hospital, nursing home, kitchen, workshop, prison, factory— that sort of place. These shoes are too expensive to be onetime disposables, but too cheap for long-term wear. And they present a couple of other curious aspects."

"Which are?"

"The SMS upper is attached to the slip-resistant sole by contact cement: very inexpensive. The bonding line is hidden by this bit of piping, here." And with the tool, Quarles pointed to a thin ribbon of material, slightly darker than the sea green of the slipper, that ran horizontally along its surface just above the sole. "We tested it and it's nothing but simple polyester. On a more expensive shoe, its use might have been decorative: a stripe to conceal the joint between the upper and the outsole. But these are of shoddy manufacture, and the stripes are not of contrasting color. They are also especially sloppy." He indicated spots where the ribbon was hanging loose from the base of the slipper or had fallen away entirely.

Pendergast nodded. "Interesting. And the other detail you can't account for?"

"It's an odd one. When we analyzed the upper,

it tested positive for antibacterial treatment. That's a common feature of 'safety shoes' you'd find in a surgical bay, a lab, a clean room—even a hotel kitchen. But such shoes almost always have EVA uppers and tend to be expensive."

"EVA. I assume you mean ethylene-vinyl acetate rubber."

"I see you've studied chemistry. Quite right: water resistant, flexible, but heavy and sturdy for protection. As you can see, this slipper isn't sturdy. And it certainly isn't heavy—the samples weigh from forty to forty-four grams. And it's not EVA."

"So why bother to protect such shoddy workmanship with antibacterial treatment?"

"Exactly."

"Very interesting, Mr. Quarles."

"That's about it. Any questions?"

A silence ensued as Pendergast became lost in thought. At last he shifted in his chair. "You're familiar with the details of the case?"

"I read the covering folder, sir."

"And there's nothing remotely like this in the NCAVC database."

Quarles nodded.

"You mentioned they were probably made in China. Can you elaborate?"

"With pleasure. There are three or four shoe-manufacturing regions scattered across China, and each specializes in a certain kind. There's Jinjiang, in Fujian Province. It's known as the 'shoe capital of China' and has facilities that are technologically advanced. Then there's Wenzhou. They have the greatest number of manufacturers but are geared toward the domestic trade. Also Dongguan, in Guangdong Province. Their factories tend to be smaller, more specialized, niche producers."

"I see," Pendergast replied. "And have you been to these places?"

"Before I joined the FBI, I was in the jobber market for three years. I was the middleman for moving overruns on big orders. Or buying and selling odd lots."

"Excellent. That familiarity, along with the remarkable knowledge of footwear you've just displayed, makes you the logical choice."

"Choice?" Quarles asked, face blank. His expression changed to one of surprise. "You don't expect me to...go to China and locate the manufacturer, do you?"

"Who else, if not you? We must find out who made these shoes."

"But that's impossible! China's footwear revenue is nearly seventy billion dollars a year. Why, Dongguan alone has fifteen hundred factories—many of them no bigger than a restaurant."

"Nevertheless, you must try. Take these samples

and show them around. Make use of your local contacts—without giving away any details, of course. *Nĭ huì shuō Zhōngwén ma?*"

"*Pŭtōnghuà*," Quarles replied absently—then looked startled, realizing he had unconsciously switched languages. "You speak Mandarin?"

"As do you, it seems. Most excellent! You'll leave immediately."

Quarles's lips worked silently a moment. "This is rather short notice—"

"I have ADC Pickett's authorization," Pendergast went on. "This won't be a shoestring operation: think of it more as a junket. I'll make sure you fly first class, stay in the hotels of your choice, have a generous expense account. Discovering the manufacturer of these shoes could be crucial in solving the case."

Quarles did not reply. But his eyes betrayed what he was imagining: a promotion and dramatic leap up the GS pay scale.

"I'll need to go back to Huntsville," Quarles said. "Pack a few things."

"Of course. Come back here—shall we say this time tomorrow?—and we'll discuss the operating parameters of your investigation. And then we'll get you on a plane from Miami. Until then, thank you once again for your invaluable—and ongoing—aid." With this, Pendergast got up and walked toward the door. When he reached it, he turned. "And, Mr. Quarles?"

Quarles, who was gathering up the evidence bags, turned toward him. "Yes?"

"Remember to pack your, ah, boxers."

15

COMMANDER BAUGH STOOD on the bridge of the USCGC *Chickering*, staring at the hazy northern coast of Cuba through a pair of binoculars. The officer at the con had brought the cutter's speed down to four knots, cruising just outside the twelve-mile limit, parallel to the low shoreline.

"Mr. Peterman, throttle down to two knots," Baugh said. "Maintain the same heading."

Baugh could feel the diesel engines slackening slightly, more a change in vibration than an actual sound. The handheld binoculars were no damn good. He laid them down and moved to the navigation bridge station, where the XO stood before an array of electronic charts, transceivers, and radar screens.

"Mr. Rama, I'd like to take a look at the prison through the electronic telescope."

"Aye, sir."

The XO busied himself with the controls and an

image of the shore sprang into view on a screen. It was a muggy day and the image was blurry, wavering in the heat. A gigantic gray prison sprawled along the shore, off the port side of the cutter. El Duende. The entrance to Mariel Bay lay a little farther on, where fishing boats could be seen coming and going, along with a small Cuban Navy warship, entering the mouth of the bay and disappearing around the point of land.

Baugh peered at the image. There was something happening on the shore in front of the prison— a group of men were clearly occupied. Inmates, it seemed, at least judging from the universal orange uniforms. And guards in green. But it was all a blur in the hazy afternoon light, the images of the people merging and blending with each other like ghosts.

"Mr. Rama, can you sharpen the image?"

"Yes, sir. I'm working on it."

The image jumped around a little bit. Whatever this group of men were doing, it didn't look ordinary. There were a bunch of people, prisoners surrounded by guards in a tight group.

"Jesus, Mr. Rama, did you see that?" Baugh couldn't believe what he had just seen. Or was it his imagination?

"I did, sir."

"Play it back in slo-mo. On screen two."

The recording jumped back a minute and then crawled forward on a second screen.

"There! Stop it!"

Good God, it looked like a decapitation. But it couldn't be—could it? "Mr. Rama, can you tell me what you think is going on?"

"Sir, I'm not sure. It looked . . . violent."

"A decapitation, maybe? Play it again."

They went through it, frame by frame. The men were moving about, fast. A man seemed to be brought up to a blurry object or wall—and then, with a jerking motion, his head appeared to separate from his shoulders, even as a man near him swung his arm around. It was too blurry to see what kind of weapon the second man might be holding—everything was still shimmering and hazy—but Baugh saw the head separate from the body and tumble to the ground: that much at least was clear.

"It could be a decapitation, sir."

"You *saw* the head come off, right?"

"I believe so, sir. A little hard to tell."

Baugh felt his blood pounding. What the hell was going on? The Cubans were long known for torture. But decapitations . . . that was more like ISIS. Could this be some sort of terrorist alliance, right here, ninety miles from the U.S.? They'd better get some serious IMINT on this, satellite and whatever. Christ almighty, it could be another Cuban Missile Crisis.

Baugh took a deep breath. "Is there *anything* you can do to get a better image?"

"I am doing everything possible, sir."

Rama worked the controls and called in another officer. The image continued to focus and blur, jiggle, zoom in and out—but nothing made it better. The haze and heat shimmer overwhelmed the image. They had to get closer.

"Double the watch," Baugh ordered. "I want OS Atcitty up here on the double, along with First Lieutenant Darby."

The orders were given.

"Mr. Rama, turn off AIS and all transponders. Initiate radio silence."

"Aye, sir."

"Okay, now paint 'em with hi-def radar."

There was a hesitation. "Sir, that may be construed as provocative," said the XO.

"Carry out the order."

The high-definition radar showed nothing more than a green smudge on the beach, worse than the visual. They were still too far away, and the heat waves were throwing back return. There was no immediate response.

Atcitty arrived on the bridge and gave the CO a smart salute. A moment later Darby, Baugh's chief of staff and overall right hand, followed.

"Look at this, Mr. Darby."

Darby, leaning his plump form forward, stared at the screen where the activity was taking place.

"What are they doing?" he asked.

"You tell me."

"There's a big crowd, it looks like. Bunched up. Moving around. Prisoners in orange, guards in dark green. But it's just too blurry. I can hardly make out individual people."

"Could it be...an execution ground?"

Darby stared. "Could be, sir. Or maybe a riot. I mean, it looks like they're fighting."

Baugh turned to the helmsman. "Mr. Peterman, rudder ten degrees to port, maintain present speed."

"Sir, our turning radius will take us inside the territorial limit."

"Make it so, Mr. Peterman."

"Aye, aye, sir."

There was a silence on the bridge. Baugh turned to the XO, who was staring at him. Baugh flashed him a reassuring smile. "Don't look so alarmed, Mr. Rama. We painted them with radar. No response. Someone's asleep at the helm. They won't even notice."

"Aye, sir."

The ten-degree rudder would give them a turn of two-mile radius, bring them within eight miles of shore. Baugh turned to the operation specialist. "Ms. Atcitty, prepare to launch a surveillance drone at closest approach. Mr. Peterman, continue turning the ship through two hundred and seventy degrees. When a heading of zero-zero-zero is achieved, accelerate to forty knots and exit Cuban waters."

More shocked silence.

"I gave an order!"

"Aye, aye, sir."

Baugh felt the cutter begin to turn. He understood the hesitation of his staff, but he also knew they didn't have his experience. There were times when standard procedures didn't apply; when unusual, even heroic, measures had to be taken. Something terrible was happening on the shore in front of the prison, and by sheer chance they had hit right on it. It might well be part of a complicated military strategy, of which the feet were an early component. If so, Washington had to be informed. They couldn't wait for sat imagery; that might take hours, if not days. He needed to document this right now. The cutter was fast—damn fast—and if the Cubans gave chase, she could outrun almost any tin-can Cuban warship.

The *Chickering* continued its slow turn. The activity on the beach continued, and Baugh swore he saw another decapitation, but it was too fast and blurry to be sure. But slowly, slowly, the picture grew clearer as they edged closer to land. As the cutter came parallel to the shore on the starboard side, still turning, Baugh said: "Ms. Atcitty, launch drone."

"Aye, aye, sir." She relayed the order and a moment later said, "Drone launched."

Baugh heard a buzzing sound and saw the drone—a helicopter type—shooting out over the water, staying low, heading toward shore. By now the cutter's bow was swinging northward.

"Sir," said the operation specialist, "if we accelerate to forty knots, we will put ourselves out of the drone's range. It won't be able to return to the ship."

"Destroy it over water, then, after transmission of footage is complete."

"Aye, aye, sir."

The bow was swinging through the compass, nearing true north.

"Increase speed to forty knots," Baugh said as the boat stabilized on its new heading.

A warning sound went off, and a moment later the cutter surged forward as the massive 4,800-horsepower twin jet diesels powered up.

The XO suddenly said, "Sir, I've got a Cuban warship at two zero nine at thirteen nautical miles, proceeding at twenty knots—diverting to intercept us and increasing speed."

"What the hell?"

"My guess is she was returning to Mariel from a routine patrol. Our bad luck, sir, that she happened on us."

"Stay the course, increase speed to max. We'll be out of territorial waters in four minutes."

"Sir, we're being painted with fire control radar!"

"General quarters, battle stations!" Baugh barked out. "Evasive maneuvers. Jamming. Prepare to launch chaff!"

All hell broke loose on the bridge—organized, focused hell. The general alarm went off. Baugh could just see the Cuban warship now, a wavering dot on the horizon at 265 degrees off the port bow. It had been coming in from the northwest and their radar hadn't picked it up—was it employing Russian stealth technology?

The *Chickering* was now moving at forty-five knots, close to full speed. They'd be back in international waters in two minutes. The son of a bitch wasn't actually going to fire on them, was he?

"It's a fast Komar-class missile boat," said the XO, peering into the scope.

"How fast?"

"Top speed rated at forty-four knots, but this one's moving at thirty."

"Armaments?"

"Two twenty-five-millimeter guns, two Styx anti-ship missiles."

At Baugh's shoulder, Lieutenant Darby swallowed loudly and painfully upon hearing this.

The *Chickering* was weaving now, executing evasive

maneuvers. Baugh gripped the console rails. The Cuban missile boat was a lot smaller than their cutter, but it had those damn Styx missiles. Christ, one of those would obliterate his ship and no amount of chaff could chase it away. But the *Chickering* couldn't fire first, especially while in Cuban waters.

"Still painting us with fire control, sir."

One minute. If they were going to launch a missile, it would be now. He hoped to God this was a bluff.

He heard a small explosion behind him and almost jumped out of his skin, then swung around. He spied a puff of smoke in the sky several miles to the rear. "What the hell was that?"

"Drone self-destructed, sir," said the OS.

"We're out," said the XO. "In international waters. Still painting us."

"Maintain evasive maneuvers."

But the Cuban boat was not pursuing. It slowed and began to turn, resuming its heading toward Mariel Harbor.

"Radar illumination ceased, sir."

The bastards had just been trying to scare him. It was a bluff after all. Maybe he should've fired on that little wise-ass and turned it into floating matchsticks. In any case, there was going to be a shitstorm over his incursion into Cuban territorial waters. But he'd let Darby handle that—the lieutenant, truth be told, was good at placing smoke screens where they'd do the most good. Besides, they had the drone footage. And the Cubans knew it. This was going to be *big*.

"Cease evasive maneuvers," he said. "Make course zero one zero at thirty knots. Stand down general quarters."

The alarm went silent and the bridge began to return to normal. Baugh realized he was sweating like a pig. He turned to the operation specialist. "Ms. Atcitty, did the drone footage come through?"

"Aye, sir."

"What can you see? What were those bastards doing?"

There was a long silence. "It appears, sir, that the prisoners and guards were playing volleyball on the beach."

16

THE LARGE SCREEN showed a detailed map of the Indian Ocean between Australia and Réunion Island east of Madagascar, bounded on the north by Borneo and Sumatra and on the south by nothing. Stretching across the center of the map was a rat's nest of pink, red, and burgundy threads, as dense and tangled as Day-Glo steel wool, surrounding a thicker black line that arced from the coast of Java to a spot in the southern Indian Ocean many thousands of miles from land.

Gladstone, standing behind Wallace Lam, stared at the image. "What makes you think this is going to help us?" she asked.

"Because this was the most expensive and sophisticated ocean drift analysis ever performed."

"Yeah, and it failed."

Lam sighed. "Lord spare me from fools and numbskulls."

"Watch out, or I'll cut your salary."

"What salary?" He sniffed. "Look. It only *failed* because the searchers didn't *interpret* it properly. But I was able to take their data and perform a different calculation."

"You're saying you know where Flight MH370 went down?"

"They spent a hundred and fifty million dollars searching this area here, and here, and over here—and were wrong every time."

Gladstone stared at the map. "Okay, but we're not looking for Flight 370. We're looking for the place where a hundred feet were dumped into the ocean."

"It's the same problem, really." Lam sighed again, this time with impatience. "Let me try to explain."

"If it wouldn't be too much of an imposition."

"I'm a glutton for punishment. Anyway, you know the story of the missing plane. On March eighth, 2014, Flight MH370 took off from Kuala Lumpur, headed for Beijing. Over the Gulf of Thailand it made a sudden turn and headed southwest, eventually flying far out over the Indian Ocean. About seven and a half hours after it took off, a satellite signal, the last contact with the plane, indicated it was somewhere in the southern Indian Ocean—and then whammo! It disappeared."

Gladstone nodded. She knew the story well.

"Investigators calculated how far it could have flown, given the fuel it carried and the speed and altitude, and estimated it ran out of fuel and went down somewhere along this arc." He gestured at the thick black line on the screen. "Which became the main search area."

"Right."

"But *then*!" Lam held up his finger. "On July twenty-ninth, a six-foot piece of the plane, a flaperon, washed up on Réunion Island. And that's when this reverse-drift study was done, backtracking to March eighth to approximate where that flaperon might have originated."

"You're not telling me anything I don't already know."

"Patience, boss lady, is a virtue. Now, shut up and listen—please. You can't just throw a virtual flaperon into the ocean off Réunion Island and then run the clock back to see where it was five months earlier. So what they did was throw five million virtual flaperons into the ocean and run them all back in time to see where they were on March eighth."

"Using what data?"

"They made a model of the flaperon, put it into a tank, and ran tests on it. They took into account the sail effect—how much wind might affect the floating object. They calculated wave action. They allowed for surface currents, tidal currents, and deeper ocean currents. And finally, they took into account the flaperon's permeability—how much it became waterlogged and degraded over the months it spent floating at sea. All that went into the model. As more debris washed up on various islands and the African mainland, they added that to the model, as well."

"So each of those colorful little kinky threads on the screen is one possible backtrail?"

"Right the first time."

Gladstone stared at countless squiggly lines. "Judging from this map, those virtual flaperons could have come from anywhere in a million square miles. This analysis didn't work at all."

"But at least it showed that some areas were more likely than others. They shifted their search after that."

"But still didn't find Flight 370."

"No."

"Like I said, their model was a failure. A total, balls-up failure."

"But like *I* said—"

"And now you want us to replicate their failure?"

"Not the *failure*." Lam rolled his eyes. "You see—"

"You want us to dump five million virtual feet into the sea off Turner Beach and backtrack them in time, to see where they started?"

This time, Lam waited until he was sure no more

questions were forthcoming before he answered. "Yes, I do."

"And why will that work for us when it didn't for them?"

"We have more data on the gulf than they had about the Indian Ocean. And we only have to backtrack twenty-five or so days, not five months. But most important, I had a new idea about a way to analyze their data. I applied it to Flight 370—and when I did, all the floating debris models from the flight converged in one approximate area on the date of the crash. Instead of a thousand."

Gladstone stared at the map. "So what's your new idea?"

"I figured if I applied Feynman sum-over-histories diagrams to the possibilities, I might be able to eliminate the least likely pathways. Not every one of these squiggly drift patterns is equally probable: some are more likely than others. So you eliminate the unlikely ones—using Feynman diagrams."

"What's a Feynman diagram?"

"I'm tired now. How much will you pay me to explain?"

Gladstone frowned. Money and mathematics were all that Lam seemed to appreciate, even though he rarely had any of the former. "I'll order extra cheese on our next pizza night. *And* onion. Okay?"

"Okay. It's a mathematical and geometric way of

diagramming the probability of particle interactions. Like in a particle collider? I just adapted the process to the ocean, treating it mathematically like a sea of interacting particles and forces. The math is terrifying and you need a supercomputer. But when it was done, *this* is what happened."

He gestured at the screen. One by one, the colorful little threads disappeared from the map until nothing was left but the black arc of the airplane's possible locations when it went down. Then, new threads began appearing on the map, all originating from Réunion Island. Some drifted one way, others jagged off in another—but they all converged, more or less, on a single spot in the ocean—on that black arc.

Gladstone shook her head. Was this another of Lam's mathematical flights of fancy? "So that's where Flight 370 is? There?" She pointed to where all the lines converged on the map.

"At the bottom of the ocean, of course."

Gladstone stared. "Are you sure?"

"Well, obviously I have no proof. But I did run several billion Feynman diagram permutations through the university's Q machine." He sniffed again. "And I ran up a rather impressive CPU bill in the process."

"How much?"

"Four grand."

Mary, mother of Jesus. "And you didn't clear it with me?"

He looked at her with an exaggeratedly wounded expression. "I didn't realize it was going to go so *high*."

"And you think you can do the same thing with floating feet?"

"Well, you've got tons of data from your floater experiments you've gathered over the past five years—much better than what they had for the Indian Ocean. I just need to figure out the floating characteristics of the actual feet to plug into the calculation."

"What exactly do you need?"

"I'll need two actual feet, along with a test tank of water with a wave and wind machine—they've got one at the oceanography lab at Eckerd."

"And how much will all this cost, even assuming I can get ahold of some feet?"

He shrugged. "Another grand?"

"Jesus. And where are we going to get the money for that?"

"Why don't you ask that FBI dude? He looked rich enough to me."

17

Roger Smithback drove his Subaru along Cypress Lagoon Drive. For the last half hour, he'd been cruising around some neighborhoods south of Fort Myers—supposedly this was the more dangerous part of town, but he had seen mostly well-kept apartment buildings, schools, bodegas, small houses, even a decent-looking country club straddling Whiskey Creek.

This wasn't what he'd expected at all.

Smithback had done his research. He knew that the tattoo he'd surreptitiously photographed was most likely a gang symbol of some kind. After he'd blown up and sharpened the image, it had become much clearer. It was definitely a cross, with lightning bolts coming out diagonally from the lower intersections of the crossbeam, and what looked like animal claws protruding from the top—although their tips were not visible, thanks to the tearing and nibbling of

the torn skin. It was surrounded by two letters: a
P on the left and an *N* on the right, done in the
usual blackletter font of gang tattoos. Its color was
the blue of prison tats, but that didn't necessarily
mean anything: it could just as well have been done
at some Central or South American tattoo parlor.
Because his research had indicated crosses done in
this particular way—with a distinctive fleur-de-lis
styling at the tips and an unusual method of decorative shading—were a trademark of gangs from south
of the border.

But conventional research could tell him nothing
further. And there were a shitload of gangs out there.
He'd done his share of guessing about what the
P and *N* could mean—Panama? Padre Nuestro?—
but if he really wanted to learn more, he'd have to
hit the pavement.

As a reporter, he'd heard back in the day about the
troubles in Fort Myers—the Latin Kings, Surf 69,
and the others: lots of drugs, lots of bad hombres
killing other bad hombres. But there had been a
concerted effort to clean this up, and the neighborhoods he'd previously heard mentioned, like
Dunbar and Pine Manor, felt safe. Now, however,
he found himself southwest of those, closer to the
Caloosahatchee River. And as the blocks passed by,
and he noticed more and more shuttered storefronts
and graffiti tags sprayed on the sun-bleached walls,

he grew confident he'd found a good place to start sniffing around.

He drove a little farther west, letting things get worse, then pulled over to the curb. He was on a block where old bungalows—the worse for wear— stood cheek by jowl with family businesses. About half the businesses were closed, windows painted white and front doors shuttered. Smashed or dented trash cans lay strewn about. Pickup trucks and a few old boat skeletons sat on cinder blocks in driveways or on front lawns, slowly moldering in the heat. A stray dog wandered by, tongue lolling. The air smelled of burnt rubber and garbage.

Smithback got out of his car and walked up to the first bungalow, which, not uncommonly in older and poorer communities, was half-hidden in overgrown tropical vegetation. The once-bright coat of paint had been reduced to faded and peeling strips. He pushed the doorbell—busted—then knocked. After a few minutes, he heard shuffling inside. Then the door opened halfway.

Hot as it was outside, he could feel even more heat radiating from the house. An old Hispanic woman in a housedress stood, peering at him in curiosity.

"*Buenos días*," Smithback said. He explained, in halting Spanish, that he was a student, working on a research project. Then he pulled out the enlarged and sharpened photo of the tattoo.

"*¿Ha visto esto antes?*" he asked.

The woman squinted in the semidarkness of the front hall, putting her face close to the image.

"*¿Qué es esto?*" Smithback asked.

Suddenly, the old woman's eyes widened. The curiosity was replaced with suspicion. "*¡Vaya!*" she spat at him, abruptly slamming the door in his face.

Smithback rapped again, then again, but there was no response. Finally, he shoved his card under the door, went back to the curb, and looked around. A few houses down, he saw a short, wiry man of about sixty mowing his lawn. Smithback walked toward him.

At his approach, the man cut the motor. He was smoking a small, foul-smelling cheroot and wore a filthy T-shirt emblazoned with the logo of a landscaping company.

Smithback nodded at him, and the man nodded back. Encouraged by the logo, the reporter launched into his explanation, in English this time. After a minute, the man interrupted him. "*No hablo inglés.*"

Smithback showed him the picture. "*¿Qué significa eso?*"

The man looked at the image—barely a glance, really—then shook his head. His face was a studied blank.

"*¿Lo ha visto antes?*" Smithback pressed.

The man shrugged. "*No hablo inglés.*"

Christ, it wasn't even English. But the man just stood there, shaking his head and shrugging, and eventually Smithback gave him his card anyway, thanked him, and turned away. Immediately, the man fired up his old mower and went back to work.

He glanced around again. A little farther down the block, another woman—slightly younger, slightly better dressed—was approaching the front door of a two-story apartment building, arms full of grocery bags. Instinctively, Smithback trotted forward in time to hold the door open for her.

"*Gracias,*" she said with a smile.

"*De nada.*" He dug out the picture of the tattoo. "*Por favor—qué es esto?*"

The woman looked at the photo. Almost immediately he saw, despite her initial friendliness, the same look the old lady had given him—a combination of suspicion and dread. As she turned to enter the building, Smithback stopped her one more time. "*Por favor, por favor. ¿Quién lo lleva?*"

From the shelter of the doorway, the woman glanced around nervously. Then she jerked her head westward, indicating a spot farther down the block. And before Smithback could give her his card or say anything more, she scurried into the apartment lobby, shutting the door behind her.

Slowly, Smithback walked back to his car. Christ, it was hot. So far he hadn't learned anything concrete.

Nevertheless, the very silence and agitation of the people spoke volumes. Starting the engine, he pulled away from the curb and began heading down the block, looking for whatever or whoever the woman with the groceries might have been indicating.

He found it at the next intersection. A dilapidated social club stood on the corner, front door open, what sounded like narco-rap filtering out from within. Three young men were lounging outside the door, dressed in T-shirts and old jeans. One sported several tattoos on his arms; the others appeared unmarked. Their expensive sneakers and gold chains looked out of place with the rest of their ratty attire.

Smithback pulled over. He had good street instincts, and at this moment they told him to keep his engine running.

He rolled down the passenger window and gestured to the youths. "*¡Hola!*" He had to say it again before one of the three pushed himself away from the wall and sauntered over.

Smithback showed him the picture of the tattoo. "*¿Qué es esto?*"

The youth looked at it for a minute, then turned to the others and muttered something Smithback couldn't understand. Now they, too, approached the car window. Smithback's sense of danger spiked dramatically.

"*¿Quién lo usa?*" he asked as calmly as possible.

Abruptly, one of the three tried to snatch the picture away. Smithback pulled it back just in time, crumpling it and throwing it in the backseat. At the same time, he put the car in gear and pulled away from the curb.

"*¡Vaya de aquí!*" said the tattooed one. "*¡Hijo de puta!*"

"*¡Pendejo!*" yelled another, spitting in the direction of the passenger door.

Smithback drove away, glancing frequently in his rearview mirror. None of the youths followed him, but it was clear they were watching him as closely as he was watching them. He took a deep breath, let it out slowly. McGregor Boulevard wasn't far away, and from there it was half an hour's drive back to the place he'd rented on Sanibel.

Had he made progress? Very likely.

Had he nearly shit his pants just now? Absolutely.

18

IN THE NEXT scheduled meeting, Chief P. B. Perelman contemplated Commander Baugh with fresh interest. The man had taken a cutter down to Cuba—a gutsy thing to do—and returned having provoked a minor diplomatic incident but with nothing tangible to show for his effort. Yet the man at the front of the briefing room didn't look chastened. Instead, he was just as self-assured as ever, just as determined, every inch the confident commander. Perelman wondered if that wasn't the very quality that had allowed him to advance so far.

Since the incident, however, the commander had shifted focus, dropping the Cuban prison idea and working instead from the hypothesis that the feet had been dumped at sea from a ship.

Perelman glanced at the back of the room, where Pendergast was standing in his usual spot, arms crossed, his expression obscured by the Panama hat that had been pulled down over his features.

Baugh cleared his throat, his gravelly voice filling the briefing room. "I would like to introduce Dr. Bob Kendry, who is a specialist in ocean currents, to explain the new line of inquiry. Dr. Kendry?"

A strikingly tall man took the podium. Bald and sixtyish, he had a lean, fit frame and wore a tailored blue suit. There was almost something of the movie star about him, and when he spoke, it was with a voice to match—deep, smooth, and calm.

"Thank you, Commander Baugh." He removed some notes from his pocket and placed them on the lectern. "Over the course of three days, one hundred and twelve feet washed up on Captiva Island—or I should say, mostly on Captiva. Two drifted into Sanibel, and two more washed up on North Captiva, one on Cayo Costa, and one on Gasparilla Island. The investigative problem can be simply stated. Can we backtrack twenty-eight, thirty days to where these feet came from? The answer is: we can."

The lights dimmed and he launched into a discussion of currents, winds, tides, and wave action, with several charts projected on the screen, along with a crude animation of how an array of floating objects the size and buoyancy of the feet would have traveled, ending on Captiva Island. After ten minutes of this, Perelman turned to Morris, who was sitting next to him. "'Confusion now hath made his masterpiece.'"

Morris rolled his eyes. "I got lost a while ago myself."

Kendry paused, and Perelman waited with hope that this signified the close.

"And so, to conclude—"

Thank you, Lord, Perelman thought.

"—as you can see, we were able to retrace the route that these feet took on their journey from the dumping point to Captiva. We zeroed in on this area, here."

An image came up of an elongated dotted oval drawn not in the gulf, but in the Caribbean Sea.

"'To unpathed waters, undreamed shores,'" Perelman murmured.

"You've got a quote for every occasion, don't you, Chief?"

"I certainly do."

"He never runs out," said Towne.

Kendry went on. "This target area is located about two hundred miles due west of the Cayman Islands— an area of approximately six hundred square miles."

"Thank you, Dr. Kendry," said Baugh, resuming the podium as the lights came back up. "Our investigation has proceeded using Dr. Kendry's analysis. Fortunately, the dotted area you see on the map lies outside the major shipping lanes. Which isn't surprising, since one wouldn't expect a ship dumping cargo of this sort to choose a well-traveled area. Using transponder AIS data, we've determined that four vessels passed through this area during the time frame in question: twenty-eight days, plus or minus three. We've also examined satellite imagery of the area and determined there were two other, smaller vessels in the area at the time not using AIS. We've managed to identify all six vessels."

Towne leaned over and murmured, "Seems like the commander has finally gotten his act together."

As Perelman was about to speak, Towne said: "Please, Chief, not more poetry."

Perelman frowned. "Philistine."

"Four ships," Baugh continued, "were large, internationally flagged carriers: the M/V *Pearl Nori*, a chemical tanker; the container ship *Empire Carrier*; the *Everest*, also a container ship; and the M/V *First Sea Lord*, an LNG tanker. The other two vessels in the area were local boats. The first was a pleasure yacht known as—" He paused, frowning. "*Monkey Sea Monkey Do.* The other was an eighty-six-foot stern trawler called F/V *Irish Wake*. Both hail from Gulf Coast ports."

He paused and looked around, squinting. "And so, the next stage of the investigation includes, among other things, tracking down and interviewing the captains of those six ships." His eye fell on

Pendergast. "Ah, Agent Pendergast, I'm glad to see you after an absence. Interviewing these captains is a perfect job for the FBI. I'd like you and the agency to take charge of that."

When Pendergast didn't respond, or even acknowledge he had heard, Baugh said, voice raised: "Agent Pendergast? Hello?"

The FBI agent was still standing with his arms crossed. It was hard to tell what he was thinking, his face still obscured by the hat. After a moment he nodded curtly.

"Any luck with the NCAVC databases?"

"It would seem this case has no precedent."

"And how is the investigation on the source of the shoes coming?"

"Very well, thank you. We have an agent in China."

The "thank you" somehow managed to sound faintly insolent, but maybe, Perelman thought, it was just his imagination.

The commander then began to dole out other assignments, and it was at this point Pendergast chose to slip out of the room like a cat.

19

I HATE TO BE crude, but that looks like...looks like..." Gladstone stopped, unsure what comparison to make.

"Well, I *love* being crude," said Lam. "It looks like an exploded merkin."

Maybe he's right, Gladstone thought as she stared at the big-screen image of the southern gulf. Thousands of squiggly black lines started at Turner Beach and then went off in every conceivable direction. "What a mess. It makes no sense."

"Well, I'm still refining the program," said Lam defensively.

"How much more did this cost us in CPU time?"

"Um, about two thousand dollars."

"Good Christ. So what's the problem?"

Lam shook his head. "Basically, most of the mathematical solutions are going into imaginary space."

"Which means?"

"The drift analysis is producing impossible results. There just doesn't seem to be a place any-where out there in the wide ocean where you could drop a hundred-plus feet and have them wash up on Turner Beach the way they did. The place just doesn't exist."

"It *has* to exist."

Lam shrugged.

"What about the garbage stinking up the back room?"

Lam pantomimed the act of vomiting. "Cataloged anything remotely identifiable. No smoking guns."

"What about the analysis? Did you work that into the equations?"

"I did. Not all of it—just select pieces to give us a broad enough sample. Same impossible results."

"But we know the feet *did* wash up!"

Lam sighed. "As I said, it's impossible."

"It can't be *impossible*," Gladstone said, feeling like tearing her hair out.

"Don't yell at me!"

"I'm not yelling. I'm emphasizing."

"Well, don't emphasize at me! You know how sensitive I am."

Gladstone rolled her eyes. "You need to figure out what's wrong and rerun the analysis."

"Okay. Fine with me. Each time I run it on the Q machine, it costs us five hundred bucks."

Gladstone paused, thinking. A temporary silence filled the lab. And then she took out her cell phone and dialed, putting it on speaker so Lam could hear.

"May I speak with Agent Pendergast?" she asked when the call was answered.

"Speaking."

"Gladstone here. I'm glad I reached you," she said. "We've been working on the analysis you asked for."

"And how is it going?"

"Um, well. Very well. We've prepared a full catalog of the debris that washed up, and we're working on our mathematical models. We're making great progress."

Lam made a face.

"Delighted to hear it."

"But the number crunching is getting expensive. We're running up quite a bill with the Q machine at the university."

"May I ask how much?"

"We're a few thousand dollars into it, and we're probably going to crack ten thousand before we get our answer."

"You have my authorization to expend up to fifteen thousand."

"Wow. Thank you, that's great. Really great." She paused. "There, um, is one other thing that would really help us refine our calculations. It's kind of critical, to be honest."

"And what might that be?"

"We need a foot. Two, actually. To accurately model drift behavior, along with several other variables."

There was an extended silence. "How long would you require them?"

She glanced at Lam. He held up two hands, fingers spread.

"Ten hours."

"I believe I can provide you with them—but it would be for half that long, at most, and I will need to be present at all times. Will that be acceptable?"

"Sweet mother of..." Lam began in a low voice. Then he went silent and, a moment later, nodded at her.

"Yes. Thank you. Thanks very much."

"In that case, I shall do my best to be there within the hour. And I sincerely hope that the additional funding will help you and Dr. Lam make better progress. Good day, Dr. Gladstone."

She lowered the phone. "I wonder how he knew we weren't making good progress?"

"I don't know, but I told you the guy had money."

"That fifteen grand isn't his own dough."

"I wouldn't be so sure about that."

* * *

Moira Crossley waited while Special Agent Pendergast finished his call and slipped the cell phone back into his pocket.

"I beg pardon for the interruption," he said.

What an odd fellow, she thought. She found his Southern gentlemanly manner and soft accent strangely soothing. But there was nothing soft or particularly gentlemanly in his keen, silvery eyes.

"Quite a few of the lab reports are back. I sent them over to your office for review."

"I've received them but would greatly appreciate a summary."

"Sure. Let's go to my office, where we can speak privately."

They were in the autopsy room and several assistants were still working on the last of the feet, carefully cutting off the shoes, looking for identifying marks, photographing, taking tissue samples, and, where necessary, dissecting and stabilizing the remains to remove dead sea creatures and small parasites that had burrowed into the flesh. Pendergast paused a moment to examine the process, restless eyes taking in everything, then returned his attention to her with a nod of apology.

She led him through the lab and into her office, with its single window overlooking the parking lot. The space was small, but she kept it meticulously neat and spare, a habit gained from years of living on a houseboat at a slip at the Cape Coral Yacht Basin.

"Please sit down."

Pendergast took a seat and she sat behind her desk. Several files were laid out with military precision. She flipped open the first.

"You had raised the question as to whether the feet had been frozen. They were—immediately following amputation. All of them we've examined so far, at least. Microsections of tissue indicate they were frozen fast at a low temperature—somewhere in the range of minus thirty degrees Celsius. That's much colder than household freezers typically go, which indicates these feet were stored in a professional-grade deep freezer, or even a laboratory freezer."

"And how do you know this?"

"In freezing, microcrystals of ice grow inside the cells and rupture various membranes. From the pattern, we can get an idea of how fast and deep the freezing was. For these feet, it was both."

Pendergast inclined his head briefly.

"And we've got some interesting results on the DNA testing," she said, removing another file. "To summarize: a majority of the individuals we've tested so far, about sixty, have varying percentages of Native American blood—from 9 percent to 90 percent, with an average around 70 percent. Of the European DNA, the majority can be traced to the Iberian

Peninsula—Spain—as well as southern and western Europe. There is also a portion of African DNA in many samples, varying from 3 to 15 percent. This mix is typical of the populations of Central America— in particular Honduras, Nicaragua, Guatemala, and El Salvador. To a lesser extent Panama and Costa Rica. Belize, Mexico, Colombia, and Venezuela are outliers, but still could be a partial match. We're in the process of analyzing mitochondrial DNA to see if any of the individuals might be related to each other, and I should have the results by tomorrow, at the latest. In any case, Central America seems the overwhelming point of origin."

Another slow nod.

"A few of the feet had tattoos. Some are generic, bracelets and the like, but others appear to be religious or gang symbols of some kind. One foot was chopped off higher above the ankle than most, and in that case we managed to retrieve almost the entire image."

"Interesting."

"The feet all came from adult individuals, in apparent good health, with a roughly fifty-fifty distribution between male and female. Some of the feet had the remnants of toenail polish. We're looking into identifying sources for that, based on chemical composition or color, but no luck so far."

She pulled over another file. "Here's something

curious. Many of the soles of the feet, and the shoes, showed signs of pesticide residue—DDT and chlordane, which have been banned in the U.S. for decades. There are significant traces of certain other compounds evident as well, such as sodium hydroxide. Beyond the pesticide residues, there is no commonality we've been able to discover."

She consulted the file, running her finger down the points. "We've collected hair, fiber, pollen, and other residues. Nothing of note except this: the pollen is a typical mix of local flora—not Central American. The pollen types point to a spring season—likely this spring, by the freshness of them."

"Please continue."

Crossley flipped over a page. "The toxicology reports all came up negative, at least for common toxins and substances. I think you have the list of what we tested for."

"I do indeed. Now, I wonder if we could go over, just once more, exactly how the feet were amputated."

She felt a stab of annoyance. "As I mentioned before, the amputations were crude, many done with repeated blows of what seems to be a hatchet, and a dull one at that, others perhaps with a heavy machete. The amputation point varies considerably from just above the ankle—by far the most common—to a few below the knee. In many cases there was no evidence of a tourniquet being employed, although others show signs that a clumsy and ineffectual tourniquet may have been tied around the limb before the amputation. There is no evidence of skilled medical care or first aid. The probability is that most of these victims bled to death."

"And the angle of the blows?"

"Most vary within, say, forty to seventy degrees from the horizontal—angling down, in other words."

"And the direction of the amputation?"

Crossley was growing more annoyed. She had discussed this with Pendergast before. "The amputation started with the anterior outside portion of the lower leg, right or left."

"The blows coming from above."

"Yes, yes. You know all this—we've gone over it."

"Indeed we have. And now, Dr. Crossley, please humor me by visualizing, in your mind, the actual amputation, taking into account all the factors as you've just described them."

Her annoyance finally got the better of her. "I fail to see the point of this."

The voice dropped in tone, smooth as honey. "Dr. Crossley, I promise that the point will become clear. I can guide you through the process to make it easier. Close your eyes, take five deep, slow breaths, and then *visualize* the process of amputation. Consider all the relevant details and make a mental film of the amputation, putting in the real person."

"That's peculiar and unscientific."

"Indulge me. Now, please..." His voice was strangely hypnotic. "Close your eyes."

Almost against her will, she closed her eyes.

"Take a slow, deep breath...Inhale..."

She did so.

"Now slowly, exhale."

She did as he guided, five times. Remarkably, she could feel annoyance and tension draining away, her mind quieting down.

He continued to murmur directions in a soothing tone. Then, after a few minutes, he began reciting the grotesque details of the amputations in the same calm, neutral voice, asking her to visualize in slow motion the hatchet descending from above; the repeated blows; the flesh being cut; the bones fracturing and splintering; the foot coming free; the gushing blood...It was almost too horrible to imagine: she had literally spent years learning to think of the autopsy as a job to be done on an inert object, rather than on beings who had once lived and suffered—there was no other way to keep her emotional equilibrium. But under Pendergast's gentle tutelage, she found at last that she was able to bring the human subject to life at the moment of the amputation.

Her eyes popped open in shocking realization. "Oh, *no!*" she gasped.

For a moment she couldn't speak. Pendergast looked at her with a mixture of curiosity and concern.

She found her voice. "These amputations were self-inflicted," she said. "Good Lord, these people chopped their own feet off!"

"That is indeed what they did," said Pendergast. "In the crudest and clumsiest way imaginable. The question is: why?"

20

PENDERGAST DROVE THE rental car northeast along Route 1, also known as the Overseas Highway. This latter moniker seemed particularly apt—in the hour it had taken him to drive up from the Key West airport, Route 1 had been more bridge than highway. Now and then it would pass over solid ground— some islands large enough to support a village, others barely more than a nubbin with palms and grass—and then the land would fall away and the road would once again stretch out over the greenish-blue ocean.

After one long stretch of water, Route 1 passed through Marathon Key and then, a few miles later, approached Islamorada. The lower Florida Keys had a tropical feel, like a land apart: a lived-in, sleepy, and weather-beaten environment that, while still reliant on tourism, was a far cry from the manicured luxury of Palm Beach. Islamorada seemed slightly more upscale than some of the other keys; as he drove, Pendergast passed several resorts monopolizing the island's beaches. The northern end, however, seemed more for locals, with a school, residential streets stretching away from the ocean, and the occasional trailer half-hidden among the trees.

Pendergast checked the GPS on his phone, and then, just before the highway arced out over the water again, he turned left and headed down one of the narrow roads cut through the scrub, half blacktop and half sand. No resorts here: just trailers and houses in various states of decrepitude; outboard motor repair shops; and small businesses, signs bleached by the sun.

Within half a dozen blocks the road ended in the gravel parking lot of a commercial fishery. Pendergast pulled up beside a row of pickup trucks and got out, glancing around. To the south, rusting hulks of old working boats had been laid on their beam-ends, forming a fence of sorts. To the north, where the land led down into a swampy shoreland area, he saw a motley collection of dwellings: lean-to sheds with corrugated roofs; shabby Airstreams with cinder blocks for wheels; one or two tiki-style huts that Gauguin might have enjoyed painting. The beach community seemed to have grown willy-nilly, like barnacles on the hull of a ship. Pendergast checked his GPS again, then made his way toward the little collection of houses.

He drew close, then stopped. Amid the scents of diesel oil, dead fish, and stagnant water, a new odor had wafted in: acrid, bitter, more appropriate for a chemical plant than a tropical island. Burnt coffee—but *burnt* hardly did it justice: coffee that had been boiled and boiled far past any trace of appeal or dignity. Pendergast put his phone away and—gingerly—began tracking the stench to its source. It was coming from one of the huts at the edge of the cleared area, where the trees ended at a strip of shoreland marsh. Beyond lay nothing but green water, the occasional sandbar, and the Gulf of Mexico.

Pendergast walked around to the front of the hut. There, reclining on a deck chair, was a young man, unshaven and unkempt. He wore a pair of cheap sunglasses and ragged sun-bleached jeans cut off midthigh. He was shirtless, displaying a muscled, bronze chest. A large scar, the stitches recently removed, ran in a thin line across his abdomen, like a stripe of pale paint against olive-colored skin. His jet-black hair had been pulled back into a tight ponytail and a red bandanna was rolled and tied around his neck. On one side of the chair stood a large mug of coffee, and on the other a half-empty bottle of Corona, beads of moisture sweating on the glass. The crackle of a police scanner sounded faintly from within the darkness of the hut.

The man, alerted to Pendergast's presence, glanced over. For a moment, the two merely exchanged a look. Then the man in the deck chair nodded. "Kemosabe," he said.

"Agent Coldmoon."

"Nice weather we're having."

"Perfectly delightful."

The man named Coldmoon gestured toward one of several empty oil drums scattered around. "Please have a seat."

"Thank you very much, but I'd prefer to stand."

"Have it your way. Some coffee, then?" He gestured toward a large steel pot that was simmering on an old ring stove in the darkness of the hut.

Pendergast didn't reply.

Coldmoon took a long pull on his beer. "Funny. I didn't expect to see you again. At least, not down here in Florida."

"I was unavoidably detained. And I might say the same about you. As I recall, you were discharged from the hospital a week ago. Why are you still here?"

Coldmoon shrugged. "I'm recuperating. The snows of Colorado can wait."

"And how did you end up in this picturesque locale?" Pendergast waved a hand at the engineless RVs, the piles of outboard motors, the sand and swamp grass.

"Just lucky, I guess. Rent's practically nothing. I got on a Greyhound headed south from Miami, looking for a place to clear my head of Mister Brokenhearts and his murders. Decided to get off here."

The capriciousness of that decision had made the search for him a great deal more difficult than it might have been.

"So you decided to finish your convalescence by going native," Pendergast said.

"Careful with that word choice, Pendergast. I'm already native—Lakota."

"Of course. But let us not forget your dear Italian mother."

Pendergast knew that Coldmoon was ambivalent about his Indian heritage being tainted by European blood.

"*Non mi rompere i coglioni*," Coldmoon replied, making an insulting Italian gesture.

"Allow me to get to the point. Have you been following the case of the curious flotsam that recently washed up on the beaches of Captiva Island?"

"The feet? What I read in the newspapers. Hear on that scanner."

Pendergast took a breath. "I have taken an interest in the matter."

"And?"

"I've found it a most baffling case indeed, perhaps even unique. Since you're still here, and knowing how you might appreciate additional experience to add to your jacket, I thought you'd find it interesting to take a day or two to observe the situation. Informally, of course. And—"

He was interrupted by Coldmoon's laughter. He wasn't a man to laugh easily, and it was an unusual, melodious sound. When he stopped, he finished the bottle of beer, then dropped it in the sandy dirt.

"Okay. Let's take apart that little speech of yours and extract the real meaning. Pickett forced you to take the case—right?"

"He did nothing of the sort," Pendergast said, annoyed. "He offered to show me the lay of the land. I accepted the case out of my own interest."

"Right, right. And now you're hip-deep in it, and you've decided you need your old partner Coldmoon to help you out."

"As you know, I don't work with a partner. I'm merely offering you the chance to consult."

"Ah, *consult*. You want my help and, given the roundabout way you're talking, that particular help is something I won't like."

"If you are accusing me of dissembling, I take exception."

"Well, maybe I 'take exception' to your interrupting my vacation. Oh, and blocking my sun, too." He looked at Pendergast, one eyebrow arched over the sunglasses.

After a brief pause, Pendergast stepped aside and perched lightly on the empty drum he'd declined before. "You have a suspicious and cynical nature. Ordinarily, I'd consider that an asset. But at the moment, I wonder if you're simply using it as a smoke screen for malingering."

Coldmoon smiled, but there was an edge when he spoke. "Malingering? You think that a bullet in the chest and a water moccasin bite is an excuse for me to goof off?"

"I think perhaps you're getting a little used to dozing in that lawn chair, drinking beer and execrable coffee, instead of consulting on an important case."

The two men fell silent. There were distant sounds of machinery, traffic; the cry of gulls and the screech of flamingos.

Finally, Coldmoon spoke. "Okay, Pendergast. What do you need me for? Just tell it straight. No bullshit."

"You have a peculiar—unorthodox—way of looking at things. A way that complements my own."

"Why don't you just say it? *'I need your help.'*"

"That's precisely what I am trying to do," Pendergast said in a frosty voice.

Coldmoon shook his head. "What does Pickett have to say about this? Your bringing me on?"

"I have his full support in making this request."

"And if I say no? Does the request change to an order?"

"Let us cross that bridge when we come to it."

Coldmoon gazed out to sea. "All right. I'm more than a little curious about all those feet washing up on the beach. Who wouldn't be? And, yes, I've got some time until I officially report to Colorado. But I'm not playing Tonto anymore. No consultancy stuff, nothing *informal*. That's a euphemism for 'dogsbody.' If I help you with this, I want in. Totally. Full partners—or nothing."

"You know my methods. What I was suggesting is something more, ah, provisional."

"Forget it."

Instead of responding, Pendergast closed his eyes. This time, the silence stretched into minutes. Then he said, eyes still closed: "The feet were previously frozen."

"That's bizarre."

"And the amputations were crudely performed, by machete or ax, without apparent medical intervention or subsequent first aid."

The silence deepened. "Now, that's some crazy shit."

"I promise you, the case presents aspects of exceptional curiosity."

"But still: *full partners or nothing.*"

Pendergast finally opened his eyes and focused on Coldmoon. "All right. For the duration of this case."

"Or until one of us gets killed."

"A lovely thought." At this, Pendergast stood up, dusted himself off in a finicky feline manner, then turned toward his rental car. "Feel free to spend the evening here, entertaining yourself in whatever meretricious manner you've grown accustomed to. But I'll expect you on Captiva Island tomorrow by lunchtime. Let's say one o'clock."

"Where?"

He opened the car door. "I'll be at the Mortlach House, just over the Blind Pass Bridge and past the beach. I've rented the house and there's plenty of room, so you needn't worry about finding a place to stay." Pendergast let his eye travel over Coldmoon's tiki hut. "If you'd be more comfortable, I could arrange for a packing box and mattress to be placed in the crawlspace under the porch."

"Ha ha."

"Do you have a mode of transportation?"

"I'll get there, don't you worry." Coldmoon grinned. "See you at one, *pard.*"

With a pained look, Pendergast slipped behind the steering wheel, closed the door, started the engine, and departed back down the dirt track, leaving behind a cloud of dust that slowly settled over the shacks and abandoned boats.

21

CONSTANCE LAY IN the old four-poster set back from the windows of a second-floor bedroom in the Mortlach House. The lawyer, Mr. Mayfield, had brought in an army of cleaners and house-dressers, and the shingle-style Victorian had been made bright and airy. Although Constance had kept a sharp eye out, she had yet to see blood seep out from behind the wallpaper, as the lawyer's secretary had assured her it did.

Her windows were open to admit the gulf breezes, and the faint thunder of waves on the still-cordoned beach reached her ears. Other than that, the house was silent. The bedrooms were all on the second floor, and she found that her sleeping quarters were closer to Aloysius's than she was used to. It was an old house, and well built, but not nearly as solid as the Riverside Drive mansion where she lived in New York City. This was their first night in the

place; Pendergast had gone to Key West this afternoon and wouldn't be getting in until half past one,
if not later.

As she lay on the bed, she watched a tendril of
moonbeam make its way across the paneled ceiling.
She felt no drowsiness. She had come to know herself
well over the many years since her birth, and there
was no mystery to her wakefulness: her senses were
on high alert and she was waiting for something
to happen.

The mystery, however, was . . . what?

Upon arrival, she had done her best to immerse
herself in Aloysius's case: doing bits of online research, expressing her opinion of his speculations and
offering a few of her own. But she found it hard to
develop an interest in the matter. A hundred human
feet, washing ashore—it was a bizarre and awful
thing, but it had little to do with the intellectual
and murderous battle of wits she so enjoyed assisting
Pendergast with in his cases. Death on this scale was
more like genocide, and genocide was never clever
or mysterious: it was just the ugliest, cruelest side of
humanity, manifesting itself in a brutal and pointless fashion. Enoch Leng, her first guardian, had
been a scholar of genocide, and through him she had
learned more about the subject than she ever would
care to have known.

She had finally admitted to Pendergast that she had

little interest in the case and would prefer to pursue other things while on the islands. But there was another reason she wanted nothing to do with the case, which she hadn't shared with Pendergast.

If one looked deep enough into the death records of late-nineteenth-century New York City, one could learn that a young married couple had died during a cholera epidemic ravaging the docklands slums. But the death certificates did not tell the full story. After the husband, a stevedore, died of the disease, his wife—out of her head with fever and despair— either fell or jumped into the East River. Two little girls, Mary and Constance, were there to see their mother's body being hoisted from the foul water with grappling hooks.

She had never told anyone, even Dr. Leng. But the memory was with her always, and she did not wish to have a hundred waterlogged feet sharpening the edges of those memories.

And so she had begun playing the role of tourist, wandering the streets, peering into shops, visiting the historical society, or sitting on the veranda of the Mortlach House, gazing toward the gulf and reading *To the Lighthouse*. She despised the book and had never been able to finish it, but now it was a martyrdom she was grimly determined to see through, like Henry IV of Germany enduring a hair shirt along the Walk to Canossa—

Constance's train of thought came to an abrupt stop.

She lay perfectly still. There it was again: a rapping sound, faint but discernible. And it wasn't from outside; it was in the house, down below—perhaps the basement, which Constance had not yet explored.

And now, lying in bed, Constance realized what she had been waiting for: evidence of the Mortlach ghost.

She sat up with a mixture of thrill and fear. Her eyes were already accustomed to the dark, and reaching over, she picked up the antique Italian stiletto that she always carried with her. She swung her legs out of the bed, rising to her feet in perfect silence while slipping into a silk robe. With equal stealth she crept to the door, then—very slowly—opened it.

The hall was empty, lit only by a single small lamp. Weapon at the ready, Constance paused again to listen.

Another tap, followed shortly by yet another: stealthy and hollow with a sense of purpose. They were definitely coming from the basement, and they sounded to Constance like someone tapping on the walls of the old mansion with a bony hand. It reminded her of the Mount Mercy Hospital for the Criminally Insane, where an inmate had been infamous for . . .

The breeze shifted and a sudden gust of wind

caught the curtains of her windows, slamming her door shut with a thunderous bang.

Constance froze. She waited, motionless, listening for a long time, but there was no more tapping.

At last she turned and—as silently as she had risen from it—she returned to her bed, laid her head back on the down pillows, and once again stared at the continuing journey of the sliver of moonlight across the ceiling.

22

THE FINAL LAB results had arrived the previous evening, just as Moira Crossley was about to close up. She had stayed until nine o'clock going through them and then returned to the office that morning at seven to finish up before that strange FBI agent, Pendergast, was due to arrive for another update. She knew he would be punctual, and there was something about him that made her nervous, giving her the feeling that she should be very careful, not make a mistake, and be ready to answer any question.

The buzzer rang just as the second hand on the clock was sweeping across twelve: OCD-level punctuality. How did he manage it with the hideous and unpredictable traffic? Did he arrive early and wait with a stopwatch? She wondered why she was so concerned about his approval. With most people, she didn't give a rip.

She opened the door and Pendergast stepped in,

wearing a beautiful lemon-colored silk suit with the same Panama hat he had worn before. He tipped his hat in an old-fashioned way, then hung it on a coat rack by the door.

"A lovely morning, Dr. Crossley," he said. "Do I need to gown up?"

"Not necessary," she said. "We can go over the new results in my office. Please come with me."

Pendergast followed and she unlocked her office.

"Take a chair," she said as they entered.

Pendergast slipped into a seat. Crossley went to her safe and punched in the combination, removing a couple of file folders. At Pendergast's suggestion, she was taking extra care with security. She placed the folders in a stack. "I'll be sending these to the FBI later today, but if you wish, we can go over them now."

"I do wish."

"Fine." She passed him the top folder, opened the second on her desk. "There's some, shall we say, *unusual* new information."

"Excellent."

At that moment the buzzer sounded again. Irritated, Crossley looked at her watch: 9:05. It wasn't Paul; he had his own key. Probably one of those goddamn reporters.

"Excuse me while I get rid of whoever that is," she said.

She went to the door. Through the wire-glass window she could see a very tall man standing ramrod straight, in a crisp blue suit, clean-shaven with a fresh buzz cut, lean and chiseled, with brown skin and striking green eyes.

This was no reporter.

"Who is it?" she asked through the microphone.

In response, the man held up a badge. "Special Agent Coldmoon, Federal Bureau of Investigation."

"Oh." Unlike Pendergast, this one looked every inch a fed. She buzzed him in. "I was just about to go over the lab results with Agent Pendergast. Are you also assigned to the case—?"

"We're partners." His dazzling smile just about bowled her over.

As she led him in, Pendergast rose.

"Good to see you, Agent Pendergast," said Coldmoon. "I see I've arrived just in time."

"I rather expected you later, Agent Coldmoon." Pendergast eyed him keenly.

An easy laugh. "We have an old Lakota saying: the early bird gets the worm."

"Indeed. And I see this early bird has new feathers."

Coldmoon tugged on his lapels. "Walmart. One hundred twenty-nine bucks."

A look of undisguised distaste flitted across Pendergast's face.

Coldmoon took an empty seat, while Crossley

resumed her place behind the desk, passed another of the folders to Coldmoon, and then began her summary. "As I was about to explain to Agent Pendergast, we've completed the DNA testing and the results are rather interesting. Earlier we determined that most of the feet came from the genetic heritage you typically find in Central and South America—mostly Native American with some European from the Iberian Peninsula, and a small portion of African. We've refined those results, and here's what we've got." She removed a large folded chart. "Many of these individuals are related, in widely varying degrees. We've got some brothers and sisters, a few parents and grown children, along with first cousins, second, third, fourth, and even fifth cousins." She slid the diagram over. "This is an attempt to show relatedness. Of course, it's extremely complicated because some first cousins are also third and fourth cousins to others, and so forth."

Coldmoon leaned forward eagerly and drew the diagram toward him, examined it, then passed it on to Pendergast.

"We're now going to submit the DNA results to several large commercial genetic testing databases to see if we can identify any of these individuals by name. That's a complicated process, but we're pushing it forward as fast as we can and should have those results soon." She cleared her throat. "In addition to the DNA results, six individuals had partial or complete tattoos, which we've now analyzed. We've identified a few as symbols related to gang or religious affiliations common to the western highlands of Guatemala. The ink used is consistent with crudely formulated tattoo inks commonly used in Central America. Unfortunately, with the proliferation of such gangs, obtaining verifiable, current information on them is difficult. We've brought in a specialist and are doing what we can. The toenail polish present on some of the feet was identifiable—cheap brands common to Central America. But perhaps the most important evidence we found is this."

She took a photo out of the folder and placed it on the desk in front of them. Once again Coldmoon eagerly snapped it up and examined it before passing it on to Pendergast.

"That's a silver toe ring displaying an image of the Virgin of Guadalupe, of a form and style typically worshiped by the Maya people of Guatemala. And engraved on the ring—" she pulled out another close-up photo— "is the name of a town in Guatemala called San Miguel Acatán."

"Where's that?" Coldmoon asked.

"A village in the western highlands, close to the Mexican border, with a mostly Maya population." She paused. "Well, that about summarizes it."

Coldmoon put down the photo. "The obvious

inference is we're dealing with a group of migrants, all from the same town—San Miguel Acatán."

Crossley nodded.

"You know how it is," Coldmoon said. "A group of people from the town get together and decide to head north to the United States. Economic refugees. And you'd expect a lot of people in a small town like that to be related. I would imagine that on their journey north they got waylaid by some bad guys, and then...well, something terrible happened to them and they got their feet chopped off."

"As Agent Pendergast brought to my attention, it appears they each amputated one of their own feet," said Crossley.

At this Coldmoon sat back. "Holy shit. They cut *their own feet off?*"

"Yes."

"Were they shackled? Was this a way to escape?"

"A good guess, but they weren't shackled. There aren't any abrasions, bruises, or scratches around their ankles you'd get from shackling. They self-amputated for some other reason."

"What could possibly make someone chop off their own foot?" Coldmoon asked incredulously.

At this Pendergast spoke. "How excellent it is that Agent Coldmoon is finally here to pose the truly arduous question."

This was followed by a brief silence.

"Is there anything else, Dr. Crossley?" Pendergast asked.

"That's all for now."

The two of them rose, and Coldmoon followed Pendergast out. A moment later, with the closing of the hall door, the lab fell silent. Moira Crossley sat in the quiet for some time. The final question Coldmoon had posed, which she had asked herself many times, seemed to have no possible answer—none at all.

23

Outside, Coldmoon followed Pendergast into the parking lot.

"Do you have a car, Agent Coldmoon?" Pendergast asked.

"Nope." Coldmoon had anticipated this. He had no intention of playing chauffeur, as he had during the Brokenhearts investigation.

"Pity. However, managing to anticipate that answer, I've acquired a vehicle myself that should prove suitable. Not only is it equipped to go across any terrain imaginable—including swamps, beaches, and bayous—but it will do so in comfort."

Coldmoon looked around the lot but didn't see any official-looking vehicle among the Ford Explorers and Jeep Cherokees that met these qualifications. Then his gaze fell on something parked at the far end of the lot.

"No," he said, staring.

"Yes," Pendergast said, slipping him the key fob.

Glistening in the sun was a factory-fresh Range Rover, an "Autobiography" edition in off-white pearl with a beautiful satin matte finish. It seemed to have every available option for arriving at an opera premiere, or the top of Everest, in style: LED headlights and desaturated taillights, rear fog lights, a badge announcing the 5.0 liter, 557-horsepower supercharged LR-V8 that sat beneath the hood—and those were just the externally visible attributes.

Coldmoon whistled. "Nice ride."

While he had been taking in the Rover's features, Pendergast had walked around the rear of the vehicle and was now getting into the passenger seat. Coldmoon looked down, saw the key fob Pendergast had put into his hand. *Son of a bitch*, he thought. But instead of refusing outright, he put his bag in the back and got into the driver's seat, immediately sinking into creamy leather. Once he'd figured out how to start the engine, he saw the car had less than fifty miles on it. In the driver's side pocket was a folded dealer's sheet, and as the interior cooled off he pulled it out curiously. The sheet ticked off such items as electronic air suspension, wade-sensing technology, hill descent control, roll stability control, and a laundry list too long to read through. At the bottom was a price: $189,500.

Coldmoon took another look at the dealer sheet,

recognizing it for what it was. "Hold on," he said. "You just *bought* this?"

"Leased, actually. After all, we don't have Axel on hand to take us around anymore, and that confiscated Mustang of yours was about as comfortable as the rail they used to ride one out of town on. When I learned you were willing to join the investigation, I decided the least we could do was prosecute the case with a degree of luxury."

Now Coldmoon understood: he was still expected to play chauffeur, but Pendergast had sweetened the deal by providing almost three tons of rolling opulence. He shrugged, then twisted the large round knob that put the vehicle in gear.

"I'd like to introduce you to the oceanographer I've privately engaged to work on the case," said Pendergast. "She's trying to backtrack the feet to where they entered the ocean—without much success yet, unfortunately."

"Sure, I'd love to meet her."

"But before that, why don't we drop off your luggage at the lodgings I've rented for the duration? My ward, Constance Greene, will be staying with us, but I think you'll find the house both commodious and private."

"Uh, sure." *Ward?* That sounded a little odd, but then, nothing about Pendergast was normal.

Pendergast gave him the address and—after some

fiddling with the touch screen on the central panel of the dashboard—he managed to punch it into the GPS.

"A/C?" Coldmoon asked.

"No, thank you." Pendergast rolled down his window and Coldmoon did the same. As they drove out of Fort Myers, taking SR 867 south, Coldmoon observed with curiosity the neighborhoods they were passing through. They were a mixture typical to Florida: some wealthy, some shabby, many in between—but all high density. It was amazing how many damn people there were in this state. In South Dakota there were stretches of highway where you could drive a hundred miles without seeing a house.

And then, quite suddenly, they passed by a checkpoint and emerged onto a causeway that curved like a scimitar over a shallow bay, the sun glittering off the water, with the low outline of Sanibel Island growing on the horizon. Considering its size and weight, the Range Rover was surprisingly responsive, and it accelerated effortlessly, sending a warm breeze coursing through the interior. For a moment, however brief, Coldmoon could understand why someone might want to live in Florida.

Once on the island, the houses moved upscale, and the farther he drove, the wealthier it got. Toward the north end of the island they came to a line of stopped cars.

"I'm afraid there's another checkpoint up ahead," said Pendergast.

But the traffic went quickly, and soon they had flashed their badges and were through. A short bridge led them across an inlet to Captiva Island. The beach and parking lot to their left had been turned into a staging ground, it seemed, with tents, trailers, container offices, and a van with satellite dishes on top. Two Coast Guard patrol boats plied the ocean beyond the line of breaking surf.

"That was where most of the feet washed up," said Pendergast as Coldmoon slowed to look. "The entire beach has been taped off as a crime scene, to the great annoyance of the inhabitants."

"I'd be annoyed, too. That's a beautiful beach."

They drove on, leaving the staging ground behind. Past the far end of the beach, Coldmoon spied a huge Victorian house, taller than the others, rising above the palms and buttonwoods, with two towers and a widow's walk, casting a long shadow across the beach. He knew right away this must be where Pendergast was staying—the house, with its faded elegance, fit his personality perfectly.

"The Mortlach House?"

"Indeed. Pull into the porte cochere, if you please, and stop by the door."

Coldmoon wasn't sure what a porte cochere was, but he turned into the driveway that ran alongside the house, looping through a sheltered overhang. He brought the SUV to a stop before a set of tall double doors with oval windows.

"Wow," said Coldmoon, stepping out and looking up, "this place looks haunted."

"Indeed," murmured Pendergast.

The doors opened and Coldmoon stopped in his tracks. A woman appeared on the landing, wearing a long dress, her dark hair bobbed, her violet eyes directed on him.

"You must be Agent Coldmoon," she said in a contralto voice, coming forward. She paused to look him up and down. "From Aloysius's description, I was expecting someone a little more...informal."

Coldmoon grinned. "Don't worry, I'm as slovenly as they come. This is just a disguise to fool my betters."

That produced a faint smile. There was something absolutely intriguing about this young woman, who seemed self-assured far beyond her years and spoke with an unusual inflection that reminded him of old films.

"Don't you have a valise?" she asked.

Coldmoon realized he'd been standing there dumb. "Right. In the back." He went around the car, opened the tailgate, and pulled out his bag.

"I'll show you to your room," said Constance, turning and heading back inside. Coldmoon followed.

"I'm retiring to my quarters," Pendergast said from behind them. "You're in good hands with Ms. Greene." He slipped away.

Entering the cool dimness of the house was like stepping back in time. The interior smelled of furniture polish, fabric, and old wood. He could see, past the entryway and down a hall, a large sitting room with Persian rugs and antique furniture. A row of windows looked out across a veranda to the sea horizon, where he could hear the distant rhythm of surf and the crying of gulls.

Constance turned and mounted a set of stairs to the right of the entryway. "This way, Agent Coldmoon."

Coldmoon followed, up to an annex that served as a small sitting room, with three rooms going off it—two bedrooms and a bath.

"The servants' quarters," said Constance. "Separate from the rest of the house."

"Servants' quarters," Coldmoon repeated in a tone of irony.

Constance again fixed those violet eyes on him. "You are Agent Pendergast's *junior* partner, are you not, Mr. Coldmoon?"

Coldmoon couldn't help but laugh at this brazen comment, so archly delivered. "I guess I am a kind of servant." He set down his bag. "By the way, you're free to call me Armstrong if you wish."

That slipped out before he even knew he'd said it. Why had he offered up this information? He almost never told people his first name.

"And you may call me Constance. Your bedroom is here. The other bedroom has a desk for you to use as a workspace." A key appeared in a delicate white hand. "Your key, Armstrong."

"Thank you, Constance." He took it. "Um, is the house really supposed to be haunted?"

"So they say."

"What's the story?"

She gave him another arch smile. "That's *my* investigation. Once I've pieced it together, we'll light a fire in the parlor and I'll regale you with the details."

24

PETER QUARLES MADE his way down the crooked, congested streets of a city that had no name. Or if it had a name, he had not been able to discover it. All he could say for certain was that he was in Guangdong Province in southern China. Dongguan, a first-tier manufacturing city, was to his east, across the Pearl River. Just to his west was Foshan, itself an agglomeration of three dozen towns that specialized in industries from chemical processing to communications equipment to biotechnology. And here he was, in a bustling no-man's-land of small-time commerce and manufacturing, situated in an anonymous district just a stone's throw from the South China Sea.

Yet Quarles felt curiously at home. He was not so many years removed from his time in import-export work, and was not so brainwashed by Bureau mentality, that he'd found it difficult to slip back into his old guise. After just one day, the crowds, the endless yammering, the smog, and the smells had all become familiar and comfortable, and he fell back into that shuffling two-step that one used to get about in the congestion. Nobody would suspect him of being anything more than a *gweilo* middleman, working at the low end of the manufacturing business—which, in fact, was true. Except that his Mandarin was perhaps a little too refined.

The only difference from back then was how Agent Pendergast had financed this investigative journey with a most lavish expense account. How he'd managed it, Quarles didn't know, but the man had made clear he would take care of everything and that Quarles should not stint on his accommodations, meals, bribes, or hiring assistants. And so Quarles had splurged, staying at the Marco Polo in Jinjiang and the Shangri-La in Wenzhou. As he'd expected, he'd had no luck in either city finding a manufacturer of anything like this odd slipper: a cheaply made, disposable product of propylene that nevertheless sported both high fluid resistance and antibacterial properties. Even Dongguan, where he'd placed most of his hopes, had initially been a dud: a big influx in Brazilian manufacturing had driven out many of the local manufacturers he thought most likely to have made these. But he soon learned those small-time manufacturers had not disappeared—they had migrated across the river into the shadow of Foshan. And so it was here—as he walked along Zhaofang Road, the towers of Lunxiang Residential District rising behind him—that he undertook his search in earnest.

He paused for a minute to wipe his brow and adjust the cheap canvas bag he'd slung across his shoulders. He'd already spoken to several mom-and-pop operations, greasing his inquiries with packets of Dunhills, Gauloises, and Camels. Though none had been able to help him directly, they'd suggested he try the neighborhood around Zhaofang Road. He glanced ahead through the crowds, taking note of a cotton factory, a sugar water shop, a school, and a salted-chicken restaurant called Every Day Is Better. He saw a couple of shopfronts of the near-ubiquitous clothing manufacturers, but no shoemakers. But that did not dissuade him—small manufacturers were often found on second floors or down narrow alleys.

He continued, careful to give a wide berth to the monolithic structure titled Central Commission for Discipline Inspection, and then—when the road took a sharp turn—found himself at the edge of a Cantonese food market. Tanks swarming with abalone, crab, and clams were everywhere, next to other vendors selling savory cuts of dog, cat, and other four-legged creatures. There were no tourists in sight, just locals—travel guides billed the food in this region as "most disagreeable" to Western palates. And yet Quarles had grown to like it. Yue cuisine put a premium on fresh ingredients, lightly cooked and seasoned. And as for the ingredients themselves, well, you got used to them after a while.

He wandered across the market, continued down Zhaofang, and then spotted exactly what he was looking for: a tiny, windowless shop with a few pieces of leather last nailed across the doorway. It lay in the shadow of the Wooden Bucket, an offal house that specialized in spicy beef soup. He stepped toward it quickly, pushed aside the improvised door, and entered.

As his eyes became accustomed to the dim interior, he saw an old man sitting behind a long wooden table. He was slicing small lines across the lower edges of shoe uppers, preparing to glue them to the soles. Behind him was an equally old woman working a sewing machine. Piles of footwear lay here and there—including, Quarles noticed, some disposable shoes not so different from the one in his satchel.

He removed his sample and stepped forward. "You good?" he asked politely in Mandarin.

The man merely nodded.

Quarles showed him the shoe. "Have you seen this handiwork before?"

Something in the man's eyes told Quarles it was familiar to him. But he simply shrugged, giving the universal gesture for not understanding what Quarles was saying.

This was ridiculous, of course, but also part of the usual dance. Even though Mandarin was primarily the language of business, Quarles switched to the Sam Yap dialect used by local Cantonese. He reached into his satchel again, this time removing a *hóng bāo*, a red envelope of cash: an equally universal gesture. He placed it against the sole of the shoe, then thrust them both toward the man. "Do you know where I can get more of these?" he asked.

The old woman, who had grown interested as soon as the red envelope made its appearance, now rose and together with the old man scrutinized the shoe carefully. Quarles waited, taking more red envelopes out of his satchel and counting them, implying that more *hóng bāo* would be forthcoming if his quest was successful.

At last the old man handed back the shoe, minus the envelope. "Try Changyou Fourth Road," he said in Sam Yap. "Down near the ancestral temple. There are still one or two factories that may produce what you seek."

"*M goi nei sin*," Quarles said. Then, putting the shoe and envelopes back into his satchel, he turned, opened the door, and was quickly carried away by the crowds thronging the street.

25

PERELMAN HAD HIS head and shoulders deep within the engine space of his boat when he heard someone approaching down the dock. But the socket wrench in his right hand was occupying all his attention, and he ignored the sound: maybe, for a change, it wasn't somebody intent on bothering him. Sure enough: there was no hull dip of someone coming aboard. He returned to wrestling with the 700 horses that had occupied him for the last ninety minutes. "This is your last chance to come out," he told the plug, raising the wrench threateningly. "Otherwise, I'm going to WD-40 your ass."

Now there came another sound, this one unmistakable: the polite clearing of a throat on the dock behind him. Suppressing a curse, he hoisted himself up from the engine well, turned, and—to his great surprise—saw Constance Greene, Agent Pendergast's niece. Is that what he'd said she was? At the time,

Perelman had still been too preoccupied with all the feet littering his beach to pay sufficient attention. But he certainly recalled her violet eyes and lithe silhouette, and her remarkable resemblance to Olive Thomas.

"Ms. Greene," he said, closing the hatch and rubbing the grease from his hands with a rag.

The young woman nodded. "Chief Perelman. How are you?"

"I'm doing battle with a platoon of spark plugs."

"And how fares the combat?"

"The spark plugs are winning. But even defeat would be a relief at this point."

She gave him a faint smile. There was a brief silence.

"Would you like to come aboard?" he asked.

"Please."

She took the proffered hand, and Perelman helped her over the gunwale and into the boat's small cockpit: back of the cabin, there were just the two seats and a padded couch behind. She thanked him, setting her handbag aside and smoothing her stylish dress as she sat down.

Perelman began to wad up the oily rag, reconsidered, and instead folded it neatly and placed it atop the engine cowling. There was something about this young woman that put him on his best behavior, and he understood himself well enough to know what it was. About a decade ago, just before he'd left the Jupiter PD for this promotion, he'd dated a high-fashion model. The two of them had had about as much in common as King Kong and Fay Wray, but in their brief time together she had educated him about some things. Among those that had nothing to do with the bedroom, she'd taught him the difference between real taste and mere gaucherie. She devoured magazines like *Grazia* and *L'Officiel*, and Perelman had followed in her path, smitten by her beauty and picking up a great deal of esoteric information. Florida was thick with both the real rich and the wannabe; being able to tell the difference was most useful in his line of work. In the case of Constance Greene, for example, he recognized her handbag was an extremely rare black-and-orange Hermès. He couldn't recall its name, but he remembered the long list of impossible tasks his ex-girlfriend had stated she'd do in order to get one. Then there was Constance's wristwatch: he recognized it as a vintage Patek Philippe Nautilus, Reference 5711, white gold with an opaline dial. Subtle, understated . . . save that, for those in the know, there was a ten-year waiting list to acquire one. He did not recognize her dress or shoes. But it was the way Constance wore these items with a casual grace, a lack of self-consciousness, that Perelman found so interesting—and unusual.

"How can I help you?" he asked.

Constance nodded again, as if appreciating his directness. "The place we're staying in—the Mortlach House."

"I heard about that. I was glad to hear the demolition had been postponed."

"As a tenant, I've taken an interest in the house's history."

"How so?" Perelman said cautiously.

"I'm curious about the murder. There's quite a lot of it that seems puzzling. I was hoping you'd assist me."

"Assist you with what?"

"Understanding what happened. Surely you participated in the investigation?"

Perelman frowned and looked away. When he did not respond, she continued.

"The body was never found, apparently, but a determination of wrongful death was made based on the sheer quantity of blood at the scene, which amounted to virtually all that would be found in a large human male. And the signs of a terrific struggle of the occupant against an intruder wielding an ax." She reached into her bag, produced a thin sheaf of glossy photographs, and handed them to Perelman.

He flipped through them quickly, surprised and annoyed to see they were official police photographs, complete with annotations. Just looking at them brought back a flood of unpleasant memories. *Where the hell did she get these?* he asked himself—but then, just as quickly, he realized the answer.

"I'd think these pictures would answer any question you might have about the murder. I'm not sure what I can add. As you know, it was never solved."

His tone had been curter than intended, and a silence fell over the boat, broken only by the cry of seagulls.

"This is an unusual boat," Constance said, changing the subject. "Does it go fast?"

Despite himself, Perelman smiled. "It's a cigarette boat. And yes, it goes very fast."

"Cigarette?"

"They were originally used during Prohibition by rumrunners trying to avoid the Coast Guard. At some point they acquired the name because they were long with a narrow beam, like a cigarette, to go as fast as possible."

"What is their purpose now, with the repeal of Prohibition?"

"Point-to-point powerboat racing is very popular today. The go-fast design proved ideal." He made a vague sweeping gesture with the back of one hand. "I bought this thirty-two-foot frame a couple of years after becoming chief. It's a relic, built in the late sixties, but it had new crate inboards that caught my attention."

"Crate inboards?"

"Engines, already fitted out with manifolds, heads, other car parts."

"Car parts? You mean this boat is powered by automobile engines?"

"Sure. They're often salvaged from car wrecks and repurposed for boats." He patted the rear hatch. "This baby has twin Corvette 454s, old big-block Chevys tweaked for additional horsepower."

"I would think boats and cars incompatible."

"The conversion isn't difficult. It's actually easier to drive them in a boat than on four wheels. No gears." He laughed. "Just turn the key, push the throttle forward, and hang on, you know."

"Actually, I don't know, but thank you for a fascinating explanation."

"You've never driven a boat?"

"I've never driven any sort of motorized vehicle."

"I—" Perelman stopped himself. This was a surprise. But it also helped highlight the fact that the interest she was showing was mere courtesy.

"Of course," he went on, changing tacks, "this particular boat spends far more time tied up at a slip than it does out in the gulf. Took me two years to finish repainting it, and I still haven't thought of a name." He turned to Constance. "Any suggestions?"

" 'Up the River'?"

He laughed. "Look, I'm sorry if I seemed a little touchy back there about the homicide. It's a sore point. When I first got here, the murder was only two months old. I was on fire to prove myself and took up the investigation with a vengeance. But we never got anywhere."

"Why?"

"Well, the killer must have entered and exited the house, but we could find no evidence of ingress or egress, no evidence of a boat landing or car arriving and leaving, no witnesses who saw anyone coming and going, not a clue as to who it might have been."

"And no body?"

"We figure he tossed it in the ocean nearby, since it would have been hard to transport it off the island without being seen, but nothing ever washed up. It was plain as day it was a homicide. Not just the amount of blood belonging to the victim, but chop marks in the wood with scalp and hair embedded, the blood spatter analysis, the cast-off spatter from a handheld weapon—not to mention the volume of blood at the scene. The blood type was the owner's, of course."

"How much blood?"

"About five liters. That's pretty much all the blood in a human body. Even losing half that amount would have put the victim into class IV hemorrhagic shock—inevitably fatal."

"Tell me about the victim."

"His name was Wilkinson. Randall Wilkinson. Late fifties, unmarried. Worked as a chemical engineer, an expert on lubricants and solvents at an automotive subcontracting company in Fort Myers. Sounds about as interesting as watching paint dry."

"Literally," Constance said faintly.

"Yeah. Anyway, he helped invent some new process. On the strength of that, he moved to Captiva and bought the Mortlach House. Then a couple of years later he was involved in some kind of chemical accident. Damaged his lungs, I think. After that, he only worked part-time. This was, oh, maybe 2004, 2005. The man always lived quietly. Polite, reclusive. Walked the beach every evening at sunset, rainy or clear. And then, one July night in 2009..." Perelman spread his hands.

"Unmarried, you said."

"That's right."

"Do you know if he had an insurance policy on his life?"

"He had a term policy, yes. Quite sizable, but nothing totally outrageous. His sister was the beneficiary. Naturally the insurance company balked but paid up in the end."

"Does she live nearby?"

"No. Massachusetts, I think." He looked at her. "You don't think she killed her own brother, do you? Not even the insurance company suspected that—

and they suspect everything. Anyway, as best I can re-member, she lived a quiet life. Never moved into the house. Died not all that long after inheriting it."

Constance smoothed her dress again. "Did he have any enemies?"

"None that we know of. Everybody imaginable was interviewed: the chemists he worked with, relatives, his roommate at UF's grad school, elementary school friends. He led a very dull, law-abiding, quiet life."

Constance nodded. "It would appear, from the photographs, that the killer dragged the body to the door."

"Right. That was really confounding. The blood smear led straight to the door and over the threshold, where it abruptly ended. We hypothesized the killer loaded the body directly into a vehicle on that spot. But damned if we could find any good tracks or witnesses who saw a car."

"I see."

Constance gazed at him with a strangely pene-trating look. For a moment, Perelman felt a totally unreasonable wish that, in some capacity or other, Constance were a member of his team.

"I know, Chief Perelman, that unsolved murder cases are never closed—they just go cold. In your time here, you must have heard innumerable specu-lations about this one. Have you, personally, found any theory to be more persuasive than the others?"

He hesitated. "The more you think about it, the less sense it makes. I've seen my share of unsolved homicides. You do everything you can and then you simply have to lay it aside. Not very satisfying, I'm afraid, but that's it." He rose from the deck cushion. "I'm going to get a beer. Can I get you something? If not beer, I've got a bottle of Beaujolais nouveau chilling in the cabin."

"Thank you, no," Constance said, rising as well. "You've been very patient. I appreciate your candor."

"If you solve the murder," he said with a wry smile, "let me know." Belatedly, he realized she'd interpreted his getting up as a cue that the meeting was over. This was a shame—he'd had enough of the subject matter, but not her company.

"Naturally." Constance placed the crime scene photos in her bag and slipped it over her shoulder. "One final question, if I may?"

"Please."

"I don't want to call your work into question. But are you *sure* it was Wilkinson's blood?"

"It's true that, at the time of the murder, Sanibel and even Fort Myers didn't have the kind of facilities they do today. However, I personally took DNA samples from half a dozen separate pieces of evidence preserved from the crime scene, including hair and blood, and carried them to the Miami PD forensics lab, which at the time had state-of-the-art

equipment, together with several known DNA samples from Randall Wilkinson collected in the house.
Everything matched the DNA of Randall Wilkinson.
That was his blood, without a doubt. And then..."
He hesitated. "Last year, I had another lab rerun
those samples, just in case the technology in 2009
wasn't up to snuff. Same results."

A mischievous smile played over the young
woman's lips. "And here I thought you'd put the
case aside."

"Touché."

"Thank you again." Then, before he could assist her,
Constance put one foot on the gunwale and sprang
lightly onto the pier. And as she turned away from
him, Perelman caught the faintest scent of perfume.
It, too, was exceedingly rare—his ex-girlfriend had
given him a lecture about it once, at an invitation-
only *parfumerie* in Palm Beach. He'd never forget the
scent, but he couldn't recall its name. It was, he
feared, a riddle that would keep him awake in his
bed far into the night.

26

PETER QUARLES OPENED the glass door leading onto the roof deck on the fourteenth floor of the Sofitel Foshan. It was a pleasant enough spot, consciously minimalistic, the flooring and furniture done in a blond wood like a Scandinavian lodge. Quarles stuck his head out and looked around. The deck was deserted—as he'd hoped, considering it was well after ten in the evening.

He stepped out, sliding the door closed behind him. He strolled past the tables and gurgling fountains toward the building's edge, where a row of wooden benches had been set into the decorative guardrail. A stiff breeze had blown the smog and soot temporarily out to sea, and below him, Quarles could see the megacity of the Pearl River Delta stretching on forever. Central highways, ribbons of red and white light, threaded their way past neighborhoods whose indifferent architecture, shot through with gloomy alleyways, formed at this height an intricate labyrinth. Here and there across the urban landscape, small clusters of tall buildings rose, as if huddled together for protection, their neon banners and illuminated signage blinking and scrolling frantically against the darkness. In other, more industrial zones, equally tall spires, grim and utilitarian by contrast, were lit only by blinking red warning lights, and by the numerous plumes of steam and smoke, along with the occasional belching gout of flame that issued from chimneys set among them.

Turning his back to the view, Quarles took a seat on one of the wooden benches, plucked from his jacket pocket a sealed burner phone, and tore off its wrapper. He reached into a different pocket, removed a SIM card, and inserted it into the phone. He plugged a portable battery into its charging port and turned the device on. Once the activation process was complete, he looked around again, dialed a long series of numbers, and put the phone to his ear.

Ten seconds of silence. And then, despite the great distance, an unmistakable voice: "Yes?"

"Agent Pendergast?"

"Ah, Mr. Quarles. What news?"

Quarles licked his lips. "I've found it."

"Are you sure?"

"Yes. It's the only one that meets all our criteria. A source, and my own observation, confirm this."

"Excellent. This is in the same location you were, ah, perambulating yesterday?"

Perambulating. They had agreed to use language that was as innocuous as possible. Quarles wasn't sure that included five-syllable words. "Yes."

"Any specifics you can share?"

Quarles thought a moment. "It's an unusual situation. The business was once much larger, but a series of unfortunate events have diminished it." In China, any number of political faux pas could easily result in "unfortunate events." "However, they retain a few of their original clients." He hoped the subtle emphasis he gave the penultimate word would be picked up on the other phone, seven thousand miles away.

"I see. Have you made direct contact?"

"Indirect."

Pendergast did not reply, and Quarles took this as a cue to provide additional information. "The subject once furnished such items to several clients in the past. Not anymore, however. This was a single order, to a single client, through a jobber."

Now Quarles fell silent, indicating he had something he wanted Pendergast to take particular note of.

"Proceed."

"Because the contact was indirect, I can confirm nothing yet. But it seems there was more than one . . . unusual request involved."

"But you don't yet know what those consist of."

"No."

"Have you a count?"

"Trio." Code for three hundred pairs of disposable shoes having been ordered. This nugget of information had cost Quarles the last of his red envelopes.

"This is exemplary work. We now need just establish the narrow end of the chopstick."

Quarles knew this was coming. He had to identify the end buyer—without raising suspicion. For some unknown reason, the tiny three-man shoemaking factory had been remarkably secretive. Already the interest he'd shown had drawn a response that was close to hostility. All this spycraft—using burner phones, speaking in code—had originally been set up as a mere contingency, standard procedure in a case like this. But it became a contingency no longer when Quarles sensed he was being followed. He had a fine-tuned radar, and the paranoia he felt now was more than just imagination.

"Finding the thin end might not be possible," he said.

Pendergast clearly picked up on Quarles's unease, because he replied: "If that's your impression, then drop the chopstick and resume your other duties. Speaking of which, have you prepared for the upcoming meeting with the tussah moth specialist?"

Quarles exhaled in relief. "Yes." Pendergast had

just cleared him to leave China at the first sign of actual danger, no matter how small.

"Good. Recall that our contacts here are interested only in wild silk. Not the usual mulberry."

The conversation continued in this innocuous and misleading vein for another thirty seconds before they said goodbye. Looking around one more time, Quarles plucked the SIM card from the phone, placed it in an ashtray, and melted it with a match, then flicked the blob over the edge of the railing. He stood up and made a single circuit of the deck, breathing the way he'd been conditioned, letting his heart rate and respiration return to normal. Heading toward the glass door leading back into the hotel, he took the burner phone in both hands, snapped it in two, and threw the sections into different trash cans. He opened the door, then glanced over his shoulder. The earlier breezes had now fallen away: already, the stench of refineries and dye factories, the greasy soot from the tanneries to the west, were once again filling the air.

He slipped inside, letting the door close behind him. It was going to be a dirty night.

27

COLDMOON GOT BEHIND the wheel of the Range Rover, with Pendergast sitting coolly in the passenger seat. He was again wearing that white linen suit with the Panama hat, an outfit no FBI agent in the entire history of the United States of America had ever put on before.

They made their way through the Blind Pass Bridge checkpoint and to the mainland, retracing the route Coldmoon had taken the day before. Fifteen minutes later, Coldmoon turned into the parking lot of the Fort Myers Police Department. The lot was packed with task force vehicles.

"Tell me more about this Commander Baugh," said Coldmoon. Pendergast had brought him up to speed on the task force the previous evening, but he'd been careful to refrain from opining or editorializing.

"You will meet him in a moment and can judge for yourself."

Coldmoon caught a note of disdain in his voice. "He's an asshole, then?"

"Such a disagreeable expression," said Pendergast. "I should think that you, with your wide-ranging intellect, might find another word."

"How about suckwad? Dripdick? Shitbag?"

"You're a veritable cornucopia of colorful expressions."

"That's just English. You should hear my Lakota."

"Perhaps another time. Have you ever considered pursuing such a rare talent on the doctoral level?"

They entered the building into a wash of air conditioning and soon found themselves at the closed door of the commander's office. Pendergast rapped.

The door was opened by a lackey in full dress uniform. "Please come in."

He stepped aside to reveal the commander, sitting behind a large desk, also in dress uniform, looking crisp and fit, with a face of granite. "Oh, Pendergast, it's you. So good of you to make an appearance."

"My partner, Special Agent Armstrong Coldmoon," said Pendergast.

Coldmoon stepped forward but the commander didn't rise to shake his hand. Instead, he said, "Partner? Glad you finally brought in help."

Coldmoon immediately felt the hairs on the back of his neck prickling. He glanced at Pendergast and was surprised to see the mild expression on his face.

"And this," said Baugh, "is my chief of staff, Lieutenant Darby."

He was a chinless wonder, thin, nervous, and slope-shouldered, with a prominent Adam's apple that bobbed as he nodded a greeting.

With this, Baugh indicated for them to sit. Darby took a seat to one side of the commander's desk. He removed a steno notebook and, pen in hand, prepared to take notes.

"I expected a report from you already. Two of the six ships in question are currently in territorial waters, right here in the gulf, and I would advise you to get warrants and swoop down on them before they sail back out."

"The warrants have been pulled," said Pendergast, "and Agent Coldmoon and I will be executing them shortly."

"Good. Now, there's another issue I want to talk to you about. What's this I hear about you hiring some oceanographer without my knowledge?"

At this, Pendergast went very still. "Where did you hear this?" he asked.

"Never mind where I heard it. Is it true?"

"Commander Baugh, are you aware of the concept of compartmentalization?"

"For Christ's sake, this isn't some CIA operation! I'm in charge of this task force. I can't have the FBI going rogue on me here."

Pendergast's silvery eyes remained for a long time on the commander. "If you're displeased with the idea of my withholding information, you'll have to take that up with Assistant Director in Charge Pickett."

"Are you telling me to my face you're withholding information? This is unacceptable. I *order* you to share your work with the task force."

Coldmoon felt his own anger, which had been growing, finally overflow. He half rose. "You don't get to *order* the FBI to do a damn thing!"

He felt Pendergast's hand on his forearm. "Agent Coldmoon?" he said placidly.

Coldmoon sat down, fuming.

"Thank you for controlling your partner," said the commander, giving Coldmoon a nasty stare.

This was messed up. Coldmoon wasn't going to tolerate one more disrespectful comment from this jumped-up jackass in uniform. He was about to say more when he caught Pendergast's warning glance.

"Commander Baugh," Pendergast said, "I will gladly share my conclusions with you *when* we have drawn them. For the time being, I will continue working in confidence."

"I promise you, Pendergast, this lack of cooperation will have consequences."

Pendergast rose, his voice still mild. "Thank you, Commander. Now, as you just pointed out, we have warrants to serve—and so we'll take our leave."

As they departed the air-conditioned haven into the sweltering parking lot, Coldmoon turned to Pendergast and exploded in anger. "That bastard! Where does he get off talking to us that way! And you *let* him!"

"Agent Coldmoon, there's a word to describe our response, and that word is *strategic*. It isn't *strategic* at the present time for us to do battle with the commander. Recall that you're still new to this task force—and its shortcomings."

Coldmoon felt some of his anger at the commander shifting over toward Pendergast and his lack of fight. "You can't let him talk to us like that. We're *FBI*, for Chrissakes."

"His day of reckoning will come. But first, it's crucial we get the drift results from Dr. Gladstone—and we must do all we can to keep her name out of the investigation. I can't imagine how Baugh learned of her involvement."

"Why? Is she in any kind of danger?"

"We are all in danger."

"What from?"

"I don't know—and *that's* what makes it so very dangerous."

28

SMITHBACK SAT IN the driver's seat of his Subaru, parked beneath a broken streetlight, half a block from the LeeTran bus stop. There was nobody on the street, and the kiosk was empty.

He glanced at his watch: quarter past ten. Christ, the guy was fifteen minutes late already. But it was the only lead he had, and he would sit here half the night if he had to. Faint sounds came to his ears: an argument in Spanish; boat traffic on the river; and a car horn braying "La cucaracha," Doppler-shifting as it passed by.

He wondered, for the thousandth time, who it was that had called him. It was a gruff voice with a Spanish accent. Smithback had lived in south Florida long enough to know there were dozens of variations on a Spanish accent, but he'd never learned to tell them apart. The voice had said to meet at this bus stop at ten in the evening—in a southwestern neighborhood of Fort Myers not far from where he'd had the unpleasant encounter with the guys in the street. He wouldn't say anything beyond that, except to tell Smithback he had information.

Information. That could mean anything. Smithback's beat was Miami; his byline wouldn't be known around here. And the call had come over his cell phone, which almost certainly meant it was from one of the cards he'd given out. But he hadn't passed out more than a dozen; most people he'd encountered in the barrio had simply refused to take them.

Just then, he saw movement on the next block. Instinctively, he crouched in his seat, watching. The shadowy figure crossed the street, coming closer, and quite abruptly Smithback recognized him. It was that old landscaper, the one he'd seen mowing the lawn who had spoken no English. What the hell was going on? Was it coincidence?

As he watched, the lean man kept coming, walking intently, looking straight ahead, until he reached the kiosk. Then he stopped, glanced around once, and took a seat: arms folded, body rigid.

Rising from behind the steering wheel, Smithback regarded him carefully. Everything about the man's body language told the reporter this wasn't a person waiting for a bus. The old man, like just about everyone else he'd encountered in that neighborhood, had been unwilling to talk, at least in public. And he knew the reason: fear. In recent years, waves of gangs had swept over these streets like plagues, hollowing them out and transforming the neighborhood into a nightmarish shadow of what it had once been, with the drug dealing, shootings, abandoned buildings, and graffiti-covered walls.

The gardener unfolded his arms long enough to take a puff on his cheroot, and as he did so, Smithback saw his fingers tremble. He was afraid, all right. It was clear the man was taking a big chance to talk to him, and Smithback wasn't going to expose him to further danger by delaying. He took another look around to make sure the street was still deserted, then started his engine and drove the half block, pulling up in front of the bus stop.

The man glanced up and their eyes met. For a moment, they just looked at each other. Then the man nodded faintly, dropped his cheroot on the pavement, rose, and got into Smithback's car, crouching down much as the reporter had done minutes earlier. He did not offer either a greeting or a name. Immediately, Smithback pulled away from the curb and they drove into the night.

"¿*Adónde?*" Smithback asked.

The man waved a hand. "Drive. *Circula.* Around."

So he did speak English—after a fashion, anyway. And Smithback recognized it as the voice he'd heard over the phone.

He'd conducted enough interviews like this to know brevity was important. "Why are you helping me?" he asked.

"*¿Eres tonto?* You crazy? You are the one looking for help. You are the one asking questions everywhere, asking for trouble for people—you *and* us. If they knew I was talking to you...*ya valió madre.*" The man shook his head.

"You say I'm making trouble for myself. Why?"

"Because you are like *pollo* scratching for corn in front of the fox's den. What are you doing, all by yourself? You are reporter, *sí*? So I tell you story. Not all, but enough. Then you go—go write your story. Maybe it help, maybe not. But you don't come back. *Gira aquí.* Turn here."

Smithback turned onto a narrow street, crowded on both sides with beat-up trailers and cars in various stages of decrepitude. They passed by small, dimly lit houses. Every now and then Smithback saw the flag of some Central American country hanging from a window.

"When I move here, there were already gangs," the man said. "Just like in El Salvador. They sell the *drogas*, handle the *juegos de dinero*—numbers, you know?—but they watch the barrio, too. Then the police, they come in, break up gangs, put the leaders in jail. Years pass. Then new gangs, they come in. But these *pandillas* much worse. Before, the gangs, they lie low, keep to themselves unless messed with. But now, these gangs like wasps, everywhere, sting everyone." He interlaced his fingers for emphasis. "Organized, *muy malas, muy sanguinarias*. They care nothing for their own people, nothing for life. To join, you kill. Anybody." He nodded out the window. "Before, people would sit out at night. There would be music, singing. Now we might as well be among the dead."

Smithback had heard similar stories about Miami gangs. "And that tattoo? The one with the *P* and the *N*?"

Quickly, the man crossed himself, muttered something under his breath.

"Is that the gang you're referring to? The gang that's so influential? So bloodthirsty?"

The man nodded once, said something else under his breath.

"Excuse me?"

"*Panteras de la noche*," the man said.

Panteras de la noche. Night panthers. This was it: the missing link, the answer to the riddle of the tattoo. Smithback tried to contain his excitement. "So: *muy mala*. But they still deal mostly in drugs, right?"

"*Sí, sí.* But before, they were—how you say it?—little fish. Now, one connected family, like I tell you. Big drugs now. The coca leaves, they grow in Colombia, Peru maybe. But the *panteras* are Guatemalan. They make everything...everything smooth."

"Smooth?"

"*Sí*, smooth."

Smithback thought a moment. "You mean, like middlemen?"

"*¡Sí, intermediarios!*" The man gestured in frustration: one cupped hand arcing over the other. "Guatemala best for shipping. Drugs come by airplane, go by boat, *caravana*, whatever. Guatemala very poor. The *panteras*, they know the *oficiales*, the *funcionarios*. *Reclutamiento* very easy. Often they are *familia*." He gave a harsh laugh.

The road ended in a T, and at a signal from his passenger Smithback turned right. This street was busier, a boulevard of sorts, with bodegas and small restaurants. For the first time in a while, Smithback saw something resembling a crowd.

This was gold. This was better than gold. Totally by accident, he'd stumbled upon a resident who was fed up with what had happened to his community—and had the stones to do something about it...even if that something was just talking to a reporter.

"This gang," he said. "These *panteras de la noche*. Where can I find them?"

The man's eyes went wide. "*¡Pinche estúpido!* Have you not heard what I have told you? You can do

nothing yourself. You write—write in your newspaper. Write about how the *policía* do nothing. But
first, go home."

"I need something more. A name, a place—
something. Otherwise, it's hearsay."

The man would not calm down. "I tell you, no!
No names!"

"Look, you need to understand. You've been talking
to me off the record. We won't print your name, even
if I knew it. But we also can't print speculation or
rumor. I have to have something hard to go on."

Despite his anxiety, the man barked a laugh.
"Something hard? No names, but..." He thought
a moment. "I will show you something. A place
where they meet. I show you, then you go. You *go.*
¿Entiende?"

"*Sí.*"

The man sighed. "Keep going. It is not far."

They drove along the boulevard, passing more
restaurants and knots of strolling people. The lights
were brighter here, the atmosphere noticeably more
relaxed. After about three blocks, Smithback felt the
man grasp his forearm. "There, on the right. Past
Pollo Fresco. You see?"

Smithback looked ahead. There, beyond a family
market and a restaurant with a garish red-and-yellow
sign, was a narrow street, a service road for the
nearby businesses.

"Turn in there. Don't stop. When we pass the entrance, I will tell you. But don't stop. Drive slowly until we get to the next road, then *vamos*."

Smithback turned in at the indicated spot. It was narrower than he expected, more an alley than a street, and darker. Ahead, he could see dented trash cans and, overhead, laundry drying on clotheslines that stretched from façade to façade. They passed one door, then another, dim gray outlines with no identifying names or numbers.

"Hey," he said, "how are you going to be able—"

Suddenly, a pair of bright headlights swung into the alley ahead of him. Smithback squinted and looked away, blinded. As he did so, he saw another pair of headlights appear in his rearview mirror. A roar of powerful engines, and the twin sets of lights came closer until his Subaru was pinned. He looked over at the landscaper in mute appeal, uncertain what to do, but to his vast surprise the man had already stepped out of the passenger seat. He was standing and talking to a large, tattooed figure . . . probably the largest and most heavily muscled man Smithback had seen in his life. He watched in a confused daze. It seemed the big man was giving a roll of money to Smithback's confidential source. The two shook hands or, more precisely, fingers. With a lurching feeling, Smithback realized he'd been set up. Then the landscaper was gone, walking off down the alley, and the huge man came strolling over and leaned in the passenger window, staring at Smithback. The reporter had just enough time to see one ham-sized hand ball into a fist before an impact like a steam piston knocked him back and into a place of unrelieved blackness.

29

COLDMOON COULD SEE the cargo ship about a mile off, an ugly, rust-streaked vessel stacked with containers of different colors, looking like a bunch of Legos. He couldn't believe a ship so overloaded wouldn't just tip over. As the chopper approached, he spied the name stenciled on the side, barely legible through peeling paint. The ship was at anchor; they had received word it was having engine trouble. No wonder, a shitcan like that.

"There it is, Agent Coldmoon," said Pendergast. "The good ship *Empire Carrier*, Liberian flagged, Ukrainian owned, crew of eighteen."

"Eighteen? A big ship like that?"

"These days, apparently, that's all that's required."

Coldmoon found his annoyance increasing as the ship loomed below. What a fool's errand this was. "If you don't mind me asking," he said, "how the hell are the two of us supposed to search that ship? It must be seven, eight hundred feet long, and most of those containers are inaccessible."

"Ah, but you see, we don't have to search it. Direct your attention to the cleared space at the bow. Do you see that lone container, sitting next to the crane? That's our target."

"Thanks for briefing me," Coldmoon said sarcastically.

"Why, Agent Coldmoon, I *am* briefing you. That container is known in the lingo of the shipping business as a 'reefer.' A reefer, contrary to the usage I am sure you're accustomed to, is a refrigerated container carrying either frozen or chilled cargo. But as you can see, it no longer appears to be connected to power, so whatever is or was in it has spoiled—or disappeared."

"Like a bunch of frozen feet?"

"Possibly." Pendergast pulled a sheaf of papers from his briefcase and handed them to Coldmoon. "Here are a series of satellite pictures of this same ship, taken five weeks ago, at the approximate time and location the commander's team thinks the feet were dumped. And as you can see, the ship did indeed dump something—from that very container. You notice, in that first photo, a vessel approaching from the north? It's a Coast Guard cutter. It appears the *Empire Carrier*'s crew thought they were about to be boarded and in a panic disposed of the cargo in this particular container. But it was a coincidental meeting. The cutter went on past and it seems they dumped the contents of the container for nothing."

Coldmoon began flipping through the pictures with growing amazement. They showed the container being lifted by crane, swung out over the stern, tipped, and a loose blurry load splashing into the ocean. "Holy shit, this is a smoking gun!"

"Not quite. There are two problems. The first is that whatever was dumped overboard sank immediately. The feet would have floated, encased as they were in buoyant shoes."

"Hmmm."

"The second issue is that while our oceanographer, Dr. Gladstone, hasn't been able to pinpoint the place where the feet were dumped, she did analyze the commander's own estimate of the location and found it has a very low probability of being accurate, at least according to her algorithms." He put away the pictures. "And now, are you ready for a surprise boarding?"

Coldmoon removed his Browning Hi-Power, checked the chamber. "Good to go."

The FBI chopper passed over the ship, and the pilot

spoke through the headphones. "There's a helipad on the stern where I can land."

"Excellent. Radio the ship and say we're coming in with a warrant and expect the captain to be ready to receive us. Then land immediately, giving them no time to react."

The chopper pilot called the ship's bridge, causing a storm of protests and threats.

"Land," said Pendergast.

The pilot swooped around and came in for a landing, just as some crew members came rushing out, waving their arms and blocking the helipad.

"Tell them to clear the pad or we'll send the Coast Guard in and arrest the captain for obstructing law enforcement."

That worked and the men backed off. The chopper came down for a landing. Pendergast hopped out with Coldmoon following, keeping low as the rotors whipped the air above them. At the edge of the helipad, several sullen sailors in greasy overalls waited with a deck officer. The officer was small and plump, with long greasy hair combed back, and he was smoking.

Pendergast presented the warrant with a flourish. "Take us to the captain."

The deck officer took the warrant and peered at it, turning it this way and that. He raised his head. "No English."

Pendergast scrutinized him. "*Italiano? Français? Hóng bāo?*"

The man shook his head again.

"Captain." Pendergast pointed to the bridge. He made a series of gestures that were unmistakable in meaning.

The man turned and in a shambling walk led them through a forest of stacked containers to the companionway up to the bridge. It was a hot climb. When they arrived at the long bridge, it was almost deserted. There was no A/C and it was sweltering. A man who was apparently the captain stood next to a person who seemed to be the helmsman, even if there wasn't anything that looked to Coldmoon like a wheel—just some levers and joysticks, along with a row of flat-panel screens displaying charts and radar. The bridge was old and shabby, the Plexiglas windows streaked and faded. It smelled of diesel fuel and vomit.

The entire bridge crew—maybe five—had ceased work and were staring with naked hostility on their faces. Coldmoon wondered how the hell this was going to turn out. Most of these people looked like criminals or thugs.

"Captain Yaroslav Oliynyk?" Pendergast said, removing his shield, Coldmoon following his lead. "Special Agent Pendergast, Federal Bureau of Investigation, United States of America. And Special Agent Coldmoon."

The deck officer handed the captain the warrant. He was a tall, lugubrious man, unshaven, with hollow cheeks and watery eyes. He took it and stared, flipping through the pages. Coldmoon got a whiff of alcohol breath. He also noted a sidearm in a holster at the captain's waist.

"Do you speak English?" Pendergast asked.

The man hesitated and Coldmoon had the distinct impression he was thinking about lying. "Yes."

"This is a judicial warrant authorizing us to search the entire ship," Pendergast said, "and requiring the assistance of such crew and officers necessary to facilitate that process, upon pain of arrest. I will remind you that the ship is in United States territorial waters and subject to our laws and regulations."

The captain took the warrant between his fingers, held it up with both hands as if to examine it more carefully, then slowly tore it in half, carefully layered the torn pieces together, tore those in half, did so a third time—and then let the pieces flutter to the ground. He looked back up at Pendergast with rheumy eyes and said: "Fuck you."

As if not having heard, Pendergast reached into his jacket and removed a small piece of paper on which a number was written. "We wish to examine this particular container. It is located at the bow of the ship."

Captain Oliynyk seemed not to have heard and did not glance at the paper. He turned to the crew members standing by and spoke sharply in a language Coldmoon couldn't identify. They suddenly surged forward as the captain stepped back and yanked out his sidearm. But before it could clear the holster, Pendergast flashed out as fast as a striking viper, jabbing the man in the face with his fist, and the captain's head snapped back, the gun going off harmlessly. Simultaneously, two crewmembers rushed Coldmoon; he kicked one in the balls as he pulled his Browning, dodged an inept punch from the second, and slashed him across the face with the barrel of his gun. Both men went down and a sudden silence fell as the rest froze. Pendergast had the captain in a hammerlock, his Les Baer 1911 pressed into his ear.

Coldmoon stepped over and picked up the captain's firearm, which had been lying on the deck—a crappy old German Luger—and covered the stunned crew with both weapons. Nobody besides the captain seemed to be armed.

"On the floor," Coldmoon said. "All of you: facedown, arms extended."

They stood stupefied, doing nothing.

Pendergast twisted the barrel of the gun in the captain's ear. "Tell them."

The captain said something and they quickly complied. *Now what?* Coldmoon wondered. *Call in backup?* They were still outnumbered and God knew how many armed men there might be elsewhere on the ship.

Pendergast spoke to the captain in a mild voice. "Are you ready to take us to that container now?"

The captain nodded.

"Good. Tell your crew to stay put. *All* of them. Anyone seen moving anywhere, at any time, will be considered a lethal threat and will therefore be shot. Make the announcement."

He released the man. The captain pulled down a mike from the console and made the announcement— at least, Coldmoon hoped it was the correct announcement.

"And now, Captain Oliynyk, lead the way. Slow and easy. Agent Coldmoon, keep an eye out for snipers."

The captain shuffled through the door of the bridge and headed down the companionway, Pendergast and Coldmoon following. They came out on deck and the captain led them toward the bow of the ship, along the outside rail next to stacks of containers. At the bow, there was a large cleared area with some cranes. The bright blue container sat there, all by itself.

Pendergast inspected the welded steel lockbox at the container's door. "Open it, Captain, if you please."

"It is empty. Nothing in there."

"Open it."

"I don't have key. I must call for key."

"Then call for the key. Make sure only one deckhand brings it, and that he comes unarmed—otherwise an unfortunate event might take place."

"Yeah," added Coldmoon. "Like you getting shot." He gestured with both the Browning and the Luger, wanting to make sure the captain understood.

The captain removed a portable walkie-talkie and spoke into it. They waited. After five minutes a man arrived and handed the captain a key. He unlocked the padlock and pulled open the door of the reefer.

"See?" the captain said. "Nothing."

The container was indeed empty. A terrible stench of rotten fish wafted out.

Pendergast sniffed a few times, an expression of disgust on his face. He turned to the captain. "You go in first, Captain, and stand in the back. We will follow."

The captain stepped inside and moved to the rear. Pendergast and Coldmoon trailed behind, the latter gagging at the nasty, stifling atmosphere. The container was filthy, splattered with sticky brown stuff on the walls and floor. God, did it stink. Coldmoon, who wasn't fond of fish to begin with, felt he was going to puke.

Pendergast slipped a small penlight from his pocket and shone it around, then bent down and examined the foul matter. He removed a small evidence collection kit, along with some minuscule test tubes with stopper-swabs. He swabbed here and there, took some samples, and sealed them up.

"Let us go outside, Agent Coldmoon," said Pendergast, sniffing again, his brow furrowed in displeasure. "You stay in the rear, Captain, until we're out, and then you may emerge."

They exited, the captain following, sweat pouring down his face. Coldmoon gulped the sultry air, feeling his nausea recede.

Pendergast was examining one of the test tubes. Suddenly, he turned to the captain with a pained expression on his face. "Captain, how *could* you? What a tragedy!"

The captain stared at Pendergast, uncomprehending.

"How many pounds were in here? Five hundred? A thousand? Good heavens! To think, to just *think*, of the waste!"

Pendergast swung toward Coldmoon, face stricken, dropping the evidence collection kit in his agitation. "Agent Coldmoon, what we had here were not human feet. Rather, this was the transportation of cargo in direct violation of U.S. sanctions."

"What cargo?"

"If I'm not mistaken, this container was filled with tins of the finest Iranian imperial gold caviar, dumped into the sea in a moment of panic. My God, I could *weep*!"

30

GLADSTONE HAD BEEN surprised when Agent Pendergast dropped by the lab unannounced, with an official partner no less. At least this new guy looked like an FBI agent. Pendergast had introduced them with the sort of formality reserved for a duke and duchess, and now they had all crowded into her cramped lab, watching while Lam ran the latest simulation. They had already racked up close to nine grand in computing time on the Q machine, but Pendergast hadn't batted an eye when he heard the figure.

When the simulation was finished, Gladstone explained its failure. "The only conclusion we can draw is that there's a gap in our data."

"What sort of gap?" Pendergast asked.

"I wish I knew. We're missing an input. To figure out what it is, I'd like to do what we call a 'rubber ducky' test in the area where we have the thinnest data sets."

"Which is?"

"The northern part of the Florida Gulf Coast. We drop about twenty-five floating buoys, each fitted with a small GPS transmitter and battery, in calculated locations, and then track them. I think with that data we could plug the gap."

"Very good." Pendergast seemed unfazed, but Agent Coldmoon was giving her the hairy eyeball.

"Rubber ducky?" he asked, his voice laden with skepticism.

Lam burst into a cackle of laughter, abruptly silenced by a glare from Gladstone.

"It's just our term for floating sensor buoys. They're yellow. The cost is a hundred dollars per buoy, plus fuel for the boat. We've already got the buoys—we keep a stock on hand—and I'd like to drop them tomorrow. Wallace has determined the locations necessary to maximize our data collection. Wallace? Please show Agent Pendergast what I'm talking about."

Lam tapped away on a keyboard and a chart of the Gulf Coast popped up. "There are eddies and currents all through here," he said, "especially at the mouths of rivers and inlets. That's where we lack high-resolution data. So we drop them in a line here, another line here, and then here. Here, too. Oh... and *here*." He smiled, immensely pleased with himself. "Five locations, five buoys."

She glanced over at the agent named Coldmoon, who was peering at the dotted lines on the screen. "Any questions?"

Coldmoon shook his head. "I wouldn't even know where to begin."

"I really believe this will fill in the missing pieces," said Gladstone, trying to muster as much confidence as she could. "Anyway," she went on hastily, "we'll be doing the buoy drop tomorrow. No reason to delay."

"I should like to join you," said Pendergast, "if it isn't too much trouble."

This brought Gladstone up short. She didn't like having landlubbers on her boat. They were always underfoot, never knew what to do, and they tended to ask a lot of dumb questions and then puke everywhere. But she could hardly say no. "If you wish. We leave early—like at five AM. It's going to be a long day. And the forecast is for a rough sea."

The briefest of pauses before Pendergast answered. "That will not be a problem."

"Well, okay. But wear foul weather gear. And bring Dramamine."

She heard Pendergast's phone vibrate. He extracted it from his pocket and, excusing himself, stepped outside. She could hear his low voice speaking beyond the door.

"Agent Coldmoon, will you be coming, too?" she asked.

He backed away, a look of horror on his face. "No, thanks. Boats, water, and me, we don't get along. I grew up two thousand miles from the ocean."

She felt relieved. The only thing worse than a guy puking off the starboard rail was another one puking off the port rail.

Pendergast returned to the lab after his call. Coldmoon was surprised at the transformation: his face was full of eagerness. He bowed to the oceanographer, saying he would see her at the dock at five the next morning, and they left.

Pendergast walked swiftly away, Coldmoon struggling to keep up. "The M.E. was able to identify one of the victims," he said, "or at least narrow it down to two people."

"As in, identify by name?"

"Yes. A foot was shown to belong to one of two sisters: either Ramona Osorio Ixquiac, thirty-five years old, or her sister, Martina, thirty-three. Both were born in San Miguel—the same Guatemalan town that toe ring came from."

"How in the world did they identify her?"

"Through a commercial genealogy website. The Ixquiac extended family has several relatives in the U.S. whose DNA is on record at a genetic testing database. Using the same techniques used to identify murderers in cold cases, Crossley was able to match the foot as belonging to one of two sisters. A brilliant piece of work."

"The sisters—where are they now? Did they disappear?"

Pendergast continued through the relentless heat at his breakneck pace. "All we know is they were born in San Miguel—and we have one of their feet. We know nothing in between those two facts. You'll be able to find out a great deal more when you're actually in San Miguel."

"Wait," Coldmoon said, halting. "When *I'm* in San Miguel? What are you talking about?"

"You leave tomorrow morning."

"Hold on here. I came to the Suncoast to work on this case with you. *Not* to go to Guatemala. No way—no way in hell!"

"According to your FBI jacket, you're the ideal choice. You speak Spanish fluently. You've been to Guatemala before, and you've traveled all over Central America. You're Native American."

"Yeah. Lakota, not Mayan! Or do all Indians look alike to you?"

"I must admit, you don't look Mayan."

"No. Or like Pancho Villa." Coldmoon paused. "Wait a minute. This was your plan all along, wasn't it?"

"I assure you, I—"

"Now it makes sense. Sooner or later in this investigation, *somebody* was going to have to go undercover in Central America—and when you realized that, my name just popped into your head. Like magic."

"Agent Coldmoon, you wrong me! The feet we're investigating are here, not in Guatemala. But the DNA evidence, the toe ring, and now the actual name—there are just too many commonalities for us to ignore."

Coldmoon didn't answer.

"I'd take your place if I could. But consider how *I* would stand out. You're the logical one for this minor divagation." He paused, and a faint smile appeared. "Or would you rather come out on the boat with me?"

Coldmoon swallowed. Yesterday's taste of the high seas had been enough—more than enough.

Pendergast uncharacteristically placed a hand on his shoulder and gave it a light squeeze. "Thank you, *partner*. This is much appreciated."

31

COLDMOON STOOD IN the main room of the "servants' quarters" of the Mortlach House—he had to smile again at the term—eyeing the open bag and articles of clothing spread across the bed. God, it seemed like he'd just unpacked—and now he was packing again. Not only that, but he was headed for Guatemala, of all places. He'd been there before. It was a beautiful country with wonderful people, but a hard place, and he wasn't particularly eager to go back, especially undercover, trying to figure out how a woman got from the streets of San Miguel Acatán to the waters off Florida's Gulf Coast—or at least how one of her feet did. There was no telling what kind of *hmunga* was waiting for him down there.

He muttered a curse. And to think he could still be recuperating on Islamorada, drinking Coronas and watching the sun set over the rusting old fishery. But Pendergast had shown up, dangling precisely the kind of juicy case he knew Coldmoon couldn't resist.

He picked up a T-shirt from the bed and threw it into the bag with disgust. In looking back on their conversation, he had the sneaking suspicion that Pendergast had known from the start that he'd insist on being a full partner in the investigation. He'd been manipulated. In retrospect, he should have remembered what his grandfather Joe had once told him: *Keep your mouth shut and let the paleface do all the talking—and then say no.* In this case "paleface" was a description so accurate it could hardly be considered insulting.

Then again, it was a juicy case—certainly the most inexplicable he'd ever handled. And high profile. Bagging this one successfully wouldn't hurt his career...not at all.

He wondered idly where the "paleface" was. It was almost midnight and Pendergast didn't seem to be the type to hang out in a bar or restaurant. Come to think of it, he had no idea where Constance was, either. She hadn't been in the library when he went down to the kitchen at ten o'clock for a root beer, and no light had shown from beneath her door as he was going back up the stairs to the servants' quarters. Maybe they were out together.

Only now did he realize he had, unconsciously but quite deliberately, looked for that light under her door.

Once again, he wondered what this "ward" business was all about. Was there something going on between those two? Coldmoon had seen some odd relationships in his day, but this one really took the cake. He didn't think the two were together in any conventionally romantic sense—although Constance was smoking hot despite her prim clothing. And yet there *was* something electric between them. When Pendergast and Constance interacted, he could almost smell the ozone in the air, like the approach of a thunderstorm.

He had never met anyone like her: so poised, reserved, cynical, erudite, quick-witted—and yet, he sensed, broken at some fundamental level. But, broken or not, she was anything but fragile: he sensed a cold-bloodedness in her, a capacity for violence. She reminded him of a big cat, a panther or tiger, fangs smiling at you while the eyes never left your throat.

For some reason, the memory of his paternal grandmother came back to him. It was a cold winter night on the Pine Ridge Reservation, he was just six or seven, and she was mending a pair of beaded slippers by the stove, her chatter veering into talk of the unseen.

"There are spirits," his grandmother told him. "Like Owl-Maker, who guards the Milky Way. And Keya, the turtle spirit. They are not of this world. But Wachiwi—Dancing Girl—she is mortal, as we are. Yet she is also different. She has lived hundreds of years and is very old and wise. No longer dancing, just watching and seeing." The next fall, Coldmoon saw Wachiwi himself, from a distance. She was walking slowly at dusk through the frozen trees, a blanket wrapped around her corduroy dress. She looked toward him briefly, and even in that short glance he saw the wisdom in her eyes.

Had he seen that same look in the eyes of Constance? *Hell with this.* He was just delaying the inevitable.

He picked up a checked shirt, tossed it into the bag, then followed it with a worn pair of chinos and his FBI day pack. He needed a game plan for Guatemala. There were ways in which he could turn what seemed like disadvantages—his obvious foreignness, his tallness, his unfamiliarity with indigenous languages and customs—to his advantage. If he told people he was from South America—Chile, perhaps—his odd Spanish and his looks would not be questioned. He didn't need a disguise—his off-duty clothes and bag were cheap and shabby already. He'd have to wing some of it, but improvisation was his strong suit. And if Pendergast didn't like it, then he could lick his *kokoyahala*, because Coldmoon planned to own this operation. This would be his, and his alone—

Suddenly, he heard something. He paused a moment, shrugged, then resumed his packing. As he did so, the sound came again. It was an unusual noise, like the knock of a bird's beak, only slow and deliberate—and oddly hollow. Where had it come from? Nobody was in the house. There was no storm outside, no wind or waving branches, and the beach was still off-limits to people.

Another faint knock. His eye fell on the hot air register in the floor. It had come from there: that explained the hollow echo. The duct, he knew, ran to the boiler in the basement.

With a sigh, he went back to his packing. Rats, probably, in the ductwork. Not a bad place to hang out, given how infrequently the heat was turned on around here.

But then the sound came again. It had a measured nature that seemed to bespeak intelligence. He thought of Tungmanito, the night woodpecker, who visited the houses of the dying, trying to get inside and steal their spirits before they could complete their journey to the lush prairies of the afterworld.

His mind was certainly running in odd circles tonight. He'd better recall he was an FBI special agent on assignment and push aside all this superstitious nonsense. There could be someone in the house, and that was something real and present—and worth investigating.

He pulled his gun from the holster hanging on the back of a chair, stuck it into the pocket of his jeans, and stepped out into the hall as silently as possible.

He glanced around, then took the back stairs that led down from the servants' rooms into the kitchen.

Walking over to the door leading to the basement, he opened it, felt along the wall beyond, found the light switch, then reconsidered. If he was going to follow through on this fool's errand, he might as well do it right. He pulled out the small tactical LED flashlight he always carried, snapped it on low power—if you could call three hundred lumens "low"—and started down the stairs.

The "basement" of the Mortlach House was, in reality, less than a full basement but more than a crawlspace. The ceiling was just high enough that he could move around with only the slightest stoop. As Coldmoon played his light around, he saw that the space was a forest of supporting beams, all covered in a moisture-resistant material of more recent vintage than the house itself, with a maze of brick alcoves built into the foundations. The air smelled of salt water, mold, and earth.

He paused once again. The tapping sound had stopped. Nevertheless, he made a thorough search of the labyrinthine space, walking among the columns and peering into various nooks and cellar rooms and vaults. His last stop was the boiler itself, which was newer than expected but, as he'd guessed, cold. Nevertheless, he gave its flank two good whacks with the flat of his hand, the sound booming out in the hollow darkness. If there were squirrels or rats— or woodpeckers, damn it—that would give them something to think about.

He made a final sweep with his light, then turned and ascended the stairs, bent on completing his packing.

The echoes of Coldmoon's footsteps faded away in the cellar, and silence returned along with the dark. The figure in the basement remained unmoving, hidden in a small alcove. After a minute it moved out of the tiny space. Constance Greene, clad all in black as if in mourning, peered around, noting that the basement was once again empty. When she was satisfied that all was as it had been before Coldmoon's disturbance, she retreated into the shadows, invisible once again, to wait...and wait.

32

ROGER SMITHBACK ROLLED over on the dirty mattress that served as his bed and—with a groan—gingerly held one hand up to the side of his face. Even now, two days later, the pain hadn't abated much. His eye was puffy and half-closed, his ear swollen, and his temple almost too tender to touch. He could only guess what a wreck he must look—there was no mirror in the grimy little storage room that made up his cell.

Two days—he'd been here two whole days. He knew this only because of a tiny barred window high up in the wall that permitted sunlight to enter. When he'd first come to after that awful sucker punch, it had still been dark. Then hours later, the sun rose, then after an interminable wait it had gone and he faced a second endless night. It had risen again, and set—for the second time.

Two days. His only food had been bags of plantain

chips, his only drink cans of tamarind soda from a pallet stored in one corner. The chips had been served to him daily, each time accompanied by a shouted warning, and a door cracked open just wide enough to toss a few bags in at the point of a shotgun. His toilet was an old galvanized pail. It had yet to be emptied.

It had taken him a long time to clear his head of the effects of the blow. Once he had, he felt overwhelmed with terror: What was going to happen to him? Was that blow to the side of the head a mere taste of things to come?

Was anyone looking for him? Since the death of his brother, Smithback had no family to speak of, and no girlfriend. He traveled so often and unpredictably, with no notice to his friends, that they wouldn't be alarmed at his disappearance. Which left Kraski as the only one who would note his absence—and he'd probably just assume his reporter was slacking off.

At least it seemed they weren't going to kill him... not right away. And he wondered: what did they want with him?

With this realization, his thoughts—as much as the blinding headache allowed—turned to the events that had led up to this. He'd been set up by that old bastard landscaper. Maybe Smithback should have seen it coming. As usual, he'd been too eager for the story.

He now had a story, all right, if he could only get out of there alive.

Given his limited Spanish, he'd been able to comprehend only a portion of the loud talk that went on beyond the locked door. As far as he could tell, he was being held prisoner in some unused back room of the *tienda guatemalteca* they'd passed just before turning into the alley. There were two male voices only, it seemed. Sometimes the two laughed coarsely, telling crude jokes and bragging about their exploits. They had speculated about some big reward being offered by someone for something. There was much talk of drugs, shootings, and smuggling. Once or twice, he thought they'd mentioned him, and the dismissive way they'd done so was chilling. Mainly, though, it seemed they were waiting for their boss to come back. Somebody they called "El Engreído."

Engreído. He'd puzzled over that one. Figuratively, Smithback thought it meant "stuck-up." Literally, he knew, it meant "Bighead" and must be a nickname. He wondered what was going to happen to him when this Bighead dude came back.

As if on cue, a commotion sounded in the passage outside his makeshift cell. He heard the two familiar voices, yammering excitedly. And then a third voice joined in: slower, deeper, full of authority.

Instinctively, Smithback slid backward on the

mattress until he was pressed against the wall farthest from the door. *Shit.*

He didn't have long to wait. There was a brief fumbling at the lock, and then the door opened. No shotgun barrel peeping in this time; no need for that. The doorway was filled by the giant figure of the tattooed man who'd coldcocked him.

Seeing Smithback, the man grinned and stepped through the door.

"*Flaco, cierra la maldita puerta,*" he said over his shoulder. The door closed behind him and then, a moment later, a wire-basket light in the ceiling came on for the first time since Smithback awoke. In the light, the man looked even bigger than he had in the alleyway. His head was shaved, and a thick rope of fat—it looked more like muscle, if that was even possible—formed a bulging ring around the back of his neck. The wifebeater he wore strained to cover his massive chest, and both arms were sleeve-tattooed from shoulder to wrist. In one spot, Smithback noticed with a spike of fear, were the *P* and *N* that had become all too familiar to him.

The wooden pallet of tamarind soda sat in one corner. Bighead pulled it toward Smithback's mattress. Though it had to contain a dozen cases of soda, the giant man slid it over as easily as if it had been a shoe box. He settled himself atop the pallet and looked at Smithback.

"Got a little boo-boo, *chiquito?*" he asked in surprisingly unaccented English.

Smithback realized that, unconsciously, he was still covering his injured temple, and he immediately lowered his hand.

"So you're the one who's been waving photos all over the barrio, asking questions about how we're inked."

"I'm a—" Smithback began, but Bighead raised his voice and spoke over him.

"I know who you are. You are Roger Smithback. Smith-*back*. A reporter."

For a moment, curiosity mingled with fear: how did this brute know that? Of course—they'd taken his wallet, looked at his driver's license. A Google search would have done the rest.

"But you're a long way from home, Smith-*back*. What are you doing so far from Miami? And why are you asking about the Panteras?"

The man's English was very good. Smithback swallowed, trying hard to keep in mind the code of journalistic integrity his father, a newspaper editor, had fiercely advocated. *What would Ernie Pyle do?* he had always asked at difficult moments. "If you know I'm a reporter," Smithback said, "then you know it's my business to ask questions. I—"

Bighead shut him up just by lifting one index finger. "I'm the one asking questions now. And you—you're no reporter anymore. You're dogshit on the sole of my boot." He paused, looking at Smithback speculatively. "Got a problem with that, *mierda de perro?*"

Journalistic integrity or not, Smithback had no problem with it.

Bighead nodded. "I think *I* would like being a reporter. You get to go everywhere, stick your nose where it doesn't belong. You talk to the cops, talk to the street, learn twice as much as anyone else. Ask all the questions you want, even if they're none of your business." He paused, mimicking the act of puzzling something out. "And if I was a smart reporter—and maybe I learned something I shouldn't have—I could ask even more questions. Like about the Panteras. And everybody would think it was just my job."

Suddenly, swift as an adder's tongue, the man's huge arm darted forward, grabbed Smithback by the collar, and pulled him bodily up from the mattress. Smithback yelped in mingled pain and surprise.

"So what's going on, *chiquito?*" he asked in a dreadfully menacing, silky voice. "I know you want to tell me. You wouldn't have such a hard-on, sniffing around here day and night, if you didn't know something. What went wrong at the meet? Where are they, *las mulas?* What's the story with all those trucks?"

Smithback's mind worked fast as the fist tightened,

but only a childlike babble escaped his lips. "What are you talking about? *Mulas*? Trucks?"

"Don't play stupid. Big trucks, government trucks. Were they full of stuff? *My* stuff?" He paused. "Something's *late*, my journalist friend. Very, very big. Very, very late. That makes my *hombres* angry. That makes my *jefe* angry."

There was a moment of silence. Then, tightening his fist still further around the collar, he lifted Smithback off the ground. With a grunt of effort, he smacked his other fist into Smithback's stomach, suspended over the mattress. A horrific pain ripped through the reporter's gut. His body instinctively tried to curl into a fetal position but, dangling as he was by the collar, his knees only jerked: once, twice. Bighead delivered another terrible blow to his midsection, then threw Smithback down onto the mattress.

Smithback doubled over, vomiting on the filthy cover.

Bighead stepped forward, straddling him. "You don't have all the shit already, *chiquito*, or you wouldn't be around here asking questions. But you know something. I think maybe it's about those trucks—the ones with their numbers painted over."

Smithback barely heard. He struggled to breathe, waves of cramping pain ripping through his guts.

"And you *will* tell me," Bighead said. "You know

why? Because people *always* tell me. Like when I spent two years in Charlotte CI. I had a thing for new fish, especially the diaper snipers. They were all soft—soft like you. I'd push their shit, just to break them in a little...and they'd start talking, right away!" Bighead laughed in mock surprise. "They'd tell me everything, every secret they ever had, every messed-up thing they'd ever done, hoping to make me stop. But I didn't stop, *chiquito*. I pushed their shit until I was fucking *finished*. Now...talk to me."

"It's the feet," Smithback groaned in agony.

"*¿Qué?*"

"The feet..." Smithback was still dribbling vomit, and he could only speak a few words at a time. "That washed up...on the beach..."

Bighead stopped straddling him, took a few paces back. "What about the feet?"

"That tattoo...it was on one of the feet..."

"What? Those feet on that beach in Captiva?"

"I got the photo from...from an autopsy...Trying to use the tattoo to...get a story...a story..."

"Shut up! My missing shipment got nothing to do with those feet! You're just trying to hustle me." Bighead cursed, then called over his shoulder. "Carlos! Flaco! *¡Pongan tus culos aquí, carajos!*"

Immediately, the door opened again and the two figures stepped inside. Through his haze of pain, Smithback saw they were both as heavily tattooed as Bighead: one tall and well-built, the other short. Turning away from Smithback, Bighead started speaking to them in low, rapid Spanish. Smithback didn't even try to understand. Something had occurred to him—something he should probably have thought of before, but it had taken this brief, vicious beating to bring it to mind. That old gardener, the spotter—when he'd driven Smithback around, he'd done a lot of talking. It sounded like the gang, the Panteras, had some kind of serious problem going on—this was what Bighead wanted to know about. But the thing Smithback couldn't get out of his mind was something a cop buddy had once said: *If you're kidnapped, and they don't wear masks, if they mention each other's names in your hearing, that means you're fucked: sooner or later, they'll put a cap in your ass.*

He realized Bighead was looking back at him. The hulking figure wore an expression Smithback couldn't read: it might be anger, it might be uncertainty—it could have been any number of things.

"That's some little story, the feet," he told Smithback. "I don't know if you're smart or stupid. I'm going to ask around. See if maybe you speak a little truth, see if there's a connection. Then I'll come back and break you in. That's when I find out whether you're lying—or, if you tell the truth, maybe you'll tell a little bit more."

"I've told you everything—" Smithback began, but Bighead had turned away and was walking toward the door. Already, he was pulling a cell phone out of his pocket. In the doorway, he paused to give his two gunmen another instruction.

"Fuck him up a little more before locking him in again," he said. Then he stepped into the narrow passageway and vanished.

33

THE R/V *LEUCOTHEA* passed under the causeway bridge as a gray dawn was creeping into a stormy sky, casting a steely light over the choppy water. As they passed the Sanibel Island Lighthouse, they left the shelter of land and began encountering a deep swell from an offshore storm, the boat riding up and down through the whitecaps, the wind whipping the spray across the windows. Pamela Gladstone headed the *Leucothea* around the southern end of the island into the rough sea.

Pendergast had taken a seat in the chair opposite the helm. He had arrived in a slicker with a yellow sou'wester, rain pants, and boots, all brand new and still smelling of the shop where he'd purchased them. She had to stifle a smile of amusement.

"Nasty day for a cruise," she said.

"Indeed."

She scanned him for signs of incipient seasickness but didn't see any. His face was as impassive and cool as ever, impossible to read. Usually they turned white before they puked, but he was already about as white as you could get.

"We'll be reaching the first drop point in about fifteen minutes. It's the inlet between Boca Grande and Cayo Costa. The second drop is off Manasota Key and the third and fourth off the Venice Inlet. The fifth is a bit farther out to sea and about ten miles north. It's pretty much a straight shot up the coast."

"Thank you for the explanation." Pendergast didn't offer to help and she wouldn't have wanted him to anyway. In these rough seas, a man overboard wasn't out of the question. The storm causing them was way out in the gulf and heading toward the delta. They were getting the fringes of it, nothing her boat couldn't handle, and nothing that was forecast to get any worse. Just your usual rough day at sea—or so she hoped.

It wasn't long before Gladstone noticed a boat on the radar, about five nautical miles back. It had been there almost since they passed Sanibel Light and it seemed to be pacing them. She enlarged the radar field and made a mental note of the other vessels in the vicinity, their positions and headings. There weren't nearly as many as usual—the nasty weather had kept the pleasure boaters in port. These were working boats. Her eye drifted back to the green blob five miles behind, going the same speed and heading as the *Leucothea*. She glanced back but could not make out the boat among the swells and white-caps, spray and mist.

Pendergast had been quiet, but now he spoke. "It seems we are being followed."

"You mean that boat at one eighty about five miles back? I noticed it, too. Could be a coincidence."

"Shall we perform a little test?" he murmured.

"How so?"

"Alter your course by ninety degrees."

"Not a bad idea." She turned the helm and brought the boat around in a wide arc to a new heading of 270 degrees.

"Hey," said Lam, calling in through the open wheelhouse door. He had been back in the stern area, preparing the first drop. "What's with the course alteration? We should be heading north."

"Just a little experiment," said Gladstone.

She watched the little green blob, Pendergast at her side. After a minute or two, it altered course to track them.

"Son of a bitch," Gladstone said.

"Does that vessel have AIS?" Pendergast asked.

She was surprised he knew about the Automatic Identification System carried by most boats. "No."

"Are you using AIS?"

"Yes." She hesitated. Glancing back, she could see that Lam, bundled up in a slicker, his red sneakers replaced by oversize green rubber boots, was fully occupied setting up his drift buoys. "Agent Pendergast, would you be willing to go aft with those binoculars and tell me what you see? Keep a hand on the grab rails—the sea's pretty rough."

"Certainly."

Pendergast exited the wheelhouse and went to the stern, raising the binoculars. She could see his bright yellow form trying to peer through the spray and wind.

She now altered course back to the original heading—and noted the other vessel soon followed suit.

Pendergast returned, shedding water. "I couldn't make it out, I'm afraid."

"Yeah, visibility sucks." Who the hell would be following her, and why?

"Would it make sense for you to turn off your own AIS?" said Pendergast.

"I could do that, but it wouldn't make any difference—that boat's already locked in on us with radar. What I'm going to do instead is call the bastard on VHF."

"Excellent idea."

Gladstone pulled down her mike. Channel 16 was

quiet, so she pressed the transmit button. "Unknown vessel, unknown vessel, this is *Leucothea*, over."

There was no response. She waited two minutes and tried again. Still no response.

"Didn't the vessel receive your message?" Pendergast asked.

"She damn well did, she's required by law to have the VHF tuned to channel 16. She's just not answering." Now Gladstone was seriously pissed off. No AIS and ignoring a call—that was not right. But they were nearing the first drop point and she had to turn her attention to that.

"Wallace, how are you doing back there?" she called through the open door.

"Ready to roll."

"On my signal."

He picked up a plastic basket of the buoys and carried them back to the transom. Gladstone throttled down to seven knots. The slackening of speed, she noticed, was soon matched by the following vessel.

Keeping an eye on the chartplotter, she held up her hand, then brought it down. She saw Lam toss the first buoy overboard. In another five hundred feet, she signaled the second drop. In five minutes, all buoys earmarked for the first drop were away.

He came back in, grinning. He used a towel hanging on a hook to dry his face and hands, and then checked an iPad mounted on a side console. "All buoys broadcasting their positions."

Gladstone throttled up. "On to Manasota Key."

The boat accelerated. She watched the following boat to see what she'd do. But that boat was now doing something different. Instead of pursuing, it was accelerating to where they had just dropped the buoys. The green blob approached the first drop point and slowed, then circled and stopped. She couldn't believe it—what were they doing?

"What the fuck!" Lam cried, staring at the radar. "That boat's picking up our buoy!"

Gladstone watched as the green blur of the boat on her radar merged with the GPS location being broadcast by one of the buoys. She throttled back down and grabbed the mike. "Unknown vessel, unknown vessel picking up our buoy, this is *Leucothea*, over."

Still no answer.

"Unknown vessel, this is *Leucothea*, get your hands off our gear or we're reporting you to the Coast Guard."

Still no answer. But now the boat was moving toward the second buoy in the drop.

"Coast Guard, Coast Guard, this is R/V *Leucothea*, over."

She waited. No response. "Coast Guard, Coast Guard, this is R/V *Leucothea*, position 26.68 north, 82.34 west, please respond, over."

This was crazy. The Coast Guard monitored channel 16 twenty-four/seven and had surely picked up her call. Why the hell weren't they answering? She checked to see if there was a problem with the radio and confirmed it was indeed broadcasting at twenty-five watts.

"The boat's picked up two buoys," Lam said. "And now ... looks like it's accelerating toward us."

Gladstone stared at the radar. Lam was right: the boat was really coming at them, now moving close to thirty knots. She looked at Pendergast. "I've never had anything like this happen before. I can't outrun that sucker."

Pendergast said, "Allow the boat to approach us."

"But they might be dangerous—drug dealers or criminals. I can't understand why the Coast Guard isn't responding to our call."

"Perhaps because that boat *is* the Coast Guard."

"What? Why the hell would they interfere with my work? I've got permits up the wazoo!"

"If I were you, I would have those permits at the ready."

Gladstone waited. She kept the throttle down, the *Leucothea* making only enough headway to keep her bow to the seas. As the green dot approached, she began to hear the distant throb of an engine, and then the vessel's shape materialized out of the mist and drizzle—the unmistakable form of an RB-M Coast

Guard patrol boat, with a Day-Glo orange hull and a 50-caliber machine gun mounted in the front.

"Christ, it *is* the Coast Guard!" She pulled down the mike again. "Hey, Coast Guard patrol, this is *Leucothea*. What's the matter—you guys deaf? Over."

The vessel slowed about a hundred feet out and a loudspeaker blared. "*We are drawing alongside. We are drawing alongside. Bring your vessel to a halt and prepare for boarding.*"

Gladstone yelled into the mike. "Coast Guard, in case you haven't noticed, the sea is a little rough for coming alongside, over."

Finally a voice came over the VHF. "*Leucothea, this is Coast Guard RB-M 5794. Move to channel nine, over.*"

Gladstone furiously punched in the channel. "Hey, what the hell are you guys doing, picking up my buoys? I'm a research vessel! And this is no sea for a safe boarding!"

"Repeat: we are coming along your port side and will board, out."

She clicked off the transmission. "Assholes. Wallace, toss out the fenders on the port side. This is messed up—we've got a six-foot swell running!" She turned to Pendergast. "You're FBI. What are you going to do?"

Pendergast returned her look. "Cooperate."

"Jeez, thanks a lot."

She brought the boat to a halt. With no headway, it began getting pushed all over the place by the sea. The Coast Guard boat now came up alongside, and a crew member tossed over a couple of lines, which Lam cleated down before racing into the hold, apparently to hide. The two boats were now tethered, heaving up and down, the inflatable gunwale of the Coast Guard boat smacking hard on their hull with each swell. The man directing the operation came out of the wheelhouse dressed in foul-weather gear, but she could see the lieutenant's bars on his sleeve. Two sailors helped him over the side and onto the deck of the *Leucothea*, then followed.

"Lieutenant Duran, United States Coast Guard," he bellowed. He was a big man, not fat but broad and solid, with a brushy mustache and icy blue eyes. The two other men came up behind him. "This is a Coast Guard boarding. Please remain in place while the vessel is searched."

"Hey, don't you guys need a warrant?" Gladstone asked.

"Title fourteen, section eighty-nine of the United States Code authorizes the U.S. Coast Guard to board vessels subject to the jurisdiction of the United States anytime, anyplace upon the high seas and upon any waterway over which the United States has authority, to make inquiries, examinations, inspections, searches, seizures, and arrests," said the lieutenant in a booming voice.

"Really? Jesus Christ."

The two men began searching the boat, rummaging through the bin of undropped buoys, opening the hatches, shining lights into the bilges, flipping cushions, opening gear lockers, throwing stuff around.

"Be careful in there!" She looked at Pendergast. "Aren't you going to show your badge?"

"They know very well who I am," he said. His face seemed even paler than usual.

Duran came back. "Okay, let's see your captain's license and registration papers."

Gladstone opened a compartment next to the helm and shoved them at him. He took them, examined them, and handed them back. "Research permits?"

She gave those to him as well. He flipped through them, not even bothering to make a show of reading. He tossed them back at her and turned to his men. "Okay. Let's go."

"Just a moment," said Pendergast quietly.

Duran turned and jutted his chin at Pendergast. "What?"

"May we know the reason for this search?"

Duran grinned. "Well, we saw shit tossed in the water, so we decided to check it out. Might have been garbage, drugs, sewage discharge—who knows? You got a problem with that, pal?"

Pendergast didn't reply.

The man's arrogant, smirking gaze rested a while longer on him; then he turned to Gladstone. "Looks like everything's in order. We'll leave your buoys on the deck. Uh, looks like one of them got a bit dinged up when we ran it over." A bigger grin. "Sorry for the inconvenience."

The man went out onto the deck with his two companions and they climbed back to their boat. Gladstone was sorry to see that none of them got thrown into the drink by the swell.

"Cast off!" Duran called.

Gladstone cast off and the Coast Guard boat revved its engine and swung away.

As Lam cautiously emerged from below, Gladstone turned to Pendergast. "What the hell was that all about?"

"Harassment," said Pendergast.

"How come you didn't pull rank on those assholes?"

"A wise man once said, 'Engage the enemy on your terms, not on his.'"

"What's that supposed to mean?"

"They wanted to provoke me at sea, where they have almost unlimited power—and I have next to none."

"So you're going to, ah, wait to engage them on land?"

"That same wise man said, 'Let your plans be dark and as impenetrable as night, and when you move, fall like a thunderbolt.'" And with this, the pale agent smiled in a ghastly way and his eyes glittered like broken glass.

34

At the mountain pass above San Miguel Acatán, Agent Coldmoon looked through the grimy window of the bus down into the valley. It was, he had to admit, a spectacular view—the snowcapped peaks of mountain ranges all around, the valley blanketed in clouds, the patchwork fields on the hills above.

There were two ways for an FBI agent to conduct an investigation in a Central American country. One was to go through official channels, using the Central American Intelligence Program, the CAIP, run out of Quantico and the State Department, which would have taken days if not weeks to set up, involving official visits with partnering government officials in Guatemala, paperwork up the wazoo, visas, dinners, photo ops, and so on. The other was to do what he had done and just go on a tourist visa. He would find what he wanted and then, if necessary, on his return, retroactively jump through all the hoops.

Staring down into that mist-shrouded mountain valley, he felt he'd arrived at the end of the earth. Soon the bus crept down the switchbacks, grinding gears, and went below the level of the clouds into a misty dreamscape. It wasn't long before they entered the town. Small pastel-colored farmhouses with tin roofs clung in clusters to the steep hills, among green patchwork fields and tattered strings of rising haze, above a roaring torrent in the ravine below. The bus came to a halt at the main square in town, fronted on one side with a whitewashed church and on the other with some tin-roofed government buildings and a small outdoor market where livestock and vegetables were being sold.

He stepped off with his backpack into the square and looked around. San Miguel Acatán was impoverished but still retained a sturdy dignity. It was easy to see why people might leave and head off to America. *God, but what a journey that must be*, he thought, looking at the endless sea of mountains stretching northward to the Mexican frontier.

He could see that everyone in the square and the little market had noted his presence and was watching him, not in an obvious way, but slyly, out of the corners of their eyes. There was a wariness here at the presence of a stranger. Although his skin was the same color as theirs, he was acutely aware of his towering height, lean physique, and craggy appearance, so different from the small stature and rounded physique of the local Maya population.

He had done what preparation he could. While there were no landline phones in San Miguel, there was, amazingly, cell phone service, and he had managed to get a list of phone numbers of twelve inhabitants in the town by the last name of Ixquiac. The name was pronounced "*Ish*-kee-ack," he reminded himself. According to the cell phone company's records, they all paid through P.O. box addresses. So he would have to find them by asking around.

He had also worked up a cover story. He knew that as soon as a stranger started going around a small, isolated town like this, asking questions, the whole place would go from wary curiosity to high alert.

Crossing the little square, with its collection of trees with whitewashed trunks, he entered the market. He went up to a woman selling guinea pigs in little wire cages, smiled, held out his hand, and introduced himself in Spanish, quickly removing one of the business cards he had printed up the evening before.

"I am Señor Lunafría," he said, "attorney-at-law."

Upon hearing this, the woman shut down, her face hardening into a mask of suspicion.

"I'm looking for Señorita Ramona Osorio Ixquiac."

He was gratified to see a flicker of recognition in

the woman's face at the name. "What do you want with her?"

"I have important news."

The woman looked at him a long time, with an impassive face—so long that he began to feel uncomfortable. Maybe this wasn't the best way to go.

Coldmoon leaned forward and lowered his voice. "If not her, is there an Ixquiac family member here that I can speak to? It's a confidential matter."

At this the woman turned and called out to a nearby seller, saying something in an Indian language. The other woman's eyes widened and she left her stall and came over. She stared at Coldmoon.

"*I* am Ramona Osorio Ixquiac. What's this all about?"

Coldmoon thought fast, stunned at how quickly he'd succeeded in finding an Ixquiac. If this was Ramona, then the foot must belong to her sister Martina. He said, "I am here about your sister, Señorita Martina."

At this her eyes widened. "My sister? Oh, thank God, we haven't heard from her in so long! Come, please come, to my house and tell me all about her, where she is, what she's doing in America!" Her eyes shone with mixed excitement and apprehension and Coldmoon's heart fell at what he would have to tell her. But maybe not everything—not just yet.

* * *

Ramona's house stood at the edge of the ravine leading down to a river. The house was surrounded by several small, terraced kitchen gardens. The mist was continuing to lift and now a streak of sunlight pierced the cloud cover, making a bright moving spot on a distant hillside.

The house was built of pale-blue-washed cinder blocks and neat as a pin, down to checked curtains and a clay jug of flowers on the kitchen table.

"Please be at home," said Ramona, offering him a seat.

Coldmoon sat and the woman busied herself with a pot of coffee simmering on a woodstove. She poured two mugs and brought them over with a bowl of sugar and a jug of cream.

Raising the mug, Coldmoon caught the scent of dark, burnt, acidic coffee. "Just the way I like it," he said, taking a sip. And it was delicious: finally, a cup of coffee resembling what he knew from growing up on the rez.

Ramona took a seat with her own cup of coffee and placed a dish of chuchitos on the table. "Please tell me all about my sister."

"I'm afraid I don't have good news," said Coldmoon. God, how much should he tell her? "Your sister seems to be missing."

"*Missing?*" Ramona held her hand to her mouth. "This is as I feared! What's happened?"

"It seems..." Coldmoon hesitated. He didn't know what to say, so he took her hand. "It seems she may be in trouble."

"Oh!" She gasped, tears springing into her eyes. "I told her not to go, I begged her, I was so afraid!"

"We don't know for sure what's happened to her. That's what I'm investigating. I need your help. Please tell me what you know."

She dabbed at her eyes. "As you can see, we're very poor here in San Miguel. My sister, she kept talking about going north, to the USA. It wasn't just her—everybody was talking about it. How rich everyone is up there, how an honest person who works hard can have a good life, that people have all the food they need and a house and maybe even a car, how every child can go to school. I knew it was a lot of exaggeration. But the desire to leave is like a fire in this town."

"When did she leave?"

"It was just before the Feast of the Immaculate Conception, in early December."

"You mean over four months ago?"

"Yes."

"Tell me how that came about."

"My sister became part of a group planning to go, and finally somebody contacted a man who knew how to get them over the border into Mexico, and from there, he knew another man who was a coyote, who could get them into the United States. It's easy getting into Mexico. The hard part is getting into the U.S."

"Who is this man?"

"His name is Zapatero. Jorge Obregón Zapatero. He got them all together—and one day they just left." And at this she dabbed her eyes again.

"How many of them were in the group?"

"About twenty. But..." She took a deep, shuddering breath. "We worried that something bad must have happened, because we've heard nothing since. Nothing. Not one person in that group has written or called. Zapatero swears he turned them over to the other coyote in Mexico. But it's as if they vanished."

"What did Zapatero charge for this service?"

"A thousand quetzals."

Coldmoon did a quick calculation—about $130. "That's not much."

"Yes, but then they had to pay another thirty thousand quetzals to the coyote in Mexico."

"I see. And who was that coyote?"

She shrugged. "Who knows?"

"Zapatero must know."

"He won't say. He says he did his job right. He thinks they were caught at the border and jailed in the United States."

"Where is Zapatero now?"

"He's organizing another group to leave in a month or so."

"Why would more people go if the others disappeared?"

There was a long silence. "Because people have hope. Here, we have no hope."

35

SMITHBACK LAY ON his mattress, staring at the ceiling. Bugs were crawling on it, and he watched their progress without interest.

The first couple of days he'd been locked up in here, he could think of nothing but escape. He'd thought of everything—breaking down the door; trying to reach the ridiculously high, ridiculously small window; yanking at the shotgun that appeared when they tossed in food, in hopes of pulling the thug in with it and overpowering him—yet nothing even remotely likely had suggested itself. But now, after his little "talk" with Bighead, he could do little but lie on the rude bed and hope for sleep. It was as if the hulking bastard and his fearsome threats had beaten all hope out of him.

Once again he cursed his own habit of sudden travel with no notice to his friends or colleagues. What the hell was Kraski doing? Calling the cops?

No, the son of a bitch was probably just bitching and moaning about his absence. Maybe he'd sent out a couple of co-reporters to sniff around. Useless bastards, they couldn't empty piss out of a boot.

At first he thought the gang boss had ruptured his internal organs. But today, his gut felt a hell of a lot better than it had the day before. And his eye, too, was clearly less swollen.

Of course, none of this mattered in the long run. He knew now that it was just a matter of time before they killed him. *I'm going to ask around. See if maybe you speak a little truth. Then I'll come back and break you in.* Somehow, instead of motivating him to escape, Bighead's words had filled him with despair.

There had been no sign of the motherfucker for a day now. Smithback still didn't know exactly what the hell was going on, but as best he could tell from the talk he heard through the door, it had to do with a shipment of drugs, cocaine, that had gone missing on the Arizona border, somehow involving trucks with their numbers painted out. And Bighead seemed to be on the hook for it. Smithback felt certain that all this was the reason the bastard was away so much of the time—trying to mitigate the damage and figure out what had gone wrong.

On top of that, more people had been coming around and talking to his two jailers. It seemed Bighead had put word out about a reward for information. One of them had been an old rummy, his voice slurred through the closed door. But he only spoke English. He demanded to talk to Bighead and he also had something to say about trucks, ten-wheelers with large drums bolted to the drivers' fenders, payloads covered in canvas. The guards had told him to come back later, when the boss was around. The rummy apparently thought they were giving him the brush-off, because he talked loudly about these trucks seen going into a place named Tate's Hole or Tate's Hall.

Smithback's unpleasant interview with Bighead had had another unexpected result. For whatever reason, the two goons, Carlos and Flaco, now showed themselves openly. The two seemed far more at ease when Bighead was away. They even came into his cell from time to time or chatted with him through the door. They didn't replace his vomit-strewn mattress, but they at least turned it over. They started giving him better food and actually emptied his improvised toilet. Not that any of this fooled Smithback, of course. The two were still his jailers, keeping him healthy enough until Bighead's next—and maybe final—interrogation.

Because he had nothing to do but listen to the conversations on the far side of his door, Smithback had learned a fair amount about his jailers. He was able to put names and personalities to them. Both of them talked tough: despite his rudimentary Spanish, Smithback had picked up boasting about women, hijackings, and shootings. The two seemed especially proud of the murders they'd committed, but Smithback had the impression a lot of their talk was bravado and exaggeration. At other times the two seemed like relatively normal young men. Carlos, the big one, had apparently worked in a moped shop in Guatemala and was fascinated with big bikes—sometimes going into incomprehensible disquisitions on technical aspects of *motocicletas*. Flaco, the shorter, thinner one—wiry, not scrawny—appeared to be a fan of graphic novels. In Bighead's absence, the two didn't even seem particularly brutal: despite the boss's instructions to kick Smithback's ass, for example, Carlos had just given him a few perfunctory smacks before turning over the mattress and one-arming him down onto it.

He heard the two of them laughing now in the passage; the slap of a high five. Carlos, it seemed, was going out on some errand. Smithback turned his gaze back to the ceiling. It surprised him, distantly, that he could look upon his captors with relative charity. Maybe it was an indication of how resigned he'd become. If they'd stayed in Guatemala, if they hadn't fallen victim to bad influences, Carlos would probably still be working in the moped shop, and Flaco—Smithback wasn't sure about Flaco. The day before, bringing in what passed for his prisoner's dinner, he'd had a graphic novel jammed into his back pocket, and when Smithback commented on it the guy had hastily dropped the plastic plate on Smithback's mattress and walked out, pushing the comic book deeper into his pocket. Only then did Smithback realize it was not a book, after all, but a manuscript—the drawings had been Flaco's own. If he was working on a graphic novel, or even just drawing in his spare time, it probably wasn't the kind of hobby his *compañeros* would think highly of.

Carlos had gone; it was late afternoon, and the little shop had grown quiet. Smithback closed his eyes, tried to shut down his thoughts and sleep. But within five minutes, he was interrupted by a scraping sound: his door, opening.

He pushed up on his elbows, wincing a bit. It was Flaco. For some reason, instead of exuding his usual cocky air, he looked nervous. He glanced up and down the passage, then—after making sure Smithback hadn't moved—he stepped in, closed the door, and approached the pallet of tamarind soda. It was still where Bighead had dragged it over twenty-four hours before.

He sat down. "You," he said in English. "You writer. *Periodista. ¿Sí?*" Flaco dug into one pocket and pulled out a folded piece of paper. He unfolded it and held it in front of Smithback. The reporter, one eye better than the other, peered at it in the dim light. With surprise, he saw that it was his first article for the *Herald* on the feet that had washed up on Captiva. Flaco pointed at the byline. "Smithback," he said. "That you, right?"

Smithback nodded. Flaco spoke better English than he had initially let on.

"You work with...with a publisher?" Flaco asked. "Newspaper publisher?"

He wondered where Flaco had gotten a copy of that article. It was blurry, like a screenshot that had been printed. All of a sudden, Smithback realized what all this would look like from the perspective of a person like Flaco. He didn't know much about the young man's background, but he almost certainly came from a small Guatemalan town where the outside world rarely intruded. To a guy like that, a reporter for a big newspaper might be seen as someone important. Smithback recalled Flaco bragging about his initiation into the Panteras. He'd been told to kill two people: a *rata*, informer, and his wife. He could kill the man any way he wanted to. But first, he had to kill the woman. He had to cut her throat— in front of the rat. That, anyway, had been the gist of the story. But the way he told it, the bragging and unlikely details, made Smithback think the whole thing was made up, or at least highly embellished.

Flaco was looking at him, question still hanging

in the air. Smithback thought quickly, pushing these speculations aside. A reporter, his name on the front page of a big city newspaper . . . to someone like Flaco, his lifestyle must seem so unimaginably distant that he might as well be from another planet.

"Yes," he said, sitting up. "Yes, I work with lots of publishers. Important publishers." A spark of hope that had died sometime during the previous night now flared to life again. He'd been like a drowning man, and all of a sudden, he'd caught sight of a life preserver. Distant, but visible nonetheless. There might, after all, be a way out of here.

"What kind of publishers?"

"All kinds. Newspapers. Magazines. Books."

As he spoke, a light gleamed briefly in Flaco's eyes. "Magazine?"

"Sure. My best friend, *mejor amigo*, he used to do cartoons for my newspaper. Now, he has his own publishing house. Right here in Fort Myers." This was a lie: Smithback hadn't known anyone in the comics section of the paper, and he personally hadn't read a comic since the *Peanuts* and *Zap Comix* of his youth.

"What kind of publish, this *amigo*?"

"He publishes . . ." Shit, what should he say? He gestured. "Graphic novels. Manga. *¿Sí?*"

Flaco became animated. "Graphic novels? *Sí. Sí.* And you say this friend, he live here? In Fort Myers?"

"Yeah. Downtown." His mind ran wild, trying to fill in the story. "He's also getting into movies. Hollywood. But this..." He made a sweeping motion that, he hoped, indicated a lateral professional move. "He helps make graphic novels get made into movies."

"You...you read graphic novels?"

"Sure. I love them. Big fan!"

Flaco, encouraged, patted one pocket of the cargo shorts he wore. "I...draw novels."

"Really? You draw graphic novels? Come on, really?" Smithback tried to inject the right mixture of admiration and incredulity—one that would flatter rather than insult.

"*Sí.* Since I was little, all I want to do...is *dibujar.*" The young gangster mimicked sketching on a pad. "My father, he beat me when he find I drawing, not working. *No me importa.*"

"Wow. Amazing." And it was amazing, in a way. Smithback always liked to find creativity in unexpected places. Bighead wouldn't be happy if he thought Flaco's ambitions ran in some direction other than dealing drugs and wiping out competition. The man was obviously starved for some sort of recognition.

"Um, can I see?"

Flaco, after a hesitation, reached into the oversize pocket of his shorts and pulled out a wad of battered pages. "You read. Tell me this good?" He held the pages out to Smithback, with an oddly tender gesture, as if they were flower petals he didn't want to damage. "You read?"

"*Sí. Con mucho gusto.*"

"Carlos, he gone one hour. You finish before then, tell me it's good."

Tell me it's good. Not if *it's good.* Smithback nodded, taking the pages gently.

Suddenly, Flaco drew a switchblade and held it at Smithback's throat. His eyes gleamed again, but with an entirely different kind of light. "You no tell Carlos. No tell Bighead."

Smithback shook his head. "No, no."

"Or I say I cut you, trying to escape. I make it hurt."

Smithback had no doubt that he would. He shook his head as vigorously as the knife would allow. "I won't tell anyone. It's our secret. *Nuestro secreto.*"

Flaco remained motionless for a moment. Then, with a slow grin, he withdrew the knife. "*Nuestro secreto. Sí.*"

Secrets, Smithback reflected, rubbing his throat as the door whispered shut, were something Flaco appreciated.

36

COLDMOON FOUND THE tiny one-room bar at the very edge of town where Zapatero was said to hang out. He slipped in, hoping to be able to order a beer and take his time getting a measure of the man, but that was a hopeless idea. As soon as he parted the beaded curtain that served as the doorway into the cinder-block barroom, the place went silent and every eye turned on him.

Well, thought Coldmoon, *the direct way is sometimes the best way*. "Señor Zapatero?"

A long silence and then a man said, "I am Zapatero."

"I would like to have a conversation with you," Coldmoon replied in Spanish. "In private, outside."

"What's this all about?"

"Outside."

"Señor, I am not used to being ordered around like a peasant."

If it was going to go that way, it would go that

way. Coldmoon approached Zapatero rapidly, before he could even rise from his chair. He towered over him, six feet, four inches, and he used his vantage point to first make sure Zapatero wasn't armed. The man had no firearm, at least none that was accessible, but a small machete was tucked into his leather belt. The man's hand went toward the handle.

"Not a smart idea," said Coldmoon.

The man's hand paused. "Why do you come here like a *cabrón*, speaking so disrespectfully to me? I do not know you."

Coldmoon realized now that his approach had been wrong and that Zapatero was more afraid of losing face in front of this crowd than he was of a confrontation.

"There is no need, señor, for concern," said Coldmoon, suddenly polite, trying to pitch his voice into a calmer register. Christ, he still had a lot to learn about dealing with people in Central America. "I have business to discuss with you, that's all, which may be to your benefit—but it's of a private nature. Forgive me if I've given offense. My name is Lunafría." He held out his hand.

Zapatero relaxed and took it, breaking into a smile. "Why didn't you say so before? Let us go outside to discuss. Gentlemen, I will leave you for a moment."

They went outside.

"Señor Lunafría? I think you are not from around here, judging by your accent and behavior."

"I am from the south. *Far* to the south." He hoped that Zapatero would accept that, given that the Spanish accents spoken in South America were highly diverse. He knew his Spanish wasn't perfect, but it was fluent enough that he might pass for someone from another Spanish-speaking country and not, he hoped, identify him as North American.

"Tell me about your business."

"I'm trying to find out what happened to Martina Osorio Ixquiac, who was in a group you led into Mexico last December."

"Mother of God, I'm sick and tired of these questions! I did for that group what I promised to do and I know nothing of what happened after that."

Coldmoon removed a thousand-quetzal note from his pocket. "I'm just looking for information, privately, and I'm willing to pay for it."

Zapatero did not take the money. "What do you want to know?"

"Tell me about that group. Who they were, why they left."

"There's not much to tell that you can't see with your own eyes. The country around here is dying. The fields are shriveling up, there are no jobs, there are no doctors, the government ignores us except

when the army comes to steal our money and livestock and threaten our wives and daughters. This is
no place for a good life. So I help people escape—
anyone who wants to go and is physically capable. I
am doing God's work, Señor Lunafría, to give people
the chance at a better life. I bring them north,
into Mexico. The Mexican border is only twenty-five
miles away, but it is through mountains and most
of them have never left this town, so they need my
guidance."

"Once you get them over the border, what happens?"

"I take them to La Gloria, a village in Chiapas along
Route 190. There I turn them over to a professional
coyote, who takes them north to the United States."

"Who is this coyote?"

"I know him only by his nickname, El Monito."

"Is he Mexican?"

"I think so. He has a Mexican accent."

"Do you have any idea what might have happened
to the group with Martina?"

"Señor, I think it is very simple: they were caught
and arrested at the border. This is common. They're
in detention in the U.S. and that is why no one has
heard anything. It used to be they were released, but
now they keep them in camps."

"El Monito—tell me about him."

"He's a businessman. He's expensive, but he does
what he promises. I wouldn't be entrusting my

people to him if I thought he was a bad man. What-ever happened to them happened once they got into the U.S."

"How can I meet El Monito?" He once again offered Zapatero the banknote and still the man ignored it.

"I think that will be difficult. He is secretive. Six months ago, we arranged for me to bring a new group of emigrants to La Gloria next month. He is supposed to be there with the vans to take them north. That's the only way I know how to meet him."

"If I went to La Gloria, where might I find him?"

Zapatero shrugged. "There is a café and bar there where I make contact with him, through a bartender named Corvacho. The bar is called Del Charro. On the north end of town."

"Thank you." Once again he offered the note, to no avail. It made Coldmoon nervous, the man not taking his money.

Zapatero looked at him. "May I ask why you're so concerned about Martina in particular?"

"Like you, I'm a man doing a job, and that job involves finding out what happened to her. I wish I could tell you more. I work for the good guys—that's all I can say."

"I accept that," he said, finally taking the banknote. He carefully folded it up and tucked it into his wallet. "Please don't tell El Monito we spoke. He is very protective of his privacy."

As Coldmoon got up to leave, he added, "And, señor: he is a very nervous man. A nervous man with a gun is not a good combination."

37

FORTY-FIVE MINUTES later, there was a light rap on the door. Then Flaco slipped back in. He said nothing, but he didn't need to: his eyes moved from Smithback to the pages, and back again. At first, he didn't approach. He was clearly burning with curiosity, but it seemed that the break had also given him a chance to reflect on the risks of consorting with prisoners.

Smithback indicated the manuscript. "You...did this? By yourself?"

"*Sí.*"

"Really? Sorry, I'm not calling you a liar, it's just..." He flipped the pages. "Really good."

Actually, it was not very good. The drawings were fair—their style seemed to have been heavily influenced by tattoo art, which was probably the case. Ironically, it was the brief little pencil sketches Flaco had done here and there, apparently placeholders for later ink drawings, that seemed to show the most skill. It was possible the youth had latent artistic talent.

The story itself sucked ass. Part of this, of course, was due to the mixture of Spanish and English that Smithback found hard at times to decipher. But translations were easy enough to arrange, and poor spelling or run-on sentences could be fixed. The major issue was the stupid and improbable storyline. It purported to be the autobiography of a macho gangbanger, embellished with bizarre and fantastical violence, implausible sex scenes, and a ludicrous hero with popping pecs out to defeat the forces of evil in a fantasy universe. Pure crap.

"It's brilliant, in fact," Smithback went on, "and the illustrations are so vivid and powerful!" He slathered on the praise, raving about the authenticity of the story and how fresh El Acero, the protagonist, seemed as a character—two critical elements, he explained, required for a great story.

"Who have you shown it to?" he asked in summation.

Flaco frowned. "*¿Qué?*"

Smithback then launched into the prerequisites of getting a graphic novel published. He explained the arduous process: preparing a sample, looking for an agent, hoping a publisher would show interest. Sending it out cold, week after week, getting rejection after rejection. All because in order to get published, you had to have *connections*. Just like in the drug business. Connections were everything.

This stroke of genius was something Flaco could understand.

Where they might catch a break, Smithback went on, interjecting *our* and *we* into his advice, was that a good number of graphic novel publishers still accepted direct submissions. And unlike commercial book publishers, they weren't all centered in New York—Drawn & Quarterly was in Canada, and Dark Horse was in Oregon, just to name two. And, of course, his friend's small publishing house right here in Florida. Steering the conversation in this direction, he played up his relationship to the publisher he'd started calling Bill Johnson, picking a name that couldn't be successfully googled. He was careful to be vague about the name of the company, because that was something Flaco could easily check. He emphasized again how publishing, like so many industries, was all about relationships. Getting in the door was half the battle.

And that, Smithback ended, was something he could easily do.

"He's on Kellogg Street," Smithback said, pulling the name of a well-tended, innocuous downtown street from his meager knowledge of Fort Myers. "We have lunch from time to time. I could get in to see him like *that*." And he snapped his fingers.

"And he read it? My book?" Flaco asked this as if he'd just been offered a skeleton key to Fort Knox.

"If I took it to him, *mi amigo*, he would read it right there. While I waited."

Flaco, who'd been looking increasingly excited during this exchange, now suddenly frowned, grew remote. After a moment, he held out his hand. "Give me book."

Smithback gave him the book back. Flaco stuffed it in his pocket, turned, and left.

Son of a bitch, thought Smithback. He almost had him.

Ten minutes later Flaco was back. "You lie. You want escape."

Smithback shook his head. "Where would I go? You know my name. You have my license—you know where I live, where I work. Look, if you don't trust me, come with me."

But Flaco shook his head. "Bighead back tomorrow afternoon. If he find out we go..."

While Smithback had been reviewing the comic, he'd also been assembling a game theory decision tree. Now he played the best of his limited options. "So I go in the morning. *We* go in the morning," he said hastily as the expression on Flaco's face changed. "You wait outside, at the corner. Better Bill not see you first, because of...you know..." And with more gestures than words, he explained how Flaco's fearsome demeanor might initially put the publisher off—though ultimately Johnson would appreciate the realism Flaco could bring to his work.

Flaco seemed to be on the fence while Smithback made his case. Then he shook his head. "No. *Demasiado peligroso*. Too dangerous."

"Look, we can make it fast. I'll go in, shake his hand, get him excited about your manuscript—give it to him and then leave. Let him read it. All it takes is a read and then he'll see the genius in your story. Then you can follow up with him yourself. You won't need me after that."

"Why not talk to him now? You call."

"Flaco, it doesn't work that way! It's all done in person! Just like in the drug business. Would you do business with someone only over the phone, that you'd never met in person? Of course not!"

Flaco seemed unconvinced; his creative ambitions were clearly at war with his cautious instincts. "*Peligroso*," he repeated.

Smithback played his last card. "You're the boss," he said. "But you'll never get another chance. This is it. He knows all the important people in Hollywood. And for a character as exciting as your El Acero, the movie tie-ins, series licenses..." He shook his head. "Bill's made a lot of artists rich."

They fell silent as someone passed by in the

corridor. Flaco pursed his lips. "We see. If Carlos go out in the morning..." He shrugged with feigned nonchalance, but Smithback could tell that he could barely contain his excitement.

"I'll need to clean myself up." Smithback indicated his wrinkled clothes, the dried vomit that was still caked to one side of his head.

"We see," Flaco said. "Meanwhile, you remember. Say anything to Carlos, and—better keep mouth shut." He took out his switchblade and pointed it at Smithback's mouth, for emphasis. Then he slipped it back into his shorts. "I get your dinner now."

And with that he turned and left the makeshift cell. The door closed and locked behind him.

38

CONSTANCE AND PENDERGAST sat in deck chairs on the wide veranda, looking westward over the gulf, watching the sun slide toward the western horizon. Pelicans, seagulls, and sandpipers cruised across their line of vision, black spots against the pink and blue and gold. On a table next to the door sat Coldmoon's police scanner, which he'd left behind when he went to Central America. It was on constantly, volume turned low, its background squawk like law enforcement Muzak. They had been relaxing for over an hour, and their conversation, despite its unhurried back-and-forth and occasional lapses into silence, had been of absorbing interest to them both. They had spoken of how Piranesi's *Carceri* had managed to influence at least three disciplines—fine art, literature, and rectilinear geometry. The topic of geometry led them, indirectly, to a debate on the house they were currently inhabiting, and whether its symmetrical façade and numerous formal touches—transoms, coffered ceilings, rococo molding—truly qualified it as an example of shingle-style Victorian architecture. Once or twice, in the subtlest of ways, Pendergast had inquired how, exactly, Constance was spending her days; each time, the question was put off with equal delicacy.

"Peculiar, isn't it," Constance said, rather abruptly.

"What is that, my dear?" Pendergast asked. The conversation had moved on to whether Campari or Aperol made for a nobler aperitif.

"The way the sun sets over the sea. At first, it seems to drop so languorously, one can barely observe its transit. But then—as it nears the horizon—it accelerates, as if pulled by some invisible elemental force."

"There's a scientific explanation for that," said Pendergast, sipping his Campari. "But I think I prefer your idea of the elemental force."

"Sunset is time for the appreciation of elemental forces, not talk of science."

Pendergast smiled slightly.

At that moment, his cell phone rang. He plucked it from the jacket of his suit pocket, examined the caller ID, which indicated nothing, then answered it. "Pendergast."

"Good," came the voice on the other end. "And you've answered your work phone: that will make things easier."

Pendergast recognized the voice as that of ADC Pickett. But it was not quite that man's normal voice: it sounded strained.

"I've just heard from our station in southern China. Specialist Quarles is dead."

For the briefest moment, Pendergast went totally still. Then he reached for his glass. "Give me the details."

"He fell from his suite at the Sofitel Foshan, in Guangdong Province. Chinese police and medical workers recovered the body and had already begun an investigation before Quarles's credentials, and his assignment, were spotted as active by Langley. By the time we reached out to the Chinese authorities and completed the necessary diplomatic dance, the autopsy was complete. We were lucky to get one of our own forensic specialists in for an examination before the body was cremated and returned to the States."

"And the findings?"

"The official Chinese verdict was death by blunt force trauma, consistent with a fall from the twentieth floor of a building. I'm sending you some encrypted images now." There was a brief pause. "Suicide was presumed. The autopsy was quite thorough, and our expert had a difficult time finding evidence to the contrary. Quarles fell from his room, all right. But..."

"Yes?"

"Our expert noticed something unusual: the man's esophagus was abraded."

"Abraded?"

"That was the word our medical examiner used in his report, yes."

"Will you send the report to me, please?"

"Just a moment." Another pause. "The Chinese M.E. brushed it off as esophageal perforation due to a preexisting—let's see—squamous cell carcinoma."

"Anything else?"

"There was no time. He did what he could before the Chinese cremated the remains—as is their usual damnable practice, covering up any hint of foul play that might befall foreigners in China."

"Do you have any images of the esophagus?"

"Sending it now."

During this exchange, Constance had risen from her chair and walked to the railing of the deck, aperitif in hand, and was looking west across the beach. The sun was now an orange ball of fire kissing the sea horizon. Pendergast decrypted the messages on his phone, then quickly scrolled through the photographs. Quarles was barely recognizable as a human being, let alone as the short, fussy man with the Eton haircut he'd met in the M.E.'s office in Fort Myers not so many days ago. That was a tall building. He scrolled forward to the U.S. doctor's report.

"It says here that both the mucosa and submucosa were involved, and that there was no indication of either eschar or debridement."

"Agent Pendergast, you're losing me with that medical terminology."

Pendergast swiped ahead to the final image—the single picture their doctor had been able to take of Quarles's esophagus.

"Traumatic injury or no, these are definitely not cancerous squamous cells," he said.

Pickett sighed audibly. "Dr. Pendergast speaks—"

"The expert from the FTG I sent to China earlier this week did *not* have advanced esophageal cancer. That much I can tell you for a fact."

"So what was it?"

"I'm saying exactly what our own medical expert is probably also implying, as diplomatically as possible under the circumstances. This damage to the esophagus wasn't caused by cancer or a fall. It was caused by full-thickness burns."

"Burns?"

"Third-degree, where tissue is destroyed down to the subcutaneous level."

This pause was longer. "And you're implying what, precisely?"

"That Specialist Quarles was tortured. A specially fitted gastroscope was inserted down his throat."

"Specially . . . fitted?"

"Yes. They can be purchased if one knows where. Medical instruments that aren't meant to heal but do the opposite. Gastroscopes can normally be fitted with lights, cameras, tiny scalpels for the taking of biopsies. But they can also be fitted with electric probes, cautery pens. A method of torture that leaves no visible exterior trace, only interior."

"Good Lord."

"Quarles called me three days ago. He said he thought he'd found the manufacturer of the shoes. It was a small company that furnished items to a limited list of clients—including a jobber that, fairly recently, had ordered three hundred pairs of our precise shoe."

"Anything else?"

"Yes. He said that there had been some unusual requests involved. He also said that he felt this was a sensitive order, and that learning more might present problems."

"And?"

"Sir, Quarles was as comfortable doing business in China as he was analyzing shoes and neckties in Huntsville. But he was not an agent, and his primary training was not in covert work. He thought he'd found the manufacturer and jobber. We wanted to identify the buyer, of course, but I told him to use his discretion, and that if he felt any danger, he should abandon the attempt and exfil the region immediately."

"Did you get the name of the manufacturer or jobber?"

"Neither. There was no reason for him to tell me more at that point—for security reasons, if nothing else."

"Security? It sounds to me like when you had this conversation, it was already too late."

"That has occurred to me as well."

"Has it also occurred to you that if they, whoever they are, went to such lengths . . . then Quarles probably gave them what they wanted to know?"

"Yes."

"He would have told them of our interest in who ordered the shoes, the name of his case agent. That is, *you*."

"The real question is: how did they know how close he was? Quarles and I took level one classified precautions."

"That is an important question. How do you want to proceed?" Pickett asked after a moment.

"I'd like to think about it overnight."

"Okay. I think it's safe to say this unfortunate development tells us one thing, at least: the people we're dealing with are sophisticated and have a surprisingly long reach. I'm warning you officially to watch your six. And tell Coldmoon to do the same."

"When I'm able to reach him, I will."

The phone went dead, and Pendergast slipped it back into his pocket. The sun had sunk below the horizon now, leaving behind it an afterglow of the purest cinnamon. Constance had taken her seat again. Pendergast had made no attempt to hide his end of the conversation from her.

She finished her drink, put it on a nearby glass table. "You lost somebody," she said.

"I'm afraid that's too kind a way of putting it. Because of my instructions, somebody was tortured—and killed."

Constance did not reply to this. Instead, she took his hand and they sat in silence as the light slowly faded.

"What was he, or she, like?" she asked at last.

"He was a courageous man who died in service." A grim look flitted across Pendergast's face. "One can offer no higher praise than that."

After another moment of silence, he turned toward Constance. "I should warn you this news is more than just tragic. It could mean we're in significant danger ourselves."

"Oh?" Constance's expression did not change. "In that case, there's something we had better do right away."

"What's that?"

"See about getting dinner. I'm famished."

They rose and—with Pendergast placing a partly affectionate, partly protective arm lightly around her waist—they made their way to the end of the porch, down the steps, and out toward the restaurants of Captiva Drive.

39

It's here," Smithback said.

Flaco turned off U.S. 41 onto Kellogg Street. Checking the road ahead, Smithback relaxed ever so slightly. It was as he'd remembered: Kellogg was one of those streets whose buildings, once large private residences, had been converted into law firms and doctors' suites, and cute office buildings with tasteful wooden signs advertising the businesses inside.

It was also, he noted grimly, just steps away from Lee Memorial Hospital.

Smithback had put everything he had, body and soul, into making sure this moment came to pass and thinking how he would pull it off. He'd suggested that a few pages of the manuscript be redrawn to improve their appearance. He'd requested a brush to put his hair into some kind of order. Anything, everything he could think of to keep Flaco—who, once Carlos returned, had clearly started to waffle— dreaming of Hollywood riches instead of Bighead's rage. As night came on and the hours crawled slowly by, Smithback had grown increasingly worried. What if Flaco lost his nerve? What if Carlos didn't go out after all? Every hour, he knew, was an hour closer to Bighead's promised return. *I'll come back and break you in.*

When Flaco silently brought him breakfast, Smith-back even resorted to demanding a portion of the imaginary profits. "Look," he said, "if El Acero really becomes big—a franchise, you know?—I think we'd better agree now on what my percentage will be. I mean, I'm the one putting you together with Bill. Right? Normally, an agent gets 15 percent. But I don't want to be greedy. I'll take 10 percent, maybe 12—we can talk about it once we get back here, after the meeting."

Flaco dropped the plate of tortillas and beans on the mattress, then turned and left without a word. Smithback didn't know if the images of wealth, his own implied willingness to return to captivity, Stockholm-style, had gotten through to the young gunman. He wasn't even sure Flaco had under-stood him.

The next two hours were the longest Smithback ever spent.

Then, suddenly, the door to his cell opened. Flaco was standing there. "We go now," he said.

"But my clothes, my face—"

"In the car, *ese*. Carlos back by noon. And you get no fucking money."

So the muscular goon *had* gone out. Smithback hurried after Flaco, down one cramped corridor and then another. After his time in the cell, it felt strange to walk more than a few steps at a time. Suddenly, Flaco opened a metal door and they stepped out into bright sunlight. Smithback stopped, momentarily blinded.

"*¡Date prisa!*" Flaco said in a low, urgent voice, pulling Smithback by the arm and flashing the butt of a pistol he'd shoved into his waistband.

They were in the alley where Smithback had initially been ambushed. Sitting outside the door was a '60s Impala coupe, butternut yellow. Smithback had seen countless vehicles like it when he'd worked the vice beat in Miami: a gangbanger's ride, chopped and shaved but still street legal. Inside, he found a paper bag with a brush, cheap sunglasses, a box of wet wipes, and a folded T-shirt with the logo of some *rock nacional* band. Flaco had pulled out onto the boulevard, then turned north on 41 while Smithback took off his filthy shirt, pulled on the tee he'd been given, and went about brushing the dirt from his pants and cleaning himself up as best he could. The mirror on the passenger visor had reflected a frightful visage: bloody, vomit-flecked, and dark with matted hair and several days' worth of stubble. There was nothing he could do about the beard, but a few wet wipes and the hairbrush restored his appearance to something resembling normalcy. The sunglasses and an artful combover did a good job of concealing his bruised face. By the time he'd finished his toilette, they were downtown and fast approaching Kellogg. Smithback put his shirt in the paper bag, rolled it up, and stuffed it between his feet just as they came up to the street. He'd had no time to steady himself for what was to come.

But what *was* to come? All his effort had been directed at this moment: getting downtown and away from that hellish prison. He hadn't known the layout of Fort Myers well enough to come up with any better plan: he'd just have to wing it. One thing he knew: he couldn't just jump out of the car and make a run for it. Flaco would gun him down without a second's hesitation, and then burn rubber back to the *tienda*, where he'd spend the time coming up with a satisfactory explanation for Smithback's demise. The only chance he had was spotting a passing cop. But as usual, there were none around when you needed one, and as the blocks went by, Smithback realized he was running out of time. About half a mile ahead, he could see the character of the neighborhood already changing: shabbier, less affluent, the well-kept buildings giving way to Florida cracker houses.

"Slow down," he told Flaco. Shit, he'd better do something, fast.

"Where is it, *cretino?*"

"It's close. Okay? These houses look familiar. I'll know it when I see it."

As Flaco slowed, Smithback scanned the surrounding buildings, doing his best to conceal a rising panic. The far side of the street, nearest Flaco, had already given way to larger commercial buildings. Many of the houses on Smithback's side still had tasteful shingles set out in front of them, but they, too, were becoming sprinkled with less attractive structures, and beyond their backyards was some kind of overgrown slough.

"There!" he cried, more out of desperation than anything else, pointing to a particularly large and ornate building whose signpost they were just approaching. Flaco drove past it, made a U-turn at the next intersection, then came back and stopped across the street from the structure.

Smithback was almost afraid to look at it. He'd had to choose one, and there had been no time to consider the relative merits of each building. It was no better than playing Russian roulette.

The signage was attractive, thank God, of lacquered

redwood with the lettering cut in bas-relief. Across the top of the sign, straddling its two posts, the main plaque read: THE FLAGLER BUILDING. Below it, screwed in vertical series between the redwood posts, was a series of names: John Kramer, DDS. Lauren Richards, DDS. Kenneth Sprague, DDM. Shirley Gupta, DDS. And then, at the bottom: ENDODONTICS.

Oh God, Smithback thought. A goddamned dentist's office. If he'd tried, he couldn't have chosen a worse place to stage his deception. He felt, more than saw, Flaco looking at him.

"Flagler Building?" Flaco said, his voice even more menacing and suspicious than usual.

"Of course. Haven't you read any of Bill's periodicals?" Smithback was suddenly beyond caring what he said: fuck this, he'd done his best and he was fresh out of ideas. "That's his company, Flagler Publications. He named it after his brother, who died young. Flagler Johnson."

"And those names? And what is Endo...endo..."

"Those are Bill's business partners. The artists. Look for yourself: John Kramer, Doctor of Drawing Studies. You really *haven't* read any of their graphic novels? 'Endodontics' is the name of the series. The superheroes all come from the planet Endodont."

"What about *la película*? The movie?"

"It comes out around Christmas." Maybe he should

just get out of the car and start running. Suicide by Flaco.

At the nadir of his despair, Flaco eased the car forward. At the next intersection, Flaco made another U-turn, then came back and pulled up in front of the Flagler Building.

"I go in with you," he said.

Smithback's heart accelerated. Flaco had just swallowed the most outrageous load of bullshit Smithback had ever flung. And it was only, he realized, because he'd stopped caring—and the fear had gone out of his voice.

"Bad idea." He pointed at Flaco's sleeved arms, the torn bandanna around his head. "We talked about this. Let me speak to Bill, show him the manuscript. After he's read it, your looks—*apariencia*—will be okay. But too early... You don't want to spook him." Smithback shook his head.

Flaco sat without moving for a moment. Then he took his right hand and reached across his own gut, toward the driver's door. At first, Smithback thought he was going for his gun. But instead, he reached into the door pocket, pulled out the manuscript, and handed it to Smithback.

"*¡Muévete!*" he said.

Smithback nodded. Then he opened his door, stuck a foot out. His sweaty shirt peeled away from the vinyl of the bucket seat.

He walked briskly toward the building, thinking fast. It was filled with dental practices. If he was lucky, that meant not just one receptionist, but several. And beyond them, several rooms, and maybe a back way out. Or places he could hide in. It all depended on Flaco staying in his car long enough for Smithback to call the cops.

Without looking back, he trotted up the steps and opened the door with as much élan as he could muster. As it closed behind him, he saw a floor of gleaming blond wood lead down a hallway ahead of him. There were open doors to the left and right. Immediately past the entrance was a staircase, the risers painted white. Flowers were set on a small table, along with several plastic holders for business cards.

Smithback raced up the stairs. There was another hallway here and, operating purely on instinct now, he followed it to a desk, behind which sat two women in white.

"Can I help you?" asked one, looking him up and down.

"May I use your phone?" he asked. "It's an emergency."

The women looked at each other. But even as they did, Smithback heard a burst of angry Spanish from downstairs and realized it was already too late. Flaco, ever suspicious, had entered the building himself.

On pure instinct, Smithback raced past the reception desk and through a partially open door beyond. He sprinted past a room in which a dentist was at work, drill whining. Another room contained a patient waiting in a reclining chair surrounded by hideous gleaming instruments. Ahead, a sign above a door read EXIT. Smithback charged through and rammed it open, finding himself in a back stairway as he heard another burst of Spanish, this one louder, longer, and angrier.

He descended to a landing, two steps at a time, down a second flight, pushed open the door the stairs dead-ended at, and found himself in the backyard of the building. He paused a second. On either side were similar structures. Ahead of him was the slough he'd noticed earlier: a dense, swampy tangle of mud, brook, and bracken that ran like a green labyrinth from right to left. Pushing himself away from the façade, he ran for it. As he did so, he heard a shot ring out behind him, followed by yelling and a scream. Reaching the edge of the slough, he practically dove into the jungle-like vegetation, rolling over once, then gaining his feet and running on into deep mud as the mazy branches of a mangrove swamp closed in overhead and the sunlight dimmed.

Suddenly, another shot rang out. Then another, whining past a few feet behind him, clipping twigs as it went. He realized he was still clutching the manuscript and immediately dropped it, pages fluttering into the muck. And then he heard the already distant Flaco, yelling at him in furious, frustrated rage: "Smithback! You a dead man. *¡Chinga tu madre!* You hear me, motherfucker? Dead! Dead! *Dead!*"

40

CHIEF P. B. PERELMAN, on his first day off since the case broke, heard his doorbell ring at noon, as he was sitting down to lunch. The ringing, once again, aroused a twist of pain for him, followed not by a flurry of eager barking, but only by silence. God, he mourned that dog every day. If only he'd closed the door properly on that fateful, awful morning...

He was surprised to find Pendergast standing on his porch. The man was so unpredictable, never turning up where you'd expect. His very capriciousness seemed to be a feature of his investigative methods.

"Lovely morning," said Perelman. "Can I offer you a cup of coffee?"

"No, thank you. I have an appointment with the commander, and I was hoping you might accompany me."

"Of course. Come in while I get ready." This was a bit strange.

Pendergast stepped into the entryway and waited while Perelman buckled on his belt and sidearm, then buttoned up and adjusted his shirt. Perelman disliked the commander and as a result always wanted to appear spit-and-polished when meeting him. Speaking of spit and polish, he noted the perfect gleam on Pendergast's shoes and checked his own.

"Just a moment."

He kept a shoe brush handy in the entryway for just this purpose, and he now pulled it out of its box and gave his shoes a swift brushing.

"What's the meeting about and, if you don't mind me asking, why do you need me?"

"I am bereft of my partner, Agent Coldmoon, who is down in Central America. Constance is out on some errand of which I am ignorant. As a result, I find myself in need of a witness. That would be you, Chief Perelman."

"A witness." He followed Pendergast out to the porch. To his surprise, a new, full-size Range Rover sat gleaming at the curb. "How so?"

"I believe our meeting with the commander might result in a small contretemps. He will be accompanied by his second, Lieutenant Darby. I, too, must have a second."

"Sounds like a duel," said Perelman with a laugh.

The laugh quickly died as he realized the man wasn't making a joke. There was a chill about him today that was quite unsettling.

Pendergast got into the driver's seat, while Perelman slid into the passenger seat.

Traffic was lighter than usual, and they sailed along the causeway and up to Fort Myers. It felt strange, somehow, to see Pendergast behind the wheel, but Perelman was very pleased with the plush interior of the vehicle. The parking lot was almost empty. Pendergast parked up close and they stepped out into the muggy air. Perelman noticed that, for the first time in his memory, Pendergast was carrying a briefcase.

The commander's door was closed, as usual, and when Pendergast knocked—at exactly 12:30—it was opened by Darby, who stepped aside in silence to let them in.

The commander rose. "Chief Perelman, this is a surprise. I was, however, hoping to have a private conversation with Agent Pendergast."

"Chief Perelman is standing in for my absent partner," said Pendergast. "You can speak in front of him as you would Agent Coldmoon."

"Well, fine. If that's the way you'd prefer it. As we get started here, I just have to warn you that what I have to say may not be things you wish others to hear, Agent Pendergast."

Pendergast said nothing and they took a seat.

Darby, Perelman noticed, sat at a chair beside Baugh like the lapdog he was. He even had a steno notebook in hand, ready to take notes.

"All right," Baugh rumbled. "Do you finally have the reports on those vessels?"

Pendergast opened his briefcase and pulled out a file, handing it over. "Unfortunately, nothing came of the searches. It appears the *Empire Carrier* was smuggling a cargo of Iranian caviar, and that's what was seen dumped in the satellite pictures. The other vessels proved even less interesting."

Commander Baugh took the file with a grunt and pushed it aside without looking at it. "Now I want to talk about this oceanographer you've been working with. Pamela Gladstone."

A chilling silence.

"I thought you'd take my gentle hint," the commander went on, "but it seems you chose to ignore it instead. I know all about it, so no more secrets. She and her crackpot ideas have no place in this investigation. I've already sent her notice of termination, and I've ordered a full accounting of her work, expenses, and results, such as they are. I've made it clear to her and her assistant that any further work in this regard will be considered interference, and I will yank her oceangoing research permits so fast her head will spin."

Silence.

"Now, what about your man in China? Anything happening there?"

"He was murdered."

"*What?* Murdered? How the hell did that happen and why wasn't I informed?"

"You were not informed because I'm growing increasingly concerned he was killed because of a mole in this investigation. Most likely on your staff."

"A mole? On *my* staff? That is an outrageous accusation! By God, Pendergast, this is a step too far. I hoped I wouldn't have to do this, but you give me no choice." He stood up, his face darkening. "I hereby terminate your involvement in this case—which, as commander of the task force, I am fully authorized to do. Pack your bags and get out. I'll be in touch with your superiors about your insubordination and obstruction—you can be sure of that."

Pendergast stood up as if to leave. Perelman was aghast. Was that it—he was just going to walk out, after getting himself kicked off the case?

But then he hesitated. "Before I take my leave," said Pendergast, "I wanted to express my sincerest condolences for your loss."

At this, Baugh exploded. "What the devil are you talking about?"

"I'm referring, of course, to the tragedy of having to put down your horse, Noble Nexus."

Perelman had never seen such a crimson color on

a human face as he now saw on Baugh's. The commander lowered his head and leaned over his desk, speaking in a whisper. "Get the hell out."

Pendergast didn't move. "Once upon a time, there was a man who purchased a lovely dressage horse. His name was Noble Nexus."

"Get—the *fuck*—out."

Pendergast stopped and said, in a voice that froze Perelman to the bone: "It is in your best interest, Commander, to hear my little fairy tale about the rider and his beautiful horse...and the tragedy that followed."

The commander fell into apoplectic silence.

"Noble Nexus was a Dutch Warmblood out of a famous lineage, bred and trained at Rocking Horse Farms in Georgetown, Kentucky. The rider purchased Noble Nexus for one hundred and twenty-five thousand dollars. The former owners were concerned about selling the horse to the rider, because they had watched him ride and weren't sure he was experienced enough to handle such a high-spirited animal. But good money is good money, and so they sold him the horse.

"The rider took the horse home to his little ranch in Palmdale, Florida, and began riding him in dressage competitions. The man, in truth, was not a good rider, but he compensated by having a highly trained horse with a strong desire to please. So, while the rider did not distinguish himself in these competitions, he did well enough. That gave our man the idea he was a far more talented dressage rider than he actually was. It also helped him qualify for the Florida Winter Equestrian Jubilee."

Perelman saw that Baugh looked almost paralyzed. His face had gone from red to palest white. Darby was sitting like a statue, still holding the steno pad and pen.

"At the jubilee, when his turn came, the man rode Noble Nexus into the dressage arena and began to perform. Noble Nexus was a marvelous horse, with spirit, beauty, and athleticism. He had a heart as big as the world, ready and willing to perform his very best. But his rider was nervous and unsure. In the arena, with all those people watching, Noble Nexus tried to understand what the rider wanted him to do, but the rider was sending him contradictory signals with the wrong leg pressure, the wrong touch, the wrong weighting. What was worse, to steady his nerves the man had taken a quick drink before the competition. Horses have an extremely keen sense of smell, and this new and ugly scent on his rider alarmed Noble Nexus. Things reached a crisis when the rider tried to get Noble Nexus to perform a difficult maneuver known as tempi changes, in which the horse changes lead in the middle of a canter, multiple times in a row."

At this Pendergast paused and tilted his head to examine Baugh with a cold eye.

"They started cantering around the arena, but Noble Nexus was confused and scared. When he didn't know what to do, the rider jabbed his spurs hard into his flanks. So Noble Nexus did what any normal horse would do: he threw his rider. In front of the entire stadium."

Another long pause.

"The rider was unhurt physically, just a little dusted up. But he was humiliated. This rider had a particular kind of personality: he was one of those men who are supremely sure of themselves, who rise in life from the ability to project absolute self-assurance to all those around them. A man who is never wrong, who has no self-reflection, a man to whom any mistake or problem must be someone else's fault. In short, he was a man who would go to any lengths to preserve his self-image. To such a man, getting thrown from a horse in front of ten thousand people could mean only one thing: the horse was at fault. More than that—the horse was *dangerous*. There was only one way the rider could prove to the world that it was the horse, and not he, who was to blame: Noble Nexus had to be put down."

Pendergast fell silent. Perelman felt horror creep up his spine.

Baugh spoke. "You're a sick man, Pendergast, if

you think this story is going to intimidate me. That *was* a dangerous horse, and I have the paperwork to prove it. A trainer certified it as dangerous, and a top-notch vet approved the certification and put it down. It was the only safe and humane thing to do, or other riders would have been put at risk."

Pendergast removed a document from his briefcase and laid it on the desk. "Here is an affidavit, sworn and notarized, from the trainer in question, stating that you bullied him, up to and including the threat of physical harm, into certifying the horse as dangerous. In the affidavit he details your intimidation and expresses his opinion that the horse was *not* dangerous and that the fault of being thrown was entirely yours. He also expresses his enormous regret at what he did and his desire to atone."

He slipped another piece of paper out of his briefcase.

"This is another sworn and notarized affidavit, from the veterinarian you engaged, who confesses to taking a five-thousand-dollar payment in order to approve the certification and put down the horse. He additionally says that you threatened to, quote, 'make sure his son would never find work as long as he lives' if the vet refused to cooperate. The son had just graduated from the U.S. Coast Guard Academy, which put that veterinarian very much in your power. And he, too, expresses enormous sorrow at the role he played in the killing of that beautiful animal."

Baugh had gone even paler. God only knew what he must be feeling. Perelman, for his part, felt sick to his stomach. The story reminded him of what he'd been forced to do to Sligo—something he would never get over as long as he lived.

A vast silence gathered in the room. Baugh seemed unable to speak.

"Commander," Pendergast said in a quiet voice. "Over the course of my career, I've dealt with many murderous and psychotic human beings. But I have rarely seen anything as abhorrent as this cold-blooded, deliberate murder of a trusting and innocent horse, merely to satisfy your inflated ego."

Finally, Baugh opened his mouth and managed to croak out: "What...are you going to do with those?"

"First, I will state my requirements. You will allow me to continue my investigation as I see fit, with your full cooperation. You will immediately rescind your termination of Dr. Gladstone's involvement in the case and issue her a letter of apology, along with a check for $101.25 to pay for the buoy Lieutenant Lickspittle—I mean Duran—intentionally damaged. You will have no further contact with Dr. Gladstone. You will maintain the compartmentalization that I have created so that the mole on your staff no longer has access to information on my activities. Pursuant to that, I will tell you nothing of my work...and *you* will not inquire."

The man's mouth worked a little before the phrase *all right* emerged.

"As for the affidavits, I will keep them in a safe place in case further problems arise."

He rose. Perelman did likewise: he couldn't wait to get the hell out of there. Pendergast had left the commander a quivering, heaving wreck.

Pendergast turned to Darby and said, in a suddenly loud voice: "Why, Lieutenant, you haven't taken any notes! Shame on you!"

And with that he strode out of the office, Perelman following. They got into the car. Perelman crawled rather than hoisted himself into the passenger seat, taking deep breaths. He had never seen a confrontation like this before—so cold, so efficient, and so devastating. "Man, you play *rough*," he finally said.

"It is not play," said Pendergast. And only then, he allowed a small smile to crease his austere face. "Let us find a place with fresh stone crabs. Cracked cold, with mustard sauce. I have worked up quite an appetite."

41

THE MORNING BUS from Acatán to the Mexican border was overloaded and stank of diesel fumes, and it had taken two hours to lurch and grind the twenty-five miles. At a sad border station it made a groaning stop, where everyone had to get off, show their papers to a Mexican border patrol agent, and get on another, but equally decrepit, bus that lumbered along the highway for another hour.

Finally, with a chuffing of brakes, the bus pulled into the town of La Gloria, Chiapas State, in southern Mexico. Coldmoon was the only one to exit, and no wonder, he thought as he looked around at the isolated town, with its limp palm trees and dust-caked bushes lining the dirt roadway. He slung his backpack over his shoulder as the bus pulled away. The driver had kindly let him off in front of Del Charro, at the outskirts of town, with its lone blinking neon light advertising Olmeca beer in the window, and the faint sound of *ranchera* music filtering out. He crossed the street and the parking lot outside the bar, almost empty at this time of day, and pushed open the door.

Inside, it was blessedly cool, and it took a moment for Coldmoon's eyes to adjust to the dimness. There was no one within except the bartender and a teenage boy sitting on a barrel at the far end of the bar.

Coldmoon sauntered over, took a seat at the bar.

"What would you like, señor?" the bartender asked in Spanish.

"Olmeca, please."

The bartender, a friendly-looking man with a colorful striped shirt and a cowboy hat, brought over the bottle. "Glass?"

"Just the bottle, thanks."

He put it down and Coldmoon took it up. "You wouldn't happen to be Señor Corvacho, would you?"

"I am."

This was encouraging. "I'm looking for a friend."

"And who might that be?"

"He calls himself El Monito."

At this Corvacho seemed to go still, and he said, just a little too quickly, "Never heard of him."

Coldmoon nodded. He took a sip of his beer—ice cold, surprisingly—while Corvacho made a show of wiping up the bar around him. Coldmoon could see the man had been deeply alarmed by the question and was trying to cover it up.

As he sipped the beer, Coldmoon considered what to do next. He could offer the man money, but he sensed somehow that would only frighten him more. Sometimes, he thought, the truth—or something close to it—worked better than an elaborate lie.

"I'm trying to find someone," Coldmoon said, "came over in December from San Miguel Acatán, part of a group heading north to the U.S. Martina Ixquiac." He took out a photo of her, given him by Ramona. "She disappeared and I'm trying to find out what happened to her."

Corvacho barely glanced at it. "Don't know anything about her."

Again, the answer came too quickly.

"Look, friend, I'm working for her family, who are worried about her. I'm just trying to find her. I really need your help."

"As I said, señor, I have never heard of this man, and I don't know anything about the group you are talking about." His voice shook from fear. "I'm sorry I can't help you." He finished up his nervous wiping and quickly disappeared into the back.

Christ, thought Coldmoon, *he's going to call El Monito now and warn him.*

But then, through the bar's window, he saw the bartender come around the corner of the bar and climb into an old pickup. He was going to warn him in person. And Coldmoon had no car, no way to follow. Coldmoon swore under his breath; El Monito was either going to make a run for it—or, just as likely, assemble a gang to return for a fight.

But as he watched, the truck didn't leave. The man, it seemed, was trying to start it. A moment later the bartender got out and slammed the truck door, and Coldmoon could hear him coming into the back room behind the bar and rummaging around— with the rattle and clink of tools.

Sensing an opportunity, Coldmoon slipped off the stool and quickly went outside into the parking lot. The truck was a single cab, nothing in the back, no way to hide unless he could hang on to the chassis underneath—which would be suicide on these pot-holed dirt roads. What to do? The bartender would be back out any moment. There was one thing: a long shot. He peered through the cab window and made a mental note of the exact mileage on the odometer.

Then he ducked into the bar just as the bartender came back out to the parking lot with a couple of tools in his hand. He threw open the hood, messed with the battery cable, slammed it, got back in, started the engine with a roar, and peeled out of the lot in a cloud of dust.

Coldmoon checked his watch. "Another beer," he said, signaling to the boy.

The boy shook his head. "Not old enough to serve beer."

"Right," said Coldmoon. "Sorry. Can you recommend a hotel?"

"There is only one, señor. Next to the plaza, the Sol y Sombra."

"Thank you."

Exactly thirty-two minutes later the bartender was back. He came in, red-faced and flustered. "You still here?"

Coldmoon gestured. "How much?"

"Fifty pesos."

He put some money on the bar and left. As he passed the truck, he noted the odometer again, did a quick mental subtraction. The truck had gone 18.4 kilometers. He also made note of the nearly bald tires with just a hint of zigzag tread left.

Bag in hand, Coldmoon walked the quarter mile into the center of town. A small plaza was flanked by an old blue-washed adobe church on one side and the hotel on the other. He was glad to see a taxi sitting in front of the hotel, windows rolled down, the driver napping inside.

He went into the hotel, booked a room, and carried his bag upstairs. It wasn't a bad room, spacious and sunny, with a bed, desk, and (thank God) A/C, which he turned on. The place also had a sluggish, intermittent semblance of Wi-Fi. He removed his iPad from the bag and loaded Google Maps, zeroing in on La Gloria. Fortunately, it was a village with not many roads radiating from it. There was a main road, Route 190, which passed by about five kilometers to the west. A dozen other roads led out from the town's small grid of streets. They were all dirt and almost all seemed to go to outlying farms or ranch houses.

Using an online tool, Coldmoon measured 9.2 kilometers from the Del Charro out each of those roads.

Bingo. There was one, and only one, that matched within half a kilometer, and that ended at a farmhouse precisely 9.2 kilometers from Del Charro.

No suspicious-looking convoy of armed men had passed through the square headed for the bar while he made these calculations. Apparently, El Monito was going to wait for trouble to come to him.

He went downstairs and exited through the lobby to the street. He tapped on the cab's window, rousing the driver.

"Are you available?"

"Of course, of course! Where do you want to go, señor?" asked the driver, sitting up and starting his car, astonished to have business.

"I'll tell you where to turn."

"All right."

"Start by taking a right at the end of the plaza."

He directed the cabdriver out of town, following

the route he had identified. It led westward into a range of low hills, past tiny farm plots and small cattle ranches.

"Where are we going, señor?" the driver asked, becoming nervous.

"I'm looking to buy land."

At one kilometer from the farmhouse in question, Coldmoon said, "I'll get out here."

"There's nothing here."

"There's land here."

By this time the driver was extremely nervous and trying not to show it. Coldmoon tipped him generously, got his business card, and arranged to be picked up at the same place in two hours' time. He wasn't sure if the driver would show up, but the man was probably frightened enough to do what he asked.

The cab pulled a U-turn and drove off. Coldmoon watched it go, and then he walked ahead and inspected the dusty road. There they were: fresh, almost bald tire prints with the faint zigzag.

Other than those prints—one set coming, another set going—there were no recent tire tracks visible.

He paused to think about how he was going to handle El Monito. He would certainly be armed. The man was a coyote, and they had a reputation for brutality equal to drug smugglers and gang members. And there might be—in fact probably were—several friends in the farmhouse. On top of all that, they'd be warned and on high alert. In short, he realized, he was about to do a completely stupid and dangerous thing.

He pondered this. He'd come a long way, the answers he wanted were in that farmhouse, and he was goddamned if he was going to walk away.

Locating his position on the iPad using Google Maps, he climbed a fence into a cornfield of dry stalks and began circling around to approach the house from an unexpected direction. The field offered excellent cover, and he was able to get within a hundred yards. He settled down to watch for a while, try to get a sense of how many people he would have to deal with. The farm was a small whitewashed building with a tin roof painted red, next to a sagging barn with holes in the roof and walls. An old Ford sat in the dirt parking area outside.

A half hour passed, and Coldmoon saw no sign of life. The house looked deserted, but with the car and the lack of recent tire tracks he was pretty sure at least one person was inside. He needed to view the house from another angle, preferably closer, where he could see into the windows.

Circling further, he came up behind the barn, which would provide cover for a closer approach. He emerged from the corn and sprinted to the back side of the barn, pressing himself against the wall and removing his Browning. Edging along, he came to a dirty window and peered inside. The barn was dark, flecks of sunlight dappling the interior through the holes in the roof and walls, and it appeared to be empty. Coldmoon edged farther around to the door and slipped inside. He crossed the length of the barn and paused next to a sliding door that opened toward the house.

The door was open and he peered around the corner. The house remained silent—but watchful. There was an open dirt expanse he would have to cross to get inside. Did he dare make a run for it? The odds were good he hadn't been seen. And even if he had, he would make a fast-moving target.

He broke cover and ran, dodging this way and that. The firing began almost immediately, wild shots kicking up dust on both sides of him. In a few seconds he had reached the back wall of the house and flattened himself against it. The firing had come from a window not five feet to his right.

Son of a bitch, now he was really screwed. He was probably outnumbered. All he had was his Browning versus their probable arsenal. Maybe he would get lucky and only the shooter would be inside.

"*Hola*, El Monito!" he called out.

Silence.

"I just want to talk!"

A voice came from the window—quavering and high. "I did everything you asked! For God's sake, leave me alone!"

This was unexpected. "I'm not going to hurt you, I promise."

"*¡Mira qué cabrón!* Hurt me? You want to *kill* me!"

While he was yelling, Coldmoon took the opportunity to slip around the edge of the house to the door.

"You can keep the money," the man shouted. "I don't want it! Just leave me alone!"

Coldmoon braced himself, then rammed his shoulder into the door. It burst open with a splintering noise and he rushed the man, who was crouching below the window. The man whipped the gun around, but he was in such a panic that he started firing even before he had aimed and Coldmoon body-slammed him, sending the gun flying. He kicked it aside and swung his Browning on the man, who was now sprawled on the floor.

"Don't!" the man cried, covering his head with his hands and drawing up his knees. "Please! Just tell me what you want me to do!"

Instead of the brutal coyote he expected to find, Coldmoon saw a small, skinny man with a wispy goatee, blubbering in fear.

"Are you El Monito?"

"Don't do it!"

"Pull yourself together. Is there anyone else in the house?"

The man shook his head.

"You're El Monito?"

A tentative nod.

"Okay, now do as I say. Stand up slowly, hands in view."

The man stood up, his thin arms held out. Coldmoon quickly searched him and removed a knife. "Okay, let's go into the kitchen. You first."

The man turned and they walked into the kitchen.

"Have a seat," said Coldmoon. He could smell burnt coffee. There was a pot on a woodstove. Damn, he could sure use a cup.

The man sat down, shaking in terror.

"Look. First of all, I'm not going to kill you."

The man said nothing.

"Second, we're going to need coffee. Two cups, please, and pour them nice and slow, keeping your hands in view. Okay?"

The man rose, took down two mugs from a wooden shelf, and poured out the coffee.

"Slide mine over here."

Coldmoon hoisted the mug, enjoyed the burnt aroma, and took a sip. He took another, bigger gulp, almost burning his mouth in his enthusiasm.

"All right," he said, putting the mug down. "You're

going to answer my questions completely and truth-fully. You understand?"

Another nod.

"Let's start by you telling me who you think I am and why you think I'm trying to kill you."

42

Two hours later, on his way to the airport, Coldmoon called Pendergast.

"Delighted to hear from you," came the smooth voice. Coldmoon, to his surprise, found it unexpectedly reassuring. "Have you made any progress?"

"A lot."

"Excellent."

"Martina Ixquiac was part of a large group of travelers headed for the United States. They left San Miguel Acatán in December. A local man guided them over the border into Mexico, where they met with a coyote, a fellow called El Monito—real name Alonzo Romero Iglesias. El Monito has been moving groups of people from southern Mexico into the U.S. for half a dozen years now. We just had quite a long talk, El Monito and me."

"What is his methodology?"

"I'll start by telling you how it *usually* works; Martina's group was handled differently."

"Very well." There was some kind of humming sound in the background, behind Pendergast's voice.

"Usually, he picks them up outside of La Gloria, in Chiapas State. It's where I am now, a little town about twenty miles from the Guatemalan border. He has vans and drivers, and he brings them north in a sort of caravan. There are certain Rurales and police he pays off to let him through the checkpoints. They go up through Oaxaca, bypass Mexico City, on through Durango, Hermosillo, and into Sonora— heading for the San Pedro River, which flows from Mexico into Arizona, just south of Palominas. That's where they bring them across. The Sonoran drug cartel controls that portion of the Mexican border, and charges a toll to the coyotes to bring people through—a thousand dollars a head. So our man has to pay off the cartel."

"How do they actually get across?"

"There's a fence along that stretch of border, but where the river flows there are only some steel tank traps that are easily climbed over. The area is heavily patrolled by ICE, but they have spotters on some hills on the Mexican side with powerful night-vision telescopes. They're able to track the coming and going of the ICE patrols. The group waits for hours, sometimes days, on the Mexican side before they find an opportunity to slip through."

"And once over?"

"El Monito takes them to a 'safe ranch' north of Palominas. There they wait before being allowed to continue on to wherever they want to go—Houston, Chicago, New York, LA. Most of them have a destination where there's family or friends. El Monito makes sure that only a few leave the safe ranch at a time, in ordinary-looking delivery vehicles or cars, so as not to arouse suspicion."

"But this isn't what happened with the group that included Martina Ixquiac."

"No, it isn't. That was special. Just after his previous trip, El Monito was contacted by an ICE official— at least someone claiming to be ICE. It scared the hell out of him that they knew who he was and how to contact him, but they told him they had a proposition. They needed to engineer a spectacular bust, something dramatic. It would not only help their careers, but also ease the difficult political climate. Or so they said. So they asked him to bring in an extra-large group so they could bust it. They would pay El Monito big money: fifty grand. The migrants would be nabbed on the U.S. side, before they reached the safety of the ranch. For fifty grand, El Monito couldn't resist.

"So: in order to get enough people to satisfy the

official, El Monito had to assemble three groups of twenty individuals each and consolidate them in Sonora. One of those groups he recruited in San Miguel, and the others in Huehuetenango. He brought them up, paid off the Sonora cartel, combined them at the border, and then brought them over—all sixty—at once. They were able to cross quickly, without any problem. At the time, El Monito figured this was part of an official plan. But it's possible that certain bad actors had instead arranged for a diversion that would draw off ICE.

"The bust was to happen where they had to cross Route 92 in Arizona. It was a moonless night, dark as a tomb, when El Monito and his two associates got the group over the border and up through the mesquite scrub. They waited along Route 92. As they were waiting, a bunch of truck headlights turned on and moments later the place was swarming with armed men in military fatigues. But something wasn't right. El Monito had a bad feeling, or so he says. These weren't ICE vehicles, but U.S. military trucks—with the logos and markings painted over. And it wasn't a normal kind of arrest either, making everyone lie down and that sort of thing. Instead, the soldiers surrounded them and just started loading them into the trucks as fast as possible. El Monito, who was in the rear driving the stragglers forward, saw them take his two associates away at gunpoint as well. So he took off back south. Some soldiers chased him, but he knows that country like the back of his hand and was able to escape and get back over the border."

"And then?"

"He was pursued into Mexico. That scared the hell out of him. These men were in military fatigues— not ICE—and they were looking for him. Not to pay him, but to kill him. He just barely escaped several times. They're determined, he says, and that's why he was hiding in a remote farmhouse outside La Gloria—where I found him."

"Still being hunted after five months?"

"Yes."

"And you believe his story?"

"I do. I was totally convinced. The guy was terrified, and when he found out I wasn't going to kill him, he just spilled his guts."

"You left him there?"

"He wouldn't come with me, and there's no way I could get him out of Mexico without his cooperation."

"It would be a setback if he were murdered. He's a vital witness."

"I realized that. I gave him almost all the rest of my money—ten thousand dollars—and told him to buy another car, get the hell away from La Gloria, and go to ground. He was very grateful."

"Agent Coldmoon, you've done outstanding work, and I thank you. How quickly can you return? This case is starting to present some unexpected developments. I am uneasy."

"I'm on my way to the airport in Tuxtla—I'll be back in Fort Myers by evening." In the silence that followed, he noticed the humming again, and now he recognized what it was: the sound of an automobile engine. "Hey. Are you in a car?"

"Yes."

"You mean, you're driving somewhere? Driving *yourself?*" Coldmoon had to laugh.

In lieu of an answer the line simply went dead.

43

PENDERGAST HAD ARRIVED suddenly and unexpectedly at the lab in the early afternoon. Gladstone was embarrassed that the A/C had once again failed and the lab was hot and stuffy, but it didn't seem to bother the FBI agent, who remained cool and dry in his linen suit. He hadn't even taken off his jacket. How did the man do it? Maybe he was part reptile. His eyes blinked infrequently enough, she thought, for it to be at least a possibility.

He wanted them to go once again through the drift models in exhaustive detail. Lam had launched into another incomprehensible explanation of chaos theory and imaginary space, but it amounted to the same thing: *nada*. The data from the buoy drop was beautiful, it had come in flawlessly, but plugging it into the models still resulted in nonsense. They were now over ten thousand dollars into CPU time on the supercomputer, with nothing to show for it.

"So there we are," Lam finished up, spreading his hands as the last drift analysis finished its run, the squiggly lines of simulated floating shoes tracing themselves from nowhere to nowhere. "Unless you'd like to apply that Ramanujan eleven-dimensional Matrix Attractor you're such an expert in."

Silence fell. Pendergast said nothing, his pale face impossible to read. He seemed quite a bit more on edge than usual—almost wary. His eyes, always busy in the slackest of times, never stopped in their movement. The noises of passing trucks roused his interest. Once or twice, he checked his phone— something she'd never seen him do before. Finally, Gladstone cleared her throat. "Now you see why we asked you to come by."

"I was planning on stopping by in any case. There is a matter, a possibly serious matter, that we need to prepare for."

Gladstone barely heard. "Everything you need to know is right there on that screen. There's really nothing to say. We've tried every imaginable varia- tion. Lam has been a workhorse, using branches of analysis I didn't even know existed to try to make the drift lines work out. But they simply don't." She paused. "I'm sorry we've wasted your money."

Pendergast thought a moment. Finally, his silvery eyes turned to her. "Failure is always useful."

"A nice thought. But personally? I think failure

sucks." Gladstone slumped down in her chair, trying to get comfortable. After so many hours, it was difficult.

"The question failure asks is: what don't we know that we don't know?"

"Whoa, man," Lam said. "That's deep."

Gladstone had to parse this for a moment. "How are we supposed to find out what we don't know? We've input every possible factor and still get nonsense."

"Except that you have not. There's a factor you haven't input—the factor that will explain this phenomenon. Because there *must* be an explanation. And the key is to find that factor."

She didn't blame the guy for being annoyed at throwing away money, but now he was starting to sound like Don Quixote. "We've racked our brains, honestly we have. We've run simulations with all the meteorological data available. Every single thing that might influence a current is in that model, even weather events over highly localized areas of the sea— isolated winds and thundershowers, for example."

"Could the meteorologists have missed something?"

Gladstone shook her head. "Not possible. They've got satellites, weather buoys, reports from ships—if a drop of rain falls into the ocean, they know it."

"Every single thing that might influence a current, you said." Pendergast frowned, and there was a long silence. "What about a land-based effect?"

"Like what?" Gladstone asked.

"Forgive the naiveté of the question, but could a storm on land affect ocean currents?"

"I don't see how."

"If it caused a flood, for example?"

Okay, now the guy was really reaching. "A flood from a river would inject a very small amount of extra water into the gulf, yes, but the effect would be minuscule. These Florida rivers are slow-moving and shallow. The effects would remain close to shore. Nothing that would push debris far enough out into the gulf to reach the Loop Current."

Pendergast nodded slowly. "And the garbage analysis? Are you sure there's nothing there?"

She sighed. "As I mentioned over the phone, what we could identify came from all over the gulf. There was no pattern to the samples we analyzed."

"Hold on," said Lam. "I just thought of something."

"What?" Gladstone said.

"You remember a few years back, when that developer up north was fined for illegally dredging the mouth of some river?"

Gladstone nodded.

"He dredged a long, straight channel that unexpectedly acted like a funnel when a big storm caused a surge of upstream water, shooting all the agricultural pollution out into the gulf, killing a bunch of fish and creating a dead zone. They fined him and made him redo the dredging into a wiggly pattern."

"Your point?"

"Well, maybe somebody else did the same thing more recently."

"Did what same thing?"

"Christ on a donkey." Lam sighed with impatience. "Dredged a channel that, in a flood of water from a storm upstream, would create dangerous currents in what should be a protected harbor. *And* push debris out into the Loop Current in the process."

Gladstone paused. It was such a far-fetched idea—especially that the force of such a flood could reach the Loop Current. But it wasn't like they had anything else to go on. And it might satisfy Pendergast. "The Army Corps of Engineers is in charge of coastal dredging. Wallace, pull up their enforcement website. Let's see if anyone's been fined recently."

Lam tapped away on the computer and they waited while the website loaded.

"Here's something."

Gladstone leaned over his shoulder. It seemed that not too long ago, a developer in Carrabelle had been fined for illegally dredging the Crooked River to his new marina. Ripped out a lot of mangroves in the process, too—a big no-no.

She felt Pendergast's presence behind her. "This

looks like the straight-dredging situation you spoke of," he said.

"Yes, but that's way the hell up in the Panhandle. I mean, this is really unlikely."

Pendergast stepped back. "If you please, bring up the analysis you prepared on the garbage."

Gladstone pulled it up on the computer, and sent a copy to the printer as well.

"There," said Pendergast, pulling sheets from the printer and pointing at the second one. "Two crab pot license tags from Carrabelle washed up with the feet."

Gladstone stared. She had dismissed those earlier, Carrabelle being so far away from any conceivable drift pattern. Besides, there were a dozen other license tags from all over the gulf, including from as far away as Texas and Louisiana. "Um, I'm not sure that's relevant."

"Perhaps, but recall the missing factor. Let us look at extreme weather events—*on land*. Specifically, did the Crooked River flood at the time period when the feet would have entered the water and that illegal dredging was still in effect?"

Lam grunted. "That's easily looked up." More gun-fire rapping of keys. Meteorological data and weather maps scrolled across the screen. "Whoa," he said. "Check that out. Massive thunderstorm over the Apalachicola National Forest on March 19—that's in the Crooked River watershed."

More tapping.

"And—yup—the river flooded. Took out a few piers, dragged some boats from their moorings. After that, they made the developer restore the river to its previous condition."

Gladstone felt her heart accelerate. This was amazing. Unlikely, unexpected, but amazing. "Wallace, plug into the model a bunch of simulated shoes being injected out of the mouth of Crooked River in a flood of that magnitude. Then let the simulation run freely and let's see where they go."

"Will do."

Lam began typing at a furious rate, and soon he had set it up. "Shall I run it? Gonna cost us more dough."

"I will cover it, naturally," said Pendergast.

Lam hit the execute button and they waited. These drift simulations ate up CPU time like it was peanut butter, but this one seemed particularly slow. Gladstone heard Lam curse under his breath.

The screen finally came to life, showing the Florida Gulf Coast. A nest of black lines—hundreds of simulated feet—arrowed out of the mouth of Crooked River into Saint George Sound, curled around Dog Island, got caught up in what looked like an eddy, circled way out into the gulf, got snagged by the Loop Current, swept down the coast... and converged on Captiva Island.

"*Holy jeez,*" breathed Lam.

Gladstone could hardly believe it. All of a sudden, her model had worked beautifully: all the squiggly lines coming out of Crooked River and twenty-five days later converging on Captiva Island.

"It appears," said Pendergast, "the feet weren't dumped at sea. They were flushed out of Crooked River in that flood. I believe we may have our factor." His eyes, still unusually restless, had been focusing on Lam. "Dr. Lam, you seemed frustrated with your computer just now. Is it operating unusually slowly?"

"Yeah, they must be running some big simulations over at the university. It's been like this for a day or two."

Pendergast went still. "A day or two?"

"Yes. I think. I didn't pay much attention at first."

"And you've noticed this on which systems, exactly?"

"All of them. At least, the ones tied into the university—which is almost everything."

"I see. Excuse me while I make a call." Pendergast slipped his cell phone out of his pocket, dialed a number, and turned away. He murmured quietly into the phone for a while. Then he turned back and handed it to Lam.

"What's up?" Lam asked.

"A computer expert in my employ, specializing in cybersecurity and cyberwarfare. His name is Mime.

He wishes to examine your system. I can assure you he is entirely trustworthy."

"Maybe. But *I'm* the computer expert around here." Even so, Lam took the phone with a puzzled expression. Gladstone watched as the person on the other end gave Lam detailed instructions, which he tapped onto the keyboard. It appeared that the anonymous person began controlling the computer remotely after a few moments, because suddenly Lam was no longer typing, just watching as his screen filled with windows dense with scrolling computer code. After ten long minutes, Lam handed the phone back to Pendergast, who spoke into it and then hung up.

"It seems your system has been hacked," Pendergast informed them as he replaced the phone in his pocket, along with the printout. "By an expert— most likely, someone with government or military expertise."

"What kind of a hack?"

"Mime called it a 'cocktail of zero-day exploits,' but the most pernicious actors were keyloggers attached to every input device."

"Son of a *bitch*," said Lam. "So some bastard has been keeping track of everything I type? Who the hell would want to steal a bunch of drift data?"

"Who, indeed?"

This was said in such an uncharacteristic tone of voice that Gladstone looked over at Pendergast.

The wariness she'd noticed earlier had turned into alarm. The FBI agent stared at both of them in turn. "I'm afraid," he said, "that the time has come for our departure."

"Departure?" Gladstone asked. "Where?"

"Away from here. And *right now*." Then, before she could react, he had taken her arm and hustled her out the door.

44

COLDMOON GRIPPED THE armrests while the plane once again rebounded in turbulence, the captain's calm voice reminding everyone to keep their seat belts fastened. Christ, he hated flying almost as much as boating. The only reasonable way to travel, he thought, was by foot or car—or horse. Everything else was bullshit.

Back on the rez, there had been a lot of horses wandering around, free for the borrowing. Most were a bit wild, unshod and half-crazy, leftovers from the days when horses were sacred to the Lakota. Now people kept them for no good reason beyond tradition and nostalgia. But Coldmoon and his friends, as a lot of kids did in those days, would occasionally rope a random horse, bridle and throw a blanket on him, and ride him somewhere—if they could stay on—as an alternative to hitchhiking or walking. There was one horse in particular Coldmoon was fond of—he called him Mop because of the massive mane of blond hair. He fed him oats from time to time, which made it easier to catch him by shaking the bucket, and he trimmed his splayed hooves and wormed him. He didn't know whom Mop belonged to, nobody did, but he wasn't a bad horse. Riding him was fun. You didn't get motion sick on a horse the way you did on a plane or boat, and you were in control, at least sort of. The idea of being thirty thousand feet up in a plane, strapped into a seat with nothing between you and the ground six miles down, where you were at the complete mercy of the pilots, and the air traffic controllers, *and* the mechanics who took care of the plane, *and* the engineers who designed it, *and* the weather, *and* bird strikes, *and* terrorists, and even to an extent the other passengers, freaked him out almost as much as the bottomless black water underneath a ship—where, with even the smallest boat, all it would take was one hole. And as boats got bigger and bigger they just had more systems that could break, or catch fire, or lose power and drift, or hit an iceberg, or fall to a rogue wave, or encounter Somali pirates, and then, boy, that's all she wrote...

Another rumble and shake abruptly brought Coldmoon out of these morbid thoughts as the plane passed through more turbulence. They were above the clouds, and great thunderheads rose all around like gigantic fairy towers of white. Clearly the pilots were trying to make their way around a stormy area, and it looked pretty bad, with some clouds flattening into an anvil shape, signifying serious thunderstorms.

Lovely.

He forced his mind back to the case. In his conversation with Pendergast, he had relayed all he'd learned from his trip to Guatemala and Mexico. It was becoming quite clear this case involved something as big as it was bizarre—backed by a powerful, well financed, and widespread organization. Who they were, and what they were up to, remained as crazy a mystery as before. A hundred and twelve feet, crudely chopped off by their owners, deep-frozen, and then set adrift at sea. Why? And how the hell did everything link up: from Guatemala, coyotes and secret border crossings, unexpected apprehensions, to hacked-off feet floating in the Gulf of Mexico? In a criminal investigation, one of the first questions you asked yourself was: who benefits from this crime? But how would anyone benefit from people chopping off their own feet? For what purpose except to free themselves from shackles in the most extreme possible way—but even that had been ruled out.

Another jolt, and the voice of the captain came over the system, announcing that, due to severe thunderstorms, the flight was being diverted from Fort

Myers to Tallahassee. There were the usual apologies while the passengers groaned and hissed.

Tallahassee. Where the hell was that in relation to Fort Myers? Coldmoon fished out the in-flight magazine and looked it up, then cursed under his breath. It was way up in the Panhandle, hundreds of miles to the north, a five-hour drive at least.

Another reason to hate flying, he thought.

45

"WHAT'S GOING ON?" Gladstone demanded as Pendergast ushered them out of the lab and into the parking lot. She noticed his piercing eyes casting about. "Are we in some sort of danger?"

Without answering, he unlocked his car: a new Range Rover, both sturdy and sleek. "Get in. Both of you."

She slid into the passenger seat while Lam got in the back. Pendergast started the engine and headed out of the lot, driving slowly.

"We're dealing," he said, "with a powerful organization. Through hacking your system, they now know that *we* know their location—somewhere up Crooked River. I have no doubt they're reacting to that information as we speak, which puts all of us in immediate danger. Both of you must go to ground."

"Why don't you call the FBI or the task force, get a team or something to protect us?"

"Because the investigation has been thoroughly penetrated. There's nobody we can trust. And there's also a time factor." Pendergast swiveled toward her. "I'm bringing you both to a bungalow in Corkscrew Swamp, south of here, where you'll be safe until further notice."

"What the hell?" Lam asked. "We're going in *there*?"

"Yes. For some time now, I've suspected we might be dealing with an adversary more formidable than anticipated. As time went on, I became increasingly convinced, just as I also grew more certain that our task force was leaking information—accidentally or otherwise. It was then I established a safe house in case things went awry; after all, you two are civilians, working at my request, and should not be exposed to danger. But it's now clear that you are. I realized neither how quickly the threat was accelerating . . . nor how breathtaking its scope had become. I can blame only myself for not treating it with greater seriousness—when it was still containable."

"Safe house? Containable? The hell with this." And Lam reached for the door handle. But just as he did, Pendergast gunned the supercharged engine, pressing his passengers back against the leather seats with the acceleration, running a red light as he headed south from Fort Myers on Route 41.

They blasted down 41 at speeds exceeding a hundred miles an hour as the sun sank toward the horizon in a blaze of orange and red thunderheads. It was one of those spectacular sunsets that looked like the end of the world. Gladstone had been frightened by Pendergast's pronouncements, but as they rocketed down the highway she wondered if it wasn't just an overreaction. He didn't seem like a dramatic sort of personality, but then again, she didn't really know him.

Before reaching Bonita Springs, Pendergast turned off the highway, and they proceeded east on an unmarked tar road that quickly left the developed areas behind, stretching like an arrow through yellow pine plantations, swamp, and cypress groves. Soon, in an orgy of blood-red clouds, the sun set and a purple twilight rose.

She noticed Pendergast accelerating still further and, glancing behind, saw a distant pair of headlights. Despite their speed, the lights appeared to be pacing them.

"You know there's a car following us," Lam said in undisguised alarm.

"Yes," Pendergast replied.

She felt a wave of panic. Christ, they were out in

the middle of nowhere. Worse, she saw Pendergast remove a massive gun from his suit and lay it on the seat next to him.

"Holy shit!" said Lam. "You really planning to use that?"

Pendergast said nothing.

How the hell had they been followed? How did anyone know where they were going? But then she heard a faint throb from above—and, a moment later, saw lights ahead. They looked stationary, blocking the road.

Even as she took notice of this, Pendergast was slowing down. Now he turned off his lights, and a moment later swung the Rover from the tar road onto a dirt lane that led away at a right angle. There was just enough twilight left in the air to see—barely—but once they were in the trees it was dark. The vehicle slammed through potholes, leaping and bucking. Gladstone had no idea how Pendergast could see where the hell he was going. The sound of throbbing rotors above increased, and through the treetops a chopper came into view, banking to the right and accelerating toward them.

"Undo your seat belts," Pendergast said.

She fumbled with the clasp, her heart pounding. In the backseat, she could hear Lam breathing loudly, hyperventilating.

"Get ready to exit. If we're still at speed, make sure to open your door completely, then jump away at an angle, tuck, and roll."

Pendergast veered off the lane onto what was little more than a track through a denser, tree-covered area. He gunned the big engine, and the Rover slewed through marshy bottoms and mud holes, once again in almost complete darkness. Now the chopper was almost on top of them, keeping pace. A brilliant beam of light stabbed through the tree cover, illuminating the area around with crazy, moving shadows.

A harsh electronic voice came from above. *"Stop your vehicle."*

Pendergast, if anything, accelerated, plunging into a low, swampy stretch, mud splattering against the windows.

"Stop or we'll fire."

Gladstone, terrified, crouched down, hands over her head.

The heavy vehicle abruptly swerved at the same time that a burst of gunfire sounded from above: a rapid *pop-pop-pop*. Gladstone screamed as the Rover sideswiped a tree. Another burst of gunfire, this time with a loud hammering sound in the rear of the vehicle, glass flying everywhere, leaves and branches shredding around them in the glaring light. In the backseat, Lam emitted a gargling scream.

Pendergast jammed on the brakes and the SUV slewed sideways to a stop. Gladstone turned back only to see Lam torn apart by gunfire, a sight so horrific that she froze. Pendergast seized her, throwing open the door and hauling her out. He turned and leaned back in, pausing briefly over Lam's mutilated body before grabbing her again and pulling her away from the scene. As he towed her into the brush, a muffled thump sounded behind as the Rover caught fire, flames leaping up even as the car settled, sizzling, into the muck. The forest lit up a lurid yellow.

Holding her hand, Pendergast pushed forward into a dense tangle of cypress trees. The chopper seemed to have lost them; its spotlight beam was swinging through the trees in a searching pattern.

Pendergast slowed, moving deliberately, still holding her hand as a warm rain began to fall: light at first, then getting heavier. The helicopter's spotlight was moving around in a more distant location and she had the sudden hope they had lost their pursuers completely. He led them into denser vegetation, the cypress trees giving way to a mangrove swamp cut by narrow, winding channels of water a foot deep. They continued as quietly as they could, wading through the watery maze. Gladstone forced away the image of Lam's body, making an intense effort to control her panic and focus on moving as quietly as possible.

At a cul-de-sac, Pendergast halted. He reached into the water and pulled up handfuls of mud with which he began coating himself, gesturing for her to do the same, in particular her blond hair. The muck smelled foul, fishy and rotten, but she complied, covering herself as thickly as she could manage. Then they turned and continued moving. But now, the thudding of the rotors was returning, the chopper widening its search pattern. No: it was hovering. Pendergast paused and they peered through the foliage. Men were roping down from the stationary chopper. In the downpour, they looked like aliens, with gray-green helmets sporting multiple stalklike goggles, and bulky body armor bristling with weapons.

Pendergast, gesturing for absolute quiet, turned and they headed away into deeper water, crouching low and pushing into the narrowest lanes among the mangroves, scrambling at last under a bundle of roots and wriggling themselves into a small pool within the densest vegetation. Pendergast leaned toward her and whispered, "Immerse yourself, just your head above water. Apply more mud."

She did as ordered, sinking into the warm water and smearing more foul mud over her head, even though the rain seemed to wash it off almost as quickly as she applied it.

Just as Gladstone began to think they might have evaded their pursuers, she saw flashlight beams cutting through the mangrove trunks. And then the lights vanished. She strained, trying to hear. Flickers of red, like fireflies, darted through the trees, and she heard a splashing sound of approaching men. She felt Pendergast's hand stiffen. He leaned to her, mouth at her ear. "Laser sights. Hold your breath. Under the water."

She took a deep breath and submerged herself in the dark, murky water. She held her breath until she could hold it no more, then tried to angle her face to expose as little as possible above the surface while she gulped in air. As she came up, brilliance flooded her eyes.

"Don't move!" cried a voice. "Raise your hands!"

She slowly rose and, a few moments later, Pendergast did likewise. Her eyes were dazzled by the sudden glare of spotlights, but could make out, backlit, half a dozen figures carrying heavy weapons.

"Come out!"

They worked their way out of the stand of mangroves. The men surrounded them. One searched Pendergast, taking his gun, a knife, other things from his person.

"Hands on head. *Move.*" The soldiers pushed them from behind and they proceeded out into the deluge. Ahead, in an island of sawgrass, the helicopter had eased down, whipping the grass into a frenzy.

"To the chopper."

With their hands on their heads, they waded out of the channel and toward the helicopter. As they approached, the cargo door opened and a woman appeared. She gazed at them for a moment, then said: "Mr. Pendergast. How unlovely to see you again."

46

IT WAS A DARK, quiet, rainy evening. The police barricades and bad weather had left Captiva Island feeling almost deserted. Turner Beach was still closed and the investigation had driven away most of the usual tourist traffic. A storm was rolling in.

North of Turner Beach, back from the water, sat the Mortlach House. Its whimsical Victorian lines stood against the dark sky. No lights gleamed in its tall windows, and no murmur of voices came from within. It stood among the sleeping dunes, and a curious no-man's-land of saltwort and sea grapes separated it from the sprawling waterfront properties that began farther to the north. The only sound was the regular susurrus of breakers along the beach, and the occasional car crossing Blind Pass Bridge.

And then a figure rose from an observation point tucked away in the dunes: the figure of a bearded man carrying a canvas duffel, moving with the utmost care. Wearing a lumpy gray raincoat, he was barely visible, approaching slowly, furtively, from the north, weaving a path through the dunes.

The man crossed the plot of wild grasses and reached the side of the Mortlach House unseen. He paused for a long moment, listening and watching, and then moved on.

On the northern side of the house, invisible beneath a stand of cabbage palms, a three-foot piece of high-density polyethylene—painted brown to resemble the surrounding soil—lay on the ground, abutting the structure and pitched at a slight angle away from it. Once he reached it, the man stopped again to listen. There was no noise other than the low crackle of the police scanner that had been left on the porch. It had been there for days now, on twenty-four/seven, with or without any human listener. If anything, its low white-noise hiss had proven useful to him. His long observation had established that the house was quiet. One man had left several days ago with luggage and the pale man had left in the morning. The girl was still in the house, her shadowy figure seen against the gauze curtains in an upstairs bedroom, reading a book.

The man knelt, grabbed hold of the thick HDPE plastic, and slowly moved the edge up to expose a hole. The material was waterproof and virtually indestructible, and he was able to swivel it sideways with relative ease. He slipped carefully down into the black hole that yawned beneath, then pulled the covering back into place overhead, precisely where it had been before he arrived.

The entire operation had been completed without noise of any kind.

Now, beneath ground level and sheltered from the rain, the man crouched. He was no longer visible to anyone: a stray passerby, a cop riding an ATV . . . or an occupant of the house itself. And yet, his heart was beating fast with anxiety. The meticulously planned successes, the many failures, all combined with long periods of brooding and fearful speculation to make this a moment of triumph mixed with the greatest apprehension. It was this apprehension, in fact, that had caused him to move up this final moment to early evening, instead of his usual nocturnal hours: he simply could not wait any longer. Besides, it was so gloomy it might just as well have been midnight— and in any case, he was no longer visible.

Ahead of him, a rude brick-lined declivity de- scended into the ground, stopping abruptly at the foundation wall of the house about six feet ahead. The walls of bricks were heavily covered by verdure and old spiderwebs, and the ground beneath him— actually steps, roughed out but never finished— was a combination of clay, sand, and brackish water seeping in from the improvised covering above. It was a messy, nasty-smelling tunnel, but he'd been here many times before and no longer noticed. It had originally been intended as a stairway up from a basement exit, but the door had never been cut in the stem walls of the house and the project had been abandoned decades before.

The soft hush of the surf was more a sensation than a sound down here. Slowly he relaxed, heart returning to its normal rhythm.

He made his way down the unfinished stone stairs until he smelled, more than saw, the foundation of the house an inch or two before him. On the far side of this wall was the basement.

He let the canvas bag slip to the damp ground, then eased it open and removed the tools of his trade: a small chisel; a rubber mallet; an ice pick; and a large filleting knife: long, cruel, and very sharp. There were others, such as a pair of brake spring pliers: normally reserved for automotive work, whose curved jaw tips resembled the fangs of a rattlesnake. Many of these tools had served him well in the hours leading up to this.

Others would be of use to him once he was inside.

After arraying his tools on the lowest step, he straightened up. Turning his attention again to the foundation wall of the house, he stretched out his fingers and ran them along the lower edge of the mucky surface until he found what he was looking for: the cake of mud that concealed his painstaking efforts. With his nails, he plucked the fragments away, catching them in his other hand and letting them drop soundlessly at his feet.

Mud removed, he took a tiny penlight from his equipment, turned it to its lowest setting, and let it travel along the newly exposed brickwork. It revealed a course of old blocks of a curious blue color, stretchers alternating with headers in the ancient masonry pattern known as Flemish bond. The mortar between the bricks had been almost completely removed along the length of three feet over a total of six courses, each directly above another. He had done this work with a chisel over many nights. Working as silently as possible had of course made the work take longer. But what awaited him on the far side of that wall—on the inside of the house—would make it all worthwhile.

The bricks above and below the section he'd worked on were the regular deep reddish color. He had intentionally chosen to work on the courses of Staffordshire blue brick—used to contain rising damp—because they were not load bearing. Nevertheless, he'd removed the mortar from between so many bricks that he'd decided to insert wooden shims to keep the wall from sagging. He'd cut the shims short so they would not show through his layer of mud, and the pliers would be necessary to pull them out. With the penlight, he carefully scrutinized the wall, wiping off mud here and there, using the edge of the chisel to pick out bits of remaining mortar, making sure everything was in readiness. Then he turned, put down the chisel, and picked up the pliers. He'd been waiting for this moment a long, long time.

Carefully, quietly, he used the pliers to pull out every other shim between the lowest two courses of bricks. Then, moving up a course, he pulled out alternating shims once again, even more carefully this time, making sure not to remove two shims from the same vertical section of brick face. Finally, he stepped back to survey his work. No sign of settling or movement. More quickly now, he removed alternating shims from the upper courses until he'd reached the sixth.

By his calculations, he had, over his nights of cautious toil, removed all but the final eighth inch of mortar from between the bricks. What remained deep within the courses—what would look, from inside the basement, like a normal brick wall—was, in reality, just an illusion of solidity. Only the night before, he'd removed the mortar from between the last few bricks, stealing away with it in the predawn hours and mixing it with beach sand, as usual, so it would not be noticed. Now that he'd removed the shims from between the damp-proofing bricks, all that remained was to knock out the remaining skin of mortar.

Using a tool he'd designed himself—a thin shaft of iron about two feet long with an angled rectangle of steel, sharpened on all sides, welded to its end— he pushed his way into the spaces between the bricks and, when he encountered resistance, gently prodded the last thin crust of mortar out through the crack formed on the far side. A faint sound echoed back through the opening—bits of old mortar falling to the basement floor—but it was barely louder than sand streaming through an hourglass. Now he moved the instrument along the lowest course of unsecured bricks, steadily pushing out the thin section of mortar at the other end as he went. It would be making a mess on the basement floor, of course, but the mortar was dry and he could deal with that later.

Once he'd finished with the first course, he used a prybar to pull the bricks away from the low foundation row beneath them. Carefully, silently, he stacked the bricks to one side of the unfinished stairway.

The second course went faster, and the third faster still. He put each brick aside until at last all the courses had been removed and six piles of bricks lay around him, outside the foundation, hidden—as he was—beneath the rain diffuser. Quickly, just in case the brickwork above the newly made opening began to sag, he removed a pair of portable steel load bars from his canvas bag, set them securely on bricks at either side of the base, then ratcheted them quietly up until they supported the upper edge of the hole.

The warm air of the basement, smelling of dust and old paper, washed over him. It was as if the house were slowly exhaling.

For a minute he crouched, motionless. At long last—after so many nights of secretive labor, unexpected delays, endless surveillance—his work was complete.

Almost complete. The most important part, the part he'd worked so hard for, lay ahead.

As he crouched, he listened. The house had remained completely still, oblivious to his labors. Now he exchanged the tools he'd been using for others: the ice pick; the rubber mallet; piano wire; a long, clear piece of tube. He pulled a 9-millimeter handgun out of the pack and stuffed it into his belt. He turned off his penlight, and the basement was plunged into almost complete darkness. He removed a Fenix 850 nm infrared flashlight. Lastly, he placed a third-generation white phosphor night-vision monocular on his head and adjusted the straps. And then, taking a deep breath, he switched on the flashlight, picked up his tools, and ducked inside.

He stepped carefully over the ragged line of mortar debris, then rose to his full height and looked around—slowly, slowly. It was now dark outside and the cellar was, of course, unlit. As he took in the features of the basement, he involuntarily expelled a deep, husky breath. There they were, repainted but unmistakable: the workbench; the storage alcove; the boiler...and the stairs leading up to the inhabited part of the house.

He realized that his heartbeat had accelerated during this penetration of the basement, and he waited another moment, allowing it to slow. As it did so, he looked around again—this time, with a single purpose. A tall, wide column, wavering slightly in the greenish shadows of the monocular, stood like a sentinel before him. Taking a firm grip on his tools, he took a step forward.

...And it was then that he felt a sylphlike limb slide up from behind his right shoulder, with a movement that was so smooth, so unexpected, he wondered briefly if he was dreaming. But there was nothing dreamlike about the way the arm suddenly tightened, viselike, beneath his jaw, or how a second arm darted in with snakelike rapidity, a short and terribly sharp blade in its hand, gleaming in his IR goggles for just an instant before pricking its point in the soft tissue above his Adam's apple.

Just when he was most confused and terrified, uncertain what was real and what was nightmare, the voice came: unmistakably feminine, but deep and strange, with an undertone of feral yet somehow courtly menace.

"Good evening, Mr. Wilkinson. Before you react in any way, allow me to offer you a choice. If you drop the gun, and then follow it with your flashlight and that ridiculous helmet, I will take my knife from your neck. If you resist, I will sever the four extrinsic muscles of your tongue, in preparation for piercing your carotid artery. It's your choice, but in your situation I would recommend the former option. You will find it much easier to explain all of this to me with your hyoglossus intact."

47

CONSTANCE CAME LIGHTLY up the basement steps, then quietly but firmly shut and locked the heavy door behind her. The kitchen, like the rest of the house, was dim, the lights off. This was as Constance had left it hours before, setting the trap—but now the gloomy emptiness made her fretful. A part of her had hoped Pendergast would have returned—she felt not so different from a cat, eager to display the prize evidence of her hunting skills to her owner.

She walked over to the sink, ran the water, took the soap from its porcelain dish, and washed her hands and forearms with great care. She took the stiletto from her hidden pocket, slid it open, and gingerly washed its razor-sharp blade with equal attention. Then, drying hands and weapon alike, she took off the black mourning cloak she'd worn during her long vigils in the basement, folded it with a few expert strokes, and laid it carefully over the back of a chair. Beneath she wore an Arc'teryx covert sweater of thin gray fleece with matching leggings: not her usual choice of apparel, but the combination allowed for quick, unrestricted movement while providing excellent concealment—and the basement had been damp and surprisingly chilly.

She paused to listen for a moment. The only sounds were the rain, the police radio—random bursts of low squawking—and the muffled cries emerging from the basement. Giving those as little attention as she'd given the radio, she stepped into the butler's pantry, filled a small cut-glass tumbler with ice, poured in a generous splash of Lillet, quartered a key lime, and dropped a segment into the glass, then wiped her hands on the nearby bar towel. She moved back into the kitchen and pushed the door open onto the back porch. She was curious to see the point of ingress the man had used and wondered how she'd managed to miss it earlier. But first, she would relax for a few moments, in the calming dark.

The cool, humid breeze coming off the gulf and the sound of the rain on the porch roof were as welcoming as they were relaxing. The beach was empty, and the large houses to her right were dark and asleep. The police scanner sat on a round table of white-painted wicker, and she moved down to a rocking chair at the far end of the porch so as to be away from it.

Now that she had caught the "ghost," her thoughts turned to her absent guardian—and to the unresolved and never-discussed nature of their relationship. His suggestion that they spend a week on a luxurious island with no name, in the wake of wrapping up the Brokenhearts case, had awakened hopes that she had long since suppressed. But then ADC Pickett, like a cruel Mercury, had appeared—just long enough to take Pendergast away, leaving her to her own devices, consumed with memories of what had been, and what might have been.

Can you love me the way I need you to? Then you've answered your own question.

She had quickly followed him here to Sanibel, eager to help—until the grisly details of the case, sharpening as they did her own dreadful memories, forced her to beg off. She had found another mystery to occupy her time, and had kept herself away from the details of Pendergast's case—especially avoiding that blond female oceanographer with whom he spent so much time. For the same reason she disliked even the scanner. It, like Coldmoon, reminded her of the case that had torn Pendergast away from their island. And so, perversely, she refused to turn it off.

She put down her glass, untouched. This was

petulance. It was beneath her. The fact was, the time she'd spent in recent days, living so near the shore—nearer even than the time she and Pendergast had spent at Exmouth, Massachusetts—had dulled her fierce childhood aversion to the sound of salt water. Her own little case, the mystery of the Mortlach House, was solved. Perhaps her place should have been at Pendergast's side: helping move his case forward, suggesting ideas, doing more of the research she was so good at...and watching his back. Allowing her own feelings to obscure this duty was weak.

Her train of thought was interrupted by the scanner. Normally, she had no difficulty ignoring it. But now it had grown unusually active.

...burned remains of a late-model Range Rover...Route 41, along a swampy preserve on the outskirts of Estero Bay...one unidentified male, young, in the rear seat, shot multiple times and burned...no other individuals in the immediate area...evidence of struggle...

Instantly, Constance leapt to her feet. Range Rover? Aloysius had recently acquired just such a vehicle. The oceanographer's assistant—Lam—was about twenty-four. Was this Pendergast's car? She listened intently as the dispatcher went on to say the license plate had melted in the fire and no identification papers could be found in the car.

...Reported by airboat fisherman...heard automatic weapons fire, helicopters...distant flames...possible abduction...all units please report, all units....

She pulled out her phone and dialed Pendergast's number, but it rolled over immediately to voice mail. She tried a second number with the same result.

Crossing the porch, she grabbed the radio scanner and studied its controls, wishing she'd paid more attention when Coldmoon had first shown her the damn thing. How did one transmit? Could one even transmit? She turned a dial, then another, succeeding only in changing the frequency and cutting off the babel of voices. In a panic, she spun the dial back and listened, but it was the same information: nothing new, no ID on car or victim. In sudden fury, she threw the radio from the porch, where it shattered upon the stone walkway below.

Coldmoon was, she believed, on his way back from Mexico. Pendergast's location was unknown. *Possible abduction...*

She had to do something.

She checked: the stiletto was already in her pocket. She needed nothing else for the moment—except an Uber.

Just as she had ordered a ride, her cell phone rang. The number was blocked—was it Pendergast? Her heart turned over in her breast.

She answered it. "Hello?"

"Who is this?" a voice demanded.

"I was contemplating the same question."

"I'm Roger Smithback. Reporter for the *Miami Herald*. I'm trying to reach Agent Pendergast."

Roger Smithback—Constance recalled Aloysius mentioning his role in the Brokenhearts investigation more than once. "How did you get this number?"

"Don't ask me. I just kept calling Pendergast's private line—the one he gave me. I have information for him."

Pendergast had several cell numbers. There was one number in particular, used only when they were working together, that would roll over to her phone on the second repeated call.

She almost hung up—she had no time to talk. But this reporter might know something.

"This is Constance Greene," she said. "What's your information?"

"Constance Greene," Smithback repeated. "Oh, sure, you're the—" Abruptly, he stopped. "Listen. You work closely with Pendergast, right? That's as much as he ever told me. You're part of his inner circle."

"Get to the point, please."

"I've been, like, locked up for days, about to have my ass...about to be killed at any moment. I need to talk to him: you see, the gang, the tattoo—"

"Mr. Smithback, if you have information, give it to me *without* the circumlocutions."

"Okay. Right." Smithback was panting slightly, as if winded. "I was looking for a story on those feet washing ashore. I got my hands on a tattoo from one of them. It looked gang related. So I started asking around. Ended up asking the wrong person—and got kidnapped by the local gang honcho, Bighead. Jesus, what a piece of work—"

"Keep to the point." She looked at her watch. Where was that bloody driver?

"Okay. So these drug dealers were all pissed off about some big drug shipment that had gone missing. A reward was being offered, heads were going to roll if the shipment wasn't recovered. It was being brought in by some smugglers hidden with a group of migrants coming over the border. They all got picked up unexpectedly and taken away in trucks. Government trucks, identical, numbers painted over...like military."

"Go on." Constance continued listening as she

pulled back the curtain and glanced out the window. A pair of headlights was approaching along Captiva Drive.

"Some old rummy told them this story about a convoy seen going into Tate's Hole, or Tate's Hall, I didn't quite catch it..."

Constance watched, listened. The headlights slowed.

"...West, past Johnson's Fork, he said. Ten-wheelers, payloads covered in canvas. With these weird drumlike things bolted in front of the driver. Sounded like they matched the trucks carrying the migrants. Pendergast needs to know all this, okay? You'll tell him? And be sure to remind him he owes me. You got that?"

The headlights stopped in front of the Mortlach House.

"I have to go." She had no idea what the significance of this information was, but nevertheless filed it away in her head.

"Where is he, by the way?" Smithback asked.

Constance hung up and ran out to the waiting car. The muffled complaints from the basement, which had died down somewhat, increased again at the sound of her footsteps.

He'll survive, Constance thought as she climbed into the idling SUV.

"Lady, if you don't mind me saying, the destination

you put out by Estero Bay is in the middle of nowhere."

"When we're on the road in the vicinity, I'll tell you where to stop."

She saw the driver frown in the rearview mirror. "You can't say where, exactly? That's a long empty road."

"It's where the police are going to be."

48

WELCOME TO TALLAHASSEE International Airport," sounded the voice of the flight attendant over the intercom. "Once again, we apologize for this weather-related diversion, and we'll make every effort to—"

The rest of the chief attendant's announcement was drowned out by the clamor of people pulling out cell phones, jumping up and opening the overhead bins, struggling with their roller bags, and pushing and shoving each other. Coldmoon just sat morosely, letting his change in fortune settle in. He'd signed in his handgun at the LEO checkpoint before boarding, and after five hours in the cramped seat it felt like a lead weight, hanging from his shoulder beneath the jacket. Fucking Tallahassee. By rights, they should be landing in Fort Myers, but now he had hours of driving through a storm to look forward to.

His gloomy reverie was interrupted by a vibration

in his jeans—and not the kind he appreciated. His phone, muted but not switched off, was ringing. That would probably be Pendergast.

He pulled out the phone. A 212 area code—a New York number he didn't recognize. It probably *was* Pendergast, ready to put Pickett on the line to applaud him. Great—sloppy seconds were his favorite kind of congratulations.

This was probably just a figment of his foul mood. He'd know soon enough. Lifting the phone to his ear, he said: "Special Agent Coldmoon."

"Agent Coldmoon," came a feminine voice, "it's—" The rest was drowned out by what sounded like a wind tunnel.

"What?" he said. "Who is this?"

He heard the same voice uttering a command to shut the window, and suddenly the wind tunnel died away. "Lady, I can't see a thing through the windshield," came a plaintive voice.

"You can open it again in a moment."

Now Coldmoon recognized the voice. It was Constance Greene, speaking to what seemed to be a driver.

"Constance?" he said.

"Yes. I've been trying to reach you for the last quarter of an hour."

"I just landed now. Tallahassee—they had to divert because of this storm. What's up? Where are you?"

"Never mind. Have you heard from Pendergast?" There was an urgency in her voice.

There was a brief commotion on the other end of the line. "Like I said," Coldmoon heard the driver tell Constance, "Estero Bay runs almost all the way to Bonita Springs. You gotta tell me where to turn off."

"As I told you: where the police are going to be!" Then, speaking to Coldmoon again: "Did he say where he was going next? What he planned to do?"

"No. Why?"

"Because I think he's been abducted."

Coldmoon, who'd been getting ready to join the queue leaving the plane, froze. "What?" This sounded crazy.

"I heard it on your police scanner. They found the burned remains of a Range Rover similar to the one he was driving. A witness mentioned helicopters, automatic weapons, some kind of firefight. A dead man was found in the rear seat, burned."

Holy shit. Coldmoon was on his feet and in the aisle now, heading for the exit. "Anything else?"

"I got a call from Roger Smithback, the journalist. He spoke of a large shipment of missing drugs, apparently stolen along with some migrants abducted at the U.S. border in Arizona. It's somehow connected to the feet."

"Wait. Did you say migrants *abducted* at the border?"

"Yes. In trucks."

"*Trucks?* What kind of trucks?"

"A convoy of government trucks, identical, their numbers painted over. Ten-wheelers. Covered in canvas. Drums bolted in front of the driver."

This matched the story he'd heard from El Monito—matched it exactly.

Coldmoon left the gate and began making his way toward the main terminal. "Those drums are air cleaners, mounted over the left front fenders. We're talking M813 troop transports, most likely equipped with side racks, troop seats, and tarpaulins. Drug gangs don't use those—the U.S. Army does. Did he say where they were going?"

"Just a moment." The phone was muffled briefly; then Coldmoon could hear Constance talking to the driver. "Over there. See the flickering orange light, just below the horizon? Head that way, as quickly as you can."

"Lady, there's no road, and I don't have pontoons. Oh, jeez, now there's red and blue lights coming on, too—looks like your cops."

Coldmoon could hear sirens passing.

"Keep driving until you find the turnoff."

"But my car—"

"I'll *purchase* your car." And then, Constance was back with Coldmoon. "I need to go."

Coldmoon said, "Are you sure the Rover was Pendergast's?"

"I'll call you back when I know more." And then the phone went silent, leaving Coldmoon standing there, looking at it, in the middle of the arrivals section of Tallahassee International Airport.

49

MARK MACREADY, ACTUARY by profession and currently between jobs, had never liked his wife's idea that he use his new Lincoln Navigator and become a driver for Uber, as a way to make ends meet during this rough patch. He liked it a whole lot less right now, driving in the rain on a gravel road, through swamps and stands of pine trees at fifty miles an hour, heading—as far as he could tell—directly toward the bay.

"Go faster," said the crazy woman in the seat behind him.

Even though it meant increasing the chances of a head-on collision with some tree, Macready complied. He knew that reasoning with this passenger from hell was useless at best, and at worst encouraged threats. She'd already agreed to pay him $1,000 extra for this ride, tossing a crumpled mass of hundred-dollar bills into the front seat. That money, which he needed dearly, was the only reason he hadn't ended the trip prematurely.

A savage bump, then the scrape of a branch along his window. "That's going to leave a scratch," he said, easing off on the accelerator.

"Maintain speed."

Another bump, this one almost bottoming out the suspension, and then suddenly the trees fell away and, through the steady rain, Macready could see there was open marshland ahead of them. They were closer to whatever was going on than he'd realized; police lights were striping the vegetation less than half a mile away. If it weren't for the dark night, he'd stick out like a sore thumb.

"Here. Stop," came the low voice from behind him.

Thank the Lord. Macready did so with a strong sense of relief.

"Thank you, Mr. Macready, for what I realize was not quite the trip you expected," the young woman said. "Now I'm going to ask you to turn off your engine and remain here until I return. It might be fifteen minutes; it might be longer—I can't be certain."

She opened the door, filling the big SUV with the sound of thrashing rain. Ignoring it, she slipped out. A moment later, she knocked on his window. Macready lowered it halfway.

"By the way: if you're thinking of stranding me

here, I'd strongly advise against it. I'm not one to forget ill treatment."

He swallowed. "I'll be here," he replied.

He turned off the engine. *Shit*. Was this for real? He watched as the woman began moving away, her gray warm-up suit quickly lost in the wind and rain. Macready closed his window, then settled in disconsolately to wait.

Constance stayed low, using the surrounding vegetation for cover as she approached the scene of police activity. She paused and could hear the distant crackle of radios and the murmurs of conversation. Bright torches lanced here and there through the soggy darkness, and one stationary light threw a bright pool of yellow onto an area just to the south.

She began moving forward again. The area was marshy bottomland, riddled with muddy holes. Activity around the scene of the crime seemed subdued. A bolt of lightning split the sky, with the crash of thunder.

She came to a place in the swampy ground where she could see a group of people had recently passed, with crushed vegetation, broken branches, and muddy footprints filled with water, all headed away from the scene. These must be the abductors. Following the trail, she came to an open area, the grass flattened in a spiral pattern and in the center, and two parallel marks that were evidently from helicopter landing gear. If Pendergast had been abducted, this was where it had happened. She looked around carefully, but could see no shell casings, no splashes of blood, no sign of struggle or violence.

She turned and followed the confusion of footprints back to a point where they neared the crime scene. Lights blazed through the pouring rain, illuminating a gutted Range Rover, half-sunk in the muck, surrounded by tape. The closest officer was standing barely twenty feet from her, drenched to the skin, shining his light around in an apathetic display of searching. Moving away from him, she circled and approached the back of the wrecked car through heavy vegetation. She knelt and crept under the crime scene tape. The rear end of the car was badly burned: scorch marks licked all the way to the front passenger door. The Rover was not torched completely—the driver's seat and engine compartment were intact, and retardant foam covered the windows, now slowly being washed away by the rain. Four police officers stood on the other side of the car, just outside the tape. They seemed to be waiting.

Constance paused, assessing the situation. Then she crept closer to the passenger side of the vehicle. She could see that the metal had been punctured by large-caliber bullets, the holes running in a neatly stitched line. The panoramic roof was a gaping mouth of glass. Stealing closer, staying low and remaining in the shadow, she approached the rear door. It was ajar, and she quickly slipped in.

The interior smelled of melted plastic, burnt wiring, scorched leather and flesh. She caught her breath as she noticed a human being, hair and clothes burned off, teeth clenched shut in a lipless smile, limbs drawn up in the strange manner of the burned. The bullet holes in the ceiling, dripping with rain, and the remains of pooled blood that had boiled away around his feet told the story of his demise. The corpse was unrecognizable, but she noticed the distinctive red sneakers on the body's feet, the only part that hadn't burned. Aloysius had mentioned those to her with amusement while discussing the postdoc working with the oceanographer: The body must be that of Wallace Lam, the technician.

Her heart froze. Despite the evidence, a part of her hadn't quite accepted the idea that this could be Pendergast's car. It seemed unlikely that anyone could successfully abduct him. But here was proof. She gingerly lowered herself onto the rear seat next to the body, the charred leather crackling.

She took a moment to think. The huddle of cops was not more than twenty feet away, but within the vehicle she was shielded from view and nobody seemed inclined to look closely. The foam and smoke on the windows also helped obscure the interior.

The body explained why the police were just standing around: they must be waiting for an M.E., an ambulance, and a CSI and forensic evidence team to process the site before they could move the car and body.

If Lam had been sitting in the rear seat, and Pendergast had been driving, it meant Lam's boss, Pamela Gladstone, would have been in the front passenger seat. In all likelihood, Pendergast had not been kidnapped alone: the oceanographer had been taken as well.

From behind, she heard the distant whoop of sirens: the rest of the cavalry was arriving. She didn't have much time.

But she didn't leave. Pendergast had led his pursuers on a chase that had ended here. Why the chase, the sudden flight? It seemed clear Pendergast had discovered something that forced the hand of whoever was behind this—and provoked a massive reaction. Whatever he'd found must have been of great importance.

Knowing he was being chased, in possession of vital information, he might have left a message with that information. That message would be somewhere in the car. The more she thought about it, the more she was certain. But there was no telling how long it would take the cops and forensic teams to find it.

She crouched in the dark interior, thinking. The car

had been on fire. He couldn't leave a scribbled note just lying inside somewhere: it would either burn up or be found by his kidnappers. He would have to place the message someplace where the fire couldn't reach it, but where he knew it would eventually be found. And he'd had mere seconds.

Loud voices, suddenly near, forced her to duck down and remain motionless. They moved a little farther away, blending with the approaching sirens. Headlights stabbed through the scorched windows. Keeping low, Constance leaned forward and popped the glove compartment. Nothing. The cup holders and console compartment were empty. She lifted the front floor mats but found nothing underneath.

The problem was, with the car on fire, all these things could have burned up. So what place *inside the car* was most likely to survive a fire?

Constance glanced around the backseat, but it was thoroughly burned, the seats charred down to the springs.

Her gaze settled on Lam. She took in his burned clothes; the seared remains of hair; his teeth, still strangely white, clenched against the heat...

There was the faintest of hesitations. And then, in a single swift movement, Constance slipped the stiletto from her pocket, forced it between Lam's teeth, and twisted.

For a moment, nothing happened. And then, with

an unpleasant cracking noise, Lam's teeth—brittle from the heat—gave way and the jaw came loose. She reached in and there it was: something hard and small, pushed deep into the throat. She withdrew it: a tiny test tube, stoppered with a rubber plug.

Now more flashing lights came into view behind her, and she could hear slamming doors. Vaguely, through the blurry windows, she made out a forensic team. Constance shoved the tube into the pocket of her leggings. Then she reached out, put her cool hand on the corpse's withered fingers. "Thank you, Dr. Lam," she murmured. The phrase *Lipsbury pinfold* came unbidden into her mind, and she was distantly surprised by the fact she could entertain such an obscure allusion at a time like this. The young scientist, in death, had provided the safest, if unlikeliest, place to protect a small article from fire, where it was certain to be found—eventually.

Constance glanced left and right, took a deep breath, and slid sideways and low out the open rear door. She dropped to her knees and crawled back under the police tape and into the thick vegetation.

Mark Macready, watching the distant proceedings with increasing alarm, almost had a heart attack when—with no notice whatsoever—the woman, soaking wet, muddy, and stinking of soot and smoke, slipped back into his rear seat.

"You may now leave, Mr. Macready," she said, her breathing fast. "The quicker, the better."

He stared at her in the rearview mirror.

"*Now*, if you please," she said.

Not until they had reached Highway 41 and were speeding northward did Constance dip into her pocket and pull out the miniature test tube. Examining it in the courtesy light, she saw it contained a rolled-up fragment of paper. She upended the test tube and let the paper fall into her palm. Opening it carefully, she found it was part of a computer printout, apparently a list of place-names. One of them had been hastily circled:

(CROOKED RIVER)

50

MOMENTS AFTER SHE restoppered the note, her phone rang.

"It's Coldmoon," came the voice when she answered. "I've been waiting for your call. What the hell's going on——?"

Constance interrupted. "Aloysius *was* abducted. They ambushed his car in the swamplands south of Fort Myers, along with that oceanographer Gladstone and her assistant, Dr. Lam; shot the car full of holes; killed and burned Lam——and took Aloysius and Gladstone."

A brief silence. "Any idea where they're taking him?"

"He left a clue. Two words: Crooked River."

"Crooked River. Let me check that." A moment later he said, "It's a river up in the Panhandle, near the town of Carrabelle."

She could hear the grinding of an engine in the background. "Where are you?"

"I'm getting onto a shuttle. Crooked River—what the hell's there?"

"There's something else. That reporter Smithback—recall him?—heard talk among his captors of a convoy of trucks."

"Yeah. The M813s."

"He overheard a tip that a convoy matching this description had been seen near a place called Tate's Hole, or perhaps Tate's Hall."

"Tate's Hole... Wait, I'm looking at a Google map of the Crooked River now... Son of a bitch, it's Tate's *Hell!* Tate's Hell State Forest—up the Crooked River. It's right here. What else did that reporter say?"

Sitting in the backseat of the Uber, Constance tried to recall the exact words. "He said... Johnson's Fork. The trucks were seen turning into Tate's Hell, west, past Johnson's Fork."

More background noises, Coldmoon murmuring to someone. Then he got back on. "I don't see any 'Johnson's Fork' on the map. The crazy river twists all over the place, but there's no Johnson's Fork."

Constance called up Tate's Hell on her own cell phone. It appeared to be endless swampy forest, through which the Crooked River flowed.

"Got it!" Coldmoon said triumphantly. "Johnson's Fork."

"Where?"

"Ten miles past Carrabelle to the north, just beyond Bucketmouth Crossing."

Constance peered at her screen again. She found Bucketmouth Crossing—literally a mere crossing of two small roads—but beyond that she saw no named places, just another twisty fork in the river, this one shaped like a dangling sausage.

"I still don't see it," she said.

"Trust me—it's that fork to the west. Look, I'm going mute; I've got to rent a car. Hold on."

Constance looked at her cell phone map but could see nothing in that expanse of swampy forest—as one would expect—with a few old logging roads and some docks along the river.

"Back on," said Coldmoon. "Waiting in a line. I've got a few more minutes."

Constance continued scrolling through Google Maps, looking for something, anything, in that forest.

"Hey," Coldmoon said. "See that big flat-roofed building next to the river? About fifteen miles northeast up the river from Carrabelle. It's the only big building in that whole region." He covered the phone again, spoke to someone else. She heard him say "four-wheel drive."

Constance found it. It was a compound of some kind in a clearing, surrounded by a wall with gates and a few docks and warehouses on the riverbank.

"What is it?" she asked. "A factory? Looks abandoned."

"Says here a sugarcane processing plant. Or it was. Bonita Sugar. Went out of business years ago."

Constance searched the web. "Here's something. Yes, you're right. The plant was using a banned chemical for sugar processing, substituting cheaper sodium hydroxide for calcium hydroxide. The state shut it down in 1967."

There was a silence on the other end of the phone. Her driver now spoke. "Okay, here we are, lady. Back at the house."

She looked up, startled. They were in the driveway, the Mortlach House looming up again. The driver had turned around. "Lady?"

"I'm getting out," she said.

She closed the door, and the car took off with a spray of sand. "Agent Coldmoon?"

Now his voice returned, excited. "You *did* say sodium hydroxide—right?"

"Right."

"I was just looking through this list of trace chemicals found on the feet. Sodium hydroxide was a chemical found on *both* the amputated feet and shoes."

Constance looked at the satellite view on her phone.

The plant itself seemed old enough—but on closer inspection, she was able to make out what appeared to be freshly cleared areas around the building, and a new surrounding wall.

"That's it," she said. "That's where they were taken."

"Damn right," Coldmoon said.

Over the phone, she heard the sound of a slamming door.

"So where are you, Agent Coldmoon?" she asked.

"I'm getting in my rental now."

"Forget the car. Get a helicopter."

"Not possible, not on such short notice. My GPS says I'm only an hour and a half away by car."

"Call your FBI contacts and get one."

"Look, nothing's flying in this weather. And if I call the FBI, you know what's going to happen? They do everything by the book, including launching a Critical Incidence Response Group assault. Six hours to authorize and plan it, six hours to equip and brief the guys, and then they go in big. That will get my partner killed for sure."

"Your partner? My *guardian*. So we do this together—now."

"We? There's no 'we' in this scenario."

"But there must be. You'll fail if you go in alone."

She heard Coldmoon take a deep breath. "You've got to be crazy. You—come with me?"

"Of course."

"That's not going to happen. Do I really have to go over the reasons why? First, you're five hours south by car. Second, there's a big storm coming and all flights are grounded. Third, you're a civilian with no business being on a mission like this."

Constance felt herself consumed with a growing rage. "Going in by yourself is madness! You've got to wait for me. If you refuse to arrange for my transport, then I'll simply arrange for it myself—"

"Absolutely not. Now, *inila yaki ye.* End of conversation."

Suddenly, Constance felt all her emotions—her fury, anxiety, self-recrimination—gather together, targeting themselves with white heat at this truculent voice on the phone. "If you go in there without me...one way or another, you're going to regret it—regret it severely."

There was a silence on the other end of the line. And then, the call disconnected with an audible click.

Constance stared at the dead phone. Then she looked up again. She needed to get there, now. But the Uber driver was long gone—he'd never return for her. It was a five-hour drive, at least—and the airports were closed.

But Pendergast was up there, held captive, his life in danger. There had to be a way to get up there. *There had to be a way.*

She waited in the dark driveway for the white heat of her anger to dissipate. But it refused to do so.

She took in a deep breath; let it out; drew in another. And then—suddenly—she raised her face to the night and let out a terrible, unearthly, unending scream of sheer feral frustration.

51

CHIEF PERELMAN DROVE past Buck Key, half-drowned and completely disgusted. He'd planned on spending the last ninety minutes in his study, warm and dry, trying to master Doc Watson's break from the '72 recording of "Way Downtown." Instead, he'd been roused from his house and sent out into the rain because some idiot tourist decided this would be the perfect weather to take a dip off Redfish Pass. By the time a hastily assembled rescue squad had located the youth, hauled him ashore, pumped the salt water out of his lungs, and finished explaining to him the difference between one-digit and two-digit IQs, Perelman didn't want to play the guitar or do anything else but go back home, wring himself dry, and crawl into bed. Tropical storms were a fact of life on the barrier islands, and Perelman was used to dealing with them. But he'd had more than his fill of bullshit lately, with all the extra hours and bureaucratic wranglings dealing with the task force. This little stunt by a jackass from Skokie was one too many.

He crossed Blind Pass Bridge to Captiva Island, following Sanibel Captiva Road. On the trip out, he'd heard some noise over the police radio about a wrecked vehicle, shooting, and homicide reported near Estero Bay, but that was far out of his jurisdiction. Besides, whatever investigation had been required was probably done and dusted by now. Still, as he'd driven back from Captiva there'd been cross-chatter over the radio. And then, suddenly, he heard:

> ...Homicide victim in rear of vehicle positively identified as Wallace Lam of Jacksonville...

Lam. That was the name of the postdoc assisting that cute scientist—the oceanographer, he recalled, whom Pendergast had been working with. And the vehicle, the dispatcher reported, was a Range Rover. Christ, Pendergast had leased one of those. Why the hell hadn't they run the plate? But that question was almost immediately answered by the report that the rear of the vehicle had burned, leaving the plate illegible, with no identifying papers inside.

Perelman pulled his vehicle to the side to do a three-point turn and get the hell to the scene of the homicide. But just as he was backing up, he heard a sound over the steady rain. It was unmistakable: the whining scream of a boat engine being revved past redline, followed by a loud thumping noise. A pause, then the racket started up again: a wild revving of twin boat engines, and then a shuddering *whump*.

He jammed on the brakes and peered into the darkness. The sound was coming from the small communal marina just beyond the road, where he housed his boat.

What fresh hell was this?

He stepped on the gas, but instead of heading for the causeway, he skidded around and went down the sandy lane that led to the marina. He left his headlights on as he jumped out.

In the glow of the headlights, he saw something astonishing. The shrieking engines were, as he'd feared, those of his own boat. The water was churning up around the vessel into a froth so thick it almost looked like lather. There was a lone figure at the wheel, unidentifiable in the downpour. As Perelman watched, the figure pushed both throttles forward. But with the stern still cleated to the pier, the boat only shot forward about half a dozen feet before running into a brace of pilings with a shuddering thump. Without turning, the figure violently thrust the throttles into reverse and repeated the process, this time ramming its stern. The bowline was loose and flapping in the water, but constrained at the stern, his boat was like an enraged bronco in a bucking chute. Perelman watched in mixed horror and anger as he saw his beautiful—if never quite finished—vessel getting beaten to hell. It was a miracle the props hadn't sheared off already.

He raced down the dock to the boat and jumped in, grabbing the throttles and shouldering the figure aside. He pulled the throttles into neutral and centered the wheel. "Hey!" he yelled. "Just what the hell do you think—!"

Abruptly, he stopped. The figure before him—rain-soaked, rivulets of mud dripping off fabric and skin alike—was Pendergast's ward, Constance Greene. The haute couture he'd seen her wearing so casually before had been replaced by tactical clothing, and she was soaking wet, covered with mud, her hair a wild dripping tangle. Only her violet eyes, and the unsettling expression on her face—mixed detachment and violence—convinced Perelman this was the same young woman who had stepped out of a limousine just days before, reminding him of the forgotten actress Olive Thomas.

"Chief Perelman." She nodded. "Good evening."

The calmness with which she greeted him was unexpected. "What the hell are you doing to my boat?" he asked angrily.

"I'm glad you're here. I need you to take me

somewhere. I don't seem to be able to operate this thing properly."

Although this exchange had been brief, it had already taken on such a fantastical quality that Perelman found his anger draining away. "What are you talking about?"

"Aloysius has been abducted."

"Aloysius—who?"

"Agent Pendergast."

The report over the police radio. Okay, now he was beginning to understand.

"He was fleeing in his car, only to be ambushed and fired on. Dr. Lam was killed and they took Aloysius and Gladstone."

"Taken—where?"

"The old Bonita sugar plant on Crooked River—north of Carrabelle."

"And how do you know this?"

She took a deep breath. "It would take too long to explain."

"But you want to use my boat to go there."

"Is there any other means of transportation, under the circumstances?"

"But...that's two hundred and fifty miles across the gulf!"

She took a step closer to him. "They found out the truth and were kidnapped. They'll die, or worse... unless we save them."

"God, if this is true . . . we need to call in the cavalry."

"*No!*" For a brief moment, Constance's eyes blazed with such intensity Perelman shrank back. "Maybe you already know that the task force has been compromised by a mole. Any word of an operation and they'll kill him immediately—you know that. You also know how these things work: even if we ignore the mole, your 'cavalry' will take perhaps ten or twelve hours simply to assemble. So you see, it's up to us to get there—and rescue him ourselves."

Perelman stared at her, his mind working fast. She was right on many levels. Baugh wasn't the man for this job, and he himself had definitely begun to smell a rat. If he called in Pickett, well, they would put together an assault—by the book. But taking the boat?

"This is crazy," he said.

A beat, and then Constance suddenly lashed out. With the speed of a striking snake, she unsnapped the Glock from his belt, pulled the weapon out, and shifted it from her left hand to her right as she stepped back. Perelman had never seen a human being move so fast. He was still blinking in disbelief as she aimed the gun, racking the slide. A bullet clattered to the floor of the cockpit.

Constance raised the Glock toward him. For a moment, nobody spoke.

"You just wasted a bullet," Perelman said.

Constance held the gun steady. "I didn't think a village constable favoring a pancake holster would walk the streets with a round already chambered."

There was a long silence, broken by nothing but the rain and the idling engines. Perelman held out his hand for the gun and, after a hesitation, Constance lowered it and gave it back. "Shooting you won't get me to Crooked River."

Perelman holstered the gun. "If Commander Baugh and the cavalry can't save Pendergast, how can we?"

Constance said nothing for a moment, seeming to withdraw into herself. Then she looked at him again. "To paraphrase Sun Tzu: 'Know yourself and you shall win every battle.'"

Perelman sighed. "Somehow I don't think Sun Tzu quite applies."

"We're wasting time. Either you help me or you don't. Because if Pendergast dies, so will I—one way or the other. You and I both know this boat is the fastest way to get to Crooked River."

The silence that followed this was shorter. "Shit," Perelman said. "All right, take a seat next to the helm and let's go."

Constance took a seat. He checked the bilge pumps and glanced into the cabin to make sure it wasn't leaking water from the previous manhandling, then uncleated the stern line and took a seat at the wheel.

"Hold on tight," he told her. "Boats don't have seat belts. The sea is calm right now, just rain, but a storm is coming and we may be in for a hell of a ride before this is over." And with that he put the starboard motor in reverse, gave it a shot of gas, maneuvered away from the dock with a little port forward, and then—when they were clear—pushed both throttles ahead, accelerating toward the mouth of the channel and the open water beyond.

52

THE CHOPPER THUDDED low over the dark ocean, the glow of the instrument panel providing the only light. Gladstone was sitting on the flight deck, cuffed back to back with Pendergast, bound with additional leg cuffs and zip ties. The numb horror of what had just happened was beginning to wear off, and her analytical mind was starting to wake up again. The brutality of what had been done to Lam terrified and sickened her, but equally frightening was the organization, the numbers, and the quiet professionalism. These were not a bunch of common criminals. With their insignia-stripped camo uniforms, whitewall haircuts, automatic weapons, and terse communications, they felt like military.

There was only one possibility that made sense: somehow, their investigation had cut too close to the bone—and triggered a massive response.

But the apparent leader of this team, the woman

who had greeted Pendergast so sarcastically, was something quite different. She, too, had an air of discipline and precision about her, but it was at odds with her aristocratic face, mane of rich mahogany hair, brown eyes, and civilian dress. The others were kitted out in body armor, helmets, night-vision gear, and assault weaponry: all she had was a string of pearls.

Who in God's name would wear a string of pearls on a mission like this?

Pendergast was uncommunicative even in normal times, but he hadn't spoken a word since the capture. She couldn't see his face and she wondered what the hell he was thinking. She tried to steel herself for the worst. It seemed unlikely they were going to get out of this thing alive. These people were deadly serious, they were ruthless, and they seemed to be involved in secret work that—at the very least—included the mutilation of over a hundred people. She was no closer to understanding that brutal fact than ever.

The chopper banked, and she could see they were just reaching land again, as the scattered lights of a coastal town passed by. They headed inland, away from the lights, into a vast, stormy darkness.

53

As HE PULLED out of the car rental lot at the Tallahassee airport, Special Agent Coldmoon resisted the urge to stomp on the accelerator. He knew where he wanted to go, but he didn't know how to get there, and he needed to take a moment to map his route and—just as important—organize his thoughts. He stopped in a sandy turnout just beyond the airport and took out his cell phone, firing up Google Maps again and zeroing in on the location of the old sugarcane processing plant. It stood about a quarter mile from the banks of the Crooked River, in the middle of a large, uninhabited area with the crazy name of Tate's Hell State Forest.

It was a straight shot to the coastal town of Carrabelle, an hour and fifteen minutes away. From there, he'd have to turn north on Highway 67, skirting the edge of Tate's Hell, and find a way in. But there didn't appear to be any marked roads into the forest, beyond what looked like a few old tracks, overgrown and probably closed off. Presumably they had led to moonshine stills or something else he'd rather not know about. He could also see the extensive out-line of the sugar plant, with what looked like two perimeter fences and a gate. But it was hard to tell where the road passing through the gate originated. He was just going to have to wing it.

With the jeep still idling, he reached back and unzipped his traveling bag. He pulled out the marine "butt pack" in woodland green camo he'd prepared for the trip to Guatemala, his FBI radio, Ka-Bar knife, and a pair of cuffs. Working fast, he yanked off his jacket, checked his Browning, found it clean, and reholstered it. He slipped two additional magazines into the knapsack, along with the knife, cuffs, water bottle, parachute cord, flashlight, binocs, and a rain shell. On second thought, he removed the cuffs—unnecessary weight.

The place was likely to be fenced and gated. Damn, if only he had wire or bolt cutters. He felt his heart racing as he thought about what might be happening to his partner—assuming he was still alive. But he tried to reassure himself by focusing on Pendergast's resourcefulness. The man had as many lives as a cat: he'd seen it for himself.

He lowered the windows, breathing deeply of the muggy air, trying to clear his head. A storm was coming for sure, but he hoped to make good time before it hit.

If you go in there without me, you're going to regret it—regret it severely. Constance's words, spoken with conviction, still rang in his head. Was that a threat? It sure sounded like one. Coldmoon had heard a million threats in his life...but this one, he sensed in his bones, wasn't idle at all. That outrageous bitch would carry it out—he knew she would.

Those thoughts were for later; right now, he had to focus on one thing: saving his partner. Leaving the radio on the seat next to him, ready to call off any cops who tried to pull him over, he gunned the engine, spinning the wheels in the gravel as he rejoined the road. He picked up speed, accelerating steadily, the wind roaring in the open window. The map said an hour and fifteen to Carrabelle, but he had to do better. The only problem was that the Jeep, designed for off-road travel, wasn't nearly as fast as he liked. He was able to push it up to about a hundred, but at least the traffic on Route 319 south was light and he could maintain that speed in the fast lane.

The land on either side of the road was flat and featureless. Lightning flickered on the distant northern horizon behind him. Within forty minutes, making good time, he bypassed Carrabelle, blew past a gigantic prison, and merged onto Highway 67. This was an even lonelier road, a straight-as-an-arrow two-lane highway running through a scrubby area of abandoned slash pine plantations, interspersed with cypress swamps. The sky was now covered with dark clouds and the wind was picking up, the trees on either side of the road thrashing and swaying.

He passed a weather-beaten sign indicating he was entering Tate's Hell State Forest. And hell was exactly what it looked like—swampy, dense, and unsettlingly dark. In another ten miles he would have to start looking for a road going west into the forest, toward the old sugar plant. He slowed down, passing a couple of logging roads blocked with berms and dense brush. Finally, he came to what appeared to be a better-maintained road, heading off at right angles to Highway 67. It, too, was blocked—this time by a metal pipe gate, too heavy to ram through, with a barbed wire fence running on either side. He stopped and, shining his headlights down the old road, examined the ground. It was covered with weeds, but it nevertheless looked drivable. And it was headed in the direction he wanted.

He got out and walked along the barbed wire fence to a spot where the trees were spaced wide enough for him to drive through. He returned to the Jeep, put it in four-wheel drive, eased it down the highway shoulder, and then put the hammer down. The car hit the fence, which sprang apart with a satisfying twang. He maneuvered the Jeep through the trees until he reached the road. It ran in a broad curve into the dark forest.

He stopped to check his GPS. He only had one bar and felt pretty sure he was going to lose that, too, so he took screenshots of the Google Maps images showing the web of old logging roads leading in the direction of the sugar plant and stored them for future reference.

As he drove on, the road became a nightmare, gullied by rain, with loose rocks, potholes, and stretches of weeds taller than his Jeep's hood. He drove as fast as he dared, hardly able to see where the road went, half-blinded by the glare of his own headlights reflecting off the wall of weeds in front of him. A few times he almost got caught in muddy spots, but thanks to the Jeep he bulled his way through even the worst muck holes. Growing up on the rez, Coldmoon had experienced his share of horrendous dirt roads, and he had an innate sense of how to handle them. It wasn't that different from driving in fresh snow. The number one rule was to keep going, never stopping or easing up, powering through.

The abandoned slash pine plantations soon gave way to a swamp of cypress trees with knobby trunks and feathery branches. As expected, he lost his GPS, but he continued navigating using the screenshots, estimating his position with dead reckoning and keeping his cell phone's compass always pointed west.

Where logging roads crossed or divided, he tried to take the better one, but he sometimes found the roads completely washed out and was forced to backtrack. And then, quite unexpectedly, he came out on a freshly graded road—one with recent tire tracks. It was well hidden beneath tall, arching cypresses. This was it, he felt sure—the road to whatever had taken the place of the old sugar plant. He turned onto it, heart pounding; then stopped, killed his headlights, and stepped out to reconnoiter. Far off, where the road headed, he could see a faint glow in the night sky, reflecting off the gathering storm clouds. He estimated it was four miles ahead.

That was where they had taken his partner.

Getting back in the car, he proceeded slowly, keeping his headlights off, holding his flashlight out the window to illuminate his way. Gradually the glow brightened until a smattering of lights could be seen rising above the treetops. He stopped and took out his binoculars. It looked like a prison: a single concrete tower with roaming klieg lights, behind which sat a low industrial structure, maybe three stories high, punctuated with the yellow squares of windows. Next to the tower was a central cube of a building, brightly lit. That, he thought, must be the heart of the operation, situated as it was in the center of the complex. Coldmoon felt his guts constrict to think of his partner in there. *The bastards.*

Feeling his anger rise, he reminded himself once again to focus. This was a large complex and there would be a lot of people in there, alert, armed, and well protected. The place had the definite smell of government about it. Once again, he was glad he had not followed his first impulse to call Pickett. Aside from the time it would take to organize an assault, even using a Critical Incident Response Group, there was no telling where the information might be transmitted—and the still unidentified mole had done enough harm already.

He continued on and turned off the flashlight: the glow from the facility provided enough light to see ahead. That, of course, meant they could probably see him. He felt certain that at some point there would be a manned checkpoint in the road, with a gate and a fence.

He'd better ditch the Jeep.

He eased the vehicle to the edge of the road. There was really no place to hide it, except by sinking it. He hesitated just a moment. Then he rolled down all the windows and left the driver's side door open; then, shifting into four low, he drove it hard into the water and muck beyond the shoulder, gunning the engine to get as much inertia as possible. As it finally got stuck and began to sink, he hoisted his pack and stepped out into the warm, murky water. The Jeep bubbled and hissed, sinking into the muck with surprising rapidity. He realized he was sinking, too, and, in a sudden panic, he thrashed and wallowed his way back to the road. His last glimpse of the Jeep was of the air rushing from the open windows, with a gurgling sound and flurry of bubbles as the black waters closed over it.

He returned to the roadbed, shook off as much mud as he could, and stared at the complex. This was insane. It was going to be a bitch just getting in there. He'd better come up with a plan, because just barging in would be pointless and stupid—not to mention suicidal.

As he looked at the concrete tower, his thoughts turned unexpectedly to his grandfather Joe Coldmoon, who had fought in the Pacific with XXIV Corps, Seventy-Seventh Infantry Division, during World War II. "We're a warrior people," he'd once told Coldmoon, explaining that *his* grandfather Rain-in-the-Face had put the fatal arrow into George Armstrong Custer at the Battle of the Greasy Grass. It had seemed at the time like a crazy contradiction, his grandfather's patriotism and love of country combined with pride in killing Custer, but there it was. Many houses on the rez had a wall of photographs devoted to family members serving in the military.

We're a warrior people. During the invasion of Leyte, Joe and his company were hunkered down in trenches opposite the Japanese, not two hundred yards of no-man's-land between the adversaries. On the darkest nights, with no moon, his grandfather would leave his gun behind, strip down to his skivvies, put a knife between his teeth, and crawl out across that no-man's-land. When he returned an hour or so later, his buddies would ask him, "How many, Joe? How many?" He never spoke, just held up fingers—one, two, three. Once Coldmoon asked his grandfather how he did it. After the longest and most uncomfortable silence he'd ever endured, his grandfather finally said: "Your spirit goes outside your body, and you become a ghost that nobody can see." He had refused to say anything more.

Those words came back to Coldmoon while he stared at the complex. He had never quite understood what they meant: to be outside your own body, become a ghost that nobody could see. If only he could manage that now.

He shook his head. That old superstitious nonsense wasn't going to help him get inside.

Or would it?

He started walking down the road.

54

As THE BOAT with no name sped north, P. B. Perelman wondered just what the hell he'd gotten himself into.

The first two hours had been smooth motoring, the flat sea allowing him to go at the boat's top speed of seventy-five knots. But as the light disappeared in the steady rain, he could feel in his bones the approaching storm, an electricity in the air. A slight swell was developing, the leading edge of worse to come, and the wind had kicked up, producing a little chop. Already the boat was starting to catch too much air, and at that speed, in the dark, it would be easy to flip over.

He throttled back.

"What the devil are you doing?" Constance asked sharply.

"I have to ease off in this sea," said Perelman. He couldn't believe her lack of fear. Any other passenger would be on the floor by now, begging him to slow down.

"Don't lose your nerve."

"I'm worried about losing my life. *Our* lives. We can't help Pendergast if we're dead."

She said nothing, but let him throttle down to fifty without further complaint. Even at that speed, the boat was starting to take a pounding, the props coming out of the water from time to time with a terrifying roar. They were making for the mouth of Crooked River, a course that took them far offshore. Christ, if they didn't get there before the storm hit, they'd be screwed no matter what speed they were going. This was no craft to weather a storm in.

He glanced over at Constance, who was standing on his left, her face barely illuminated by the dim red light of the helm. She was looking straight ahead, her short hair whipped by the wind: a crazy girl, he thought, with such peculiar mannerisms and old-fashioned speech. Although the look in her violet eyes wasn't crazy—not exactly. They were more the eyes of a stone killer than of a young woman—eyes that had seen everything and, as a result, were surprised by nothing.

This whole business had taken a bizarre turn, and done so very suddenly. Looking back, he could see in retrospect the signs that the task force had been compromised. Whoever these people were, kidnapping a fed like that was the height of insanity—unless they were an arm of the government themselves. *An arm of the government*. Incredible as that might seem, it was really the only thing that made sense. That meant the only way to keep Pendergast alive was to make them think they'd gotten away with it; that nobody knew their location, that the cavalry hadn't been called in. Of course, the chances that Pendergast was still alive were vanishingly low.

The bow hit a particularly steep swell and the boat lurched upward, the props screaming, then came back down at a tilt that scared the shit out of him. He eased a little more off the throttle, only to receive another sharp rebuke from Constance.

She was clueless of how go-fast boats handled, but there was no point arguing with her now.

"You'd better hold on tighter than ever," he warned her instead. "Because it's only going to get rougher."

55

AFTER THE CHOPPER had landed in what appeared to be the inner courtyard of an industrial plant, they had been carried out, still bound, and placed in wheelchairs, to which they were additionally strapped. Escorted by half a dozen men carrying rifles and automatic weapons, they'd been pushed through seemingly endless cinder-block hallways and up an elevator, to arrive at a strikingly elegant room— Persian rugs, a massive desk flanked by flags, with paintings on the walls and gilded furniture.

Behind the desk sat an old man wearing military fatigues. Their escort halted them twenty feet from the desk. The old man rose slowly, painfully. Gladstone could see that where his name, rank, and service would have been on his fatigues; the labels had been removed, leaving darker patches. His collar sported three torn holes on each side. The man's square, granite face was careworn, and tiny veins sprinkled his cheeks. He looked eighty, maybe older. What little hair he had left, fringing a liver-spotted pate, had been cut so short he seemed almost bald. Outside, the storm had intensified tremendously, but the thick concrete walls shielded them to the point where only a faint, muffled moaning came through.

"Welcome," the man said, his voice anything but welcoming. "I am General Smith."

Gladstone said nothing and neither did Pendergast. She glanced at the FBI agent. His face was pale, unreadable.

"I'm sorry about what happened to your lab associate, Dr. Gladstone."

"What 'happened' is that you murdered him."

He sighed and gave a small shrug. "Our work here is of the utmost importance. Regrettable things sometimes happen."

Gladstone started to speak again but the general overrode her. "We have so little time, and much important work that needs doing. I shall escort you both to the laboratory. That will be much more convenient." He turned and walked slowly to the far door of the room. Soldiers pushed their wheelchairs, following the old man out of the elegant room and down a hallway, through a set of double doors and into a dazzling laboratory, brightly lit, with gleaming medical equipment such as one would find in an intensive care unit. Two orderlies and a male nurse were in the lab and they glanced up, apparently surprised to see them. Another man stepped through a metal door in the back of the lab. He cradled a small plastic case in his arms. The place smelled strongly of methyl alcohol and iodopovidone.

The general turned. "It is my pleasure to introduce Dr. Smith."

"Lot of Smiths around here," Gladstone said sarcastically.

"Names are immaterial."

Dr. Smith stepped forward. He was small and brisk, with round tortoiseshell glasses slightly smoked, dressed in dazzling white. With a shock of brilliantined black hair and an upturned nose, he made Gladstone think of a malignant, mincing leprechaun. An eager smile creased his small face. He gave a short bow, eyes blinking like an owl's behind the thick lenses. "Pleased."

"Dr. Smith, could you prepare the patient?"

"Yes, sir." The doctor turned to one of the orderlies. "Bring the IV."

The orderly took some items from a cabinet and placed them on the tray of a rolling IV pole, then pushed it toward Gladstone.

A strange, detached sense of curiosity and outrage was suddenly replaced by a spike of fear. "Get the fuck away from me."

The doctor continued to work as if nothing had been said. He slid a pair of scissors beneath her sleeve and started cutting.

"Stop! No!" She struggled in the chair, but everything was strapped down fast.

The doctor swabbed her exposed forearm.

"No!" she cried. As the doctor bent over her arm, she could smell his hair tonic. "*No!*"

"Dr. Gladstone," said the general, standing behind her, "if you continue to make a disturbance I will have you gagged. I can't tolerate noise."

She felt the sting as the IV needle went into her vein, and she struggled uselessly again. The doctor secured the catheter, got blood, flushed it, depressed the sterile spike of the drip chamber, then taped the setup in place and stood back. She looked once more at Pendergast, but his face remained shut down, only his eyes glittering, like pale diamonds.

"Now for step two," said the general.

Gladstone watched as the doctor opened the small plastic case, removed a syringe and glass vial, stuck the syringe into the vial, and filled it with a colorless liquid.

"What is that?" she heard herself ask.

"Dr. Gladstone, one more word from you and I will carry out my threat."

Gladstone, filled with terror, shut her mouth, her

heart beating wildly. She realized she was hyperventilating.

The doctor inserted the needle into the IV's injection port.

"Hold it there." The general now looked up at
Pendergast. "As you can see, Dr. Smith is poised
to inject your associate. Now I will ask you some
questions and I *will* receive answers. If not, he will
inject her. Do you understand?"

Gladstone made a huge effort not to speak or make
noise. Pendergast, for his part, remained silent.

The general turned his eyes to her, then back to
Pendergast. "I'm sorry it's come to this," he said.
"We're all on the same side, you see." He sighed, as if
used to dealing with people who didn't understand.
"It would be so much better if we could communicate
like reasonable people. Unlike, I fear, your man in
China. He wasn't reasonable. Not reasonable at all."

Finally, Pendergast spoke. "Is it reasonable to
murder an innocent scientist and kidnap another at
gunpoint? Torture a man in the most awful way
imaginable? Dismember over a hundred people?
And now, to proceed with this brutality?"

"It is all in service of a vital cause."

"Stalin said much the same thing."

The old general waved his hand. "Enough banter.
My questions are few, but I need complete answers.
Who else knows the location of this facility?"

Pendergast didn't answer.

The man turned. "Dr. Gladstone? I give you permission to speak in order to answer the question."

She said nothing.

"You've got nerves of steel," said the general, not without a touch of admiration. "Would you remain so brave if I told you the drug Dr. Smith will inject produces a most terrifying result?" A pause. "Now, Agent Pendergast: in order to prevent this tragedy, I need to know if anyone else has discovered the location of this facility—or has traced the source of the, ah, feet. We were keeping them for later analysis, and could never have anticipated that a freak deluge would cause the river to flood, destroying our dock and outbuildings—including the frozen storage locker—and sending the feet out into the gulf. We hoped they would decay, or be eaten, or sink for one reason or another; clearly, that did not come to pass. Even so, we never imagined they could be traced back here..." Another pause. "Obviously, we can't have others coming to the same conclusion that you did. We've made a huge investment in this facility; worked very hard to make sure the cost was buried in dark military budgets and appropriations bills; and the research we're doing here is now at too advanced a stage to be moved. You will give me the answers to these questions eventually—so why not now rather than later, when your associate will have already crossed into a land of horror? Are you truly so eager for a Pyrrhic victory?"

Gladstone stared at the man. The tired, almost bored look in his eyes made his words all the more believable. She felt herself trembling all over. "Please, Agent Pendergast. Answer his question."

The general turned to Pendergast. "You heard her plea."

"You mentioned we were all on the same side," said Pendergast, his voice cool. "Perhaps if you helped us understand the vital work you are doing here, we might be willing to cooperate without coercion."

The general looked at him a long time.

Now the woman in the pearls, who had been standing in the back during this exchange, spoke up. "General, I've had dealings with this man before. Take care with him—and don't answer his questions."

Pendergast spoke again, voice still mild. "I see you were a military man—a three-star, if I'm not mistaken. And Ms. Alves-Vettoretto—" he nodded to the woman standing to one side— "also strikes me as a person who was once military. So let us observe military correctness. Before you do this, it's only honorable to try persuading us first."

"General, I strongly advise against conversing

with this man," said the woman named Alves-Vettoretto.

Another impatient wave. "It's a reasonable request. We're all patriotic Americans here, after all."

He sat back in a nearby chair and tented his fingers. "Are you familiar with Project MK-Ultra?"

56

THE ROAD THROUGH the swamp was like a tunnel in the darkness, at the end of which Coldmoon could now see the cluster of lights of a gate and guard station. He would have to get around that.

Moving as silently as possible, trying to become his grandfather Joe's ghost, he exited the roadway and slipped into the warm, swampy water. Mosquitoes rose up around him, whining in his ears. The air was fetid with the smell of rotting wood and swamp gas. He had seen the occasional alligator as he'd driven in, and he was all too aware there were also snakes and God only knew what else in back bayous like these. He hadn't been especially afraid of poisonous snakes while growing up. With a little care, you could avoid rattlers. But that was before he'd been bitten by a water moccasin on his first assignment with Pendergast. Christ, had that been less than a month ago? At the time, he'd promised himself he'd never look at a swamp again, let alone go near one. There were no swamps in Colorado: that's one of the reasons he'd requested the position. And look at him now.

He'd heard one could see the reflection of a gator's eyes in a flashlight beam, but he was in no position to turn his on. It was the blackest of nights, the only light being reflected from the brightly lit facility. The water was only a foot or two deep; below that, another foot of sucking mud, which made moving difficult and exhausting.

He slogged about a half mile from the road perpendicular to the facility, then made a ninety-degree turn and continued toward it. At any moment, he expected to feel fangs sink into his leg, or hear the sudden thrash of water as an alligator ambushed him. He glimpsed, from time to time through the cypress trunks, a flicker of lights of the guard station. Soon he had drawn almost even with it—and then, to his surprise, came up against a chain-link fence. A channel had been cleared on the far side, providing access for an airboat, probably operated by the guards at the gate. Incredible to think they had fenced a facility that was already isolated in a deep swamp in the middle of nowhere.

He took out his flashlight and—keeping the beam low—examined the fence, being careful not to touch it. He spied three wires along the top, running through insulated clips. The fence was electrified and, no doubt, alarmed as well.

He paused, thinking. A fence like this, running miles through a swamp, with dead trees, snags, birds, and animals, would probably generate a lot of false alarms. Not only that, but the storm was still picking up, the treetops swaying overhead. Even as he stood there, a smattering of heavy raindrops came down, hitting him in the face. He waded along the fence for another hundred yards until he found what he was looking for: a rotten tree standing close to the fence. He gave it a heave and, with a nasty mushy sound, it sagged into the fence, touching the wires. A few sparks popped.

Coldmoon retreated into the darkness, submerged himself in the water, and waited.

Sure enough: about ten minutes later, he heard the whir of an airboat and saw a spotlight pierce the murk. Two guards. They came to the leaning tree and illuminated it with their spotlight, accompanied by muttered cursing and the hiss of the radios. One of the men, wearing hip waders, got out and, using a hooked pole, pulled the rotten trunk free and shoved it over into the water.

After they left, Coldmoon continued walking alongside the fence, soon coming across another rotten candidate, this time on the far side of the fence. The wind was now blowing harder, along with gusts of rain, so the guards were unlikely to question why two trees fell onto the fence in quick succession.

Taking a piece of nylon parachute cord from his pack, Coldmoon climbed partway up the fence, looped the cord over the wires, then climbed back down. He then gave the cord a mighty pull, popping the wires out of their plastic clips, sparks flying in several directions. This time, he quickly climbed over the fence, avoiding the dangling live wires, then dropped down on the other side and gave the rotten tree a shove toward the fence. But this one wasn't as rotten as the first, and he had a moment of panic when it refused to topple over. He laid his shoulder into it and, abruptly, the rotten upper portion broke off and came crashing down on the fence. He leapt aside, just missing getting clobbered.

The trunk ended up tangled in the wires. Coldmoon almost laughed—he couldn't have asked for a better setup.

He headed on, slogging through the blackness as fast as he could move. In the distance, he heard the whine of the airboat returning to investigate. He wondered when he would encounter the next perimeter—and how hard it would be to penetrate that one.

He sure hoped he wouldn't have to kill anybody.

57

THE BOAT LUNGED and bucked as the waves got steeper, the offshore wind rising near the coast of the Panhandle. The wind and tide were producing a steep chop, and it began to rain harder: big, heavy drops that felt like hail.

Perelman had the VHF turned to the weather channel, which had been regularly broadcasting ever more dire small-craft warnings, but now it announced general tornado warnings. He'd been forced to drop his speed even further, much to his passenger's displeasure. It was pitch dark on the water, and Perelman's boat had no radar. He just hoped the small-craft warnings had cleared the coast of boats. Only a crazy person would be out in this weather. If they could get into the protection of the river before the main force of the storm hit...he recited a quick Baruch HaShem in his head, and then another, thanking God for having gotten them this far. *Just a little bit farther, please?*

The booming of the water against the hull and the whine of the engine, combined with the hammering of drops on the windscreen and the howling of the wind, created an almost deafening noise in the cockpit. *Blow, winds, and crack your cheeks.* He glanced at the chartplotter. They were about six miles from Dog Island. Constance was still standing to his left, staring into the darkness with an implacable expression on her face, a real-life Joan of Arc.

Four more miles to go. The wind was really getting crazy. He throttled down again. At least this time Constance didn't respond. To his immense relief he started to see a few faint lights from Dog Island, appearing and disappearing in the murk. The sea got worse as they headed toward the northern end of the island. Now the lights of Carrabelle came into view, smeared and blurry in the tempest. And then, rising to the west of the town, he saw the powerful beacon of the Crooked River Lighthouse, strong and clear, which flooded him with relief. They were almost there.

Entering Saint George Sound, he took a bearing off the light, heading to a point of land east of the lighthouse where his charts indicated the mouth of the Carrabelle River debouched into the gulf. God, it was a relief to see that lighthouse blinking away, steady as a rock, through the howling murk. But with the change of heading the sea was now almost broadside, pitching the boat from side to side and occasionally shoving it askew, the gray water sweeping across the enclosed bows and slopping over the gunwales. The cockpit floor was awash in seawater on its way out the scuppers. The VHF was still broadcasting tornado warnings to the north. If they could only get in the damn river and out of this brutal sea, they'd be safe. Or safer, at least.

Finally, he espied what looked like the broad mouth of the river, the lights of the town casting an eerie glow through the shifting rainsqualls. Squinting and peering, he made out the blinking lights of the channel buoys. As they entered the mouth of the river, the steep swells vanished into windblown chop and spume, easily cut through by the big boat. He wondered what people on shore must think as they watched the running lights of his speedboat heading up the river. Then he realized he didn't need to wonder: they'd surely think he was crazy. And maybe he was crazy. He should never have let this woman talk him into something so insane.

As if responding to his thoughts, Constance spoke: "Speed up."

He throttled up a little, ignoring the "no wake" zone. The wind was lashing the water so hard that it was all foamy and white, with no distinct surface. But no more awful swell, at least. He pushed on, the lights of the town passing on either side of him now. Going under the Davis Island bridge, he went through the great S-curve to where the water divided into the New River and the Crooked River.

Now the VHF channel went from general tornado warnings to the specific: an emergency broadcast of probable tornadoes spotted by radar in the region of Tate's Hell State Forest—precisely where they were headed.

"Did you hear that?" Constance asked.

"Yes," said Perelman. "There's nothing we can do now—except turn around, of course."

"We're not turning around."

"Then we pray that we don't run into it."

"I don't pray," she said.

"Well," he replied, annoyed, "I sure as hell do, and I hope you won't mind if I indulge."

She said nothing, just stared straight ahead, her face illuminated from beneath by the red light of the chartplotter.

They had now left the town behind and were winding their way up the Crooked River, which quickly lived up to its name, carrying them around one deep horseshoe bend after another. The channel markers disappeared and he continued to navigate by chartplotter, glad the boat drew only twenty-four inches. Despite the storm, they were not making bad time up the channel, but Perelman's relief was starting to be overshadowed by the thought of what would happen when they reached the facility. Fighting the sea for the past few hours had pushed that out of his mind.

"When we get there," he said, "we're just going to scope out the situation and call in the cavalry. We can't handle this by ourselves."

"I've already explained why that is a poor idea. We can't trust anyone. The investigation has been compromised . . . and we don't know how, why, or by whom. It would take too long to collect, organize, and mount your charge of the light brigade. Pendergast may be at risk of death already, but he will surely die if they see that coming."

Perelman felt a rising exasperation. "So what's the plan?"

"I don't know what *your* plan is," she said. "*My* plan is to go in there, neutralize the people who kidnapped Pendergast, and bring him out."

He really was dealing with a psychopath. "With what weapon, may I ask?"

She removed what appeared to be an ornate, antique stiletto from the pocket of her leggings and showed it to him.

"You're out of your mind." He checked the chartplotter and saw they were nearing their destination, the old sugar plant on the river. At that moment, the wind suddenly and shockingly increased, the trees on either side of the river lashing about in all directions.

Simultaneously, he heard and felt a strange vibration in the air.

Son of a bitch.

As the boat swung around yet another deep bend, lights appeared—a pier and dock along the riverbank, with a loading crane and a launch. And rising behind the trees was an unsettling sight: a grim guard tower with roaming spotlights and the buildings of an industrial complex. It was so much bigger than he'd imagined. They were in deep, way deep, and this was something neither one of them could possibly handle.

But his attention was torn away by a dramatic rising scream of wind coming out of the blackness, upstream of the starboard side. He stared in horror. Something began to resolve from the howling murk: a thrashing mass of blackness against blackness, a sinuous form whipping and writhing this way and that as it advanced on them. It chewed through the trees on the far bank, reducing them to whirling splinters.

Perelman immediately swung the boat around, hoping to outrun it, gunning the engine. But the river channel was narrow and the boat's turning radius too large, and he ran aground on the muck about ten yards from the embankment.

"Out! Out of the boat!"

Even as he cried, the tornado moved out over

the river and blossomed a dirty brown as it sucked up water, its sound changing from a high-pitched scream to something monstrously deeper. Encountering the water caused it to swerve away from them, barreling directly into the docks and blowing them up like a bomb, sparks arcing through the night as the power poles went down. Perelman felt the heavy boat beneath him move in an impossible way. He clutched the wheel as they spun about, the windscreen being plucked off the hull like a child's toy and disappearing into the roaring tumult. Perelman seized Constance and pulled her out of the boat and into the muck.

The waterspout was almost on top of them, whirling so fast now that it looked like static on a television set. Perelman's ears popped excruciatingly as he grasped Constance tighter and hauled her through the mucky shallows, trying to reach the shelter of trees along the embankment. And then the roaring, shrieking column was on top of them, and his body was wrenched away, spinning, utterly helpless, before all went black.

58

"I AM FAMILIAR with Project MK-Ultra," Pendergast said. "In fact, I'd begun to wonder if this wasn't a continuation of it, in some form or other. But if we're going to converse, could you kindly ask the doctor to remove that needle?"

The general turned. "Dr. Smith, please remove the needle for the time being."

With a faint look of disappointment, the doctor extracted the needle from the IV injection port and stepped back. Gladstone felt a flood of relief. Her senses were heightened in the extreme; she could hear the storm faintly, still raging outside, along with the whisper of the HVAC and the ticking of a clock somewhere. The IV in her arm throbbed. There were no windows in the lab, only a long, horizontal mirror high along one wall.

"The idea behind MK-Ultra," the general continued, "was to seek ways to manipulate an individual's mental state—mind control, if you will—using drugs and behavior modification techniques. It was primarily meant as a battlefield weapon, employed to confuse or disable an enemy, or as a tool for interrogation. It was launched in 1953 and officially shut down in 1973, after some lily-livered government bureaucrats got cold feet." He shook his head with a mixture of dismay and disgust.

Alves-Vettoretto spoke up. "General, I'm stating for the record that you should not be engaging with this man, in particular by providing him information."

"Oh, come now. He made a reasonable request. Perhaps he will cooperate."

"He'll never cooperate."

"We shall see. Now, where was I? Most of MK-Ultra involved the testing of various psychoactive drugs. We were seeking compounds that would cause mental confusion, lower a person's efficiency, make them sick or drunk, induce amnesia, paralysis, and so forth. In short, to incapacitate them. One branch of the division also focused on potentially positive drugs, ones that would enhance thinking, clarity, or physical strength, or reduce the need for sleep without negative side effects."

He stood up and walked slowly around the lab.

"Some of us devoted our lives to this project. It was run by the CIA, but it had a military component as well. I was part of that latter section. We provided the manpower and facilities necessary to do the testing, as well as the subjects. When the CIA shut it down, several of us from the military component were devastated. We knew other countries had similar and very active programs of their own. It was insane for the United States to unilaterally disarm—especially since we were chasing a potential breakthrough. I was a young officer then, and a group of us resolved to keep it going. We resigned our commissions. But we had friends, many friends, who felt as we did, so we were able to secure black funding channeled to us through military purchasing. That funding allowed us to acquire, transform, and disguise the nature of this facility."

He turned toward the doctor. "Dr. Smith was instrumental in the development of the breakthrough drug. Doctor, would you care to take over?"

"Delighted," said the doctor, stepping forward with a grin. He removed his glasses and gave them a careful polishing with a white handkerchief tugged from his pocket. His bright, greenish-amber eyes flickered about the room, passing over Gladstone as if she didn't exist.

"By 1973, the group had identified a class of powerful psychoactive drugs derived from a genus of parasites called *Toxoplasma*. These compounds were already known to have peculiar effects on the brain. *Extremely* peculiar effects. Of course, this was before my time." He poked the handkerchief back into his pocket and perched the glasses on his nose once again, adjusting the frames behind each ear with a finicky gesture. "The pharmaceutical biologists on the team struggled to understand the mechanism. They had almost given up when I joined, back in '89."

He gave a little chuckle. "The parasite in question is not uncommon: *Toxoplasma gondii*, which causes a disease in humans known as toxoplasmosis. The illness is usually mild, with flulike symptoms, and it's common in households that have cats, which are widespread carriers. We were interested in this parasite because it appeared to have the power to alter mammal behavior. Mice infected with toxoplasmosis not only lose their fear of cats, but actually seek out cats—and subsequently get killed and eaten. This is how the parasite reproduces and spreads among cats—by altering the mouse's behavior. In addition, studies showed that people infected with toxoplasmosis also experience altered behavior. It causes, for example, 'crazy cat-lady syndrome.' It can also trigger bizarre risk-taking and even schizophrenia."

He chuckled again and inhaled with a long noisy sniff. "Consider that. A single-celled parasite with no mind of its own, no brain or nervous system, is able to take over the mind of a mouse—*or a human*—and control its behavior. Truly remarkable!"

Another strange inhaling sound as he gathered

more air to continue speaking. His voice was high, loud, and pedantic; the voice of the lecture hall.

"How does it do this? That was the question!" He raised a tiny finger. "When I arrived, I redirected the research program and we were soon able to discover a suite of complex neurotropic compounds released by the parasite. These compounds attached to certain lipoproteins in the brain and altered the firing of specific neurons. This in turn caused a range of bizarre human behaviors, mostly in the obsessive-compulsive realm. Endless handwashing, for example, or hoarding, or the sudden appearance of phobias. It even triggered, in some subjects, a compulsive nibbling or eating of the body, or violent sexual behaviors. Heady days indeed!"

His voice had climbed in pitch and excitement until it was almost squeaking. He halted and took another long, snuffling breath.

"One exploration of these compounds produced an especially strange reaction. It triggered a bizarre psychiatric condition known as body integrity identity disorder, or BIID. We called this drug H12K, after the batch number of its production."

The general spoke. "Mr. Pendergast, are you familiar with BIID?"

"No."

"I'm not surprised, since it has yet to receive diagnostic criteria in psychiatric circles. It's an extremely rare and perplexing psychological condition—so strange as to be scarcely believable. I'll never forget the first time I saw a test subject in the grips of it. At first we didn't know what was happening to him. He claimed that his left leg, from the knee down, was foreign. *An alien thing*, is what he called it. He loudly exclaimed to all within hearing that it was evil and had to be removed. This despite the fact that the limb was normal and apparently healthy. For days he was tormented by this hideous attachment, literally begging for help. We didn't understand at first how this was going to work out—until we found him later in his cell, bleeding copiously. He had sharpened a piece of metal he'd unscrewed from his bedframe and had tried to hack off his own leg."

A long sniff of triumph and another chuckle from the doctor. "And that was when I understood this drug was special—*truly* special!"

The chuckle, Gladstone realized, was a nervous tic, not an actual laugh. The sound of it made her blood run cold.

"Here is the most amazing part," the doctor continued. "Amputation is, in fact, the only cure for BIID. Nothing else works. There are doctors out there who quietly perform these amputations—and psychiatrists who sanction them. The feeling of bodily alienation is so strong, the individuals who get the amputations are relieved, even ecstatic, that the limb is gone. They are cured completely."

"How interesting," said Pendergast. The agent's voice was so calm, so neutral, that Gladstone wondered what he was thinking.

"Interesting indeed!" the doctor said excitedly, his voice high and piercing. "We refined H12K to make it faster acting and more powerful. Best of all—it can be aerosolized!"

He grasped his hands together and made that same wet chuckling sound.

The general took over. "One can only imagine the effects of dispersing H12K over an enemy's battlefield or city. Within an hour it would produce a scene of chaos, with hospitals and medical workers overwhelmed, inhabitants bleeding to death, utter bedlam. This is far better than a nuclear weapon, because it leaves infrastructure intact. It's far more reliable than nerve gas, which remains in the region for a long time and can drift in the wrong direction when the wind shifts. H12K degrades within two hours in the environment. You simply administer it, wait half a day, and enter the area unopposed. Admittedly, our own refinement, the drug that brings on the dysphoria, does not replicate a subject's *long-term* need to be rid of a hated, alien limb—the need is relatively brief, but more than sufficient to do the trick. Nor have we progressed to a point where we can specify *which* limb is considered alien: for now, all subjects present with the same symptoms. In a war situation, of course, these aren't concerns. Just think of how we might have deployed this in Vietnam or the Middle East! It is truly the ideal weapon."

"Ideal," echoed Pendergast.

"I'm glad you see it our way."

"I understand you've been collecting your test subjects from among undocumented people arriving at the southern border."

"*Undocumented people.*" The general frowned. "You mean illegal aliens? They suit our purposes very well. No one is likely to come looking for them. They're a self-selected group, if you think about it—deserving of no consideration."

"You're a sick fuck," said Gladstone, straining at her bonds.

"Another unsolicited outburst. Please gag her."

Gladstone did her best to resist, but the waiting soldiers stepped forward and, holding her head immobile, stuffed a cloth in her mouth and wrapped duct tape around it.

The general kept his gaze on Pendergast. "Perhaps my explanation has persuaded you to cooperate?"

Pendergast said nothing.

"You seemed interested."

"I am interested—interested in the profoundly

psychotic pathology I see on display in both you and the doctor."

"I'm sorry to hear that."

"It's remarkable you've managed to brainwash so many soldiers with this folie à deux. Or perhaps they don't know the extent of the atrocities committed here?"

"I warned you," said Alves-Vettoretto. "He's a snake."

"We didn't need to brainwash anyone. When we first established this operation, we were careful to identify soldiers disaffected with the transformation of the U.S. Army—disgusted with the loosening of discipline, the admittance of homosexuals, the placing of women in combat roles, and the indiscriminate mixing of races." His voice rose in volume. "We selected patriotic, tough, God-fearing boys who obey orders without question, not the sniveling, politically correct enlisted men you see in today's—" He caught himself, took a deep breath, exhaled. "I'm getting off subject. Our soldiers are well aware of what we're doing—and support it one hundred percent."

"It seems you and your men were born seventy-five years too late, and in the wrong country," said Pendergast.

The general ignored this. "We're on a schedule here, and all this is wasting precious time. You will now answer my questions or the good doctor will inject your associate with the drug. Dr. Smith? Reinsert the needle, but hold off the injection until I give the command."

Smith picked up the needle again, examined it, then stepped forward. He slid it into the IV port and looked up at the general with anticipation.

"I will ask again: who knows about this facility?"

Gladstone stared pleadingly at Pendergast. But he didn't answer.

"You know what's going to happen, of course. Surely you aren't going to put her through this? It will be on your shoulders."

Silence.

"We normally just let them bleed to death. And you will be watching."

"I can only ask you: please, do not do this," said Pendergast.

"Then answer my question."

A long silence. *Son of a bitch, answer him!* Gladstone thought, moaning and squirming.

The general sighed, then nodded to the doctor. "Inject."

"Wait," said Pendergast sharply.

The general glanced back at him.

"Very well. I'll answer your questions: you have my word."

The general smiled and gestured to Smith to pause.

Pendergast went on. "Nobody knows of this facility but me, Dr. Gladstone, and the late Dr. Lam."

The general arched his eyebrows. "Nobody?"

"That's correct."

"What about your partner? We know you're not working alone."

"He is en route from Mexico to the U.S. and I wasn't able to contact him."

"Why didn't you tell the task force?"

"No time. More to the point: We'd become sure there was a mole in the investigation, someone very close to the center. I couldn't trust anyone."

The general smiled. "Now, *how* did you identify the source of the amputated feet?"

"It was a drift analysis program, developed by Drs. Lam and Gladstone."

"In their lab?"

"Yes."

"Does anyone else have it?"

"No."

"An unfortunate fire will take care of that. Well, I'm relieved to know we're safe—at least for now. Dr. Smith, you may remove the needle."

Alves-Vettoretto spoke. "How do you know he's telling us the truth?"

"An excellent question! You haven't been around long enough to appreciate my methods. The fact is, we will know soon enough if Mr. Pendergast has lied or not."

Gladstone, moaning and struggling, saw Alves-Vettoretto frown in confusion.

"You're wondering how I can be so sure," the general said. "Because he is about to witness, with his own eyes, the effects of the drug on a subject. You see—Dr. Smith *already administered the H12K to Dr. Gladstone.* He did that when he first inserted the IV. There's nothing in that other needle but saline. Once Mr. Pendergast sees what happens…and knows the same will happen to him…then he will be totally forthcoming, if he has not been already." He turned to Pendergast with a smile and checked his watch. "It takes about an hour for the drug to act on the brain. Almost forty minutes have gone by since Dr. Smith inserted the IV. That means we have another twenty until the show begins." He gestured at the long mirror on the wall. "It can get rather messy, unfortunately, so let us retire to the observation room and watch from there."

He turned. "Ms. Alves-Vettoretto. You haven't seen the results of the drug in action yet, have you?"

She shook her head.

"Then, by all means, please join us."

59

WHEN COLDMOON WAS about two hundred yards from the main building, the swamp gave way to a thin forest of sickly pines growing upon sand. The storm had finally broken for real. A heavy rain came down, accompanied by lightning, booming thunder, and gusts of wind that pressed the trees down and almost blew him off his feet. Coldmoon was glad of it. Even though he was soaked, the night was muggy and warm and he was grateful for the rain now washing away the mud from his skin and clothes. It also provided excellent cover—there was almost no chance that, in this chaos, he would be seen or heard.

He walked through the forest and soon came to a looming cinder-block wall, about fifteen feet high, with spikes along its top. It was too smooth and high to climb, and the trees on either side had been cleared back at least a hundred feet.

He'd have to go in through the gate. What a shame...for the guards.

He moved back into the forest and walked parallel to the wall until he could see the cluster of lights that must represent a gate.

How many were on guard?

Keeping away from the road, moving with greater caution now, he approached and paused in a thicket about fifty feet from the gate. He could see a single man—a soldier—inside a gatehouse, brightly lit. He raised his binocs. The man was thumbing through an issue of *Maxim*, looking bored. Could it be there was only one? That would be most convenient. Of course, there were also cameras mounted above the gate, four of them, providing full coverage. Someone would be monitoring those.

He circled closer, creeping on his belly, until he was within fifteen feet. The water was lashing the windows of the guardhouse, making it hard for the guard to see out even if he were looking, which he wasn't. It really did look as if there was only one.

Coldmoon continued crawling until he was at the guardhouse itself. The door was shut, as was the sliding window. But was it locked?

Moving with infinite care, glad of the noise of the storm, he edged around to the door and reached up. The wind was shaking the flimsy metal shack.

There was really only one way to do this.

He stood up and peeked through the door window. The guard's back was turned, hunched over the magazine as he flipped a page.

He picked up a stick and whacked it against the guardhouse window.

The guard jumped like he'd been shot, stood up, and peered out the window. He could, of course, see nothing. The guard sat down again. Coldmoon knew exactly what he was thinking—a branch, blown by the wind. Not even worth checking out.

Coldmoon smacked the window again, even harder.

The guard got up again, went to the window, peered out, and then, looking uncertain, stepped outside.

Instantly, Coldmoon grabbed the man by the hair and pulled his head back, while at the same time yanking him behind the guardhouse, where he couldn't be seen from the camera array, and cutting his throat. He skipped back as the body tumbled to the ground, neck jetting blood.

So much for not killing anybody.

Coldmoon waited a minute for the body to bleed out. Then he quickly removed the guard's coat and hat, put them on, went back in the guardhouse, and opened the magazine, slouching down in the chair, all for the benefit of the cameras. He'd taken care to stay out of camera view as much as possible, but if someone had seen him, he'd rather know now than later. He remained for a few minutes, flipping pages;

then he laid down the magazine and sauntered out of the guardhouse, playing idly with his fly, as if on his way to take a piss.

He slipped through the gate and walked along the inside wall, pausing in a dark angle. He felt shaken by what he'd done...what he'd *had* to do. He'd killed before—once—but it hadn't been in cold blood...

He stomped hard on those feelings. Not now. Not until his partner was out.

He couldn't be sure the cameras hadn't picked him up, but in the driving rain the view would have been poor. In any case, nobody had come running, no alarms had gone off, and no lights had started flashing. After getting his heart rate under control, he crept farther along the inside wall, moving into an area that was darker still. The tower spotlights roamed about, but their movement was desultory and repetitive. Nobody expected an intruder to show up on a night like this. He pulled out his binocs to reconnoiter.

The main facility lay across a cracked and weed-infested apron of concrete, a solid two-story factory-like building with rows of small windows punched into a cinder-block façade. The windows looked new and there were other signs of renovations, especially evident in a freshly painted three-story building to one side. Past the gate, the road went straight on into the building, beneath a tall archway, also with a gate, into what looked like an interior courtyard. On either side of the courtyard, parking areas were visible.

Crouching, Coldmoon waited for the klieg lights to circle around on their route—and then he sprinted for the archway leading into the building.

60

Her mind swam back into consciousness and for a moment she braced herself instinctively, assuming the worst, hand tightening around a stiletto that wasn't there. Then everything came flooding back: the roaring noise, being picked up and tumbled about like a rag doll . . . and then blackness.

All was eerily quiet except for a steady falling rain. Constance raised her head, annoyed to find she was almost completely covered in mud for a second time that evening, but the warm rain was already washing it off. She lay on the river embankment, giving herself a minute to recover. The docks and outbuildings had been torn to pieces, an unrecognizable shambles of splintered piers and roofless structures. Their boat lay overturned where the waterspout had thrown it, about a hundred yards downstream, half on the embankment and half in the water, its hull split.

But where was Perelman?

She struggled to sit up, body aching. It was so dark she could barely make out anything on the ground beyond the nearby gleam of her stiletto.

"Chief Perelman?" she called in a weak voice, and then louder: *"Perelman?"*

"Over here."

The strained reply came from the blackness about twenty feet from her. She gingerly rose to her feet, wincing.

"Are you okay?" Perelman asked.

"I believe so. But are you?"

"I'm afraid not."

She carefully felt her way toward his voice. A sudden flash of lightning illuminated him, sprawled on the muddy embankment. One leg was twisted beneath him in an ugly, unnatural way.

She knelt by his side. "Your leg?"

"Broken, as you can see. Can you...help me out of this mud?"

"Yes." Constance put her arms under his and pulled him up the embankment and to a grassy area within a grove of trees.

"My poor boat," he said.

Constance laid a hand on his forehead. It was clammy. He would be going into shock.

"Get my cell phone out of my pocket," he said. "I've got to make a call."

She reached in and took it out of his slicker

pocket. It was smashed to pieces and dripping water. He fished a flashlight out of his other pocket and turned it on.

"Oh shit. What about your phone?"

"Gone."

"Looks like we're out of commission."

"*You're* out of commission," said Constance. "*I'm* still in commission."

"You?" He groaned. "What are you going to do now?"

Once again, in a swift movement Constance unsnapped his gun from the holster and slipped it out.

"What the hell do you plan to do with that?"

"It's going to prove more useful than a stiletto."

"You can't go in there alone. It's suicide. We need to get out of here and call in a massive raid. Which is what we should have done in the first place."

Constance tucked the gun into her waistband, saying nothing.

"Constance, please listen to me. There's no way you can do this without getting killed. You've got to get help. Call Pendergast's boss at the FBI, what's his name, Pickett."

Constance tightened his slicker around him, making the chief as comfortable as possible. Then she stood up and stared at the lights of the facility rising above the trees. "We've been over this before, and there's no more time. Pendergast is in that compound. If you call in a raid, they'll kill him. I'm going in alone."

"No." A pause of disbelief. "No, no, that's totally insane."

"I'm sorry to leave you. I expect you'll survive."

"Constance, I beg you *for your own sake* not to go in there."

Without giving any indication she'd heard him, she turned and slipped into the trees, heading for the complex. Perelman's protests were quickly lost in the sound of wind and rain.

61

WEARING THE RAIN slicker and hat of the guard he had killed—the coat unpleasantly sticky inside with blood, the outside washed clean by rain—Coldmoon observed the archway leading to the interior court-yard. The second checkpoint was manned by multiple guards and bristling with cameras. There was no way he could get through that.

There were other doors in the building's long façade. He crossed an open area, walking calmly and deliberately, hoping that from a distance he looked unremarkable. He arrived at a walkway along the perimeter of the building. The doors in the façade were locked, with no handles on the outside, but as he reconnoitered, he saw a guard exit one of the doors near the far end of the building, then turn and walk away, his back to Coldmoon. He headed in that direction and paused in an area of darkness just short of the door, wondering if anyone else would come out. The lights from the tower roamed over the outer area and the wall but didn't seem to stray along the façade itself.

He waited. He hoped to God that where one person came out, a second person might as well. He waited and waited and then—in a paroxysm of frustration— decided this was a waste of time. He needed another plan to get in.

At the corner of the building stood a heavy copper drainpipe, carrying rainwater from the roof and directing it away from the building into a concrete drainage ditch. He examined the pipe closely. Every four feet, heavy brackets held it in place against the cinder-block wall; he could use those brackets as hand- and footholds for climbing. There was a narrow ledge along the second floor he could get onto from the pipe—and the windows on the second floor were unbarred.

However, he would be totally exposed while climbing, a dark figure moving against the beige façade. At least he'd be partially cloaked by the gusting rain.

The odds weren't great, but he figured he was unlikely to get any better ones.

He walked along the building façade until he reached the bottom of the pipe. Glancing around, he saw people at the main gate, a few guards walking here and there, and—goddamn it—the tower with its roaming spotlights. But everyone seemed hunched against the rain, hurrying along. His chances were not bad...as long as nobody went out to relieve the guard whose throat he'd cut.

He grasped the pipe and swung up, finding a foothold on the bottom bracket and grabbing the one above. The rain made the metal slippery. As he climbed, he could hear the water thrumming through the pipe. Reaching up to the next bracket, he hoisted himself up, then up again. One slip sent his heart rate soaring, but he dangled for only a moment by his hands before he was able to find fresh purchase for his feet. In a few minutes he had reached the ledge. Leaving the pipe, he crept along it toward the first window. Thank God, fear of heights was one phobia he didn't have. But now he was absurdly exposed—anyone even glancing up in his direction would see him. And yet, nobody glanced; they just hustled along, heads down against the rain.

He crept to the window and peered inside. Beyond was a bleak corridor, brightly lit—and empty. It was an old casement window, with the latch inside.

Using the butt of his Browning, he broke the window as quietly as he could, knocked away the shards of glass, reached inside, and lifted the lever to unlatch the window. He wrestled it open and forced his body through the narrow opening. Once inside, he quickly shut the window.

The corridor ran about fifty feet before turning

right. As he waited, he heard footsteps rapping on the linoleum floor. He sprinted forward as quietly as possible, then flattened himself against the corner.

Almost immediately a guard came around; Coldmoon tripped him while bringing his knife into position, and the man fell onto it, Coldmoon slashing upward and cutting his throat. With a gurgle, the man fell to the floor. Coldmoon paused to look around the corner. Empty.

Crouching, he rapidly searched the guard, pocketing a magnetic key card and a Beretta 9mm pistol. He pulled off the soaked hat and shirt he was wearing, took the guard's shirt, belt, and waist pouch, and put them on. Hiding the body as best he could, he moved fast along the second corridor, then took another branching corridor that he figured headed toward the interior of the building, where the tower block was. He passed a couple of workers, but he kept his head down and they were busy with their own business and didn't take notice.

The corridor ended in a locked door with a porthole window. He looked through and made out a large open space, with what looked like cells on either wall. He could hear muffled sounds: voices, cries, yelling, sobbing—classic prison sounds.

When he held the guard's magnetic key to the plate, the door clicked and the lock went green.

He pushed it open, the sounds louder now. Reaching

an initial row of cell doors with barred windows, he stopped to peer in. Each cell held three or four people—to him, they looked Central American—men and women, all wearing hospital gowns. And those same green shoes. They were filthy and neglected, their beds consisting of plywood boards without mattresses. When he looked in, they shrank from him in fear.

"Lo siento de verdad," he said, getting blank stares of terror in return. *"Soy un amigo."*

No reaction: just silent, frightened faces.

Coldmoon backed away from them and turned, heading toward the exit at the far end of the hall. There was nothing he could do for them now, he thought as he hastened away. He had to keep his mind on the main focus; this horror, however reprehensible, would have to wait.

But then he paused at the barred window of the last cell. There were three men inside, wearing loose hospital gowns and the same green footwear.

"Hola, amigos."

They stared at him suspiciously.

"I'm a friend," he continued in Spanish. "I'm here to help you." He removed his FBI badge and showed it to them.

The men looked at each other. Finally, one approached the door. "Yes?"

"Are any of you gentlemen from San Miguel Acatán?"

A suspicious silence.

"I'm a friend of the Ixquiac family."

This produced a huge reaction. "Ixquiac?" All three rose and crowded around the window.

Coldmoon placed his finger to his lips. "Quiet. Very quiet now."

They nodded.

"I need information," Coldmoon went on. "What is going on here? What are they doing to you?"

They all began speaking at once and Coldmoon pointed to the closest person. "You speak. How did you get here?"

The man told of the journey from Guatemala across the border into Mexico, meeting with the coyote, the journey to the U.S. border and across— then getting suddenly herded into trucks at gunpoint and driven to this godforsaken place. It was basically the same story Coldmoon had already heard from the coyote's lips.

"What are they doing to you here?" he asked the man.

"I don't know. Experiments."

"What kind of experiments?"

The man shook his head. "They took our clothes and gave us these. At first, we lived in a dormitory. Then they took us and moved us into these cells. Everyone was given a number."

"When was this?"

"Five weeks ago. Maybe six. That was the time of the first experiment."

"The first?"

"Yes. Every ninety minutes during that experiment, they would come to take someone new. Someone from the last cell. When the last cell was empty, everyone moved up a row."

"You're in the last cell now."

"Yes."

"Where were they taken?"

"I don't know."

"And when did they come back?"

"They never came back."

"You don't know what happened next?"

"Once, we saw bodies wheeled by. Mutilated bodies. And there were rumors. Rumors of torture. Of a drug that makes you crazy."

"How long did this experiment go on?"

"Off and on for two weeks."

"And after that?"

"Nothing. Except now, they have just begun another experiment."

"A second?"

"Yes."

"How many more have they taken?"

"Only one so far."

"From this cell?"

"Yes."

"When are they going to take the next one?" Coldmoon asked.

"Any moment. They are already late."

Shit. "Who's it going to be?"

The man paused, then pointed to one of the other two. "Luís. They go according to the numbers."

Coldmoon stared at the man named Luís. He was tall and thin, about fifty, with dark eyes and—like the others—a haunted look. He was shorter than Coldmoon, but not by much.

"I'm coming in," said Coldmoon. "Move back, please."

Coldmoon took out the magnetic key and held it to the plate in the door. With a click the light went green. He ducked inside, then turned to face the men.

"I'm here to help you get free. But you need to do exactly as I say."

The men looked at each other for a moment. Then, in unison, they nodded.

62

THE SOLDIERS WHEELED Pendergast out of the lab, the general following. They passed through another door that led into a dimly lit observation room. It was empty except for a carpeted ramp up to a row of chairs facing the long window, which gave an expansive view of the laboratory.

"Park him right in front," said the general. He sat down next to Pendergast. "Ms. Alves-Vettoretto, sit over there, if you please. We'll be comfortable here. As you can see, our view is unobstructed, and we'll be able to hear what's happening over the intercom system."

Pendergast watched as the orderlies wheeled the struggling Gladstone into the center of the room and placed her over a large drain in the tiled floor.

He said, "General, I promise you one thing."

"And what is that?"

"You will not live to see the sun rise."

The general fluttered his hand as if waving away a mosquito. "No need for clichés. As Ayn Rand said, 'Throughout the centuries there were men who took first steps down new roads armed with nothing but their own vision.' As an FBI agent you are a mere cog in the status quo, a participant in the feckless bureaucracy known as the United States government, designed to impede such men as Rand spoke of."

"Which would be you, of course."

The general smiled. "I have a few preparations to attend to, so I will leave you here, Mr. Pendergast, as a witness. And of course Ms. Alves-Vettoretto will remain: she has been asking to observe this for some time."

The woman nodded.

"The guards will stay, as well. Just to make sure nothing untoward occurs." He turned and barked out an order. "Corporal, go fetch a parang, freshly sharpened, and bring it to the lab. Smartly."

A soldier saluted, then exited.

The general smiled at Pendergast. "In our testing, we supplied the subjects with all kinds of weapons: sharp, dull, pieces of metal, saws—the sorts of objects that might be close at hand to someone seized with BIID. Sometimes they would botch the job, with the kind of results you can imagine. A razor-sharp parang is the most compassionate instrument under the circumstances. Normally our subjects simply bleed to death or are put out of their suffering, but in this case we'll give Dr. Gladstone emergency medical care to save her life."

"How humane of you."

"And now, I will take my leave."

Pendergast turned his attention to the window. Gladstone was in the middle of the lab, above the drain, still immobile in her wheelchair. She looked utterly terrified. The doctor was standing to one side, an eager look on his face, with the two orderlies on the other, waiting. Once again the doctor removed and cleaned his glasses.

Pendergast turned his face toward Alves-Vettoretto. The woman returned his look with a cool one of her own.

"Isabel, you've made quite the journey. The last time I saw you was in a most elegant New York office, where you were counselor to a wealthy entrepreneur—now deceased, alas. How interesting to find you here, deep in the swamps of Florida, surrounded by a band of mercenary soldiers."

The woman merely arched her eyebrows.

"I see you are following your own excellent advice in not conversing with me. Even so, I hope you won't mind if I say a few words."

No response, save to look away.

Pendergast went on, his voice gentle. "I can't help but admire you. You are the ultimate survivor."

Still no response.

"I imagine you must have experienced a serious betrayal at some point in your career," he said quietly. "Otherwise, I wouldn't have expected you to adopt the general's views."

She stroked her pearls.

"I made a mistake back there, however, in saying you were military. I think 'government' would be more accurate. Most likely CIA." He peered at her with curious intensity. "Iraq?"

Her lips tightened.

"I can guess how it went. They were all killed, weren't they?"

No reaction.

"You were a good handler. I imagine you became quite close to them and their families."

She stroked her pearls again, this time with a faint nervousness.

"They learned to trust you, and you them. But when the U.S. pulled out, ISIS moved in and killed all the operatives and informants—along with their families. It's an old story."

"How do you know this?" she finally asked in a low voice.

"You tried to save them," he went on. "But they were abandoned by the administration, refused the promised exit visas. This is the source of your disillusionment."

Now she turned to him. "If you don't stop playing Svengali, I'll have the soldiers gag you, as well."

"And no one in the CIA was willing to help. They told you, *It's war. People die.* I heard similar words, once upon a time in a former career."

"So what?" Alves-Vettoretto said with sudden vehemence. "People *do* die in war. End of story."

"In the great sweep of history, those lives hardly matter. That's what you were told—correct? Warfare is about winning and losing. Morality should never be a factor in warfare."

"Of course it shouldn't," she said. "The goal is to kill."

"Which brings me to this weapon of yours," said Pendergast. "It is, in its own way, admirable in its simplicity. Its capacity to leave the infrastructure intact...if a bit sticky."

"What's the difference between a land mine blowing an enemy's leg off, or forcing them to chop it off themselves?"

"Both are equally appalling."

"That's right, and it's gross hypocrisy to pretend to be horrified by this drug, when war itself is all about killing, burning, and maiming. You think this is somehow less humane than napalming a village, burning everyone alive?"

"Napalm is certainly as cruel, if not more so." Pendergast's voice was calm, almost hypnotic.

"So why not cooperate? I'm only here because this drug is going to end warfare as we know it."

"That's what Alfred Nobel said when he invented dynamite. But you overlook one thing."

"Which is?"

"You can choose *not* to participate in the cruelty of war."

"You mean, be a pacifist? Now, there's a lame philosophy if ever there was one."

"An individual doesn't have to be a pacifist to oppose the stupidities of war. You, for example. You have the choice to opt out. You don't have to be here, in this room, observing this depraved act of cruelty."

She shook her head. "You're not making any headway with me, Pendergast, so save your breath."

A muffled sound came from Gladstone, a moan as she tried to speak with the gag on. And then another. She was starting to twist in her bonds, snorting, moaning, shaking her head. He could see her eyes had changed. They were wider, deeper, and they carried an odd, chilling look.

"In that case," Pendergast told Alves-Vettoretto in

a low tone, "you'll find the next half an hour most instructive."

The general returned. "Ah, just in time!" He sat down as if in a movie theater, leaned forward, and pressed the intercom button. "Doctor, please remove her gag."

63

PAMELA GLADSTONE SAT in the gleaming white laboratory, bound to the wheelchair. Her lips tingled faintly from the tape the doctor had just pulled away. He'd done it carefully, to cause as little discomfort as possible. Odd how such a demon of a man could nevertheless act with a doctor's habitual gentleness.

Somehow the gag had been the worst, worse even than the binding of her arms and legs. She opened her mouth wide, gulping in air, then willing herself to stop hyperventilating. The desperate need to cry out abated. The racing of her heart slowed...but only slightly.

Over the last several hours, Gladstone had felt herself veering between mounting terror and a detached disbelief. Everything had happened so fast—the sudden flight, that awful chase through the swamp, the spotlights and stutter of machine guns,

Wallace's horrible death, the helicopter ride...and now this.

She had always prided herself on her courage and independence. Back there she'd put on as brave a show as possible. But this injection...She hoped desperately it was some ruse to force them to talk. Despite the terror of the last few hours, one thought had kept her going: that somehow Pendergast would save them. She had sensed from the beginning that he was a man of rare competence. But now Pendergast had been taken away and only the doctor and his orderlies remained, watching her and waiting...waiting. And her wheelchair had been placed in the middle of the room...where the tiled floor sloped slightly down to a large, gleaming industrial drain.

A sudden wave of terror flooded through her. "Pendergast!" she cried, struggling with her bonds. *"Pendergast!"*

Silence for a moment. Then, the amplified voice of the general, coming over a speaker high in the wall: "Bring in the parang. Then follow standard procedures."

She was hyperventilating again, and this time she had a more difficult time overcoming it.

She could do this. She'd overcome worse. It was absurd to think that she could be forced to amputate her own leg. She thought back to the time when her kayak had capsized off Sitka Sound. Or five years ago, skiing off-piste on the glaciers of La Grave, when one of their party had fallen in a crevasse and dislocated a shoulder, and she had roped up and gone in to bring her out. It was all about keeping her cool; keeping control.

Everything depended on keeping control.

A steel door in one side of the lab opened, and an orderly wheeled in a gurney. An object lay upon it, covered with a hospital sheet. She watched as the orderly placed the gurney five feet from her, locked its wheels, whisked off the sheet, and walked back toward the door. A large knife lay on the gurney: a sort of machete but heavier and longer, with a blade that took an odd bend about a quarter of the way down its length. The edge was sharpened to a silvery gleam, but the body and spine of the blade were a mottled grayish-black. Its shape reminded her of a giant slug. The end was encased in a derringer-shaped handle of wood, well worn...

She looked away, toward the doctor and two orderlies.

The doctor nodded at one, who came over behind her and began undoing the leather straps that bound her. She suddenly had a thought: as soon as she was free, she could seize the blade and use it to escape. As the orderly unbuckled her ankles, legs, and elbows, she began to plot out each movement in her mind.

But then the other orderly came over and pinned her arms even as she was being freed, holding her immobile. She struggled, but he held her fast in what felt like a long-practiced maneuver.

"You bastards, let me go!" she cried, struggling again.

"Soon," the doctor said in a high, penetrating voice. "Very soon."

They stood her up, and one orderly whisked the wheelchair away while the other continued to hold her in an iron grip. He leaned in toward her ear. "I'm going to release you. Stop struggling."

She went quiet and felt his grip ease. Then, after a brief fumbling, the orderly quickly stepped back. She hesitated, then took a step toward the weapon.

"*Not yet*," said the other orderly sharply. He held a gun, pointing it at her.

She froze as the doctor and the two orderlies backed up toward the metal door, one keeping the gun trained on her. The other grasped a cabinet on wheels and moved it away. As they reached the steel door, the doctor glanced back at her. His hazel eyes had lost none of their brightness, and they regarded her with a brief, intense curiosity. Then he turned and followed the others through the door, which closed quietly behind him.

She turned away again, and as she did her eyes once more fell on the blade—what the general had called a parang. Its full import—why it was there, what it was intended for—fell on her like an iron cloak. She limped back to the far wall, all the time staring at the gurney and its blade. It was still a potential weapon of defense, of rescue. She wanted to touch it, to take it up and use it against those who had done this to her, to get out of this hellish place. But the logical part of her mind said to her, *Don't touch it.*

"No," she said aloud. "No, no, no...!"

With great effort she rallied her thoughts, pushing away the fear and despair in an effort to logically assess her situation. *Everything depends on keeping control.*

The serum had been administered to her—what? Forty-five minutes ago? The doctor said it took an hour to take effect.

Dear God, it was hard to think rationally...

Everyone in the room had left. She glanced up at the long mirrored window. On the other side, they were watching. Waiting...

Don't. She had to put all irrelevant thoughts aside, confront the situation head-on, if she hoped to have any chance of beating this—

No. That was wrong. She *would* beat this. The idea that she would cut herself with that cruel-looking thing was crazy.

She looked around. The lab was fully equipped with IV racks and monitors and just about any other kind of equipment necessary to run an ER. There were

cabinets along the wall that might contain pharma-
ceuticals and syringes. If she could arm herself with
a scalpel, or better yet several, maybe she could hide
them in her clothing, and when they came back
in...Except for that damned one-way mirror. There
was no place in the lab out of its view. They were all
watching, watching her every movement. Still...

She walked to the wall with the cabinets. Why was
it so difficult to move?

Then she realized: it was the limp. It had first
manifested when she'd left the wheelchair: now, five
minutes later, it was far more pronounced. It must
have been from the tight bonds that held her in the
chair, or maybe she'd hurt herself during the chase
or in one of the struggles that followed.

She stopped in midstride and glanced down at her
right leg. She could see nothing wrong with it. She
raised it, swung it back and forth at the knee, like a
pendulum. No pain, no restriction of movement. She
returned it to the floor, ready to continue forward,
and it was only as the sole of her foot touched the
cold tile that she realized something was wrong. It
was strange, leaden, and from a tingling line above
the ankle it didn't look or feel right.

It was not her foot. They had done something to
it. They had grafted—

For a moment, she froze in terror. And then she
realized: this thought was completely insane. *Of course*

it was her foot. She forced the perverse idea from her head and continued to the cabinets. They were unlocked, but she found nothing inside them but gauze, gowns, surgical cloths, hairnets, and masks.

She kept looking. It occurred to her that if she couldn't find a weapon, she might find a drug—a tranquilizer, or a strong narcotic, or even anesthesia: something that would put her out of commission until whatever strange feeling was creeping over her had passed.

Nothing. The cart that orderly had wheeled out probably contained anything that might be of use to her. To hurt someone—or even medicate herself.

Her eye stole back over to the parang, gleaming on the table. Now, that was a fearsome weapon. It would disembowel any of those bastards with a single swipe...

Don't touch it.

With a stab of fear and frustration, she turned away, heading across the room toward the mirror. The limp was even more pronounced now. And then it became clear that *limp* wasn't really the right term. She simply could not stand the sensation of that thing touching the ground.

That thing. That "thing" was her foot. Her *own* foot. *Everything depends on keeping control...*

She stared up at the mirror. She knew the general was staring back at her, and perhaps the doctor as well. She wanted to curse them, but Christ, she felt strange. She slumped down and heard a clattering beside her. It was the parang. Its long cruel blade, exquisitely sharp, lay beside her, edge glistening in the lights.

How did it get there?

She must have picked it up on her way past the gurney.

She edged away from it. "Pendergast!" she yelled at the mirror. "Are you there? *Pendergast!*"

With great effort, she mastered herself again. This did not need to happen. She was not like those victims who had cut off their own feet. She *knew* what the drug did. That knowledge was power.

But even as she told herself this, she found herself looking toward the foot at the end of her right leg. Strange how she'd never realized before. How could she have lived so many years without noticing the mistake? That foot wasn't hers. It was hot and dull, as if infected. In fact, she could even feel the pathogens crawling up the blood vessels like tiny insects, attempting to make their way into her otherwise healthy body . . .

No, she told herself.

She tried to summon her thoughts, but she couldn't focus. Try as she might, her old memories and her sense of control were being overwhelmed by that alien lump. She examined it closely, trying to detect exactly what was wrong, unable to look away. It was like driving past a car accident, where you didn't really want to see, but you couldn't help staring.

They had done something. Replaced her foot, grafted something on there. Something that felt—in an awful way she had no words to describe—too *much*. Her body didn't need it. Her body didn't want it. She...

"*NO!*" This time, she yelled aloud. She glanced up at the clock: more than an hour had passed.

They were watching, the sick bastards. She wasn't going to give them the show they wanted. She tried to take deep breaths, empty her mind of the fear and revulsion.

Don't do it. Don't do it. Don't do it.

Even as she repeated this to herself, she realized she was still staring at the foot.

DON'T DO IT. DON'T DO IT. DON'T DO IT...

Without her knowing it, the parang was now back in her hand. She gave a shriek and scrambled back, but somehow it remained in a grip she was unable to loosen. But when that right foot hit the ground, the soft revulsive sensation overwhelmed her with nausea.

It's just the drug, she told herself. *That's your real foot. It's normal, not some infected piece of meat.*

She had to move her focus away from it. With an immense force of will, she went back to a game she had played in her childhood. She'd been tall for her age in grade school, and gangly, and people made fun of her. But she could escape the humiliation by tuning that out and retreating into a private garden of her imagination: a Technicolor glade where the grass was a bright green, the foliage lush and parti-colored, and in which she herself was a white horse with a flowing mane, running free and wild.

It had worked when she was young, and as she concentrated it worked again now—she was able to slow the breath that escaped in gasps, open her hand, and drop the weapon. It fell to the tile floor with a loud ringing sound. Taking a step back, she closed her eyes tight against the brightness, the madden-ingly regular rows of tile. She was able to control her breathing. She opened her eyes again and looked up at that mirrored window behind which the general watched as if she were a mouse in a cage. "Fuck you," she said out loud. "It's not working."

No answer, no reaction. Well, no matter. She could resist this. She was going to win. She'd sit down in a corner of the lab, the parang in hand, wait there until someone came back, and then she'd overpower them and escape. She'd use the parang on them instead of herself.

The parang was at hand—she picked it up, stood, and walked toward the corner. But this fresh effort at walking was pure horror, every step like squeezing a bag of poison into her body. She staggered and, unable to balance, abruptly sat down on the tile floor.

DON'T DO IT. DON'T DO IT. DON'T DO IT. DON'T DO IT...

She was gasping again, sweat beading her brow, slicking her palms as she slowly, deliberately, held up the blade and turned it in the light. Another wave of nausea swept over her, and she choked and doubled over in pain. There was poison in that foot and it was going to kill her—it *was* killing her.

DON'T. DON'T. DON'T...

With a supreme effort of will, she tried to recall the white horse again, the enchanted garden of her childhood. But all that came was a white and green fog of confusion, into which a rotting horse staggered, oozing fluids from its eyes. Her entire consciousness, every particle of energy, was fixated on that disgusting thing attached to her. She drew it up toward her thigh, horrified at the thought that others might see it. Oh God, if only she were free of it...

Free.

She looked at it, breathing even faster now. She could see where the parasitic thing had attached itself. She could see the very spot: just an inch or so above her ankle.

Free yourself. Free yourself. Free yourself...

It was incredible that she could have missed it. She could actually see, *feel*, like an invisible line across her skin, the precise area where the pores and freckles became no longer hers. Abhorrence rose in her like a tidal wave. It was unbearable.

She heard, in her mind, the rotting horse pause, issue a scream of fear.

FREE YOURSELF. FREE YOURSELF. FREE YOURSELF...

A terrible anger rose in her as she looked at the foot. The parang was in her hand, the long, sharp edge glittering in the light, a thing of beauty. It wasn't a weapon. It was an instrument—an instrument of freedom.

FREE YOURSELF. FREE YOURSELF. FREE YOURSELF...

She brought it over, laid its blade on the skin of her calf. It felt cool. It felt empowering. Now she lifted it and slid it gently along the spot where the alien foot had attached itself to her body. She repeated the motion, drawing the edge across with just a little more pressure. A thin line of red appeared, and she felt a flood of relief. It hadn't hurt at all. The sense of freedom was enormous, overwhelming. This was the solution, she now realized. Having the leg drawn up like this made things easier. Best to excise the parasite quickly. She steeled herself. She knew she could do it. In times of crisis, she'd always acted decisively.

She took a deep breath, then raised the parang

above her head. She felt the muscles of her hand tighten around the handle. She could save herself from this. It was all a matter of self-determination and control. *Everything depends on keeping control...*

She took in another long, shuddering breath. And then, as she brought the blade down with all her strength, an image flickered briefly across her mind's eye: a beautiful white horse, restored to health and vigor once again, running through a verdant garden, proud and free—and then, abruptly, stumbling as its fragile front legs cracked like brittle sticks, the animal screaming in pain as it fell into a cloud of dark, miasmic dust.

64

SITTING IN THE wheelchair, bound and immobile, Pendergast watched Pamela Gladstone through the observation window. He saw her move away from the wheelchair, back up against the wall. The intercom amplified the sound of her gasping, her terrified breathing.

"No," he heard her suddenly cry out in a voice full of anguish and frustration. "No, no, no...!"

It would have been easy for him to tune this out; to use his arsenal of meditative techniques to retreat from the reality of the present moment. But he would not allow himself to do that; he would not allow himself that escape.

He watched as she made her way to the other side of the lab, searching the medical cabinets for—he surmised—some kind of tool or improvised weapon. Finding none, she retreated to her corner. He noticed her begin to limp.

He would not allow himself that escape because he felt the terrible weight of responsibility for what was happening to her. He had brought Gladstone and Lam into his investigation. Naturally, he had not known the true nature of the conspiracy they unearthed or the extent of the danger they were in. But even in the final days, when it became increasingly clear there was a mole in the commander's inner circle, he had taken insufficient precautions. After Quarles's death he had arranged for the safe house and taken certain private measures to protect Constance—but he had not realized he was up against such a powerful and tentacled enemy.

A cry echoed in the room. "Pendergast!" It was Gladstone calling out for him, amplified by the sound system. He felt himself flinch.

The general, observing him, nodded to himself with satisfaction. Alves-Vettoretto remained still and silent, as she had through the entire proceeding.

"No!" came another cry through the speaker.

The general checked the chronograph on his wrist. "One hour and twelve minutes. She's taking longer than any from the last test group. I shall have to speak to the doctor about this. The process was supposed to be accelerated. It seems her foreknowledge has had a retarding effect. If so, we shall have to compensate."

Now Gladstone was no longer crying out. Gasps, as if of great effort, came through the speaker at irregular intervals. Pendergast watched fixedly as she raised the parang. A retreat into his memory palace, which he could reach in mere moments through the mental exercise of *stong pa nyid*, beckoned. But he resisted, forcing himself to watch.

It took less time than he expected. After an initial tentative cut, the blade was brought down with tremendous determination and precision. The first sound he heard Gladstone utter was a high crooning that seemed almost exultant. Despite the blow, it wasn't enough to take the foot off. Only in the later, hacking cuts through the bone did the resolution she had initially shown begin to flag. But she persisted, screaming ferociously, until once more the parang came down, and this time went all the way through, striking the tiled floor with a ringing sound, the limb abruptly coming free.

The general leaned forward and flicked a button. Abruptly, the cries from below were cut off. He flicked another button. "Doctor? She may be removed now."

Pendergast looked toward his companions. Alves-Vettoretto seemed rooted in place, eyes wide, one hand over her mouth. Meanwhile, General Smith was looking directly at him, with an expression almost of encouragement. The orderlies came in and collected her, strapping her on to a gurney and hustling out the rear door, leaving the room empty.

A final orderly scooped up the foot and placed it in a medical waste bag.

"Give them a few moments to clean up the mess down there," the general said. "And then we can proceed. We won't have long to wait."

65

THE ORDERLIES SWIFTLY returned with mops, squeegees, and disinfectant, cleaning up the splattered and pooled blood with alarming efficiency while the doctor watched, arms crossed. They took the parang from the floor, wiped it down, disinfected it with alcohol, and placed it back on a gurney, covering it with a white cloth. And then the doctor gestured to an orderly, who exited the lab and, a moment later, opened the door to the observation room.

"The doctor wants the next subject for the second round of experiments," he said.

The general ignored this and looked instead at Pendergast. "Care to make an observation?"

Pendergast didn't reply.

"I'd imagine you're wondering if you could resist the overwhelming compulsion of that drug. She was quite resistant, until the end. Could you do better? I admit to being intrigued myself. It will make an interesting experiment."

Silence.

"Nothing at all to say?"

Pendergast fixed his eyes on the general. "You and I know perfectly well this is a charade. You're going to test the drug on me regardless of what I do or say."

"What makes you think that?"

"The expression of zeal on the good doctor's face. And, of course, the simple fact that you cannot let me out of here alive."

"Your latter statement is, I'm afraid, true. As for the doctor, the eagerness you note is an eagerness to get back to his second round of experiments—which your arrival has interrupted. However, I'm sure he won't protest this further delay when I explain to him that a man like you will prove the ultimate test. I've read your jacket, you see—and I'm aware of what you did while in the military. Administering the drug to a person who truly possesses a will of iron and, aware of what is to come, knows what he must prepare for—will you be able to resist? If not, we can be confident the drug has been perfected." The general turned to the soldiers. "Take him into the lab."

One soldier grasped the wheelchair while another

stood behind and wheeled him out the door, down the hall, and into the lab. A moment later Pendergast was parked in the center of the room, over the drain. The doctor was holding a phone connected to a wall, no doubt an inside line to the general in the observation room. Finally, the doctor hung up, brought over a pair of scissors, and cut the sleeve away from Pendergast's right forearm. He didn't bother to swab, but inserted the IV needle, got blood, and taped it down.

"A vial of H12K, please," he said to an orderly.

"Doctor," the orderly said, "just so you know: that's the last of the initial new batch."

"So?"

"Well, it was earmarked for subject 714, who's next on the list and has been waiting in the prep room."

"This one is more important," the doctor snapped. "Get me the vial and send 714 back to his cell."

"Yes, Doctor."

The orderly opened a tabletop refrigerator, took out a vial, and handed it to the doctor, along with a freshly unsealed syringe.

The doctor inserted the needle through the cap of the vial, drew out a precisely measured amount, then held the needle up and depressed the plunger until a clear drop appeared, quivering at the hollow tip. He looked up at the one-way mirror with an anticipatory expression.

"Pendergast?" came the general's voice over the intercom. "Last chance to speak."

There was a long silence. Then the general's voice sounded again. "Inject him."

66

OVER AN HOUR ago they'd brought Coldmoon up from the cell, blindfolded, cuffed to one of the two guards, and wearing the filthy hospital gown belonging to Luís, stenciled over the chest with the number 714. After a circuitous journey, they took off the blindfold and he found himself in a small room—a sort of annex, it seemed—in beige cinder block, with two benches screwed to the floor, along with a locked medical cabinet. He had been seated on a bench, the guard he was cuffed to beside him. The other guard took the seat opposite, his M16 laid across his lap. Both guards were bored, clearly used to this routine. Coldmoon was careful to maintain a defeated attitude, adopting a listless shuffle that had annoyed the guards into prodding him forward more than once.

As the minutes had passed, Coldmoon had marveled

at how silent the room was. There was a large, stout door in the opposite wall that, he figured, led to the laboratory where the inmates were experimented on. He had no idea what those experiments might be, although he assumed they involved the horror of self-amputation. If this was the waiting room, then soundproofing made sense—he imagined what came next would be a pretty noisy ordeal.

As the minutes passed, Coldmoon considered his next step. On the one hand, he could continue to wait until he was called. The imprisoned man had told him there were ninety minutes between appointments—for want of a better word—and as far as he could tell, his own ninety were nearly up. A better course of action would be to take charge now and force the action himself, when he knew the lay of the land and his adversaries were least prepared. The guard sitting next to him was half-asleep, and the other beginning to nod off as well.

He'd never get a better—or even another—opportunity.

Pretending to be weary himself, Coldmoon leaned forward, elbows on his knees, head nodding, arms drooping down. He yawned quietly, resignedly. Slowly, he reached one arm under the hospital gown he was wearing and grasped the butt of the Browning he'd strapped to his upper calf. He freed it from its holster, careful to make no noise. And then, with a smooth, unhurried motion, he brought it up and fired point-blank at the guard next to him, the sound of the shot deafeningly loud in the confined space, spraying the cinder-block wall with gore. The other guard jerked his head up just in time to receive a bullet in the face. He slammed backward against the wall, then rolled onto the floor.

Soundproofing or not, Coldmoon knew the tremendous loudness of the shots would probably generate a response. His own ears were ringing. Laying the Browning aside, he grabbed the guard's M16 with his free arm and crouched, aiming at the stout door.

A second or two later, the door slammed open and Coldmoon let loose a burst, taking down a uniformed guard who had come to investigate. With the weapon clutched under his right arm, still aimed at the door, he knelt down, plucked the handcuff key from the dead guard on the bench, and unlocked the cuffs. Then he moved forward toward the door, waited a moment, and kicked it wide.

He found himself in a large, dazzlingly lit laboratory. There, to his astonishment, was Pendergast, strapped and tied to a wheelchair, an IV rack beside him. Two orderlies and a doctor fell back in confusion and horror, the doctor dropping a syringe. Two soldiers who were overseeing the proceedings began to turn toward Coldmoon. He dropped them both with one long burst.

"Behind that mirror!" said Pendergast with a nod. *"Kill everyone but the woman."*

Glancing in the indicated direction, comprehending immediately the mirror was a one-way observation window, Coldmoon trained the weapon on it and raked it with a two-second burst. The glass shattered in a huge spray, plates falling free, and behind it he saw a military officer in camo struggling to stand up, next to a woman. A third burst stitched its way up the general's trunk from groin to throat, and he pitched forward, falling from the ruined window into the laboratory below with the sound of wet meat hitting the floor, as the woman scrambled away in panic. Coldmoon swung the M16 around to take out the doctor and orderlies—but they had already escaped out one of the lab doors.

Sirens went off in the room.

"The parang," said Pendergast, pointing at it with his eyes.

Coldmoon snatched up the parang and used it to slice Pendergast free of the wheelchair. Pendergast ripped the IV from his arm and leapt to his feet, seizing an M16 from one of the dead soldiers.

The sirens continued to sound. And now a red light in the ceiling began to revolve.

Pendergast turned to Coldmoon. "Shall we take our leave?"

"Hell, yes."

67

As THEY BURST through the back door, they saw the woman staggering out of the observation room and into the hall in front of them.

She turned. Coldmoon saw her face was streaming blood, cut by flying glass.

"I can't...I can't believe..." She gasped, wiping blood from her face. "I had no idea..."

"Pull yourself together," Pendergast said. "You're going to show us the way out of this chamber of horrors, Ms. Alves-Vettoretto."

"I have limited passkey privileges. But..." She swayed and Pendergast grasped her arm to keep her from collapsing. "The doctor...he ran by and went in there." She pointed to a closet door with a bloody hand. "He has full access."

"Stand back." Pendergast went to the door and tried the knob. Finding it locked, he fired the M16 into the lock and kicked the door open.

The doctor was crouching behind a set of shelves with glass bottles, the orderlies trying to hide on either side.

Pendergast strode forward. The orderlies, unarmed, shrank back as he seized the doctor and hauled him to his feet, knocking the shelves over with a crash. The man cringed and burbled with fear. "Don't, please don't kill me. I didn't want to do any of it; they forced me—"

Pendergast shook him like a rag doll. "You're going to lead us out of here."

"Yes! I will, of course I will," the doctor babbled, his eyes blinking in servile agreement, head nodding.

Pendergast shoved him out through the door. "Best way out, no trickery." He turned to the woman. "You too."

"Best way out." The doctor nodded, his look of servile terror morphing into a grotesque grin. "This way." He scurried down the hall, and they followed.

The doctor used his passkey to open a door at the far end. "Through here."

They went through the door into another hallway that led off to both the left and the right. The doctor turned down the right passage.

"What's the route?" Pendergast asked.

"I'm going to take you out past the barracks. Fewer guards."

"That's a lie!" the woman named Alves-Vettoretto blurted out.

Pendergast and Coldmoon turned toward her.

She seemed as surprised at her outburst as they did. She took a deep, shuddering breath. "The barracks will be a hornet's nest. You should go out the side entrance, through the old river gate."

Pendergast turned back to the doctor, weapon raised in menacing inquiry.

The doctor hesitated. Then, with a hiss and an evil glance at Alves-Vettoretto, he turned and led the way down the left-hand passage until it ended in another door. The doctor used his passkey to unlock it, revealing a stairwell beyond.

Pendergast cracked the door open and listened. Loud voices echoed upward, along with the sound of pounding feet.

He slipped onto the landing, followed by Coldmoon. They heard the group of soldiers ascending rapidly.

Pendergast glanced at Coldmoon, who nodded his understanding. He hoisted his weapon over the railing just as Coldmoon called out in a loud, harsh voice: "Hey, you guys! Look down! They're at the bottom of the stairwell, trapped!"

Five heads popped out from the landing below and Pendergast fired a long burst down the stairwell.

"Dumb bastards," said Coldmoon as they ran past

the bodies of five guards, sprawled and hung over the railings. Alves-Vettoretto stumbled along, Coldmoon sometimes holding her up. Another landing, and they arrived at the bottom.

"Go right, then straight," the doctor said. "That passes through the holding cells."

Pendergast turned his weapon toward the doctor again and the man cringed back. "It *does!* I swear it does!"

Pendergast looked at Alves-Vettoretto. She nodded.

They followed the directions, jogging down a maze of cinder-block halls until they came to the large open area where Coldmoon had found the prisoners. They were pressed against the bars.

"*¿Qué pasa?*" several of them cried. "*¿Qué pasa?*"

"You'll be free soon," Coldmoon replied in Spanish.

They jogged along, leaving behind a hubbub of excitement.

"We've got to go down one more level," said the doctor. "There are crash doors we can use to get out the back of the building."

He directed them to another stairwell, down one more level, and through another maze of corridors, encountering only one guard, who was so frightened he dropped his rifle in surprise and tried to surrender. Coldmoon took the magazine from his rifle, put one warning finger to his lips, and then left him. Finally, at the end of a short hall, they came to a crash door.

"This is it," the doctor said.

"Where does it go?"

"It leads through a parking lot, through a gate, and to the road to the river."

Pendergast turned to Alves-Vettoretto. She shrugged and shook her head. He leaned into the door, opened it a crack, and peered out. Then he pushed it open and gestured for them to follow, weapons raised. As the door opened wide, Coldmoon could hear the wail of sirens grow suddenly louder.

"You don't need me anymore," said the doctor, beginning to scurry off.

"Not so fast," Coldmoon said, grabbing the man and giving him a hard shove. "You're staying with us."

They came out into a side parking lot, with rows of jeeps, Humvees, and transport trucks. Rain was falling, blown in gusts, and a flash of lightning lit up the clouds, followed by a distant rumble. Klieg lights from the tower above were roaming over the area. They pressed themselves against the wall of the building as a beam passed.

Pendergast looked at Alves-Vettoretto. "Are you going to be able to do this?"

She nodded mutely.

"Stay close," said Pendergast. He darted out across an open area and crouched beside a truck as the others followed. Another light passed nearby and

Coldmoon could see a line of soldiers moving along the far wall, arms at the ready.

"Where's the gate?" Pendergast asked the doctor.

"In that far wall," the doctor replied. "Beyond the big truck, to the right."

"Is it guarded?"

"Yes, but it's the least defended gate into the complex."

"And beyond that?"

"Nothing but a ruined courtyard. Then the road down to the river."

Pendergast and Coldmoon rose cautiously and peered over the hood of the truck. Through the rain they could see the gate, lit up, manned by four soldiers on high alert. Another patrol, jogging alongside the wall, rounded the corner and they ducked down.

"Beyond that courtyard, how far to the river?" Pendergast asked.

"About a quarter mile."

Pendergast, crouching, moved alongside the truck, then sprinted across another open area to hunker down behind a Humvee. The rest caught up behind him. The tower lights roamed this way and that. After waiting a moment for the lights to pass, they dashed to another vehicle, and then another, approaching the gate.

Now the patrolling squad of soldiers appeared

again, moving through the center of the parking lot, the men spread out with portable spotlights, probing among the dark array of vehicles.

Pendergast gestured for them all to crouch down and wait.

The soldiers wound through the vehicles, every once in a while shining a beam inside or underneath one. They were speaking to each other by radio in low voices, moving swiftly.

As the soldiers neared their hiding place, Cold-moon braced himself; if they were discovered, there would be nothing for it but to engage in a firefight, two against ten. But discovery wasn't a given—at the rate they were moving, there were many more vehicles than the soldiers could inspect thoroughly. It was a fast sweep.

He held his breath as he heard, through the sound of the rain, the murmuring of the soldiers into their walkie-talkies.

Suddenly, the doctor jumped up, waving his arms and crying out shrilly. "It's me, Dr. Smith! Don't shoot, I'm the chief doctor. I have hostages—!"

Two simultaneous bursts of gunfire cut him almost in half, opening him up like a ripe papaya. But the doctor's treachery had caused the soldiers to pause, giving Coldmoon and Pendergast an opportunity to return fire. They dropped two soldiers before the others dove for cover.

Pendergast skittered around one side of the vehicle and fired again, gunning down one of the soldiers at the checkpoint.

"To the gate!" he shouted, taking Alves-Vettoretto by the arm and hauling her along.

But even as he spoke, a klieg light locked on them, bathing them in brilliant light and blocking their ability to see into the darkness beyond. They dove for cover behind a truck as the soldiers opened fire again, the rounds hammering through the metal above their heads, showering them with chips of paint and bits of canvas.

"If we can get past that gate, there'll be cover in the woods," Pendergast said to Coldmoon. "We'll alternate movements. Lay down suppressing fire while I try to clear the gate. You first, then I'll take her." He turned to Alves-Vettoretto. "Are you ready?"

She nodded.

As Coldmoon gathered himself for a dash, Pendergast rose and fired once over the hood at the soldiers, forcing them to take cover again. Coldmoon dashed to the next vehicle, then readied himself to cover Pendergast and Alves-Vettoretto as they made their own dash. The gate was just two vehicles away now, and Coldmoon watched as Pendergast dropped another of its guards.

Coldmoon let loose with several bursts of suppressing fire as Pendergast scurried across, pulling

Alves-Vettoretto along as he sprayed the gate with a dozen rounds of his own, dispatching its last two guards. Now all the klieg lights were on them as they crouched by the side of the last truck. It was brighter than day. More soldiers were surely on their way to the firefight.

"Ammo?" Pendergast asked.

He swiftly checked his magazine. "Christ, only one left. You?"

"One also. But the gate is clear."

Just as he spoke, Coldmoon heard the crackle of a walkie-talkie on the far side of the gate. *Shit.* And behind them, he could see the soldiers in the parking lot moving toward them, spread out, darting from cover to cover.

"We're surrounded," Coldmoon said. "Only two rounds, and the bastards aren't likely to let us surrender."

"They're going to kill us?" Alves-Vettoretto asked.

"What do you think?" said Coldmoon sarcastically.

There was brief moment of silence, a pause, as they stared at each other.

"Well," said Pendergast, extending his hand. "You've been a fine partner."

"You weren't half-bad, either."

They shook hands.

"You won't tell anyone I said that, I presume?" Pendergast asked.

Despite their situation, Coldmoon laughed. "You wouldn't have told me that if you thought I'd have a chance to repeat it."

Another burst of fire tore into the truck they were crouching behind as the soldiers in the parking lot made a coordinated rush. Pendergast said, "Get ready," and aimed his rifle, not at the approaching soldiers, but at the truck's gas tank. He fired a round into it.

"What the——?" Coldmoon scrambled back as the truck erupted in fire, ready to blow. Pendergast grabbed Alves-Vettoretto and ran past the smoke and flame through the gate, Coldmoon following, firing his last round into the darkness ahead. As they came out the other side, into the old courtyard, a voice rang out.

"Drop your weapons! Hands up! *Now!*"

They had practically run into a squad of soldiers stationed just outside the gate, arranged in a semicircle, their weapons aimed squarely at the little group of three. Coldmoon looked around in a panic for a way to escape. Broken walls of weathered stone rose on two sides amid pallets of bricks, long forgotten and covered with kudzu. The gleam of the searchlight cast a ghostly pallor over everything. They were trapped.

"Drop your weapons!" barked the voice. "I won't ask again!"

Pendergast and Coldmoon placed their now-empty

weapons on the ground. Then they raised their hands over their heads. Behind them, Coldmoon could hear soldiers from the first squad coming through the parking lot and past the gate.

They were surrounded, with approximately twenty weapons pointed at them.

The figure that had spoken stepped forward. He was tall and muscular, with an acne-pitted face. Unlike most of the other soldiers, he wore the markings of a full-bird colonel, along with a name tag: Kormann.

He looked from Pendergast, to Coldmoon, to Alves-Vettoretto, with a mixture of disdain and hatred. "Which one of you shot Harrigan?" he asked, jerking one thumb toward a prone figure directly behind him. Coldmoon noticed the colonel's boots were freshly splattered with what must have been the dead man's blood.

"I had that privilege," Coldmoon said.

The man named Kormann stepped up to Coldmoon. He smiled lazily. Coldmoon smiled back.

Kormann lashed out with a fist, catching Coldmoon on the jaw. Coldmoon staggered under the blow but didn't fall. As he raised himself back to full height, the colonel spat in his face, then buried the fist in Coldmoon's gut. He doubled over, groaning, and Kormann connected with a wicked haymaker that knocked him prone.

Pendergast must have made some attempt to intercede, because Coldmoon, as if from far away, heard the clatter of weapons and an order from Kormann: "As you were."

There was a brief silence. Then Kormann laughed. "You're the one called Pendergast, aren't you? Well, look at you now."

Coldmoon, full consciousness returning, saw Kormann turn to one of his men. "Let's take them back to the barracks—and have some fun."

Coldmoon grabbed a stone from the rubble-strewn ground and, half rising, tried to smash Kormann with it. But the colonel dodged the blow easily, kicked him brutally back onto the ground, and then—with a brief laugh—began to close in.

68

COLDMOON—DAZED AND bleeding—could only turn his face from the crushing blow he knew was coming. But there was nothing. Instead, a strange silence fell, a hush, like a collective intake of breath.

"Well," he heard Kormann say. "And just what the fuck do we have here?"

The hush was broken by a low murmuring among some of the soldiers. Everyone had turned to look at a curious figure standing in the ruined archway at the far end of the courtyard.

Coldmoon blinked the blood out of his eyes and tried to focus. He wondered if he was seeing things. It looked like some woodland elf, petite, girlish, smeared with mud. Bits of leaves and plant fronds were plastered here and there, one fern flapping back and forth in the wind. The figure itself remained motionless, in a posture that seemed easy and confident, even relaxed. It held a dagger in one hand.

"Who's this?" Kormann said. "Catwoman to the rescue?"

One soldier laughed. The rest remained tense, on guard.

The figure had been looking around the courtyard, as if memorizing it. Now it stared directly at the colonel and spoke. Coldmoon wasn't sure what he recognized first—the violet eyes or the voice: calm and unusually deep for such a small frame.

Constance Greene.

"Let them go," she said.

This was so ludicrous a demand, so unexpected, that several soldiers laughed this time.

Kormann issued a sarcastic laugh of his own. "Is that all?"

Constance remained impassive.

"Is there anyone with you? Batman, perhaps, or a squad of SEALs?"

Constance shook her head.

"In that case, I'd be happy to release them," Kormann went on. "There's just one thing."

"Yes?"

"You forgot to say 'please.'"

More snickers from the soldiers. Coldmoon used the moment to rise to his feet. This unexpected interruption, he noticed, had diffused a little of the tension and perhaps lessened their own immediate danger. As astonished as he was to see her, it was still a futile and almost ridiculous situation, surrounded by twenty soldiers, with more surely on the way. He looked at Pendergast to see his reaction, but his face was, as usual, unreadable.

Still, she just stood there. Constance... He had no idea what she might do next, armed with only a thin-bladed knife. What the hell was going through her mind? All she could do was provide a little sport for the soldiers before dying. But there was something catlike about her, an apex predator.

"I don't beg from cowards like you," she said. "Men who are all swagger and tough talk—all very easy when backed up by thugs with automatic weapons."

Nettled, Kormann said: "Why don't you come in and join your friends for their final, painful moments on earth?"

"Not quite yet," she said—and then, with a sudden flash of movement, she disappeared.

This caused almost as much consternation as her initial appearance. Except for a few soldiers, who kept their weapons trained on Pendergast and Coldmoon, everyone was staring out through the broken archway, now empty.

And then, abruptly, Constance reappeared. Only this time she was lugging something heavy across her shoulders, and also awkwardly carrying two ammo boxes. Coldmoon looked on, incredulous.

A murmur, like a rustling of grass, swept through the platoon.

With a grunt of effort, Constance put down the two ammunition boxes—green, with the standard yellow stenciling—and shrugged what was obviously a weapon off her shoulders, staggering as it slipped from her grasp and fell to the ground.

At the appearance of the gun, the soldiers instinctively trained their weapons on her, and one fired a shot that whined past Constance. Coldmoon stared; he recognized the thing she'd dropped as a military machine gun, an M240 hybrid with an integrated bipod assembly. One of the cartridge boxes was open, its belt already fed into the M240.

"Hold fire!" Kormann said. He could, of course, take her out at any moment, but he didn't seem to be in a hurry. He smiled, as if ready to play a game. "Well, now," he said mockingly. "So Tinker Bell has gotten herself a machine gun."

"I found it on my way up from the river," Constance replied. "I hope you don't mind my appropriating it."

The soldiers were on edge, but her retort only seemed to goad Kormann on. "What are you going to do now, Tinker Bell?" he asked. "Shoot us all with that thing?" As he spoke, his hand crept down, unholstering his handgun. "You can't even lift it. You could never hold it steady long enough to get off a single burst. Besides, you probably don't even know which end to point." He paused. "But touch it again, and we'll open fire."

Constance looked toward Pendergast. "I'm sorry I couldn't arrive sooner, Aloysius." She nodded at the machine gun. "He may be a Neanderthal, but the brute's right about one thing: this is heavier than I expected."

A mocking tone had entered her voice. Kormann flushed, turned toward Pendergast. "Aloysius, is it? So you know little Tinker Bell here?" He stepped toward the FBI agent. "She's awfully young to be out playing in the swamp with guns. You should spank her. I mean, you must be her *daddy*—right?"

Pendergast said nothing.

"I asked you a question!" And, raising his arm, the colonel dealt Pendergast a savage blow across the face with the back of his hand.

"Don't," Constance said instantly.

Several of the men laughed. Emboldened, Kormann leaned in closer. "So. Are you her daddy? Her *sugar* daddy, maybe?" And he slapped Pendergast again, harder. A trickle of blood appeared at the edge of the agent's mouth.

"*Don't*," Constance said again, in a voice that would freeze steel.

"I knew it," Kormann said, spitting at Pendergast's feet. "You're her sugar daddy. A sugar daddy who likes his pussy *extra sweet*." And he drew his hand back for another blow.

In a blur of motion, Constance raised one hand—the gleaming tip of her stiletto appearing between her fingers—and whipped the knife at him even as she appeared to drop straight down and out of sight.

There was a moment of stunned disbelief, a fresh rattling of weapons, several shots fired into the darkness where Constance had stood. And then silence. Nothing seemed to have happened—until Kormann staggered slightly and made an odd gesture, lifting his hand to his throat. And it was only then Coldmoon made out the handle of Constance's stiletto. It was buried to the hilt in Kormann's neck, just beneath the jaw.

Kormann tried to speak, but only a gurgling noise emerged. He took one step and crumpled onto the stone floor of the courtyard.

69

THEN ALL HELL broke loose.

Instantly, the soldiers opened fire at the spot where Constance had been, all their attention focused on the archway. It gave Pendergast and Coldmoon a split-second opening. Pendergast grabbed Alves-Vettoretto and yanked her toward the broken wall, while Coldmoon followed, all of them diving over it and taking cover behind.

The courtyard was a scene of mass confusion, the soldiers firing indiscriminately through the archway as they rushed forward. But then, to Coldmoon's infinite surprise, the M240 suddenly opened fire, its bark deeper and slower than the chattering assault weapons of the defenders. It enfiladed the courtyard, mowing down some and sending others into a panic, diving and scrambling for cover, including two who, mortally shot, tumbled over the low wall and almost into Coldmoon's lap.

He seized one of their weapons and poked his head up. To his right he could see Constance flat on the ground behind the machine gun, in a depression that gave her cover, gripping the weapon with furious purpose, her entire body shaking as the disintegrating links of the belt-fed cartridges flew away in a gathering pall of smoke. In a flash, he realized that Constance, while pretending to lose her grip and drop the gun, had instead contrived to set it atop a hummock that acted as a natural revetment, exposing only its barrel and bipod. He and Pendergast, who had grabbed the gun from the other dead soldier, fired from behind the wall, further decimating a panicked mob of soldiers within, running and scrambling in every direction as, one after another, they were shot to pieces.

But many other soldiers had taken cover and began shooting back in a more organized fashion. Coldmoon could see that Constance, with the barest of cover, wasn't going to last long against the increasing rain of fire.

It seemed Pendergast realized the same thing, because he locked eyes with Coldmoon, then glanced over their covering wall. Immediately, Coldmoon understood. They leapt over the wall together, firing across the courtyard to where the soldiers were taking cover behind pallets of bricks.

They divided, and Coldmoon ducked down behind

a pile of stones just as a series of high-velocity rounds ricocheted past him. Constance apparently took notice, because the deep *thunk* of her weapon turned his way and he saw a fusillade of 7.62 mm NATO rounds stitch a line along the wall about five feet from him, cutting down two soldiers who'd been aiming in his direction. They fell to the ground, jerking like spastic marionettes as the bullets tore through them. Another soldier rose to return fire, only to get torn apart by the M240, blood and brains mushrooming against the courtyard wall.

"This way," he heard Pendergast shout, barely audible over the din.

They dashed across an exposed area to another pallet of bricks about twenty yards from the archway. Together, they rose just high enough to see over the pallet, then sent off twin bursts of fire at the soldiers, dropping two more.

Coldmoon noticed that Constance was firing in bursts, pausing every few seconds to choose a new target before firing again. Now and then, a tracer round from her gun flashed across the courtyard. Consciously or not, she was pacing her shots; but even so, he knew the barrel of her weapon would overheat within minutes. The soldiers were firing at her now in a more coordinated fashion, bullets striking all around her, throwing up gouts of dirt. Coldmoon heard one round ricochet off the half-empty cartridge box.

A few more bullets whined over his head, hitting the pallet of bricks. Pendergast popped up and fired off several bursts of his own, suppressing their fire. The incoming rounds stopped, but now Coldmoon could hear fire from somewhere else, above, pattering around them like hail—the tower. Pendergast turned and fired upward, burst after burst, and it abruptly grew darker as some of the klieg lights were shot out. Finally, with another burst, darkness fell completely, the only light now coming from the indirect glow of the complex.

Coldmoon risked another glance over the bricks. The courtyard looked like a slaughterhouse. Bodies lay everywhere: sprawled over terraces, slumped against walls. Blood ran in rivulets across the old stones. A soldier was dragging himself through the courtyard, crying out for help.

Suddenly, the deep bark of Constance's weapon ceased. For a second, Coldmoon heard the patter of spent casings falling in the foliage around her. Then that, too, stopped. For a moment, he thought she'd been killed. Then he realized what had happened: she'd expended her two-hundred-round belt, and the ammunition box was empty.

Quickly, he glanced back over the courtyard. A dozen, perhaps more, soldiers were out of commission. But there were still several who were taking advantage of this pause to find better defensive positions—almost all of them behind and atop a stone parapet on the far side of the courtyard. With its advantage of height, and crenellations for shelter, that wall made for a formidable firing position.

Constance was almost entirely obscured by smoke, but Coldmoon could just make out movement. She had risen from her prone position and, as he watched, he could see her—barely more than a shadow—open the weapon's cover assembly, sweep out the feeding tray, then start loading in a fresh ammunition belt from the second cartridge box. She botched it and, with an impatient gesture, started trying to feed it in again. If he could only get around to help her... but there was open ground between them, sure suicide.

A burst of fire came from the broken wall, more gouts of dirt spitting up all around Constance as she struggled with reloading. The remaining soldiers were organized—and they were shooting from an elevated position at the increasingly exposed figure fumbling with the gun.

"Cover me," Pendergast said.

Coldmoon laid down suppressing fire while, in a sudden break, Pendergast ran at a crouch across the courtyard to get a better line to the parapet. Rising himself, Coldmoon also took aim at the parapet. The shooting from the soldiers temporarily abated while Constance cleared the feed tray and succeeded at reseating the belt. Out of the corner of his eye,

Coldmoon saw her close the cover and yank the charging handle into position. A moment later, the deep, powerful cadence of her weapon began raining death upon the parapet. Huge pieces of stone fell from its walls, like an exhalation of ruin, a web of cracks spreading as the wall itself began to crumble. And then, abruptly, the entire structure collapsed, sending soldiers and stones alike down into a cloud of brick dust and powdered mortar.

"*Move*," said Pendergast. They both leapt up and, trading off suppressing fire, ran along the edge of the courtyard until they reached the ruins of the archway, then took up positions on either side, flanking Constance.

She seemed unaware of their presence, all her attention fixed on the courtyard. And then, Coldmoon saw a man rise, hands in the air. Now more men began to stand up, hands raised. Still Constance gripped the machine gun, stock pressed against her shoulder, the barrel of the weapon smoking and steaming in the rain. She took aim, breathing heavily.

Pendergast put a hand on her shoulder. "Constance?" He gave her a gentle shake. "You can stop shooting now."

For a moment she remained motionless in the gathering silence; then she eased her finger from the trigger. Silence fell as more soldiers rose up, shakily, some splattered with their comrades' blood.

Although her face remained composed, her eyes were afire—a wraithlike, mud-covered specter of death.

"We'd better get the hell out," Coldmoon said. Even as he spoke there was a scattering of fire in the parking lot beyond the courtyard. The soldiers who had surrendered, seeing their comrades arriving, hesitated, and some broke into a run to get away.

In an incongruously courteous gesture, Pendergast motioned down a faint road into the dark swamp. "Constance, if you'd kindly lead the way?"

They ran down the track and were soon enveloped in protective darkness. A few random shots rang out behind them, but nobody, it seemed, cared to follow.

"Where's that woman?" Coldmoon asked abruptly.

"Alves-Vettoretto? Gone," Pendergast replied. Then: "She's a survivor; she can take care of herself."

"Why did you take her with us, anyway?"

"I believed I saw something worth saving. Chalk it up to a personal weakness, perhaps."

70

THEY JOGGED DOWN the muddy path toward the docks, Constance in the lead.

In his entire law enforcement career, Coldmoon had never seen anything remotely like what this woman had just done. He wondered if she was really Pendergast's "ward"—this crazed angel of death, in her torn and filthy clothes—or instead some kind of homicidal bodyguard the man had trained for his own protection. For a moment, his thoughts strayed back to his grandmother, and her description of Wachiwi. He recalled seeing Dancing Girl with his own eyes, walking through the frozen trees, her thin form wrapped in a blanket. *She is mortal, as we are. Yet she is also different.*

Pendergast had taken a spotlight from one of the dead soldiers, and it now illuminated a grisly sight: three dead guards in a rude pillbox made of earth and bricks, their bodies sprawled and splayed in various attitudes of death.

"Your handiwork, Constance?" Pendergast asked.

"I needed their weapon."

"How did you do that with only a stiletto?"

"Chief Perelman lent me his gun. Not voluntarily, of course. He's down at the river, with a broken leg. We were caught in a tornado as we were landing."

They proceeded through the dark trees and around a bend in the lane. Ahead now, Coldmoon could see the black mass of the river through a tangle of wrecked docks, piers, and metal buildings. Constance veered off the road and they made their way to the embankment.

"I left him here," she said as they came to a small grove of trees. Pendergast shone the light around.

"Over here," came a faint voice from downriver.

They worked their way along the embankment to find Chief Perelman lying on his side next to his wrecked boat. He had the mike of a VHF in his hand, the radio next to him, wired to a marine battery from the boat.

"Dragged myself over," he said, gasping, his face smeared with mud and dripping with rainwater. "When I heard all that shooting, I figured you wouldn't mind if I called in the cavalry."

As if on cue, Coldmoon heard the distant rumble of rotors and saw—above the treetops in the east—

a line of choppers moving fast and low. A moment later, lights appeared downriver, with a rising drone of outboard engines, as a phalanx of Coast Guard patrol boats materialized out of the darkness, moving at high speed, their spotlights playing along the shore.

"That was fast," Coldmoon said.

"I told them federal agents were engaged in a firefight, with a man down. That did the trick." Perelman lay back, looking at Constance. "I can't believe it—you actually went in there alone and *rescued* these two?"

"I only did what I said I would do," she said simply.

"*Only*," the chief said, shaking his head and lying back with a wince. He glanced in the direction of the river. "I hope to hell they're bringing painkillers."

Coldmoon watched the helicopters pass overhead. The first patrol boat made a ground landing and several men and women in body armor jumped out, their lights flashing, armed to the teeth with assault rifles, mortars, and RPGs. Its complement deployed, the boat backed away, making room for the next vessel.

"I'm going back," said Pendergast, moving toward the troops.

"What the hell for?" Coldmoon asked. "We did our part. Let them do the mopping up."

"I have to get Dr. Gladstone. They gave her the drug . . . and she amputated her own foot."

"Oh my God..." Coldmoon swallowed. "I'm coming with you, then."

Pendergast nodded. "Thank you."

They joined the stream of men clambering off the boats. "This way," Pendergast cried to them. "Follow me!" And moments later, the assembled group set off toward the glowing complex rising beyond the trees, as the choppers hovered above, fast-roping down SWAT teams and exchanging fire with the rogue troops inside the facility.

71

AFTER THE SOUND and fury of the previous night, it was a remarkably quiet group that rode in Perelman's Explorer the following morning. Towne drove while the chief reclined in the front passenger seat, his leg in a splint. Coldmoon, Pendergast, and Constance Greene sat in the back. The storm was spent, giving way to freshly washed blue sky.

"It's very good of you to drop us at the house," Pendergast said, with a voice as tranquil as if they'd just been shopping at the local mall.

"Least I could do," came the response from the front seat.

Coldmoon was too exhausted to speak. The dawn helicopter ride back from Crooked River to Fort Myers, the obligatory medical exams, the initial debriefing, and paperwork had passed in a blur. Now Perelman was driving them home, and all Coldmoon could think of was crawling into bed. As the Explorer bumped over Blind Pass Bridge onto Captiva, he thought it was as beautiful a place as he'd ever visited in his life—but he was too tired to appreciate it.

Pendergast sat beside him, as pale and still as a marble statue. Constance was on the far side. Constance—what was he to make of her now? She hadn't spoken to him since they left the complex, and he could feel the tension radiating from her when he was around. He once again recalled her warning when he'd refused to bring her along on the rescue mission. He hoped it was only a brief expression of anger and not an actual threat. Unfortunately, it didn't feel that way. Maybe he could convince Pendergast to talk to her—he doubted anybody else could change her mind.

As the Explorer approached the Mortlach House, the radio squawked. "Explorer One, Explorer One. P.B., acknowledge."

With a grunt, Perelman reached forward and plucked the handset from its cradle. "Priscilla, what is it?"

"Chief Caspar wants an update. And Commander Baugh's been calling and call—"

"Nothing until after my nap," he interrupted, replacing the handset and turning to Towne. "Just like I predicted, all those souls who did nothing, and even the ones who screwed up, are going to crawl out into the light, eager to share in the glory. Just wait."

The car slowed as it turned in to the Mortlach driveway. Pendergast turned to Perelman. "I wonder if you might satisfy my curiosity on one small point."

"Of course," the chief replied.

"What does 'P.B.' stand for?"

There was an awkward pause. Perelman turned to Towne. "Lewis, would you mind waiting for us in front of the house?"

Perelman waited until Towne had exited the vehicle, then waited some more. He turned to Pendergast. "Percy Bysshe."

"Marvelous! You must have had literary parents."

"*Not* marvelous. Bloody awful. Especially to a thirteen-year-old kid."

"It seems to have done you no harm in later life."

"That's because nobody knows about it. And I hope to hell you can keep my secret." Perelman opened his door, getting out with difficulty, Pendergast handing him his crutches.

Coldmoon followed the others up the steps and into the Mortlach House. The old boards creaked under their feet. This was immediately followed by a muffled sound coming from the bowels of the house—sounding like a drawn out wail.

Perelman halted in surprise. "What fresh hell is that?"

"That," Constance said, "is the Mortlach ghost."

Coldmoon stared, aghast, as another sound, a sort of groan, came through the floorboards.

"If you'd care to follow me into the basement, gentlemen, I'll be happy to introduce you." She led the way through the house to the basement door, opened it, turned on the lights, and descended the stairs. Coldmoon followed the others. He'd only been down in the basement once before, and it was as close and stuffy as he remembered it.

There was, however, one major change. A hole had been broken through a far section of the exterior wall, bricks and dirt scattered over the floor. And at the sound of their voices, another howl of protest issued from a dark corner, a sound so full of misery that Coldmoon felt his hair prickle.

Constance walked over and, removing a skeleton key from her pocket, opened a heavy wooden door in the alcove, revealing a tiny, windowless room. A man stumbled out into the light, dressed in muddy clothes, with wild hair and a massive dirty beard. He looked around at them with confused, pleading eyes.

"Wait—I think I know this man," Perelman said. "He's that old fellow who's been hanging around Silver Key Beach." He stared at Constance. "Who is he and what's he doing here?"

"His name is Randall Wilkinson."

"Randall Wilkinson," Perelman repeated, balancing on his crutches. "But that's...that's impossible! Wilkinson was the murder victim who..." His voice trailed off.

"That's right," Constance continued for him. "The victim himself, murdered in this house ten years ago, his body never found. That's what everyone was supposed to believe. But it's a little more complicated than that—isn't it, Mr. Wilkinson? Would you care to tell everyone what you told me yesterday?"

The man said nothing.

"Then, if you'll forgive the liberty, I will." She turned back to the three. "Mr. Wilkinson once worked as a chemical engineer and did quite well for himself—well enough to buy this house. But then he was involved in an industrial accident that kept him from doing full-time work. His employer claimed the accident was his fault and refused to pay more than a marginal disability benefit—and then fired him. Over the next few years he accrued heavy debts, and it looked like he might lose the house. Finally, in desperation, he turned to his widowed sister, a former nurse who had become a forensic artist. Together, they devised a plan. Mr. Wilkinson took out a large life insurance policy on himself, with his sister as beneficiary. He knew that, if the life insurance was to be paid out, his death would have to be incontestable—even without a body. And so, over a span of many months, he withdrew pints of his own blood, until at last he had roughly six quarts: the amount normally present in the human body. His sister, who lived in Massachusetts, came down to assist from time to time. It was all done in this basement, in secret. In between blood draws, he would conceal the medical apparatus in a hollow pillar."

She turned to the man. "Correct so far?"

When he didn't respond, she continued. "One night, when they had finally collected enough blood, they went to work. His sister knew about blood spatter and crime scene analysis, and so she was able to make everything look very credible. She artfully created spatter patterns on the walls and furniture, then poured the rest across the floor—in such profusion that it would have to be considered fatal. Mr. Wilkinson carved a small piece from his scalp; embedded it into a chair back with the blow of an ax; then broke up some furniture to ensure it appeared as if a struggle had occurred. Using blood soaked into his own clothes, they made smear marks to the back door, down the steps, and into a pickup truck. Then they drove away, split up a few days later, and Mr. Wilkinson established a new identity. He lay low for several years in a remote part of Utah—although I suppose 'a remote part of Utah' is redundant. In any case, the insurance company, after some initial resistance, eventually paid the sister, who split the money with Mr. Wilkinson. And she, of course, inherited the house. She never lived there, perhaps for obvious reasons, and later died of cancer. Her estate sold the place, and that should have been the end of the story. But it wasn't."

She glanced at the man again. "Are you sure you wouldn't care to take over the story?"

He hung his head.

"Everything had worked out beautifully. Mr. Wilkinson had a new identity and enough money to live without working. But things gradually went awry. After Mr. Wilkinson's sister died and the house was put up for sale, he began to brood. He couldn't stop thinking about that hollow pillar and the blood donor equipment hidden inside, contaminated with his own blood. In the frenzy of preparing his own death, he hadn't thought to remove it. If that were ever found, it might expose his entire scheme. The insurance company had been reluctant to pay and the adjuster had been a barracuda. Although he tried to push those worries aside, the concerns only got worse. Not unlike in Poe's short story 'The Tell-Tale Heart,' his fears grew into a full-blown obsession. That obsession grew worse when he learned the wealthy New Yorker who'd bought the house planned to renovate it. Now Mr. Wilkinson's obsessive fears suddenly became grounded in reality. He decided there was only one solution: to break in and remove the *instrumenta sceleris* from the hollow pillar. And so one night he returned to Captiva, with all the equipment he would need to remove the evidence. But being back in town proved mentally distressing. Even though he'd aged and changed his appearance and dress to that of a vagabond, he became paranoid that he'd be recognized. Worse, when he actually tried to break into the house, he disturbed a couple of squatters. He escaped the island, traumatized, while the squatters circulated a story of ghosts, knocking noises, and chains."

"Ah, the source of the ghostly rumors," Perelman said.

"My thinking exactly. In any case, the renovation took place but the hidden equipment was not exposed. This was of course a huge relief to Mr. Wilkinson—until a few years later, when the New Yorker couldn't make a go of the inn he'd dreamed of opening and received a very attractive offer from a developer. After a long fight with the historical society, the house was scheduled for demolition. All of Wilkinson's fears roared back in force—now his blood kit was sure to be found. He had no choice but to return and try again to get it."

She paused briefly, examining her audience. "This time, however, he was more careful. He knew of a brick-lined ditch along the hidden side of the house, where an exit door had been planned for the basement but never built. He got the necessary tools and practiced with them. Then—just days before the demolition was to take place, to ensure there would be no squatters this time—he returned in his cover as a vagabond. Imagine his consternation when he found that, instead of squatters, the house had renters—viz., ourselves. But it was too late to back out. And so he was forced to work very slowly and quietly...unseen, usually at night. Unfortunately for him, I heard the faint tapping. And since I find the idea of spirits curious rather than frightening—and had time on my hands—I decided to investigate. And here we are."

She nodded toward the man. "Gentlemen, Randall Wilkinson."

There was a brief silence following this explanation. Then, Pendergast said: "Constance, *brava*."

"Incredible to think he's been alive all this time," Perelman said.

Constance waved a hand at Wilkinson. "Ecce homo."

"What do we do with him now?" Perelman asked after a moment. "I can think of many laws that were broken here: insurance fraud, conspiracy, tax evasion, contributing to the forgery of a death certificate, financial fraud...the list of felonies is downright staggering."

Constance turned to Wilkinson. "How much profit did you make?"

The man spoke for the first time. He had, Coldmoon

noted, a low, almost melodious voice. "Two million dollars from the insurance. My sister got the house—that was part of the deal, plus half a million. I kept one and a half million."

"What happened to your sister's portion after her death?"

"When she found she had cancer, she started wiring amounts to an offshore account, which I later collected. She had no children, you see."

"You certainly had a devoted sister," said Pendergast.

"We were very close."

"And how much do you have left?" Constance inquired.

A hesitation. "About a million two."

Constance turned toward Perelman. "Chief Perelman, do you know approximately how much money the historical society still needs to raise to purchase and restore the house?"

Another brief pause, during which Coldmoon heard Pendergast say something in Latin to Constance. She smiled as if complimented.

Perelman spoke. "About a million. Give or take."

"Interesting coincidence," Constance said. "I wonder how Mr. Wilkinson would feel about making an anonymous gift to the historical society, in order to save the house, in return for being allowed to go free?"

Nobody spoke for a minute. Perelman finally said: "I sweated bullets trying to solve this case. I failed, and it was humiliating. I'm not sure I'm so willing to let it go."

"Consider the alternative," Pendergast interjected smoothly. "If you arrest him, all that money will go back to the insurance company—and ticky-tacky condos will replace this beautiful old mansion. Captiva Island will never be the same."

Perelman swallowed. He looked around the room. All eyes were on him. "Doesn't that make us all conspirators to defraud the insurance company?"

"Naturally," said Pendergast. "But sometimes a little bending of the law to the greater good is the wiser option. The insurance company wrote off the loss long ago. The town you serve will benefit. Most important, we can keep a secret—can't we, gentlemen? Constance?"

A long silence ensued. Then, slowly, Perelman nodded. "I imagine an anonymous gift would be very well received by the historical society."

Constance looked at Wilkinson. "We'll hold this medical equipment in trust until the donation clears. And then we will turn it over to you to dispose of."

Wilkinson clasped his hands together, as if in prayer. "Thank you." It was probably Coldmoon's imagination, but, quite suddenly, the air in the basement seemed to lift.

"Excellent," Pendergast said to Constance. "Most excellent."

"There's just one thing," Perelman said with a half smile.

Everyone glanced his way.

"If this means the passing of the Mortlach ghost... well, shouldn't we have an exorcism?"

"No," said Coldmoon immediately.

"Yes," Constance said at the same time.

"A small ritual does seem appropriate," Pendergast said. "But first, I imagine Mr. Wilkinson is both tired and in need of refreshments."

"And a bathroom," Wilkinson said.

"Naturally. In that case, while Mr. Wilkinson is making use of the facilities, and someone is getting him a drink, I shall scour the manse for a bell, book, and candle." And with that he turned and vanished up the stairs.

72

THE BELL 429 SKIMMED low above coral reefs and emerald waters, Assistant Director in Charge Pickett once again peering out the copilot's window. The mysterious island, awash in tropical green, came into view on the horizon, set like a gem on the wide expanse of sea. As they drew closer, he made out the ornamental ranks of palm trees, the boathouse, the gleaming white marble walkways and buildings, and the helipads beyond. One helipad was occupied: an AgustaWestland 109 Grand sat upon it, sleek and luxurious, with a top speed nearly double that of his ride. The 429 settled down near it. As Pickett opened the door, he felt like he was stepping out of a Yugo parked next to a Rolls.

The same two men were waiting for him in their starched and pressed uniforms. They led him along the crushed-shell paths and up the staircases of white marble. But this time, they went not along the covered passage to the courtyard where he had initially met Pendergast, but rather in another direction entirely, to arrive at a large temple-like structure built of the same bone-white marble. It was surrounded on all four sides by Corinthian colonnades, topped with entablatures and a trapezoidal roof. This, Pickett thought, was so outrageous it could only be the island's main house.

The attendants brought him up to a front portico, where he found Pendergast and Coldmoon seated in chairs, waiting for him. A refreshing breeze blew among the columns, rustling the royal palms nearby and bringing with it the scent of honeysuckle. Pendergast was dressed once again in his trademark black suit, his face and silver-blue eyes pale in the bright sun. Coldmoon also was in traditional mufti: old jeans and a plaid shirt. To one side lay a curious assortment of luggage: elegant, slab-sided Louis Vuitton suitcases beside a pair of beat-up, dirty backpacks. Pickett noticed the junior agent looked completely, even ridiculously, out of place in these surroundings—and his face betrayed his discomfort.

"ADC Pickett," Pendergast said, rising to shake his hand as he came up the steps. "How nice of you to see us off like this."

This was spoken with the casual tone of a tourist about to board a cruise ship. To observe Pendergast's manner, one would think the last frantic week had never happened: the inquiries, depositions, arrests, warrants, and raids, all done under a cloak of secrecy. Pickett had kept a tight lid on the story even within the FBI, doing his best to bury the proceedings in the bureaucratic red tape his department was so good at providing.

"I couldn't very well let you go without giving you a summary of what's happened since you left to, ah, finish your interrupted vacation," Pickett said.

"Thank you; we're most anxious to hear about it." Pendergast motioned him to a chair in the shade next to them.

Pickett whisked a newspaper from beneath his arm and laid it to one side as he sat down. "As you might imagine, there's been a massive reckoning in Lee County. Commander Baugh has been relieved of his post, pending an official Coast Guard inquiry; the police chief of Fort Myers has been reprimanded; and Baugh's aide-de-camp, a certain Lieutenant Darby, has been arrested on charges of espionage, along with another Coast Guard officer named Duran. There are many more arrests to come. It's early days still."

"And how has the good town of Sanibel taken all this?" Pendergast asked.

"We've managed to bury most of the details. Chief Perelman has been most cooperative. He's even become some kind of local hero. Nobody in town knows why, exactly, but he's generally being given credit for clearing things up...even though he's the picture of humility and professes to know nothing." Pickett chuckled.

"What's the official story?" Coldmoon asked.

"What we're saying about the amputated feet is that it was an evil experiment by a clandestine organization, and we're leaving it at that. Behind the scenes, of course, there's hell to pay and much to be done—identifying the dead, compensation to those migrants held prisoner, determining how best to move forward...it's been a nightmare for us."

"It wasn't too pleasant for them, either," Coldmoon said.

"Of course not. And we'll do absolutely everything in our power to make things right."

"While we're on the subject, what is the current status of a certain installation north of Carrabelle?" Pendergast asked.

"Completely emptied and locked down. We've spread word that there was an outbreak of hantavirus in the vicinity to keep people away. The remoteness of its location and the storm worked in our favor—nobody seems to have noted anything that evening beyond some unusual helicopter activity. Once the investigation into this rogue operation is complete, the facility will be razed to the ground. And we're getting 100 percent cooperation from the Pentagon:

they're aghast at what was being done by former U.S. military personnel, supposedly in the name of patriotism. *Former* is the operative word here: the U.S. armed forces had nothing to do with this."

Pickett paused.

"What's that you brought along?" Coldmoon asked, pointing at the newspaper.

"I thought perhaps you hadn't seen it yet." Picking up the newspaper, Pickett unfolded it, displaying the front page. The two agents leaned in. It was the *Miami Herald*, and its headline screamed in seventy-two-point type that its star reporter, Roger Smithback, had been awarded a key to the city of Fort Myers by the mayor for not only assisting with the investigation on Captiva Island, but for publishing a series of daring exposés that precipitated a raid on one of the worst gangs in the city, Panteras de la Noche. The gang had been rolled up and its leader, nicknamed Bighead, taken into protective custody. He was rumored to have flipped, and the Central American cartels had placed a massive bounty on his head. Despite this breathless reportage, the article was remarkably light on details and specifics.

"I do have a question," Pickett said, putting the newspaper aside. "It might be a little delicate. The oceanographer that you rescued from that facility, Dr. Gladstone. She's making a full recovery, despite the trauma of losing a foot, and I'm told by doctors and psychiatrists that she won't experience any lasting psychological damage."

Pickett noticed that, at the mention of Gladstone's name, a shadow passed across Pendergast's face. "What was your question?" he asked.

"She claims to have no recollection of that night's events. She remembers being chased down a road by helicopters...and then, nothing until she awoke in a hospital bed. It seems incredible she could have been induced to amputate her own foot."

Pendergast's face had gone still as granite. "It's a mercy she can't remember. What happened is all in my debriefing. That is—*was*, I hope—a perfectly malign drug. The remorse I feel at involving her and Dr. Lam is something that will haunt me."

"You couldn't have known," Coldmoon said.

If Pendergast heard this, he did not show it. "For what it's worth, I can tell you that once she is ready to return to work, a foundation I'm associated with—Vita Brevis—has offered to endow an academic chair for her at the oceanographic institute of her choice."

Pickett nodded. "She deserves as much." He glanced at the pile of luggage. "So: you're returning to New York?"

"With as much alacrity as possible."

"And you," Pickett said, turning to Coldmoon. "I understand the papers came through from the Colorado field office?"

Coldmoon patted the breast pocket of his shirt.

"Then I'm happy for you both." He paused. "It is a shame, however, because I've just learned of the most peculiar incident that took place last night, north of Savannah—"

"Forget it," Coldmoon interrupted. "Sir."

Pendergast, too, frowned at this unwelcome advance.

"Well." Pickett sighed. "I'm not going to issue any orders, considering what you've both been through. But it's a shame, because—"

He was interrupted again, this time by the light sound of footsteps coming up a nearby path. A moment later, Constance Greene emerged from the palms into the bright tropical light. She wore a large sun hat, linen blouse, and pleated white skirt. Her strange violet eyes were covered by a pair of Ray-Ban Wayfarers.

"Mr. Pickett," she said, offering her hand.

"Ms. Greene," he said, standing and taking it.

"I'm sorry I wasn't here to receive you properly on your arrival. I was just taking care of some last-minute business before our departure."

"And what might that have been?" Pendergast inquired.

"Nothing important. I was just giving the security chief a token of our appreciation." She turned to Pickett. "He was kind enough to give me some weaponry demonstrations after you'd spirited Aloysius away. Merely for my amusement, of course."

This was followed by a brief silence. Then Pickett glanced at Coldmoon. "Walk with me," he said.

They made their way down the steps of the temple-like structure and along a lane of crushed shells that led to an overlook. Pickett took a moment to get his thoughts in order. Then he turned to Coldmoon. "I've read over your transcripts," he said.

Coldmoon nodded.

"I've read Pendergast's too, of course. Everything that I didn't observe myself, in fact, I read. Read carefully. I realize that, in the mayhem of that night, given the nature of that rogue military encampment, your memory might not be crystal clear. But one thing has been troubling me."

"What might that be, sir?"

"It's—well, it's Constance Greene."

A look came over Coldmoon's face that Pickett hadn't seen on the man before, but he continued anyway. "She's the one variable in the equation I can't figure out. First responders mentioned a young woman among your party, dressed in filthy tactical clothes. I also heard reports that someone matching her description was on the rescue helicopter that brought all of you back to Fort Myers. Oddly enough, post-landing records for your group do not include such a person."

"No?" asked Coldmoon.

"Not only that, but a heavy machine gun was found near your exit point that—on trying to reconstruct exactly what happened during your final escape—we can't quite factor in. Who was manning that? It had recently run through over three hundred rounds."

"It was so chaotic, I really can't recall."

"Right. And another thing—Chief Perelman explained how, knowing only that Pendergast had been kidnapped, he undertook a rescue mission with his boat. But the tornado that wrecked that boat and almost killed him has brought on a degree of amnesia of a different sort than Dr. Gladstone's. He can't recall much that happened leading up to the tornado—in particular, whether he was alone on the boat or had a passenger." He paused. "Meanwhile, you were flying in from Mexico, forced to land at Tallahassee. Any idea where Ms. Greene was in all of this?"

"I don't know. At home?"

"*Right*. Well, let's say I'd hate to be the one who ever had to interrogate that woman." Even though the overlook was deserted, Pickett glanced around before continuing. "This isn't an avenue anybody else is following up, you understand. But I know you, and I know Pendergast better, and . . . well, I just like the cases under my command to add up."

"I understand, sir."

"And so do I." Pickett's eyes met Coldmoon's in

a curious gaze that was interrupted by a chorus of voices from behind them.

"Those must be the island staff," Coldmoon said with something like relief. "Making their way down to the helipad with our luggage."

"Of course," Pickett said. "Let's not keep them waiting any longer."

Ten minutes later, both helicopters were warming up, their blades whipping the humid air. Constance got into the plush, leather-lined interior of the AgustaWestland first, keeping her hat in place with one hand while shaking Pickett's with the other. Coldmoon—whom they would be dropping off on the mainland for his flight to Colorado—followed next. Last was Pendergast.

"Well, sir," he said to Pickett, leaning in at the door. "Last time you were here, it was with a request to 'have a look at the scene.' I hope you found my perusal to be helpful."

"Helpful? You solved the case."

"I'll say farewell, then. Agent Coldmoon is eager to get to his new post. And, in return for your kind words just now, I would only add that Constance and I are eager to get back to New York...without further delay." He gave the last three words an unmistakable emphasis.

"Then I'd be the last person to detain you."

And Pickett stepped back while the luggage was loaded into the rear of the passenger compartment. A moment later, the door closed; the chopper rose swiftly and then, with a roar of its powerful engines, it banked to the northwest and sped away.

Pickett watched the bird vanish into the brilliant blue sky. Then, stepping back from the prop wash of his own helicopter, he reached for his phone and dialed.

"Dispatch One?" he said when it was answered. "This is ADC Pickett. The craft I told you about is an AW109, tail number Z-513227. Yes, that's right. Please forward my instructions to divert it to Savannah, as discussed earlier. If necessary, I'll talk to the pilot myself."

And without saying anything further, he slipped his phone back into his suit; took one final look around at the unreal paradise that rose behind him; then, folding his copy of the *Miami Herald*, he ducked under the rotors and got into his own helicopter. A minute later, it rose into the pearlescent sky, following Pendergast's ride at a more dignified, stately, government-approved rate of speed.

The authors wish to thank Wes Miller, Kallie Shimek, Eric Simonoff, Michael Pietsch, Ben Sevier, Nadine Waddell, and Claudia Rülke. They would also like to underscore that all characters depicted in the book are imaginary, and that in places they have taken liberties with the geography of Florida and its cities to accommodate the novel's logistical demands. Finally, they wish to praise Sanibel and Captiva, both for their beauty and for their efforts to preserve the natural ecology and wildlife of the barrier islands. The authors in particular recommend the magnificent beaches on which—in their personal experience—the only things of note to have washed ashore are the beautiful shells in their private collections.

ABOUT THE AUTHORS

The thrillers of **DOUGLAS PRESTON** and **LINCOLN CHILD** "stand head and shoulders above their rivals" (*Publishers Weekly*). Preston and Child's *Relic* and *The Cabinet of Curiosities* were chosen by readers in a National Public Radio poll as being among the one hundred greatest thrillers ever written, and *Relic* was made into a number one box office hit movie. They are coauthors of the famed Pendergast series, and their recent novels include *Old Bones*, *Verses for the Dead*, *City of Endless Night*, *The Obsidian Chamber*, and *Blue Labyrinth*. In addition to his novels and nonfiction works (such as *The Lost City of the Monkey God*), Preston writes about archaeology for *The New Yorker* and *National Geographic* magazines. Lincoln Child is a Florida resident and former book editor who has published seven novels of his own, including such bestsellers as *Full Wolf Moon* and *Deep*

Storm. Readers can sign up for The Pendergast File, a "strangely entertaining" newsletter from the authors, at their website, PrestonChild.com. The authors welcome visitors to their Facebook page, where they post regularly.